THE SOCIALITE AND THE BODYGUARD

BY

DANA MARTON

With sincere appreciation for Allison Lyons and
Denise Zaza and the whole Intrigue team

Dana Marton is the author of more than a dozen fast-paced, action-adventure romantic suspense novels and a winner of the Daphne du Maurier Award of Excellence. She loves writing books of international intrigue, filled with dangerous plots that try her tough-as-nails heroes and the special women they fall in love with. Her books have been published in seven languages in eleven countries around the world. When not writing or reading, she loves to browse antiques shops and enjoys working in her sizable flower garden where she searches for "bad" bugs with the skills of a superspy and vanquishes them with the agility of a commando soldier. Every day in her garden is a thriller. To find more information on her books, please visit www.danamarton.com. She loves to hear from her readers and can be reached via e-mail at the following address: DanaMarton@DanaMarton.com.

Chapter One

Nash Wilder stood still in the darkness and listened to the sounds the bumbling intruder was making downstairs. Instinct—and everything he was—pushed him forward, into the confrontation. He pulled back instead, until he reached Ally Whitman's bedroom door at the end of the hall in the east wing of her Pennsylvania mansion.

The antique copper handle turned easily under his hand; the door didn't creak. He stepped in, onto the plush carpet, without making a sound.

She woke anyway, a light sleeper—no surprise after what she'd been through. She saw him and sat up in bed, her lips opening.

He lifted his index finger to caution her to silence as he mouthed, "He's here."

She always slept with a reading light on, and was nodding now to let him know that she'd seen and understood his words. As she clutched the cover to her chest, the sleeves of her pajama top slid back.

A nasty scar ran from her wrist to her elbow, evidence of a serious operation to piece together the bone beneath. Not that she would ever share that story with anyone. She was a very private person, not a complainer, tough in her own way. Nash had read about the injury— one of many she'd suffered in the past twenty years— in her file.

His job was to make sure it was her last.

Sleep was quickly disappearing from her eyes as she clutched the blanket tighter and drew a slow breath, spoke in a whisper. "You'll take care of him."

Her confidence was hard-won. She wasn't a woman to give her trust easily. Getting to this point had taken two months of them being together 24/7.

He wanted to protect her, but she needed more. His assignment here was over when her divorce was final in three days. After that there was no reason for her ex to come back. He would have what he'd gotten from her and no more. At least, that was what Ally thought. Nash wasn't that optimistic.

He held her gaze as he shook his head. *"You'll* take care of him."

She needed to know without a doubt that she could. And her bastard of a soon-to-be-ex–husband needed to know that, too.

Her eyes went wide, and for a moment she was frozen to the spot, but then she nodded and pushed the cover back.

Good girl.

Not that Ally Whitman was a girl. She was a grown woman who'd seen the darker side of life during her twenty miserable years of marriage. She'd been a beauty in her day. He'd seen the wedding photo that had hung above the fireplace before he moved it, at her request, to the basement on his first day on the job. She'd been young and innocent, the sheltered daughter of a wealthy venture capitalist. Easy pickings.

His anger kicked into gear. He had a thing about violent bastards exploiting and brutalizing those weaker than themselves. He moved toward the door while she put on her robe. At fifty-two, Ally was still a striking woman.

As he waited, he heard rubber-soled shoes squeak on the marble tile downstairs. "In the kitchen," he whispered when Ally came up next to him.

He walked her to the main staircase and handed her his gun. He'd made sure during the last two months that she knew how to handle it. He waited until she made her way down, then he headed to the other end of the hallway and stole down the back stairs, ignoring the sudden shot of pain that went through his bad leg. Enough moonlight filtered in through the windows that he could navigate the familiar landscape of the house without trouble.

"Hello, Jason," he heard her say as he moved toward the kitchen from the back.

A chair rattled as someone bumped it.

"What are you sneaking around in the middle of the night for?" Anger flared in the loudly spoken response. Her ex would probably have preferred to surprise her in her sleep. Scare her a little.

"I want you to leave my house."

So far, so good. Nash crept closer. A few months ago, she would have asked the bastard what he wanted and in her desperation to be rid of him, would have given it.

"Like hell." The man's tone grew belligerent. "It's my house, too. If you think you're going to push me out—"

"The judge decided."

"To hell with the judge. I lived here for twenty years. You can't kick me out like that."

A moment passed before Ally said, "I already have."

Nash moved into position in time to see Jason Whitman step forward with fury on his fleshy face. "You bitch, if you think—"

He was ready to intercept when Ally pulled the gun from her robe pocket.

That slowed the bastard right down. "What the hell?" A stunned pause followed, then, "Put that down, dammit. You're not gonna shoot me. Don't be ridiculous." But he didn't sound too sure of himself as he nervously adjusted the jacket of his linen suit. Dressed for a break-in like he was going to a luncheon at the country club.

The light color of the fabric made him an easy target. He wouldn't think of something like that. Jason Whitman wasn't used to being in the crosshairs. He was used to being the hunter.

"I want you to go. I mean it." Ally stood firm.

Moonlight glinted off the white marble counters, off the etched glass of the top cabinets. Industrial chrome appliances gleamed, standing tall, standing witness.

The man hesitated for a moment. Nash could nearly hear the wheels turning in his head. Meeting with resistance for the first time was usually a shock to the abuser's system, especially when he'd gotten away with the abuse for decades. He could either back down or erupt in violence.

Ally grabbed the gun with both hands, put her feet a foot or so apart in the stance Nash had taught her. And something in that show of strength set Whitman off. He flew forward.

Not as fast as Nash.

He had the guy's arm twisted up behind his back in the next second, brought him to a halt as the man howled in pain. "Let me go, you lowlife sonuvabitch. How in hell did you get here?"

He had suspected the man might put in an appearance if he thought the coast was clear, so Nash had parked his car a couple of streets down. He wanted the confrontation to be over with. He wanted to be sure the threat to Ally was neutralized before he left the job.

"You can't protect her forever," Whitman growled and tried to elbow Nash in the stomach with his free arm, which Nash easily evaded.

"I'm protecting *you*. Take a good look at her."

And damn, but Ally Whitman looked fine, *Make My Day* about stamped on her forehead—her eyes narrowed, her hands steady, her mouth grim.

"I'd be only too happy to have her take care of you. But I don't want her to go through all the police business afterward. Not that they'd give her much trouble. Intruder in the middle of the night. Clear case of self-defense."

And for a split second he wondered if it might not be better if things went that way. People with a bullet in the head didn't come back. Guaranteed. But he had gotten to know Ally enough over the last two months to know that she would have a hard time living with that.

Not him.

He would have needed hardly any provocation at all to reach up and break the bastard's neck.

Ally was stepping closer. Nash restrained the man's other arm. She didn't stop until the barrel was mere inches from her ex-husband's forehead.

"You've had all you're ever going to get from me, Jason. This is the last time I'm going to say this. Go away. Far away. And don't ever come back. I'm not the same woman you remember."

And from the fierce look on her face, it was plenty clear that she meant what she said.

Nash felt Whitman go limp. "Hey, okay. I didn't mean anything. I just thought—you know, that we could work things out. I just—"

She lowered the gun, but not all the way. "You just get the hell out of here." Her voice went deeper. Her chin lifted. She held the bastard's gaze without a blink.

This was it, the moment when the woman found her own power at last, and from behind Whitman, who was so doomed if he made another move, Nash smiled. He yanked the man aside and finally let him go. Whitman—not as stupid as he looked—ran for the door.

And for the first time in the weeks since he'd been her bodyguard, Nash heard Ally Whitman laugh.

Four days later

NASH HAD skirted orders now and then during his military career, but this was going to be the first time he refused a direct order from his superior officer. He didn't have to worry about a court-martial, neither he nor Brian Welkins were in the military anymore. But he couldn't rightly say he wasn't worried. Welkins had spent four years locked in a tiger cage, the prisoner of guerillas in the Malaysian jungle. He broke free and fought his way out of that jungle, saving other hostages in the process. He was the toughest guy Nash knew. Definitely not a man to cross.

Which was why he was careful when he said, "Can't do that, sir."

The sparse office was all wood and steel. Security film shielded the windows, keeping out the worst of the sun as well as any prying eyes. Nash considered the simple office chair but decided against sitting.

The only indication that Welkins heard him was a short pause of his hand before he resumed moving his pen across paper. "You will report to duty at eighteen-hundred hours." He picked up the case file with his left hand and held it out for Nash without removing his attention from whatever he was working on.

He ran Welkins Security Services like a military organization, leading his team to success. WSS had started as an outfit that offered survival-type team-building retreats to major corporations, hiring commando and military men who had left active duty for one reason or another. They were all tough bastards, to the last, who soon realized that nudging yuppies through the Arizona desert or the deep forests of the Adirondacks was too mild an entertainment for them. So the company expanded into the bodyguard business, which offered live-wire action to those who missed it. Like Nash.

He stood his ground. "I'm going to pass on this assignment, sir." He liked working in private security where he had options like that. *Or not,* judging from Welkins's expression when he looked up at last.

His pen hand stilled. "Is there a problem, soldier?"

Apparently. Since they were now all civilians, the boss only called one of the team members "soldier" if he was majorly ticked off.

"I'm not the right man for this assignment." Taking a few weeks and fixing up that half-empty rat hole he called home was starting to sound good all of a sudden.

"You think the assignment is beneath you?"

Damn right. "I'm not doing security detail for— I'm not working for a dog, sir."

"You'll be working for Miss Landon."

And that was the other reason he had to say no, a bigger reason really than the dog.

"Miss Landon specifically wants someone from our team."

"Maybe someone—"

"Everyone else is on assignment. It's four days. Quick work. Easy money."

He liked that last bit, but the answer was still no. "It's punishment for messing up the Whitman case, isn't it?"

Welkins didn't say anything for a full minute, but Nash caught a nearly imperceptible twitch at the corner of the man's mouth.

"You were supposed to be protecting Mrs. Whitman from her ex-husband, not holding him down while she put a gun to his head. His lawyer is frothing at the mouth. Do you know how much this could cost the company?"

He had a fair idea. And it burned his ass that the law

would probably take Whitman's side after all the years it had failed to protect his wife from him.

It had taken two decades of misery for Mrs. Whitman to gather up enough courage to file for divorce. She had money in spades. But money couldn't buy her happiness. Thank God she'd finally realized that it could buy her some serious protection.

Whitman wouldn't go anywhere near her again. But he'd decided to pick another fight, this time with WSS, hiding behind his fancy lawyers.

"I should have taken him out," Nash said, looking at his feet and shaking his head, talking more to himself than Welkins.

"You should *not* have taken him out. You're no longer in the mountains of Afghanistan. You are in the protection business. Do you understand that?" Welkins watched him as if he weren't sure whether Nash really did, as if Nash might not be a good fit for the team after all.

And maybe he wasn't. He was trained as a killing machine. Maybe he wasn't good for anything else.

"You need to learn to pull back." Welkins's tone was more subdued as he said that.

A moment of silence passed between them while Nash thought over the incident. "I can't regret anything I did on that assignment, sir. But I do regret if my actions caused any difficulties for the company and the team," he said at last.

"Then take one for the team." Welkins's sharp gaze cut to him.

And Nash knew he was sunk. Loyalty was the one thing he would never go around, the trait he appreciated most in others, the one value he would never compromise on.

His lungs deflated. He hung his head and rubbed his hand over his face for a second.

Four cursed days at the Vegas Dog Show, guarding celebrity heiress and media darling Kayla Landon's puff poodle, Tsini. If the boss wanted to unman him, it would have been easier to castrate him and be done with it.

The one ray of hope in the deal was that Kayla Landon had a host of assistants. She probably had a professional team showing off her dog for her, so he wouldn't actually have to come face-to-face with her and the hordes of paparazzi that usually followed.

What kind of dog received death threats anyway? He couldn't see something like that happening to a real dog like a rottweiler or a German shepherd.

"All right." He pushed the words past his teeth with effort. "I don't think a consultation with Miss Landon will be necessary." Please. If there was a God.

"No, indeed. I have already consulted with her."

For the first time since he'd walked into the office, Nash relaxed. Then Welkins smiled.

Terrible suspicion raised its ugly head.

The heavy smell of doom hung in the air.

"There's more to this, isn't there?"

"Because of the threats, Miss Landon will be traveling with her dog-show team to Vegas. You'll be working with her 24/7."

He closed his eyes for a minute. Her nickname was Popcorn Princess. Seriously. And he was going to have to take orders from her. Oh, hell. Was it too late to go back to the military and sign up for active duty in some combat zone instead?

"Let me spell this out. Don't try to fix the client's life. Don't make this personal. Go in, get the job done, get out and collect the payment." Welkins looked at Nash with something akin to regret. "You can't afford to tick off anyone else."

Meaning if he didn't please Miss Landon, he would probably not have a job when he came back.

And the demand for washed-up commando soldiers wasn't exactly great in the current job market. Especially for those with a near-blank résumé, since one hundred percent of his missions for the government had been top secret.

He was no longer fit for that job, or most others. But he had to keep working. Because if he stood still long enough without anything to do and occupy his mind, the darkness tended to catch up with him.

He thanked Welkins and walked out, knowing one thing for sure. Empty-headed socialites and puffy-haired poodles notwithstanding, no matter what happened, he couldn't mess up this assignment. If he lost Welkins and WSS, he'd have nothing left.

"So CLOSE to perfect it's scary. I'm definitely a genius." Elvis, her makeup artist, focused critically on her left eyebrow and did a last-minute touch-up with the spoolie. "*Ay mios dio.* You're so fabulous, no one will pay any attention to the food."

Her penthouse condo, in the most exclusive part of Philadelphia, was buzzing with activity. Kayla Landon worked on blocking out all the distractions. And kept failing.

"Let's hope I don't mess up any ingredients." Not that she thought she would. She was feeling decidedly optimistic today, or rather *had been*. She normally used makeup time to relax, but now found herself watching the new bodyguard from the corners of her eyes instead.

Her uncle had insisted on him. She half regretted already that she'd caved. She didn't want to have to deal with him, with the adjustment of a new man on her team.

He was gorgeous, in a scary sort of way. Six feet two inches of sinew and hard muscle, and a don't-mess-with-me look in his amazing gold eyes. That and a strong dislike for her.

She wasn't surprised.

Most men she met either hated her or wanted to screw her on sight. For the moment, she didn't know whether to feel relieved or disappointed that Nash Wilder seemed unequivocally in the first camp.

He was taking stock of her, her home and her people.

She made him wait, mostly because she could tell that it annoyed him, and also because she needed a few moments to gather herself before she faced all that raw, masculine power.

"Hey." Her younger brother, Greg, ambled by. He gave her a sweet smile and dropped a kiss on her hair, careful not to mess up her makeup.

In a couple of hours, The Cooking Channel would be recording a show in her kitchen as part of their *Celebrity Cooks at Home* series. They were setting up already, making a royal mess. People she'd never seen before traipsed all over everything.

She wasn't thrilled about opening her home to the public once again, but the show was doing a special for a charity that stood close to her heart, one that funded Asperger's research. Greg had that mild form of autism, among a host of other issues.

He was looking at all the people, his arms crossed. He hated crowds. Not that he would act out as he used to. Now that he was a grown man, he'd learned to control his impulses. For the most part. He'd definitely gotten worse since they'd lost their parents and their older brother. Maybe tonight, after everyone was gone, she'd try to talk to him about that again.

But for now, all she did was slip the white envelope off her dressing table and hand it to him. He stuffed it into his back pocket. She wanted to ask what he wanted the money for this time, but didn't want to humiliate him the way their father had done so often in the past. Money was a touchy issue for Greg.

Someone dropped a cookie sheet in the kitchen. The metal clanging on tiles drew her attention for a moment.

"Wish they'd let me cook what I wanted. Frilly finger food is not really my thing." She stifled her discontent. "I suppose that's what everyone expects from me. Easy and fancy."

"You do what you want to do." Greg was as supportive and protective of her as she was of him.

"I have to trust them to know what's best for the show. We want to raise serious money."

"Don't trust anyone but yourself."

He sounded so much like their father as he said that. *Don't trust anyone but yourself* had been one of Will Landon's favorite sayings.

Kayla was beginning to make it hers these days. She wondered what brought it to Greg's mind. She'd been careful to keep all her worries and doubts from him. Still, Greg must have picked up on the increasing tension in the air.

She forced a smile. "Don't worry about any of this. They'll be done in a couple of hours and then they'll be out of here."

Greg gave a solemn nod. "I'll be back later."

She closed her eyes for a second as the sable brush dusted her face. Her brother was gone by the time she opened them.

"God has never made a prettier face." Elvis smiled from ear to ear. "She must be so proud of you, *querida*." He stepped behind her, a hand on his slim hip, glowing with pride as he looked her over in the mirror.

She looked for the pimple that had blossomed in the middle of her chin overnight. Vanished. She blew a kiss to Elvis. "You're the best. Thanks."

He whisked away the white cloth that had been protecting her clothes. "You're welcome. Who's the hottie over there? *Yo quiero* some of that." His gaze darted that way in the mirror.

"He'll be watching out for Tsini for the next couple of days."

"*Ay dios mio.* Makes me want to write myself death threats." Elvis fanned himself with his hand and gave her a sly look.

They grinned at each other in the mirror before he turned her swivel chair. "Go knock 'em dead."

"It's a culinary show. I think they expect me to cook for them."

She glanced at her agent and manager chatting at the other end of the den, probably discussing the dog show. A couple of vendors who'd found out that she would be there had already made contact about the possibility of celebrity product endorsement. Her agent was for it, her manager against. She was undecided. She had plenty on her schedule already, but there were a couple of free animal clinics she knew to which she could donate the income from the ads.

She pushed all that from her mind for now and slid off the chair, full of nervous energy despite the fabulous yoga session she'd had that morning. She headed for the living room, waving her security back when they moved to follow. Mike and Dave were great guys, but they were a little miffed over the new security guard, and she wanted to have her first meeting with him without their interference.

"Mr. Wilder? I'm Kayla." She offered him her hand, even as she thought, *Wilder than what?* And knew from the looks of him that the answer had to be, *Wilder than just about any other thing she'd ever met up with.*

He held her fingers gently in his large hand. Didn't feel the need to impress her with his strength. So far so good. There was hope yet.

"Please, call me Nash," he said.

She hadn't been prepared for his voice. Sexy as sin.

His tone was deep-timbered, and tickled something behind her breast bone as it vibrated through her.

She put up her invisible professional force field, which protected her from an attraction toward hot men. Attraction could lead to letting her guard down. And letting her guard down always led to disaster. She was done with that. She'd learned her lesson a couple of times over.

"We can talk in here." She motioned toward her sprawling living room overlooking Memorial Park, which was outfitted with a state-of-the-art sound system. Soft music floated in the background, the latest album of one of her friends.

"We'll need everyone on set in fifteen minutes," the producer called out in warning from the kitchen.

Plenty of time for a brief tête-à-tête. She settled into a space-age style red-leather pod and crossed her legs.

Nash eyed the pod across from hers then picked the ultra-modern couch instead, sat as if expecting it to break under him. He didn't even try to disguise the derision in his eyes as he looked around. Probably didn't expect her to notice.

People who equated her with the airhead-heiress media image used to drive her to frustration. These days, since she only stayed alive because her enemies continued to underestimate her, she didn't mind any longer, had come to count on it, in fact.

But still, Nash Wilder sitting there and judging her before they'd ever exchanged two words got under her skin.

"So you're the great pet detective?" She couldn't help herself.

He focused back on her, fixed her with a glare that was probably supposed to put her in her place.

His short hair was near-black, his eyes dark gold whiskey. The two-inch scar along his jawline gave him a fierce look. The sleeves of his black T-shirt stretched across impressive biceps. He had *Semper Fi* tattooed on one and some sort of a shield on the other.

"I'm a bodyguard, Miss Landon," he was saying. "I'm *not* a pet detective."

And I'm not an airhead blonde, she wanted to tell him, but didn't. Nobody ever believed her anyway.

"There are a few things I'm going to need from you." He moved on. "A copy of your employee files, with pictures. A list of close associates. Your schedule for the past month. Your hour-by-hour schedule for the next four days of the show. The threats. The originals if the police didn't take them."

"I didn't call the police."

The police had done nothing when she'd gone to them for help about her parents' and her brother's deaths. *Accidents.* She hated that word with a hot red passion, but that was all they would tell her. They sure weren't going to bother themselves about her pet.

"You can have a list of my employees with their pictures, but not their employee files. That would be a breach of confidentiality."

He glared, obviously not liking that she pushed back. Tough for him. She expected a better plan for Tsini's protection than him harassing her employees.

Other than Greg and her uncle, she had barely any family left. Her staff was her family. They looked out for her, took care of her, defended her from the paparazzi and kept her secrets. She trusted them implicitly and she wasn't going to hand them over for any sort of interrogation by Mr. Hot and Overzealous here.

Wilder kept going with the narrow-eyed look. If he thought he could browbeat her into doing whatever he wanted, he was setting himself up for steep disappointment.

"You do that so well, Mr. Wilder. Do they teach mean looks in pet-detective school?" she began, then decided to stop there. She shouldn't antagonize him. But she knew that he'd judged her and judged her unfairly from the moment he'd set eyes on her, probably from the moment he'd taken on the job, or before. She resented it and felt some perverse need to put him in his place. Stupid. She needed to let go of that. Whatever he thought of her, he'd come to help.

Still, every inch of him exuded how much he didn't want to be here. The restraint that kept him in his seat was admirable. "Miss Landon—"

"Kayla."

"All I want is to figure out where the threats came from. It would make my job easier."

He was hired to keep an eye on Tsini for the next four days. Was he going above and beyond to impress her, or did he really care?

He didn't look as if her good opinion mattered one whit to him, for sure. But how could he care? He didn't know her and hadn't even met Tsini yet.

"I like doing my job as well as I can," he said.

That was it, then. A dedicated man. Her father would have liked him.

Tsini chose that moment to wander out of her bedroom and mosey in. She went straight to the stranger in the room and gave him a few cursory sniffs.

"And this would be my job?" He looked the standard poodle over.

"We prefer to call her Tsini." Kayla petted her when Tsini finally made her way to the pod chair. Her gleaming white hair was done in show clip, ready for the competition. They were leaving for Vegas in the morning. "Aren't you pretty today?"

Nash leaned back on the couch, watching the two of them. "So how much would one of these fancy things run a person?"

Not much at all. She'd rescued the abused poodle from a shelter. Some despicable breeder had been shut down just days before and about two dozen purebred poodles had ended up crammed into the already overcrowded cages. Kayla had gone there for a guard dog— right after her older brother's death. But then she'd seen Tsini with her badly broken leg, the cutest puppy that ever lived, and when she'd been told that the surgery to reset it would cost too much so she'd have to be put down, Kayla had snapped her up quicker than the ASPCA guy could ask for her autograph.

She'd paid for the surgeries, rehabilitation and regular grooming, wanting to erase the frightened, sick mess Tsini had been. And she had succeeded at least in this one thing in her life.

Tsini had turned out to be a real girl. She liked to look

pretty and liked to show it off. And it was a pleasure to take her to shows and let her. After Kayla tracked down and obtained the dog's papers.

None of that would interest Nash who'd strutted into her home with his thinly veiled prejudices, determined to believe her a spoiled brat. "Tsini is priceless," she said.

She reached for the star-shaped wireless phone on the see-through acrylic coffee table and rang her office as Tsini settled in at her feet. Her secretary picked up on the second ring.

"Could you please send over my schedule for the last month and the next four days? The official schedule of the dog show, too? Thanks."

She hung up then walked over to the built-in cabinetry that was camouflaged in the wall paneling. She pressed a panel and a deep drawer slid out. She pulled out the plastic bag inside and carried it back to Nash, tossed it on his lap.

Tsini had followed her there and back, taking her time to resettle again. She was a sweet, good-natured dog. Unconditional love. Complete acceptance.

Nash opened the bag with care then pulled out the contents. "What's this?"

She leaned down for Tsini, lifted her up and hugged her close as even the last bit of her good mood for the day disappeared. "The last *message* I got. Day before yesterday."

It still gave her shivers.

Chapter Two

Nash looked the thing over. "Did a note come with it?"

"No."

"So basically this is your death threat?" He did his best not to laugh. Someone sends her an electric-blue fur coat and she runs crying for help. Women.

The job was looking easier by the minute. He didn't know whether to be relieved or disappointed. Some challenge would have at least kept him from being bored to death.

Maybe she could put the damned coat on, not that there was much of it, just a strip of back and the sleeves. He thought, but wasn't sure, that they called this sort of thing a bolero jacket. Partially completed clothing seemed to be her thing. There had to be parts missing from the dress she wore. The white silk clung to curves that were made to tempt a man. Tempt him and drive him mad.

She had a perfect figure, which the paparazzi loved, big blue eyes and silky blond hair that tumbled down all the way to her pert little behind.

Temptation in a designer dress, if outside appearances were all a man cared about. But he'd been burned one time too many to be taken in by any of that.

He'd been burned and Bobby was dead. He pushed that thought away, still not ready to deal with it. He'd done many stupid things in his life, but for this one, for "Pounder"—Bobby Smith had been a wizard with heavy artillery—Nash would never forgive himself.

He watched dispassionately as Kayla Landon's luscious, hot-pink, glazed lips tightened.

"That coat is made of dog fur." She emphasized the last two words. "Same breed as Tsini, dyed blue. The decoration around the neckline is exactly the same as the collar Tsini has."

Okay, he could see that now. He dropped the thing back into the bag. He had friends who could go over it for any clues, although he didn't hold out much hope for anything usable. Likely everyone and their PR manager had already had their hands on it. Kayla Landon worked with a large staff.

"How would you feel—" her blue eyes flashed "—if someone sent you a coat made of human skin with tattoos exactly like yours?"

Point taken. He glanced at Tsini at Kayla's feet, then back at the blue coat, then at Kayla again.

And got seriously ticked when he saw the lines of concern around her eyes, and the fear behind them. And he knew in that instant what he'd stepped in the middle of here.

This wasn't about the dog.

The threats were about her. Someone wanted to scare her. And if the bastard was anything like some Nash had

had to deal with in the past, harming her would be the next step. Only, her incompetent bodyguards had been too busy brushing lint off their designer suits to realize that. He'd seen them and wasn't impressed. They'd let him into the penthouse on his word. Nobody had checked that he was who he'd claimed to be. Amateurs, the both of them.

Not my problem, his brand-new resolution smacked him upside the head the next moment. He'd been hired to protect the dog. He wasn't here to solve all of Kayla Landon's problems.

That held him back for about thirty seconds. Then his mind crept back to the issue again.

Someone was out there with Kayla in his sights. Nash watched her closely, as analytically as he had ever considered any mission.

There was a vulnerability about her that didn't come through on the television screen or show in her frequent pictures in the tabloids. Predictably, he found himself responding.

Don't go there.

He was a sucker for women in jeopardy—his one weakness. Hadn't he just gotten into trouble over that? Exactly how he'd ended up with the damned "pet-detective" assignment in the first place.

If he sank any lower, he'd be doing cat shows next.

He'd shoot himself first, he decided.

He couldn't afford to get involved in Kayla Landon's life chin-deep. Welkins would have his head on a platter. But he could do two things for her, at the very least: the first was to convince her that she was in a lot more danger than her dog, the second was to put the fear of God into her bodyguards so they would step up their vigilance. While protecting the poodle and navigating the Vegas Dog Show. All this in the next four days, which was the duration of his assignment.

And during that time, Kayla would be in an environment that was impossible to control, even discounting the media circus that was bound to follow her around. Best thing would be to convince her not to go to the show, but he had nothing save his instincts to take to her, and she had no reason to trust him.

Hell, it would probably take four days just to convince her that she was in any kind of danger. Media-darling socialite. She probably thought the whole world loved her.

He watched as she bent to kiss the dog's head, caught the curve of a breast, dropped his gaze only to land on her mile-long legs.

A target who didn't know she was in danger. A woman who was definitely tempting him on a raw, primal level, but who came with a "strictly forbidden" sticker.

"I'm a little worried that a new person will throw off the team," she said.

Great. She didn't even want him there.

"I wish there were another solution."

He wished for the simplicity of armed combat. He didn't think it'd be prudent to tell her that.

SHE HATED that she would feel rattled under his scrutiny. As a businesswoman, Kayla had fought her way through a top-notch MBA, then into a corner office at

Landon Enterprises at last. As a public persona, since people seemed fascinated with her, she'd been dragged through the tabloids over and over again. She had her protective shields firmly in place on every level. She didn't like the fact that Nash Wilder was able to get to her with a glance.

"Don't worry about anything. I'm going to take care of this," he said.

"Excellent," Kayla told him, all snooty like he would expect. Sometimes that was easiest. "That's what I'm paying you for." She flashed a saccharine smile.

And watched his Adam's apple bob up, then down.

She was getting to him, too. And how childish was it to gain pleasure from that? She needed to get away from him, away from his penetrating gaze. She wished they would call her to the kitchen.

"I'd prefer if we took the Landon jet to Vegas," he said, focusing back on the work at hand. Apparently, he'd read the detailed file her secretary had sent over to Welkins's office.

"The team is flying commercial. First class. I already have the tickets." The corporate jet would be too easily set up for another accident if her parents' and brother's murderer decided to use the opportunity to take her out.

Whoever the bastard was, she didn't think he would blow up a passenger jet and kill hundreds of people just to get to her.

Greg's voice filtered in from the den. She glanced that way. Back already? She wished Nash would finish their question-and-answer session so she could talk to her brother. But Greg seemed to be leaving again with a quick wave to her. He'd probably come back for something he'd forgotten. He was often absentminded.

"The corporate jet would give me a smaller environment to control. It'd make my job easier," Nash was saying.

Obviously, he expected her to rearrange her life to his specifications. She knew bodyguards like that. Her aunt had fallen prey to a similar man when Kayla had been a teenager. The guy had come in, made Aunt Carmella completely paranoid, got her to where she wouldn't trust anyone but him. She ended up leaving Uncle Al and marrying that man. He left her after a year, taking half of the family fortune with him.

"Your job is to protect Tsini. My job is to live my life, not to make yours easy," she spelled it out for Nash.

He considered her with a lazy look that she was pretty sure hid fury. "As you pointed out before, you're paying me to protect you—" He cleared his throat. "Your dog. Are you going to fight me on everything I recommend?"

He didn't seem like a guy who was used to taking no for an answer. He probably scared the breath out of the average person. He would have scared the breath out of her, too, if her life hadn't been in constant jeopardy in the past year.

She flashed her best debutante-millionaire-heiress smile. "Of course not, just when we don't agree." Then she thought, *shouldn't have said that.*

He looked in control, but she wasn't sure whether it was the kind of control that would easily snap. For all she knew, he was getting ready to strangle her for standing up to him. Her father had been like that. Bore no opposition from anyone. How quickly she'd forgotten.

But Nash threw his head back and laughed.

The sound was warm and genuine, reached right across the distance between them. The harsh lines of his face crinkled into a look of mirth. Not staring with her jaw hanging open took effort. The man was beyond belief good-looking.

"You're not like I expected," he said, his demeanor turning friendlier.

"And you think you know all about me now after what, five minutes?" She didn't want to admit that he was quickly disarming her.

"I know that spunk and a sense of humor rarely accompany an empty head."

Score one for Nash. He was more observant than ninety-nine percent of the people she usually met.

"Imagine that." She couldn't help the sarcasm, but for the first time in a long time, she wanted to.

He didn't seem to take offense. "I want you on your own plane because I can control a ten-person team easier than I can a commercial flight with hundreds on it." He considered her for a long moment, the look on his face turning serious. Then he seemed to have reached a decision at last and leaned forward, his voice dropping as he said, "I think you're in danger."

The slew of emotions that washed through her was bewildering. She'd been saying that for how long now? And nobody had ever believed her.

He was a complete stranger. She didn't trust him yet, might never trust him. He was the last person she wanted knowing about her personal problems. He could easily take them to the press. Confidentiality clauses tended to be forgotten when tabloids offered tens of thousands of dollars for any gossip about her.

She wanted to act as though she didn't know what he was talking about.

Failing that, she wanted to act like "yeah, I'm in danger, but I'm cool with that."

Failing that— She would have wanted to do anything but what she did do.

She burst into tears.

In front of a total outsider.

Who was probably beginning to think she was certifiable.

She didn't dare look up at him. God, she was a mess.

"Five-minute warning," Fisk, her agent, called out behind her.

She didn't turn, only lifted a hand to indicate that she heard him.

"All right, guys, let's get this party started. She's coming in a sec," he said to the producer in the kitchen as he walked back.

Nash was by her side the second Fisk left the den.

"We're going to talk someplace private," he said, then took her hand and gently pulled her up from the pod chair.

The line of potted palms between the living room and the den kept them out of sight of the staff as he led her to her bedroom, his hand at the small of her back as if he were her escort at some posh party, walking her down the red carpet.

He steered her to her reading chaise, plucked the box

of tissues off the bookshelf and dropped it in her lap, then went back and, after letting Tsini in, closed the door.

She blew her nose then drew Tsini onto her lap.

He stood between her and the door, scanning her bedroom. He made no disparaging remarks, although the place currently looked like a movie set. Her uncle's interior decorator had had it redone a week ago, in time for a magazine shoot. The cooking show was making a major promo push, highlighting their special angle that the celebs would be filmed in their homes, some for the first time. Her bookshelves and chaise had had to be taken out for the pictures. They'd finally gotten dragged back that morning, after she'd repeatedly asked.

"I think there are things you need to tell me." Nash stood tall and strong, as if standing between her and the world.

At the moment, the thought was incredibly comforting, even if it was only a fantasy.

"We don't have much time before they call you, so go ahead." His voice was steady, his gaze attentive, his demeanor calm. His stance radiated self-confidence.

The power structure had shifted between them. When he'd shown up, she was the boss and he was a hired man. Now he was—

She couldn't find the right word, but the man was clearly in his element.

"Do you know who's after you?" he asked.

"Tsini—"

"You," he corrected with a stubborn look.

She shook her head.

"Other than the death threats involving the dog—"

He looked at Tsini. "And I want all of them, with the exact circumstances of how and when they were received. What else happened?"

Here came the part where she told him, and he would think her crazy, just as the police had.

"I felt at times that I was being followed." She waited for him to roll his eyes.

He listened without giving his opinion away. "What else?"

She drew a deep breath. "A couple of times, I thought someone might have been in the apartment when we were all out. Things were out of place. I don't think it was Angie, the woman who cleans."

"You asked?"

"Yes."

"I'll talk to her. I want to talk to your whole staff."

Just what she didn't need. "Mike and Dave are going to hate that."

Her bodyguards were protective of her and their jobs. They'd been with her for close to three years.

"What extra security measures have they put in place since you told them all this?" Nash's gaze was direct, his tone honed steel.

Point taken. Mike and Dave agreed with the police that the stress of the paparazzi was getting to her. They all thought she was getting paranoid as a result of living under constant stress.

Still, Mike and Dave were not going to let Nash walk all over their work and start to interfere. Yes, she was probably in danger. But she had a strategy and she was working it. And, so far, nothing had happened.

Except that now she was getting those death threats for Tsini. Which really was unacceptable.

"Maybe you could snoop around under the radar. Without them noticing that you're checking into things." She didn't need a power struggle among her staff.

He lifted a dark eyebrow. Here came the part where he would demand full command, she thought. Alpha male was written all over the man.

For a long second, he just watched her. Then he surprised her by saying, "All right. I can do that."

DAMN, he was in so much trouble here. He hadn't been inside Kayla Landon's penthouse for a full hour yet and he was already getting sucked in, getting involved on what felt suspiciously like a personal level. Nash scratched the underside of his chin.

At least he had taken her suggestion. That was something. He was protecting the client without completely taking over her life. Welkins would be proud of him.

"I don't want any of my staff interrogated or inconvenienced," Kayla was saying.

On the other hand, she did need to face reality.

"Do you want to stay alive?" Sometimes a man had to put things bluntly.

She paled. And something else. It was as if she wasn't all that surprised by the severity of her situation. He noted the way she sat—stiff, on guard even in her own bedroom—and wondered what else was going on that he didn't know about, what else had happened that she wasn't telling him.

"You really think my life is in immediate danger?"

She seemed to be holding her breath as she waited for the answer. She was so beautiful, those big blue eyes hanging on him.

For a moment, his mind went blank. Not good.

He focused back on her question. "Someone wants to scare you. His desire to harm you in other ways is not that huge a leap. The fur coat is disturbing. This guy could be a psycho." He drew a deep breath and brought up the issue that had been on his mind for the last ten minutes. "Tell me about the deaths of your parents and your brother."

She blinked, hesitating a moment before she started. "Two years ago, my parents died in a car accident. My father had just gotten a new Porsche. The police said he was driving way too fast. Probably testing its power and all that." Her full lips trembled.

Some lips.

He wasn't going to notice them. He lifted his gaze to her eyes. "What else?"

"Last year my brother died in a skiing accident. Smashed into a tree and broke his neck. His blood alcohol levels were pretty high. He was on a slope that had been shut down due to dangerous conditions." She pressed those tempting lips into a thin line. "He was always a daredevil."

He took in the information, turned it over in his brain. It wasn't all new to him. He'd heard the stories at the time, although he'd paid little attention. Then the facts had come back again when he'd run a quick background check on her. Police reports were cut and dry. Nothing there had piqued his instincts.

Was it unusual to have two lethal accidents in a family within two years? Maybe. But the Landon family wasn't exactly average. Most people didn't drive superpowered Porsches. Most people didn't have the kind of pull to have a closed slope open for their private night-skiing pleasure. You could do a hell of a lot more with money than without, and some of those things were dangerous.

Back when he'd thought this was nothing bigger than some idiot fan trying to get Kayla's attention by sending her dog death threats, he hadn't seen any connection to the family deaths. But she clearly thought there was a connection and she was rattled. And after he'd seen that blue fur coat, he did get that cold feeling in the pit of his stomach. His instincts said there was something more here than what showed on the surface.

"My father wasn't a reckless driver. Lance was never a heavy drinker," she added in a soft voice.

And she would know them best. The uneasy feeling in his gut grew. What she'd just told him changed everything. "If someone's after your family," he told her, "then both you *and* your brother are in danger."

She surprised him by slumping back in the chaise and saying, "I know that."

"How was your day?" Kayla asked Greg over dinner.

Her brother ignored her for a moment, doing Sudoku on the side, next to his plate.

She didn't tell him to put it away. He wouldn't. He had a thing about that. Always had to finish what he started.

Her back ached from being on her feet all day. Sitting up straight and looking upbeat took effort. And she still had other commitments, a business meeting over drinks at a popular restaurant nearby, although she'd cut way back on going out since the threatening notes began to arrive for Tsini. She didn't want to leave the dog alone in the apartment in the evenings.

"Boring, like work always is." Greg finished the puzzle at last and closed the book, then meticulously arranged and rearranged his utensils and his napkin until they were lined up with military precision.

"Do you want me to talk to Uncle Al about that?"

Lance, their older brother, had been a director at the company. Their father had made Kayla financial consultant when she'd received her MBA. He'd put Greg in Human Resources, where he'd said his younger son would do the least damage. Greg was entering old employee files into the computer system, an insult to the twenty-five-year-old with a degree in Organizational Management.

Uncle Al had immediately moved Kayla up in the ranks after their parents' death, to the appropriate level for her education and experience, but had left Greg in HR. Which Greg hated.

"I'm fine." He tugged on his Eagles jersey, a gift she'd recently gotten him, signed by the whole team. "I don't want any more family arguments about this."

Neither did she. God knew, they'd had plenty of that in the past. She hadn't always seen eye-to-eye with her father. But she missed him now that he was gone, and she wished she could take some of those fights back. She'd grown up a lot in the past two years. Maybe they could have discussions now on a different level. Maybe she could make him see reason. Maybe she could engineer some sort of true relationship between him and Greg.

But her father was gone, and she couldn't take back anything they'd said to each other. It was too late to make anything better. She would have felt guilty even if she didn't think that she might have played a role in their parents' and brother's death, something she hadn't told Nash.

The man had thrown her for a loop on more than one level. He was fast. Lightning. In every way. Caught on immediately. And he was hot beyond words, although that part she was going to ignore if it killed her.

"I'm flying out for the dog show tomorrow," she reminded her brother, wanting to switch to a topic that would distract both of them. "I'm so nervous for Tsini. Would you come with us?"

She needed to convince him to tag along. Nash had insisted on that. He didn't want the two of them to separate. He wanted to be able to keep an eye on both of them.

Right now he was down in the parking garage under the building, surveying it for possible security breaches or whatever.

That he believed her and was coming up with a plan to protect them was a relief, even if they didn't agree on anything else. He thought her current security was worthless. She was proud of herself for standing up to him and not letting him ride roughshod over Mike and Dave.

"You'll have fun. If it gets to be too much, you can always hang out in the suite. I reserved the best one they had."

"I hate crowds. I'd rather have a couple of quiet evenings here instead." Greg gave her a sheepish smile.

She would have done anything to see him smile more often. She would have done anything to protect her brother.

For a moment she hesitated on the verge of telling him everything. But as competent and highly functioning as Greg was, he did get stressed easily and when he was stressed, his disability became more pronounced. For that reason, she'd never discussed her suspicions about the "accidents" with him. And though he knew that some sick person out there had threatened Tsini, she hadn't given him any details beyond that.

Something else she'd meant to talk to him about popped into her mind. "I'm thinking about a little get-together for your birthday when we come back. Just family and friends." It'd give her a chance to meet some of the new people he hung out with these days.

His eyes lit up. "Okay."

"You can give me a list of who you want to invite." She hated that she had to keep track of his friends, but past experience had shown that sometimes people took advantage of him and befriended him for monetary gain. All they saw in him was the Landon name.

Even at the company. Their father had had to fire a security guard shortly after Greg had gone to work there. Yancy had quickly become Greg's friend and had taken him to parties after work. To parties and other places. Greg had lost a ton of money betting on illegal street races, which were Yancy's secret passion. Thank God that creep was no longer in the picture.

But Greg had new friends Kayla knew little about,

friends who worried her, considering how much money Greg was borrowing from her lately. She needed to figure out what was going on there, and needed to do it diplomatically, without making Greg feel that she thought he was a child who needed watching over.

"Tsini could use the extra support at the show this year," she told him, returning to that bit again.

Truth was, even before she'd talked to Nash, she hadn't felt comfortable leaving Greg alone, had already talked to the housekeeper about spending more time at the apartment for the next four days. And back then, all she'd had were her own fears and suspicions, since everyone she'd ever told was telling her that she was wrong. And since she wanted to believe that, she'd half talked herself into thinking that they were right and all the stress of the last two years had made her paranoid.

But Nash agreed with her.

And, more than any of the cops she'd brought the issues up to, he looked as though he knew what he was doing.

So most likely there really was someone out there after her family.

Which meant she couldn't leave Greg behind.

He pushed the peas aside on his plate, away from the potatoes. "I'll like staying here."

Of course he would, she thought, ashamed for a moment. He'd never had much autonomy. He'd gone to a small local private college, at their parents' insistence, and had commuted from home every day. Their mother had been overprotective of him. Their father had never had any confidence in his abilities. From the moment he'd been diagnosed, he'd become damaged goods in

Will Landon's eyes. If his son could be of no use in his father's quest to build his empire, Greg was good for nothing. Worse than that, he was ballast.

And as much as she loved him, Kayla hadn't been much better, had not encouraged him to become more independent after their parents' death. He'd been so distraught. She'd insisted on him moving in with her, pleaded with him, telling him she needed him. Then, after his brother's death Greg had become depressed. She should have helped him build his own life, but she was worried about him, so she kept him tethered to hers instead.

And to keep him safe now, she had to continue doing that.

She patted his hand on the table. He had long, slim fingers like their mother's, the blond coloring that Kayla had inherited, as well. He had a slight body, had never been into sports or anything physical. He looked younger than his age, but he was smarter than most people expected. He'd gone through college with the help of a private tutor their father had hired, and had received a degree he'd worked hard for and earned.

He did deserve a normal life. A better life than she was making for him, she thought, and decided to help him become more independent once she was sure they were past all danger. But she needed to keep him close until then.

"I'm nervous. It's a big show for us. I don't know what I'll do without you. I need you there. You don't have to go to any of the big events if you don't want to. Just come along. Please."

And to her relief, Greg nodded.

Chapter Three

He was okay with his assignment changing when it had barely begun. That happened all the time. He didn't mind being responsible for Kayla Landon, her brother and her poodle all of a sudden—especially since she was turning out to be different than what he'd expected. That someone wanted the client in his protection dead and Nash had few clues, no leads beyond the dog's death threats, was par for the course. He liked a good challenge.

But that Kayla wouldn't openly acknowledge him as her bodyguard bugged the hell out of him. He couldn't take charge in any capacity. Even Dave and Mike outranked him.

"You've been in the dog business long?" Mike asked as he made his way toward him, down the aisle between rows of seats, Dave not far behind as the plane flew above a solid layer of clouds toward Las Vegas.

The two men looked enough alike to be related, maybe cousins. They had the bodies of linebackers, plus the whole Secret Service haircut and body language. But Nash had seen plenty of badasses to know that deep down these two weren't real tough guys. The best that could be said about them was that they would look good playing tough guys on TV.

Which meant he was pretty much alone on the job. He felt like someone entering a high-speed chase while being forced to drive from the backseat.

"You two ever been in the service?" He folded his arms, putting his tattoos in plain sight, letting the two men draw their own conclusions, showing an admirable amount of self-restraint.

Resist the urge to take over everything, had been the last thing Welkins had told him, and, *keep the client happy.*

He was doing good so far. They were going to Vegas, not that he didn't absolutely hate the whole dog-show business. At least he'd prevailed in having the entire first-class section reserved for Kayla and her staff.

A flight attendant came by with drinks, drawing Mike and Dave's attention temporarily.

They were on a commercial airline with 231 possible villains—to give himself a break, Nash wasn't counting the crew, just the regular passengers. It was enough to give a man a headache. But Kayla had put her foot down and insisted that on the Landon jet she would have been an even easier target. And at the end he'd agreed. Sometimes there *was* safety in numbers.

"I'll beat the pants off you in blackjack," Elvis, the makeup artist, said, joking around with Fisk, Kayla's agent, and Ivan, her manager, up front.

The two had tagged along because at the last minute she had decided that she would agree to some advertising deals. Since the full amount of income from the ads would go to dog-related charities, her agent and manager were coming to lay the groundwork and take advantage of the media coverage that would already be present.

"Just as long as you know that everything under my pants belongs to my wife," Ivan, a stocky black man, countered with a good-natured laugh.

Greg, Kayla's brother, had been playing some video game obsessively since they'd boarded. He sat in the first row, keeping out of the conversation.

Tsini was gently snoring in the middle of the aisle, not impressed by any of the grand plans for Sin City that were being hatched by the humans. Tom, Tsini's professional handler, was watching an action movie, pretty much ignoring everybody.

Nash was currently running background checks on each of them, plus on the staff who had stayed in Philly: Kayla's secretary, her stylist, everyone she met with regularly, even her uncle. He should have the results by the time the day was out. Her immediate environment seemed like a good place to start looking. Then, as he uncovered more clues, he could widen the circle.

"Semi-pro football," Dave put in, resuming their conversation once the flight attendant passed. "Same as war. Man-to-man combat."

Nash thought of some of the fights he'd bled through where he'd cut people's throats without a second thought and put more bullets through more hearts than he'd cared to count. "I'm sure."

Kayla slept in her window seat next to him in the back. Since he was the newest member of the team, he'd wanted to spend some time with her going over concerns and questions, which they had done for the first hour or so after the plane had taken off. Then she'd passed out from exhaustion.

He would have thought she'd overdone the partying the night before, but her manager had mentioned a late meeting with some business partners.

Her laptop stood open on the beverage tray in front of her. From the corner of his eye, Nash caught a small window opening on the screen. *You have a new message.*

"Civilian life is different than the military." Mike puffed his chest out. "Just watch what we do and you'll be all right."

"Thanks."

"And don't push her." Dave nodded toward Kayla. "She doesn't like that. She has plenty of other stuff to deal with. She needs her staff to be in her corner."

"She needs her staff to protect her," Nash put in.

She looked too young and more innocent than perhaps she'd ever been. If the tabloids could be believed, she'd had enough lovers to fill a football stadium. But right now she looked like a little girl who'd gotten into her mother's makeup and her older sister's closet. If that older sister were a pole dancer.

"She ever get threatening messages?" he asked the men.

"Just the dog. All she gets is fan mail," Mike said.

Dave rolled his eyes. "Tons of it."

"Who processes that?"

Mike gave him a narrow-eyed look that transmitted a clear *back off* message, but did answer his question. "Her secretary."

Next to Nash, Kayla shifted in her sleep.

He turned his head to get her out of his peripheral vision.

He didn't need another flash of those long legs, or creamy thighs. Hell, creamy everything. Enough of her breasts were uncovered for him to bury his face between them. He tamped down the heat that was beginning to tingle to life in the bottom half of his body.

Her stylist should be strangled. Or given a bonus. His opinion on that flip-flopped about once a second.

She was hot. Scorching. There was no denying that. But there was more to her than showed on the surface.

He had a feeling that what he'd thought she was, what he'd seen of her on TV, was going to turn out to be her organization, a persona made up by a full staff. Her organization—the people around her, her schedule, her image—was like a machine. Since they'd met yesterday afternoon, he'd caught glimpses of the woman inside that machine, and was beginning to wonder if she wasn't trapped in there.

Don't get sucked in.

He took a drink of mineral water as Mike and Dave returned to their favorite subject and went on about the bloody combat that football really was, and how they were all warriors. Part of him itched to set them straight—if only to distract himself from Kayla—but another part of him knew it wasn't worth it.

Stick to the job, Welkins had said.

Trouble was, *she* was the job. And he would have liked only too much to stick real close to her.

If he had any brains, he would leave her to Dave

and Mike, walk on back to coach and ask the first pretty woman he saw if she wanted to join the mile-high club with him. He had to get this restlessness out from under his skin.

Except, with Kayla Landon next to him, he didn't feel like walking away.

"I'm thinking the threats to the dog might have something to do with her. Could be someone wants us distracted while he goes after Kayla," he told the two men, interrupting a playoff story.

There was a brief pause as they gave him some hard looks.

"*We* protect her. You stay out of the way and keep your eyes on Tsini," Mike's eyes flashed as he issued his warning at last, the true reason for their coming over.

The two had been eyeing him since he'd shown up at the apartment last night. They obviously didn't like the idea of anyone sticking his nose in their business.

Nash ground his teeth, but somehow managed a nod, silently cursing his latest assignment all the way to Hades. Ivan prevented further friction by calling the two bodyguards to the front to settle some dispute between him and Fisk. Then Nash was finally able to turn his attention to the e-mail.

He'd seen her type in her password earlier and had no trouble getting in now. She had only one unread message.

The sender field was blank. The subject field said: Did you like my gift?

He could have waited until she woke and asked her to open the message and let him look at it. Instead, he reached over and clicked.

No text, only an attachment. He had to wait until the program ran a virus scan before he could open the picture file.

The image was grainy, but good enough to make out what was important. The picture showed Kayla's living room with her sitting in her pod chair and Nash on the couch, holding up the blue fur coat.

Could have been taken with a cell phone. By someone who'd been in Kayla's apartment yesterday when he'd arrived. Which meant all the people who traveled with them in first class right this minute. The cooking-show crew had stayed in the kitchen the whole time. Her staff had been coming and going from the den. And this picture had been taken from there.

By one of her people. One of her friends.

Oh, hell. She was really going to hate him for telling her that, he thought as his blood heated. If there was one thing he couldn't forgive, it was betrayal. In his eyes, maybe because at the core he would always remain a marine, betrayal of a teammate was the ultimate sin. He couldn't stand the thought that a member of her own staff would betray her.

And he couldn't even talk to her about this right away. He needed a chance to observe her interacting with the staff first. Once she realized that whoever was harassing her was one of them, she would relate to them differently. He wanted to get a fair assessment of her relationship with each and every person before suspicion hit her and she pulled back.

He looked at the people in first class. Nobody was watching him. The message had been sent in the last couple of minutes. But anyone could have sent a saved message with a surreptitious click on their cell phone, just reaching for a second into their pockets. Or they could have timed delivery set up from a remote computer.

That was a trail Dave and Mike might not have been able to trace back, but Nash had his sources. He forwarded the note to his own e-mail account, then deleted the original.

He didn't have the previous threatening notes with him. They were already at a lab, along with the fur coat, to be dusted for fingerprints. They weren't much to start with—pictures of poodles printed off the Internet, *DIE* in big block letters printed underneath. But now he had one more clue.

It should have made him happy. Except that one thing about this whole setup bugged him. Why would the bastard send a picture like that? Sure, the photo would make Kayla nervous, would make her feel she wasn't safe even in her own home. But it also narrowed the field of suspects considerably. And that was decidedly not to the sender's advantage.

HE DIDN'T WANT to kill her. He looked out the plane's window and saw her face even in the clouds. He loved her. He'd hoped that harassing that dumb dog of hers would distract her from the "accidents."

But she wasn't distracted, she was thinking, thinking, thinking. He could see it in her eyes every time he looked at her. And she was smart. He couldn't let her figure it all out. She would never forgive him.

He'd set up a last warning for her this morning, but

as she was talking with the new guy, Nash, in the back while the pilot announced that soon they would be landing, he saw that fire in her eyes. And he knew what they were talking about. She was never going to quit.

He reached for his cell phone and sent a text message. He couldn't say he didn't regret it, but it really was time for plan B.

NASH LOOKED around the show area on the first floor of the hotel, checking out the various stations, the seating section for the audience and the ring. Special lighting, microphones, the judges' table—the setup was fancy enough for a Miss America pageant. Except this show was for dogs.

A waste of pageantry as far as he was concerned. Who would want to look at furry canines when they could be looking at hot women in bikinis?

He finished recon and walked back toward the handful of smaller meeting rooms that were set up as storage areas for the dog show. Tom, the handler, had put some hair product for Tsini in his carry-on by accident, and since it was over the allowed ounces, airport security had confiscated the bottle. Tsini needed the special coat-shine spray or whatever for tomorrow so everyone was scrambling around. Tom and Dave were scouring the city's specialty pet shops while Mike and Kayla went to the storage rooms that contained extra supplies for cases just like this.

Nash headed to the back to find them and met Mike halfway there.

"Got it?"

Mike shook his head. "Kayla sent me off to find one of the organizers. Maybe they could tell us if there's any and where exactly it's at. Everything's a mess back there."

"I'll help her." He quickened his pace. Mike shouldn't have left her alone, not even for a few minutes.

Kayla had specifically forbidden him to put the fear of God in her staff. She didn't want everyone nervous, didn't want Greg nervous, didn't want anyone on her staff offended. They were supposed to protect her, but from where he was standing it looked as though so far she was doing all the protecting.

And someone on her staff didn't deserve protection.

Not that the e-mail had turned out to be much of a clue. Nick, an old friend and now business partner, had tracked it. Timed delivery had been set up from Kayla's home office. To which her entire entourage had access.

He opened the first door with a National Canine Club sign. Grooming stations lined the walls, buckets, brushes and about a million stacked boxes filled the place. But Kayla wasn't there.

He moved on to the next room and found her in the back. Way in the back. The room was long and narrow, stacks of dog-show accessories piled six feet high in places.

"Hey, need a hand?"

She turned and brushed her hair out of her face. Silky locks, slim frame, endless legs. She really was stunning. Just didn't have a bad side. No wonder the paparazzi loved photographing her. She was standing on one of the dog crates that were piled high in the back. Some people came with a whole pack of dogs and keeping all their crates in the hotel room would have been impossible, so they were brought down for storage.

"I'm almost there." She scaled another crate, moving higher.

He strode her way. "Let me do that."

Either she couldn't hear him or didn't want his help because she took another big step up. The pile of cages rattled.

He broke into a run. "Kayla!"

She reached for the cardboard box on top that sported a picture of purple spray bottles on the side. Still too high. She climbed another crate. "I think I found the secret stash." She grinned back at him.

He was almost there.

She grabbed the box at last and showed it to him with triumph in her blue eyes. "Just what we needed."

Her leg wobbled, the crate shifted, bumping against another. And then, before he could warn her, before he could reach her, the whole tower came tumbling down, taking her with it.

He dove forward, got clipped in the jaw and saw a couple of stars. A cross hook in the boxing ring couldn't have been more effective. He ignored the pain and went for her, saw her roll as a steel crate crashed to the ground inches from her head.

"Nash!"

Then he was there, using his body to protect as much of her as he could. But still, by the time the avalanche stopped, she was half-buried.

He heaved a heavy crate off her. "Are you hurting anywhere?"

"What do you think?" She was still holding the damn cardboard box.

"Don't move. When I get you clear, just give me a minute to assess the damage." He lifted another crate off her. "You think you broke anything?"

She sat up. "Give it up, Nash. I'm not going to give you an excuse to ship me back home. I came for Tsini and I'm staying here."

He crouched next to her and put his hand gently on the foot closest to him, pulled off her sandals. Bit back a curse. He loved women, but would never understand them. Why on earth would anyone scale perilously stacked crates in four-inch heels? He put some pressure on her toes. "Tell me if this hurts."

When she said nothing, he moved on to the next foot. Then the ankles. One of her knees was bruised. His jaw tightened at the sight. He moved on to the rest of her legs, examining her as close to the edge of her indecently short skirt as he dared. He ignored how smooth her skin was, how toned her muscles, the light scent of her sophisticated perfume. He would rather have stood in front of a firing squad than acknowledge that a fluff piece like Kayla Landon could get him all hot and bothered.

"Your arms?" He kept his voice professional.

She flexed her fingers, rolled her wrists, bent her elbows then shrugged her shoulders. "I'm telling you, nothing's broken. You're overreacting."

"Look at me." He checked her irises, looking deep into her blue eyes, which were tinged with a touch of green, the color of seawater near the surface, the way it looked when you came up after a long dive, toward the sun and air. He blinked.

He was probably too close to her if he could see all that detail. His gaze dipped to her lips, which were glossed with something that smelled like strawberries. *Definitely too close,* his brain said. *Not close enough,* another part of his anatomy insisted.

He pulled back with effort. "Did you hit your head?"

She gave a rueful smile, those tempting lips curving. "Came down on my over-photographed behind."

Definitely a body part of hers that he wasn't going to think about in any detail. "All right," he said brusquely and stepped away from her. "I don't think you have a concussion. Stand up carefully and let me know if you're dizzy."

She rolled her eyes at him and refused his extended hand.

She was a piece of work all right. He had a feeling that the key to keeping her safe was going to be not letting her get to him. He picked up the cardboard box that she'd set down while he'd been examining her. The damn thing held nothing but a jumble of leashes. He tossed it aside. "I'm taking you back to your room."

He went up in the elevator with her, handed her over to Dave, then made his way down into that storage room for another look. He pushed behind the crates, to the wall, and found a door to a back hallway. Empty at the moment, save for all the National Canine Club posters.

But somebody could have been back there earlier. Somebody could have pushed a crate to make sure she fell.

And if Nash hadn't shown up after Mike had left, if

Kayla had been here alone, who knew what else the bastard would have done to her.

Nash scanned every nook of the area as cold fury filled him.

He'd promised Welkins that he wasn't going to go overboard on this mission. He'd promised Kayla that he wouldn't upset her staff.

To hell with that.

He wasn't going let anything happen to Kayla or Greg Landon. And no sick bastard was going to make a coat of the poodle.

BY THE TIME the knock sounded on the door of the adjoining room that night, Kayla was exhausted and sore from her tumble earlier. She had a suite with three bedrooms, plus adjoining rooms on each side. Her brother had a room in the suite, so did her bodyguards. One would use the room, the other would hang out in the living room, for most of the night anyway. Elvis was in one of the adjoining rooms, Nash was in the other. Tom, Ivan and Fisk had their own rooms across the hall.

"Come in."

She put down the show's welcome packet she was reading, flinching when her bruised knee came in contact with the coffee table. Thank God the injury was pretty minor. She was grateful that she hadn't gotten hurt worse than she had. She was determined to enjoy the show despite the stupid threats. Tsini deserved to have her fun. And they *were* going to have fun. Both of them.

"Actually, I was hoping that you would come over." Nash stood in the open doorway.

Mike rose to go with her, but she shook her head so he sat back down in front of the TV. He'd taken it hard that she'd fallen when he hadn't been there. Especially because Nash had been. Some kind of a rivalry was going on there, but she didn't have the energy to deal with it right now.

She padded across the plush carpet barefooted, feeling a twinge of discomfort when Nash closed the door behind her. She was more than aware of the king-size bed that dominated the room, and of how close he was standing. The only way to get away from him was to walk toward the bed.

The room was neat almost to the point of looking unlived-in. He'd already unpacked and put everything away.

"What is it?" she asked as she turned to face him.

He nodded toward his open laptop on the desk, the only sign that the room had an occupant. "You got an e-mail message today."

A second passed before she understood what he was saying. "You hacked into my e-mail?" She looked over, then saw that the sign-in on the screen was his. The inbox was empty save a single item. How had her e-mail ended up in his inbox? And where did he keep his own messages?

"You left your e-mail on while you slept on the plane." He was infuriatingly nonchalant, six foot two of insolent male.

"And you thought it was a good idea to pry into my private life?" Truth be told, she liked his tough-guy attitude, she definitely liked his tough-guy looks, but it was clear that they were going to have to redefine some boundaries.

"If you want something from me, you have to ask before you take." She kept her voice measured to let him know that this point was non-negotiable. He could either respect her privacy or start packing and checking on flights back to Philly. Mike and Dave were capable of watching over both her and Tsini. And Tom was here as well. Plus her manager, plus her agent. She felt pretty well-protected.

Those insolent eyes watched her without blinking. "You might want to look at this."

She had to find a way to reestablish that *she* was the boss.

For one, if Nash wanted something from her, he would need to come to her and not the other way around. It'd been a mistake for her to come here, into his personal space where he held every advantage. Where the air was filled with his faint masculine scent, distracting her. "I'll look at it on my own laptop." By the time she'd woken up on the plane they were landing, and she hadn't had time to check her e-mail.

"You'll want to look at it here."

Something in his voice stopped her. She was practically next to the laptop anyway. She reached over and clicked to open the message, then the attachment.

"This is from last night. I don't understand." But then she began to. She felt chilled suddenly. "It was taken by someone inside the apartment."

He nodded.

"The TV crew was there." She scrambled to think of all the names and faces.

"They stayed in your kitchen."

"I was too distracted. I didn't keep track of them." She tried to remember.

"I did."

"But it doesn't make sense. Someone must have snuck into the den when you weren't looking. One of them snapped this picture, obviously."

"Or one of your staff." He flashed a loaded look toward the closed door behind him. "Motive would be the next question. Have you had any trouble with any of them lately?"

She stammered out a stunned, "No."

"Any trouble ever?"

"They're my family," she snapped.

"Family can do nasty things to a person," he told her, and she wondered if he was speaking from experience.

"Not mine." Not beyond her father's refusal to take his two younger children seriously, and her mother's inability to ever stand up for them. Her parents had been who they had been. They hadn't been perfect, but they hadn't been terrible either.

"First thing tomorrow morning, before we head out for our fun adventure of the day, I'm going to question your staff." His face was set in a mask of determination. He wasn't asking. He was laying down the law for her.

She stuck her chin out. "No."

He considered her. "Did you know there was a door behind those crates you fell off of? Could be someone pushed them."

That gave her pause, but only for a moment. "If anyone was there, I would have seen him. I climbed too high. That was my fault. I didn't pay attention."

He didn't seem impressed with her explanation. "We don't know for sure where any of your staff was at that point."

Anyone who messed with her people messed with her. She walked up and stopped a short foot from him. "You're wasting your energy going in this direction. You need to find the people who don't like my family, not bug people who love me. I'm not going to let you make me paranoid. These are my people. I trust them more than I trust you. You're welcome to investigate anything. I'd be glad for your help, I really would be. But you're *not* to harass my staff." She drew a longer breath at last and pulled her spine ramrod-straight. "Is that clear?"

He had the gall to look amused. "It's often the people who are closest—"

"Listen to me. My staff is my solid base. They're my only support system."

"Your security blanket?" he inquired dispassionately.

She couldn't believe he was mocking her. She jabbed her index finger right into the middle of his mile-wide chest. "Leave them alone. I mean it."

As quick as a striking cobra, he grabbed her wrist and pulled her closer, nose to nose. A dangerous light came into his eyes. The air seemed so thick with tension she half expected lightning. For a second she thought he was going to kiss her.

How irrational was that?

It wasn't as if he'd shown any sign that he was attracted to her. Her gaze dipped to his lips anyway, firm and masculine and way too close. She could smell on his breath the mint candy the hotel provided in the rooms. She could smell his soap, noticed the wet ends at the back of his hair. He must have already showered.

His eyes were dark gold whiskey and focused on her one hundred percent. "As of now, I'm your head of security."

Thoughts of kissing flew out the window.

"I. Am. The. Boss," she spelled out for him as she tugged herself from his grip. "You were hired to keep an eye on Tsini. I'm glad that we agree, and you share my suspicions that someone is after my family. But you're not taking over my life. And you're not going after my staff. You're wrong about this."

He looked ready to fight her, but then backed down, with effort, almost visibly talking himself out of it. But he still looked grim as he said, "Fine. Have it your way. Just think about this, the finger that pushed the camera button could have just as easily pulled a trigger."

She was certain the picture had been taken by one of the camera crew, someone hired by her enemies. Still, even if the threat wasn't as immediate as Nash thought, it was there. Someone who meant her harm *had* been inside her home. And now she had proof, which she was going to take to the police once they got back home.

She thought long and hard about that later that night, before falling asleep. But her final thought was of Nash, their lips separated by mere inches.

There'd been heat. A full-blown solar flare she couldn't deny but was going to ignore with all her power.

A fling in Vegas with the hottest bodyguard in existence. Elvis would approve. But she knew from experience that this was exactly the kind of idea that sounded better than it could ever turn out. And she was so much smarter than to ever think it would be worth the inevitable grief she'd catch at the end.

Nash was all male, but he wasn't for her. He was going to drive her nuts before this was over. And yet, for all his annoying pigheadedness and reading her e-mail, she wasn't going to send him packing first thing in the morning. She was going to keep him.

He was solid and competent, came highly recommended. All she had to do was establish firm control and make him understand that as far as her life and her team were concerned, she was the one making the decisions.

Once he got that, the rest should be easy.

Chapter Four

Dog show was another way of saying *hell overrun by prissy canines.* Someone should have told him that.

And Nash was stuck in the poodle section, the place obviously reserved for the darkest sinners, because it was for sure the darkest corner of hell. The dogs had hairdos. Some had their own calendars—no joke—and pinup posters that were being sold to fans. There were dogs with leashes that matched the dresses of their owners. Who in their right mind would think of something like that?

"I think we might win a ribbon this year. I really do," Kayla was enthusing to Elvis, routinely ignoring the open looks in her direction. She'd fielded the earlier influx of people wanting autographs with grace and class, and they were beginning to dwindle at last.

She let anyone and everyone just walk up to her. The woman was a bodyguard's worst nightmare. He wanted to take over so badly his teeth ached. But he kept his macho drive to control every situation in check. He couldn't afford to be kicked off the job.

Every penny he'd ever saved had been invested, in a weak moment, in some new program a buddy of his had invented. Nick Tarasov and his wife, Carly, were a couple of geniuses when it came to computer codes. They regularly worked on top-secret projects for the U.S. government. But they had yet to crack the commercial market. So Nash's money could be as good as flushed down the swirly bowl or, if he were lucky, he might get back some of it by the time he was ready to retire.

Not something he worried a lot about since in his line of work, chances were better than good that he wasn't going to live that long. When your job was to step between a bullet and its intended recipient, sooner or later you were going to be tapped, for sure.

Ducking bullets seemed a hell of a lot more fun than his current "entertainment," he thought, then bit back a groan when Kayla kicked his already dark mood another notch lower.

She pulled Tsini's pink brush from her bag and handed it to him. "Hold this."

Lack of funds or not, when he was done here, he was going to have to retire. There was no coming back from this. By the end of the show, he was going to be irreversibly damaged.

Thank God there was no chance whatsoever that he would run into anyone he knew. If there were, he'd have to go into witness protection to get away from the merciless ribbing. There were things no man could live down. Not on his team.

He was holding a pink poodle brush. If that wasn't the low point of his life, he didn't want to know what was.

Nash watched Kayla who—God help him—actually looked excited to be here. Women were a mystery. That was one of the profound truths of life. No doubt about it.

"Isn't this fun?" She beamed as she took the brush back from him and fluffed up Tsini's fur on the shoulders. "You should really try to enjoy it."

He thought, *three more days and counting*.

They were at a meet-and-greet thingy, the competition wouldn't start until tomorrow morning, but he recognized tonight's event for what it was—assessing the enemy.

On the surface, there were enough smiles for an Oscar ceremony. Emotions ran deep behind those toothy grins, however. He detected amazing amounts of hostility. His senses were on alert.

And he wasn't the only one.

People watched, calculated, dropped the occasional snide remark, or else killed with kindness. There was as much tension in the air as before any battle he'd seen.

If it weren't for the cell-phone photo, he would have been sure the source of the threatening messages was someone from here. Could still be. Could be some dog-show rival paid someone on Kayla's staff. Something to definitely consider. Maybe the threats to Tsini had nothing to do with Kayla's family tragedies.

Except that wasn't what his gut was telling him.

He'd been watching the staff on the plane, and every chance he'd gotten since their arrival. He'd searched their luggage, one by one, as they left their rooms on errands. He made a point of talking with them, measuring them up, waiting for a dropped word or any hint in body language that they were not who they seemed to be.

Nothing had jumped out at him so far.

He planned on keeping up the vigilance. Sooner or later, the bastard was going to trip.

Most of the staff had come down to the meet-and-greet to check out the competition and give Kayla advice and moral support, supposedly.

Elvis held her hand. He seemed pretty protective of her. True friend or pretending? He went on the maybe list.

Dave was eyeing the statuesque brunette who was giving the welcome speech up front. Mike had stayed up in the suite with Greg, who hadn't wanted to come down. He'd bought a giant puzzle of the Vegas Strip in the hotel's gift shop, and wouldn't move from that until it was finished. *Can't before I finish,* seemed to be his mantra.

Both bodyguards had been in the apartment when the photo had been taken. But for now, Nash was keeping them on the trusted list. They had an official record in the trade. Clean. They were from a reputable outfit. The personal-protection business to the stars—the circle they ran in—was still small enough that everyone knew pretty much everyone else, the players relying heavily on references.

Then there was Tom, Tsini's handler. His job was to carry Tsini when she was crated. He was also responsible for exercising the dog and working on all aspects of the show, including Tsini's styling. When Tsini had to go in front of the judges, Tom would be the one walking her. Kayla Landon in the ring would be way too distracting.

Nor would Nash have allowed it.

Tom was about the same age as Nash, with gym

muscles and shifty eyes, scars all over that he explained as old dog bites. He tried to dress to the upscale image the rest of Kayla's team projected, but fell short despite his expensive slacks and shirt.

His record had a few blemishes, but nothing serious and nothing recent. A couple of bar fights that had gotten out of hand. As far as Nash could tell, the man had turned his life around years ago. Still, given his background and going by sheer looks alone, he would have been Nash's number-one suspect, except that he hadn't been at the apartment last night, so he couldn't have taken that picture.

Nash kept an eye on him anyway. Especially around Greg. He'd seen Kayla slip an envelope to her brother the day before, and he had an idea it'd held cold, hard cash. Greg needed money for something or someone. And Tom had clothes way more expensive than his fees would support. Could be he was taking advantage of Greg in some way. Another thing to be investigated.

He went down his mental list of suspects so far: Fisk, Ivan and Elvis. And Elvis was allowed around Kayla with sharp instruments. When on the road, in addition to her makeup, he also did her hair.

The speaker up front made an industry joke Nash didn't get. But all around him people laughed.

"*Ay mios dio!* How true is that!" Elvis clapped with as much grace as a princess.

He spoke fluent Spanish, not that he had a single drop of Latin blood in him. He volunteered at an inner-city community center, giving unemployed people make-overs before they went for interviews. He'd even produced an educational video at one point about the connection between appearance, self-respect and success. He was currently single, having just broken up with his longtime boyfriend. He didn't seem any the worse for wear. But he was perpetually broke, although Kayla paid him well. He tended to give his money away. Didn't believe in worrying about finances. He was one of those always cheerful people Nash couldn't relate to. Highly excitable by nature.

Nash glanced at Tsini, who handled the excitement with dignity. She must have felt Nash watching her, because she turned to look at him then licked his hand. He petted her, but kept his attention on Kayla's entourage.

Since his instincts didn't point in any specific direction, he would keep an eye on all of them. He wished he could have done that anywhere but here. The show, with its thousands of people, hundreds of dogs and incomprehensible rules, was a chaotic mess already and it had barely started.

He caught a tall, bald guy to his left giving Kayla furtive looks. The man greeted people here and there, smiled, shuffled, all the while coming closer and closer. Pink polo shirt and khaki slacks, no telltale bulge around his waist that might indicate a weapon. He had his right hand in his pocket. Not a big enough bulge there either for a gun, but he could have a knife. Nash stepped between him and Kayla, keeping one eye on the man while glancing around, making sure he was alone.

He kept coming. Then he was close enough for Nash to make a quick turn and bump into him as if by accident, brushing an arm against the back of his waist.

"Sorry." Definitely no gun there.

The guy pulled his hand from his pocket.

Nash's hand went to his back as if to adjust his jacket, but his fingertips were touching his Beretta.

Then the guy's hand came free. Empty. And Nash left his weapon where it was for the time being.

He watched as the guy weaseled around the team and ended up on Kayla's other side. Nash stepped into position behind him. She still hadn't noticed anything, but the man noticed everything about her. He kept stealing glances when he thought nobody was looking. Then he reached out and stuck his fingers into the pink bag Kayla had left unzipped.

A pickpocket?

Nash moved to grab him, but Kayla turned first, her eyes going wide.

"Marcus? I didn't see you. Showing Bella again?"

The man snatched his hands back. "Her daughter, actually." He gave another glance to the pink bag. "Any new secret weapons this year?"

Kayla stiffened as she looked at her open bag. Then with a level look to the man, she pulled the zipper closed. "Are you spying on me again?" Her voice held no fear, only annoyance. She gave a back-off look to Nash over the guy's shoulder.

Nash stayed where he was.

"Of course not," the man was saying. "Just came over to wish you good luck."

Kayla held the bag tighter under her arm. "Good luck to you, too." She grimaced at Marcus's back as he left.

A dog-show spy.

All Nash could do was shake his head. And simmer in frustration that he didn't have full run of the show here. He hated that Welkins had about tied his hands and Kayla had finished the job, pretty much making a bow on the end of the ropes.

She was not safe in this crowd. Yet, short of throwing her over his shoulder and carrying her back to her room, there was nothing he could do. She didn't realize the impossibility of their situation. Sure, keeping an eye on her staff when they were near her was not that difficult. But he kept having this feeling that there was more to all this.

Everyone on her staff was better off if she were alive. The money came from her. If any of them killed her, that would be the end of their job. Unless they had a promise for more money from someone else. Or they hated the whole Landon family so much that they simply didn't care what taking them out would cost.

The brunette up front, apparently the show chairman, finished her welcome speech and walked off the small stage to another round of applause.

"Let's mingle," Kayla said.

"Let's not," Nash responded, but she was already moving out as if she hadn't even heard him, Dave a few paces behind her.

Fisk joined them.

Ivan was off to network, not the type to waste a minute. Elvis was chatting up Marcus. Tom headed off toward the vendor booths.

Nash took one last look at them then went with Kayla, Fisk and Dave, his blood pressure inching up with every step. Looked like they needed to have another talk about her safety. She needed to stop pushing. She still didn't seem to understand that the fact that her life was in danger meant that she needed to do what he said so he could keep her safe. But this was neither the time nor the place for that talk, so Nash turned his attention to other business.

"How long have you been working for her?" he asked Fisk. He used every chance he got to talk to her staff. Sooner or later the bastard who'd taken that photo would slip up. They always did.

"Four years." The man stretched his neck to look around, although he was a head taller than everyone else in their vicinity.

He was in his late twenties, skinny and well-dressed. According to his record, he was a self-made man. Came from a poor Canadian family and pulled himself up by his bootstraps. His younger sister was a ballerina with the Ottawa Institute of Ballet. Both his parents were dead. No criminal record. No financial difficulties now either. In fact, he had zero outstanding debt. Kayla seemed to get along great with him.

"She could be a major star by now if she wanted to, you know. Modeling, movies, whatever she wanted. She gets offers all the time. She could be one of those supercelebrities."

"She doesn't want to be?" That was news to Nash.

"She hates the whole circus," Fisk said with slight resignation.

She did? Nobody could be on the cover page of the tabloids as much as she was without doing everything in her power to get there, could they? He'd always figured her as the kind who would do anything for attention.

"She does as few appearances and ads as possible, just enough to keep her charities in cash." Fisk waved at someone in the distance.

So she gave her celebrity income away. Big deal. She still had Daddy's empire to live off of. William Landon had built the regional popcorn business he'd inherited into a confectionary powerhouse that dominated the national market. And from the time she'd blossomed into a showstopper as a young adult, Kayla had been the face of the business. She became the Popcorn Princess.

"She gives away millions of dollars every year," Fisk was saying.

That brought Nash up short. He wouldn't have guessed that. In fact, she'd always been featured in the media as rather self-centered. He figured she only played at the whole charity bit to counteract that. But several millions of dollars was no play.

To earn that much money took serious commitment. To give it away took a genuine, caring heart.

Kayla Landon.

He'd be damned.

She could have easily let the truth be known. The paparazzi was always hungry for any news of her. But for some reason she kept her impressive charity contributions to herself, letting only some surface bits show. Almost as if she played down her good side in public and played up the bad.

Most people Nash knew did just the opposite.

So who was the real Kayla? And why was she pretending?

He watched her hips sway as she walked up front with Tsini, the hem of her skirt barely reaching midthigh. Her toned legs went on forever. His muscles tightened. He'd been in a state of semiarousal since he'd set foot in her apartment. She was enough of a woman to push any man over the edge.

Except him. Not him. He wasn't going to go there, no sir. She was a client. He as much as laid a finger on her and Welkins would have his head—or some other, more sensitive body part—on a platter. He'd definitely never work in private security again.

He needed to focus on the job.

"Must be frustrating to work for someone like her," he remarked to Fisk. "You want to take her as far as possible and she doesn't want to go. Is that what agents call a nightmare client?"

"Nah, man." Fisk laughed. "She's the best. She's my favorite. Down-to-earth, good head on her shoulders. She's plenty big as it is. More wouldn't make her happier. You know what I mean?"

There wasn't an ounce of animosity in the guy's tone or body language. And he didn't have much of a motive, either. If Fisk resented that Kayla didn't bring in enough money because she held back, killing her would have earned him even less. And the murder of her parents and older brother wouldn't have made any sense whatsoever.

"There's a guy over there that I need to talk to." Fisk was waving again at someone over the crowd. "You keep an eye on my girls."

"That's why I'm here." And *not* to look at Kayla's assets, he reminded himself, taking his gaze elsewhere. Then he nearly blew his top as she sent Dave off on some errand.

"So we agree that your life is in danger and you send Dave off. How smart is that?" He came up next to her.

"I still have you and Tsini."

Damn right, she did. He scanned the room for her staff, for anyone else who might be watching, maybe an outsider who had paid off one of the staff to take that picture. Still not having a good handle on that bugged him to hell.

"Hang on to these, I'm going to try on that top." She handed him the big pink shoulder bag that carried Tsini's accessories. Then she gave him the end of the dog's pink leash. The leather was covered in sparkles.

Before he could protest, she was taking a skimpy shirt from a vendor's table and stepping into a makeshift changing booth.

"I don't want you out of sight," he called after her.

"You can see my feet under the curtain."

Yes, he could. But he still had half a mind to go in there after her. Especially as the people who walked by gave him the once-over. Some smiled, some gave him come-hither looks. And not just the women! Man, oh, man, he needed to get out of here. He needed a smoky bar, a big cigar and a tumbler of twelve-year-old malt in his hand. He wanted a big-screen TV with a game on in the corner and a woman on his lap.

But even as he thought that, it was Kayla Landon's face and tempting body that flashed into his mind.

Tsini gave him a questioning look as he swore under his breath.

"It's not easy being a man," he told her. "You wouldn't understand."

Kayla popped out of the changing booth just then. The top she had on sported a winking dog outlined in glitter. He'd known her long enough now and was a good enough judge of character to know that she wasn't a bimbo. But she definitely dressed like one and acted like one in public. Did she need attention that badly?

"What do you think?" She tilted her head.

The white fabric was so sheer he could practically see her nipples. Hell, he could practically taste them. Predictably, his body responded.

"Or would you prefer the black?"

He would have preferred to get the hell out of there. "This one's fine." His voice came out thicker than he'd intended.

"Fine?" Kayla seemed disappointed as she pulled back behind the curtain.

She was out in another minute or two, back in her own top that was just as provocative as the one she'd just taken off. Nash practically threw the pink bag and leash at her.

"Well, I like it." She paid for the shirt and signed an autograph for the vendor before they moved on.

Kayla handed him the plastic bag. White with pink dogs on it. Tsini gave a high-pitched bark that sounded suspiciously like laughter.

"Don't forget who's watching your back," Nash warned the dog. He could have sworn she was grinning. Did dogs do that? Man, he was so far out of his element here…

"Oh, hi, you're here this year. It's so great to see you again." An older woman came up to Kayla with a warm smile. "Tsini's been doing better and better hasn't she? I think this year she's going for a win."

Nash fell a few steps back to give them the illusion of privacy, watching every move the woman made, his right hand free to go for his gun at a moment's notice. After the woman moved on, a tall, buff guy chatted Kayla up, his eyes all over her body. She was all smiles, didn't seem to mind. Nash certainly did.

She talked to dozens of people as they moved around the room. That was what everybody was doing. This was, after all, a networking event. The buzz of conversations filled the large arena. He kept a careful eye on each person who approached her, and those who watched her from afar. He always stayed within reach, ready.

Picking the serious players out of a crowd wasn't that difficult. Men like him always watched, were always ready for action. They could be relaxed on the surface, but their muscles were wound, waiting to deflect or deliver an attack. When they had to carry something, they carried it in their left hand. Their right was always empty. Basically, he looked for his own mirror image out there in the crowd—someone whose level of alertness was a notch above everybody else's. But for the next hour or so, he found no one suspicious, nothing extraordinary.

Then Kayla wanted to go up to her room for a bite. He had insisted that she take her meals in her suite. For once she'd relented, if only because she wasn't keen on people staring at her while she ate, and constantly interrupting her meal for autographs.

They had the elevator all to themselves on the way up. Tsini lay at her feet.

"So how are you surviving your first day at the dog show?" she asked in a tone that told him she knew very well he hated the damn thing. She probably enjoyed every moment of his misery.

"All in all, I think I'd prefer armed combat."

She grinned, her face lighting up with humor, her strawberry-glossed lips stretching wide. "I bet."

He needed to focus on something other than those lips. "You don't always come. Why are you here this year?"

The smile slid off her face. "I didn't want Tsini to come without me. I know we kind of think that those notes and the coat are about me, but if she's in any danger, I'm not going to let her go across the country without me being there." She shrugged. "Some work came in, too. Everyone's here in one place. It's convenient. Fisk and Ivan can make their deals."

"You trust both of them?"

"Yes." She didn't hesitate as much as a tenth of a second.

He followed her out of the elevator and down the hall, held his hand out for her room key.

She gave it with a roll of her eyes. "We're in a conference hotel with thousands of people around. Nobody is going to be stupid enough to try to hurt me here."

Maybe she was right and maybe she wasn't. Her parents and brother had been killed when they'd been alone, no witnesses. But Nash wasn't about to take any chances. He scanned the rooms. "Where's Greg?"

"Probably went down to look for us. I'll call his

cell." She dialed. "Hey, I just came up with Nash. We're going to order some food. Want to eat with us? Okay. Have fun."

"All clear." Nash told her when he was finished checking the room.

"He's in the casino. He won't be long. He doesn't like places with a lot of people." Kayla let Tsini off her leash and headed for her bedroom. "He decided to try out the slot machines. Mike is with him. I hope he'll win at least a little and have fun." Then she thought for a minute. "Or maybe not. A couple of years ago he had some trouble with gambling."

"A casino rat?" He couldn't see it. He was having some difficulty pinning Greg down. In fact, he had trouble getting near him. Kayla was superprotective of her brother.

"Illegal street racing." She shook her head, all wide-eyed. "Can you believe that?" she asked as she disappeared behind her door.

"Sounds more fun than pushing coins into a machine," he called after her. Maybe Greg wasn't as done with it as Kayla thought either. He'd asked her for money for something. Nash still needed to look into that.

He picked up the room-service menu from the desk, but had barely opened the thing when Kayla screamed.

He had to fight Tsini to get through the door first. He had his gun out, grabbed Kayla with his left hand and pushed her behind his back, ready to face anything. Then he saw what had scared her.

Someone had sliced open her pillow. Feathers were all over her bed.

She had probably pulled the comforter back when she'd come in. It had been in place when he'd checked the room, so he hadn't seen any of this mess.

He swore under his breath as he stashed his gun back into his waistband. "Don't touch anything." He backed out of the room with her, already calling Mike and Dave to get up there and bring Greg with them.

"He's here." Kayla's eyes were huge in her face, her voice broken. "You were right."

Her admission gave him no pleasure. "It has to be one of the staff." She had to accept that.

"They were all down with us except for Mike and Greg," she said, stubborn to the end.

"I couldn't keep an eye on everyone every minute. Any one of them could have snuck back up here after Greg and Mike left."

"Other than me, Greg, Mike and you, only Dave has a key card."

Definitely something to consider. Along with the gall of the bastard. That he would do this right under Nash's nose. His blood heated.

"Hotel doors are easier to open than you'd think. Fire them all. Now. Send them home." He could protect her, Greg and Tsini for the rest of the show, or ask Welkins to send in more men. They'd figure out what to do once they got back to Philly. He could even take her to a safe house while he launched a serious investigation into who among the staff was responsible.

"No."

Man, she loved that word. "One of them is out to get you."

"Maybe. But the rest aren't. They've been loyal to me for years. I'm not going to dump them. They deserve more than that."

She was loyal. He couldn't say he didn't like it, even if just now the quality was to her detriment. "You deserve to stay alive. You can't be surrounded by people we can't trust. Fire them. Seriously."

"Somebody else could have gotten in here."

He couldn't argue with that. He'd broken into more hotel rooms than he cared to count.

"My staff stays." The fire in her eyes told Nash she really meant it.

Someday he was going to have to ignore her wishes and save her despite herself. And get fired shortly after, most likely. But today was not that day. He could humor her a little longer. He was with her round the clock. The cocky bastard wouldn't be able to help himself. He'd do something else to scare her, and Nash would be ready.

He rubbed a hand over his face. "Fine. But I'm taking over your security. No more hiding that I'm here to protect you. I can't keep you safe with a hand tied behind my back. I *will* talk to everyone. They *will* answer my questions."

She glanced at the feathers on her bed, the vicious slice in the pristine white pillow cover. "All right," she agreed at last with a haunted look on her face that twisted something inside his chest.

"But you can't be rough on them. I still think they have nothing to do with this."

"Of course you do," he told her, having just figured out something about her. "You're a middle child. You're a peacemaker. I work differently."

"Going after everyone who moves?" she accused him.

"Just the enemy. Look, I used to be military. Find the bastards, kill the bastards. That's pretty much me." And he wasn't going to apologize for it.

"You're a warrior," she summed up with a dismayed look that said she wasn't the least impressed by him.

Which shouldn't have bothered him nearly as much as it did.

KAYLA SAT on the edge of the couch, a bundle of nerves as she watched Nash take apart her staff, one by one. Nobody had an alibi for the time when her pillow had been sliced. Everyone had been off doing their own thing, except for Mike and Greg, but even they had split up for a while in the casino. Which she didn't like in the least. Mike should have been more careful than that. She couldn't bear if anything happened to Greg.

She couldn't help but think that Nash would never have been that careless. He hadn't let her out of his sight save for their bathroom breaks. And then he'd arranged for backup.

"Who the hell are you to question my loyalty to Kayla?" Mike was getting right in Nash's face on the other side of the living room.

She half lifted from the couch, ready to intervene if they came to blows, but Nash stood completely still, the epitome of calm strength. And she sank back down.

She would have been lying if she said that his strength didn't draw her. Her father had been a powerful man. Not as physically powerful as Nash, but powerful in other ways. But her father had always used his strength to dominate other people for his own good. Nash was using his strength to protect her.

Mike threw his hands in the air and walked away from him, giving up at last.

Everyone was tired. Nash had been questioning them about the photo and the sliced pillow for over two hours, as they came back into the suite for dinner, one by one. Dinner was artfully arranged on the table, food that nobody touched. Kayla wasn't hungry either. Her stomach felt as if it had a lead ball sitting in it.

"Who the hell do you think you are to bust his chops like that?" Dave took Nash to task, standing up for Mike.

They were second cousins, had worked together forever. Those two made a tight team and didn't take it well when their authority was challenged.

"I'm the new head of security." Nash looked around the room, daring anyone to challenge him as he broke the news at last.

All eyes flew to her for confirmation, and then went wide with dismay as she gave a weary nod. "I don't know what else to do. I don't think anyone here has anything to do with this, but if someone is out to get me, any of you could get hurt. Nash has the most experience."

"He knows nothing about you," Dave protested, taking a couple of steps toward her, his muscles rigid with anger, his neck turning red.

"For now." She tried to placate him, placate all of them. "We'll figure out the long-term plan when we get back home."

The day was almost over. Only three more to go. Tomorrow Tsini would attend the Group Ring and compete for the Best of Group title in the Non-Sporting category. Then, if she did well, she'd be in the Best of Show competition on Sunday afternoon. There was nothing but the closing gala after that, then various club meetings Monday morning before everyone headed out.

Kayla normally enjoyed these events. They were the only public functions she attended where the attention wasn't on her. Everyone who came here came for the dogs, was fanatical about the competition, and seeing someone famous was nothing but a minor ripple in the day. She liked these shows and unless she had conflicting engagements, she made a point to be here for Tsini. But this time around, try as she might, she couldn't get into all the excitement and anticipation as she usually did. Her nerves were on edge.

As if sensing that, Tsini came over and put her head in Kayla's lap.

"Starting tonight, I'll be sleeping in the living room here." Nash pointed at the couch Kayla was sitting on. "Mike can have my room."

Mike glared at him. Animosity simmered in the air. She hated how her safe inner circle had gotten turned upside down in the past two hours. Everyone was filled with negative energy all of a sudden.

She still couldn't believe that any of them would betray her, wouldn't believe it until she saw solid proof. She prayed that would never happen.

"I'm going to be with Kayla full-time," Nash went on. "Dave and Mike will back me up and watch Greg. Everyone else, keep your eyes open. And don't forget about Tsini either. She shouldn't be left alone for a minute, not even in the suite. Obviously," he added.

He'd asked them all a lot of questions and had reshuffled the power structure of the team, but he hadn't outright accused anyone. He'd said that technically anyone could have gotten into her room. He'd mentioned the picture from her home, as well, but had left open the possibility that whoever was behind all this could have paid off a member of the camera crew who had been there that night. He didn't want her team to know that he suspected one of them.

Not yet.

Lull the bastard into a sense of complacency, were the words he'd used when they'd discussed his approach earlier, although *discuss* was a rather strong word for what had really happened—he'd told her what he was going to do, and this time he hadn't listened to any of her objections.

She'd been crazy to ever think that she could keep him in check. Nobody was the boss of Nash Wilder. He stood in the middle of the room now like a general mustering the troops. He watched, assessed, gave orders.

She knew a ridiculous number of powerful people. But their power came from the outside—from their companies, their money, their social and political connections. Nash's power came from within, and every other man she knew simply paled in comparison.

On a very basic, primal level, the incredible maleness of him spoke to her feminine core. She found it difficult to take her eyes off the man. Trouble was his middle name. And his first. And his last. That her heart beat faster every time she looked at him was completely ridiculous. They had *nothing* in common.

If she got involved with him, the media scandal would be out of this world. Popcorn Princess Takes Bodyguard as Lover. She flinched at the imagined headline. But at the same time, the thought of them being lovers stirred something deep inside. She was a woman. That was it. Nothing more. She couldn't imagine any woman not responding to all that male energy. But he was not what she needed.

She'd made so many mistakes in her past relationships. Painful mistakes. Public mistakes. Figuring out what she needed, what she wanted in a man, had taken a long time, but she had it now at last. Nash Wilder was definitely not that man.

She wanted someone in her own social circle, someone who would be less likely to be interested in her money. She wanted someone with a business background who would help her run the company. *Help her.* Not take over. A sensitive, diplomatic, wonderful beta male. Nothing like Nash Wilder.

Okay, maybe similar in looks and sexiness. But not as sexy. She couldn't imagine anyone as sexy as Nash. Which was fine. For a sensitive, quiet man who supported her every step of the way, she was willing to give up the washboard abs and those wide shoulders.

"Kayla?"

His voice snapped her out of her musings.

"Did you want to add anything?" One dark eyebrow arched. He watched her as if trying to figure out what she'd been daydreaming about.

God, she hoped her face didn't give anything away. "No. That's it. Thanks."

"All right." He turned to the rest of the team. "I know this was difficult. I appreciate everyone answering all my questions. Let's grab something to eat then get to bed. We have a big day tomorrow."

His attention being focused elsewhere, the tension in her shoulders eased, and she got up to check on Greg. She'd talked him into staying in his room while Nash talked to the others. Being in a strange environment was already hard enough on him. She didn't want to add any more stress on top of that.

She walked in after knocking. "How is the movie?"

"Almost over. Pretty much everyone's dead."

Greg had developed a fondness for mafia flicks of late. She couldn't figure out what the appeal was. Maybe the rules that governed them. Greg liked rules. They made him feel safe. He liked any kind of orderliness in general.

His room was as superclean and organized as Nash's. Greg didn't deal well with a mess. He was so highly functional in other areas that his small idiosyncrasies took people by surprise sometimes, but Kayla was used to them.

She went over to the armchair where he sat and pressed a kiss to his head. "Good night."

"Good night, sis." He patted her hand on his shoulder, but didn't take his eyes off the screen.

She might not have liked Nash shaking everything up, but she did appreciate that he'd brought Greg under his umbrella of protection. She'd been telling herself that nobody could possibly consider Greg any sort of a threat. He was barely involved at the company, he didn't even have full say over his own trust fund, but under the layers of denial she'd been worried. She couldn't stand it if anything happened to Greg. He was the only close family she had left.

She stepped back out into the living room, her hand on the doorknob.

"You should leave that open," Nash told her from the couch. "Yours, too."

"We're on the sixty-third floor. What do you think the chances are of someone coming through the window?"

He watched her unblinking. "Even if it's one in a million, I want to be prepared."

He was always prepared, she had no doubt about that. She was the one who'd been caught unawares. But then again, she doubted anything could have prepared her for Nash Wilder.

He'd come to keep an eye on Tsini, and then he had taken over.

She understood that all this was for her own good, but on some level she resented the intrusion in her comfortable life. He was changing everything, making her question herself, making her question her staff. Making her want him, dammit.

That was the hardest admission to make.

Even if she lost complete control of her surroundings, she liked to think that she, at least, always had control over herself. She hated the feeling that she was losing that. Nash was getting to her without half trying. She didn't want to think about what would happen if he ever actually put his mind to it and came after her.

She rolled over and tangled herself in the sheets, kicked to free her legs.

Her awareness of him was driving her nuts.

And there was no getting away from him. Even now, from the couch, he could see her in her bed. She could see him. How on earth was she supposed to fall asleep like that?

Chapter Five

Nash sat between Kayla and Ivan as they watched Tom lead Tsini around the ring. Greg sat on Kayla's other side, playing on his iPhone, looking up now and then to keep track of the show's progress. Dave sat on Greg's left, while Mike had a seat in front of them. Their side of the arena was set up as the Group Ring. The other side was for the Breed Classes. Tsini didn't participate in that. Thank God.

Everything took forever as it was. They'd waited all morning for the Non-Sporting group, the group in which standard poodles competed, to have their turn.

He scanned the people around them, looking for anything suspicious. Everyone else's attention was riveted on the dogs in the ring as they walked in a circle, led by their handlers. The crowd quieted as the dogs stopped and lined up for the judge.

A couple of handlers held up their dogs' tails to offer the perfect stand.

Nash shook his head.

"I know what you mean," Ivan said under his breath, low enough so Kayla wouldn't hear.

Nash had noticed that she was rather sensitive to anyone making fun of the whole dog-show business. She was prepared to take all this completely seriously for Tsini.

"In my world, you can't hold up your own tail, you get no prize," he told Ivan and they shared a manly laugh.

Predictably, Kayla glared at them.

He cleared his throat. "Excellent showmanship." He'd heard the phrase a few times while they waited all morning for their turn.

Ivan was shaking his head now. He was short and round, bald, a genial black man in his late thirties. He was a family man through and through with little twin girls and a toddler son. A dyed-in-the-wool hockey fan. He was in the middle of having a new house built in the suburbs, trading in his condo so each of the kids could have their separate bedrooms when they were older. He did have a mortgage, but nothing unmanageable. Nash could find no financial motive for him to be involved in anything against the Landon family. He handled a lot of money for Kayla, and as far as Nash could tell, not a penny of it was missing.

For this show, between Ivan and Fisk, they had scared up about a million dollars worth of advertising gigs with nothing left to do but finalize details. They had a couple of meetings that afternoon.

Tsini had nothing else to do for the rest of the day. The afternoon Group Ring belonged to the Sporting, Working and Toy categories. Whatever that meant.

Kayla was leaning forward in her chair, drawing Nash's attention to the ring.

The judge called four dogs out of the lineup. Tsini was one of them. Was that good or bad?

Good, he figured when Kayla grabbed Greg's hand with her left and his with her right. She was squeezing as she waited, perched on the edge of her chair as if she were about to fly away, oblivious to everything else.

He couldn't say he minded her touching him. He could have stood a lot more of it, in fact. Sleeping on the couch, being up half the night and watching her sleep in her sprawling bed, had put a few improper and unprofessional ideas in his head.

Images that he tried hard to forget.

She was a client, he reminded himself for the umpteenth time.

He'd already done the whole celebrity-heiress thing and it had led to nothing but trouble. He'd lost his head before, and because of that, Bobby was dead. He was never going to forgive himself for that.

The last thing he needed in his life was Kayla Landon. They had nothing in common. She was bossy as hell. Flashy. She'd want everything her way for sure.

He was definitely not going to go there.

And to make sure of that, he was looking straight ahead, not at her, not at her low-cut shirt and her breasts that were about spilling over as she leaned even more forward, holding her breath.

The four dogs had to walk another circle around the judge who only looked at them this time. She'd touched them all over when they'd first started. Even examined their private places, which struck Nash as rather odd, not that Tsini seemed to mind. She took everything like a pro.

He'd been skeptical about the whole show, feeling sorry for the dogs, to be frank. But watching closely all morning, he had to admit most of the animals seemed to thrive under all that attention.

Even now, Tsini practically pranced around the ring, her head held high, eating up the attention. She must have known on some level that all the excitement was about her, that she was doing well. She was eating it all up.

Then the judge pointed at her. "First." Then at the dogs that walked behind her, a Dalmatian and a Boston terrier. "Second, third. In that order."

Kayla was on her feet.

He jumped up to pull her back to her seat. Security was pretty tight, but he personally knew a number of snipers who could have easily gotten by the hotel security that worked the event.

"You need to sit. Don't make yourself an easy target."

Instead, she flew into his arms and folded her slim arms around his neck.

A couple of cameras flashed.

Great. Just what he needed.

"She won!" Kayla jumped up and down while still holding on to him, creating more frontal friction than he was comfortable with and a lot less than he needed. "She's Best of Group!" She let him go, then turned to hug Greg who was grinning from ear to ear.

Then Nash succeeded in pulling her back into her seat at last.

"Oh, my God. Wasn't she fantastic? Did you see that?"

People were still clapping as Tom took Tsini for her victory lap.

"She's great." If the judge said so, who was he to

argue? Frankly, he thought all the dogs looked pretty good. He couldn't really tell any difference. Not that he was stupid enough to tell Kayla that. "Definitely the best."

He watched her clap her heart out, practically jumping out of her seat again. It was the first time he'd seen her face light up with true joy. If he weren't sitting, that smile could have knocked him off his feet.

No wonder A-list celebrities stood in line to date her.

The announcer congratulated the morning's winners and released everyone for lunch. The spectators began to file out. Kayla wanted to go and see Tom and Tsini. Nash and Mike went with her. Dave was going up to the room with Ivan and Greg where they were all going to have lunch together.

They pushed through the crowd and then Tom and Tsini were there and Kayla was hugging the dog. "What a good girl you are. You're a champion!"

"Not bad," Nash said when Tsini pranced over to him. He produced a treat he'd stashed in his pocket earlier. He petted the dog, then pulled back, embarrassed when he caught Kayla beaming at him.

Then the treat was gone and Tsini went back to Kayla, jumping on her in excitement. Kayla was grinning from ear to ear, the dog's paws on her shoulders. She hummed some song as they went around in a small circle. Craziest thing he'd ever seen.

"She loves to dance. Want to try?" she asked.

Dancing in public with a poodle? Not for a million dollars. "I think I'll pass."

Was that hurt in her eyes? Did she think he would? He cleared his throat. "Ready to go up?"

"I need to stay a few more minutes for pictures and to sign paperwork," Tom said.

Nash looked at Mike. "You stay with him." The death threats had been for Tsini after all and, at this stage, he didn't want any member of the team going anywhere alone, not even Tom, who looked like he could more than take care of himself. There was definitely a bad apple among them, but Kayla was right. The others should be protected.

"I'll take Kayla up," he told Mike, who glowered at him, but didn't protest.

Now that the event was over, Nash wanted her out of that crowd as soon as possible. The location would have been extremely hard to control if someone had tried to do her harm here. Coming to see Tsini was one thing. Needlessly lingering was just plain stupid.

He took the shortest route to the elevators. Two elderly ladies got in with them, but they got off on the twentieth floor.

Kayla was still grinning, rocking to the tips of her toes and back. "I'm so happy for her. I know you think this is all craziness, but she likes to win and she knows when she does."

"I believe you," he said, surprising himself, as he considered the enigma of the woman in front of him.

So far he'd seen her act the complete bimbo in front of the cameras when they'd filmed in her apartment. Then he'd seen a tough, mature woman who stood up to him, defending her staff. And now she was like a young girl, carefree and happy as could be because her dog had won a ribbon. She was a complex woman.

Trouble was, he never even understood the simple ones. He definitely had deficiencies in that department.

The elevator jerked, cutting off his musings.

He put a hand out to steady Kayla.

"She has a chance at Best of Show. I think this is her year," she enthused as the elevator came to a complete halt.

But the door didn't open.

"What's wrong with this?" She pushed the open door button.

"We're not there yet. We stopped between floors."

"Oh." She sounded a little breathless.

"It happens. They'll restart it in a second."

Two minutes later, he pushed the call button. That wasn't working either. "They're working on it," he reassured Kayla, but his instincts prickled.

He called Mike on his cell while Kayla fidgeted next to him. "We're stuck in the elevator. Call building services."

"Which elevator?"

"Last on the right in the main lobby. We're above the sixtieth floor."

"Okay. I'm on it."

He pushed his phone back into his pocket.

"How long do you think this is going to take?" Kayla sat on the floor cross-legged, her back resting against the wall. She wrapped her arms around herself, nervous but doing her best not to show it.

"Ten minutes."

"Do you think we'll have to climb out on top?"

"That only works in action flicks and with really old elevators. These new ones are fully secured." He hid a smile at her look of utter relief. "Ten minutes. Tops," he said again, and sat next to her.

They weren't touching, but he was close enough to catch the faint scent of her barely there perfume. He would have lied if he'd said he wasn't aware of her as a woman. He had been from the beginning, and it had ticked him off back when he'd thought her all fluff and no substance. Now that he was getting to know her better and like her a hell of a lot more, his awareness spelled trouble.

To their right, there was a mirror, to their left a poster of a famous singer who was performing that night at the hotel. She was looking at that, leaning ever so slightly closer to him. The elevator seemed to have shrunk all of a sudden.

She had an annoyed look on her face as her gaze ran down the show-time listings on the poster.

He understood how much she hated to give up her freedom, but he needed to keep her secure. "It'd be better if you stayed in your room. Whoever is after you, we know he's here and we know he has the ability to get close. You can go see as many shows as you want once this is over."

She shrugged as she turned to him. "I've seen him in concert more than enough. We've dated."

Her admission didn't surprise him in the least. "You date a lot."

"Past tense. I'm not my reputation."

"But you have one," he observed, and it bothered him to think of all the men she'd belonged to in the past. Which was really stupid. But not half as stupid as wanting Kayla Landon for himself.

She was a high-class, high-society woman. She was one of the "pretty people" and went out with others from that circle. Anger flashed through him for a split second. Not at her, but at himself because even knowing all that couldn't stop him from wanting her.

He should know better. He'd made that mistake before, a mistake that had cost the life of his best friend.

"Don't believe everything you read in the tabloids." She closed her eyes for a split second. "Or do. Everyone does anyway."

He hated the resignation in her voice. And he hated that as much as he'd watched her in the last two days, he still couldn't pin her down, although he was beginning to have a basic understanding. "I know you're not a brainless socialite."

She turned to him. "Since when?"

"Since I read your file after signing up for the job. You have an MBA. From a damn fine university. I don't think even your daddy could buy that."

"I tried to prove to my father that I was fit for the family business." She leaned her head against the wall. Her neck was slim and long, her skin like smooth cream, the definition of kissable.

Focus. "Did you impress him?"

"Nobody could ever impress him but Lance."

Her older brother who'd died in the skiing accident. He'd been an up-and-coming star of the business world according to *Forbes* magazine.

"Lance was the golden boy," she was saying, her tone thoughtful, her eyes looking into the past. "I was free advertising, once I started getting into all the tabloids."

"Your father should have protected you from that."

"It was the only thing I've ever done that my father liked. Any publicity was good publicity for him. He loved when they started calling me the Popcorn Princess. He brought me into the business because of that. I was the face of the company all of a sudden."

"And Greg?"

She looked down at her hands. "Greg was his one mistake. He actually said that. He was embarrassed by Greg."

And Kayla fiercely loved her brother because of that. Nash was beginning to understand the family dynamics. Hell, he'd always thought rich people had it easy. But from what she was telling him, her family was almost as messed up as his.

Almost. Her mother hadn't driven her father to drink himself to death. He pushed his own dark memories away.

"If he liked publicity, he must have really loved you." He'd read every piece of news he could get on her, going back a couple of years. Every gossip rag covered her. According to them, she was a hellcat in high heels. That side of her hadn't come out yet, although he would have been lying if he said he wouldn't have liked to see it.

"People know my family's name. Landon Enterprises is a big deal. Back in college, boys figured out that if they took me to wild parties where there were paparazzi, they could get their pictures in the papers the next day."

He didn't like her tone of voice. He hadn't considered before that maybe she hadn't sought the limelight on purpose. "So you got taken to a lot of wild parties."

"I guess I wasn't as smart as I thought. I kept thinking they liked me for myself."

They should have. She was bright and she was tough. She was loyal to the point of blindness. She had plenty to offer a man. That they had used her when she'd been young and didn't know better ticked him off and awoke his protective instincts. He exhaled, letting that go. Maybe she was just giving him the poor-little-rich-girl act. Could be that was how she always got what she wanted. He'd known another woman like that.

His expression must have said as much, because she launched into an explanation.

"I was raised in a sheltered environment. Industry leaders tend to stick together and socialize together. College was very different. Took me a while to figure it out and find a way to fit in."

Okay. He could see that. "You were too trusting."

"And now I don't trust anyone."

He had to laugh at that. "*I* don't trust anyone," he told her. "You don't trust some imaginary boogeyman stranger. But the second you get to know someone and like them, you give your full trust without reservations."

She'd defended her friends and staff against the slightest suspicion on his part and had reasserted over and over how much she trusted them.

"Name one person that you know closely and don't trust," he put out the challenge.

She struggled. "I don't trust any man who asks me out."

"That's a good start." He bit back a grin. "Babe in the woods." He shook his head.

"I have you to protect me now, don't I?" She rolled her eyes at him.

"And how long did it take to talk you into that? From the moment we met and were complete strangers until you trusted me with your life…twenty-four hours."

"Maybe I should take that trust back and fire you," she mumbled.

"You're too smart to do that. You might cultivate the dumb-blonde image, but you're far from it. You found a way to become director at the company. You raise millions for charity each year. You were smart enough to figure out that you were in danger and smart enough to keep up the clueless socialite act so whoever went after your parents and Lance wouldn't know that you had a clue, wouldn't come after you." He'd figured that out at one point in the last twenty-four hours.

She pulled up her legs and rested her arms on her knees. Her short skirt slid up to reveal enough of her creamy thighs to make him swallow hard.

For a second he considered whether she was doing it on purpose, to distract him. But she seemed completely unaware of the hunger that had been building in him, her face guileless.

"But he did come after me," she said.

"So you slipped up somewhere. Were you still pushing a police investigation?"

"Gave that up. Figured out that they were never going to believe me and if I kept insisting, I'd place myself in the killer's crosshairs."

"But you talked to someone about it." Now that he knew her better, he didn't think she was the kind who could give up something like this. She was too loyal for that. She would want to know what had happened to her older brother and her parents.

"I told my uncle so he could keep an eye out." Her expression changed. She closed her eyes while she drew a long breath. Then looked at him with hesitation in her gaze. "Okay, I haven't told you everything."

He tamped back his annoyance. She trusted everyone around her except him, the one person who could keep her safe. How messed up was that? "I'm listening."

"I might have something to do with— I might be the reason why my parents and Lance died." She pressed her lips together, a pained expression on her face, misery sitting in her blue eyes. "When my father hired me, he gave me a low-level job in finance." She paused as if still undecided about how much to say.

"We're on the same team here," he reminded her.

"I found a bunch of old travel-expense reports in a drawer and they weren't stamped. So I wanted to make sure they'd been claimed by the tax coordinators on the other side of the finance department."

"And?"

"They didn't have time to bother with what they thought was a negligible amount. To keep me busy and off their backs, one gave me access to the system so I could check it out for myself."

"You found that money was missing somewhere."

Her azure eyes went wide. "How did you know that?"

"Money and murder go hand in hand. How much?"

"A little over a million dollars."

"And nobody noticed?"

"It was taken in small amounts, disguised as travel expenses and on-the-spot employee bonuses. We give those out for good work throughout the year."

"You took that information to your father." A picture was beginning to gel in his brain.

She looked at her feet. "He was going to look into it. He and my mom were in a car accident two weeks later."

"What did you do next?"

"I didn't connect the dots at first. I was so devastated by the accident. Months passed before I thought of the missing money again. I told everything to Lance."

"Then he died."

She nodded. "I talked to the police, but the deaths were all ruled accidents. Half the time they thought I was loopy from grief, the other half they were accusing me of wanting more media attention."

His jaw tightened. "But you told your uncle, too, and nothing happened to him."

"He didn't believe me. My father did—he was going to investigate the company records. So was Lance. My uncle is too trusting. He thought I just needed some rest."

"How long ago did you talk to him?"

"Almost a year."

"And you haven't brought it up since?"

"Once I figured out that looking into the missing money might have led to the accidents, I didn't dare."

Her uncle might not have taken her murder theory seriously, but he cared enough to talk her into getting an extra guard when Tsini had been threatened. And he'd been smart enough to recommend Welkins's group. "Your uncle leads the company now?"

"He's one of the VPs."

"And he handles Greg's trust fund." That had come up at one point in his research. "Did you ever say anything about your suspicions to Greg?"

"No. There's no point. It would just upset him."

"But you think all this is somehow connected to the company." He'd spent hours considering that and always came to the conclusion that Landon Enterprises and the hundreds of millions of dollars it represented was the most likely motive.

He couldn't figure out, however, what someone might get out of killing the family. The stockholders owned the company, although both Greg and Kayla— and, he assumed, their uncle—owned considerable stock. There was no power struggle as far as he could tell, no bad blood between the CEO and any of the VPs.

"So the motive is to cover up a past crime, embezzlement." It was all too possible.

"Or it could have nothing to do with the missing money. Maybe a business competitor figures that if Landon Enterprises gets decapitated and falls apart, they can snap up the market share," Kayla said in a way that showed that she'd given this considerable thought.

"None of your competitors were in your apartment the night before last. And no Landon Enterprises employees were either, other than you and Greg."

"But someone could have bribed one of my staff."

He could see in her tight face that saying those words

cost her. This was the first time she'd admitted that one of them had probably betrayed her. The blue-ribbon spark was gone from her eyes. She looked so sad, he couldn't take it.

"Hey—" He leaned toward her and tucked a stray lock of blond hair behind her ear, and nearly drowned in her ocean-blue eyes. "Whatever it takes, I'm going to get you out of this mess." *And keep my hands off you.*

They were sitting so damn close that their lips were separated by inches.

She was everything he couldn't have. And he was a hairline away from not giving a damn. All he would have to do was dip his head. In another second, as she looked at him with those wide blue eyes, he might have.

But someone banged on the elevator shaft door below them, startling him back to sanity.

"You in there?" Mike's voice filtered through. "Everything okay?"

Nash stood, rolling his shoulders, never happier for an interruption in his life. Mike had just saved him from making a colossal mistake. He owed the man.

"When are they going to get this thing moving?" The sooner the better. No room to escape the scent of her perfume in here. No matter how far he tried to pull away from her, she was always within reach. He needed to clear his head.

"They're working on it. Something's wrong with the computer."

"Are all the elevators out?"

"Just this one."

That gave him pause. He didn't believe in coincidence. He looked at the door. Mike was here. Between the two of them they could…

"I'm going to force the inner door open and hold it. You do the same with the outer door. If there's enough room, Kayla can slip out."

He didn't trust the elevator all of a sudden. And maybe he was right, because out of the blue, the damn thing jostled.

He pried the tips of his fingers into the crack and strained his muscles pulling. He could hear Mike swearing outside. Progress was slow, inch by inch. Kayla stepped out of her heels, getting ready. Then Mike began to gain some headway at last, as well. When they both had a gap about a foot wide, Kayla slipped out, landing on the floor with a thump. The bottom of the elevator was at least three feet above floor level outside.

"Now you," she said immediately, before even putting her shoes back on.

The elevator jerked and dropped a foot.

She yelped, rushing to give Mike a hand. "Hurry."

Nash nearly lost his hold on the door as the damn thing shook. "If I let go of the door, it'll close on me. I can't." She was safe. Maybe the elevator wouldn't fall. He would have to chance it.

From the look of utter desperation that came into her eyes, she didn't agree. "What are you talking about?" She was looking around wildly.

"You can let that close," Nash was saying to Mike, getting ready to let his own end go.

"Wait," she interrupted, running off already. "I'll be right back."

And true to her word, she was back in a minute, just when Nash's back was beginning to ache from the effort of holding the inner door open. She shoved a fire extinguisher into the crack. Must have gotten it from the fire stairs.

Damn, but he could really come to like this woman. She was so much more than a pretty face. Seemed stupid now that he'd ever thought that of her.

"Good thinking." He grinned at her and slipped through, going at an angle to get his shoulders past the narrow crack.

Then Mike let the doors close, flexing his arms afterwards. He was strong, had to give him that.

"Thanks." Nash clapped him on the back. There was still some animosity between them, but now he knew that Mike could be counted on to put all that aside and come through in a pinch.

The man was sweating. "That's my job, and—"

The elevator rattled, cutting him off. Then there was a loud hissing sound that went on for long seconds. Then a crash that seemed to shake the building.

Kayla went white.

Nash sprang into action. "You take her to the suite. Don't open the door to anyone but me. Keep your gun handy," he told Mike and began running as a sudden idea popped into his head.

If anyone wanted to mess with the elevator, they could either do that through the main computer at the security office—which would be pretty hard to get into—or at the backup panel and the manual override that was usually at the bottom of the shaft. In the basement.

He took the stairs two at a time. Swore. He was never going to make it down there at this rate.

He left the fire stairs on the next floor and went back to the elevator bank, pushed the button. According to Mike, none of the other elevators were affected. And this was his only chance.

Still, time seemed to crawl by the time he reached the lobby level. Going below that on the elevator required a special key. He got off and looked for the stairs, found them. The steel door to the basement would have normally been locked, but personnel were rushing in and out now. The elevator crash had definitely been heard and felt.

He sneaked by them, acting as though he belonged there. He'd had plenty of practice at this sort of thing. He could be damn near invisible if the occasion called for it.

He moved toward the sounds of people barking commands. Everyone was in uniform, everyone looked like part of a team assessing damage and trying to figure out if the elevator had been empty. Storage areas took up this side of the space, boxes piled against the bare cement walls. A jumble of pipes of various sizes ran along the ceiling.

He scanned the section of the huge basement that he could see. A lot of it was partitioned off. There was a door in the back that was swinging as if someone had just passed through there. He took off running that way. With all eyes on the elevator and the damage it caused, nobody paid him any attention.

The swinging door led to another set of stairs. He ran up and found himself in a long corridor somewhere in the back of the building. A man in hotel uniform was hurrying toward the door at the end.

"Stop," Nash called out. "Stop right there."

The man broke into a run. He was lithe and quick, around thirty if that.

Nash tore after him, ignoring the pain in his bad leg, and pushed through the door. Loading docks. Empty, save for the guy he was chasing. Probably everyone was at lunch or gawking at the elevator accident. The guy up ahead turned for a second. Nash was gaining on him.

He caught him in the far corner as he slipped through a gap between a parked truck and the wall. Nash couldn't go after him; he was bigger and wouldn't fit through the crack. But he had a firm hold of the man's shirt.

He yanked the guy hard against the corner of the truck. Blond hair, green eyes, a narrow face with an unhealthy tan and crooked teeth. "Who do you work for?" He tried to pull the man back in, but the guy twisted right out of his loose uniform shirt and dashed forward, out of reach.

Then all Nash could hear was the screech of tires and a thump. By the time he made his way around the truck, the man was sprawled in a pool of his own blood on the ground. His lifeless eyes stared right at Nash.

"Damn." He swore a blue streak as he moved closer, pulling his cell phone from his pocket.

"I didn't see him. He jumped out of nowhere." The white-faced driver of the delivery truck that had clipped the bastard was climbing down from his cab. His voice shook so hard, he almost sounded as if he was speaking with an accent.

Nash hit the speed dial for Mike. Before he did anything else, he needed to know if Kayla and Greg were all right.

She'd saved his life back at that elevator.

Whatever everyone else thought about her, Kayla Landon was a helluva woman.

And he was not going to let anything happen to her. He let go all of his resolutions then and there. To hell with not getting in up to his eyebrows. To hell with professional distance. To hell with making sure the job stayed just a job. As of now, this was personal.

Chapter Six

She couldn't sleep. The elevator had been a close call. Her whole body still vibrated with tension. Nash lying there, within view, didn't help either. His presence was impossible to ignore, day *or* night. Kayla pushed back the covers and got up. She needed to get rid of some nervous energy. If she were at home, she would have had yoga with Ilona today. The popular instructor came to her house three times a week.

She needed exercise, to exhaust herself to the point of passing out. Her laboring mind and jittery body might never get any rest otherwise.

She grabbed a pair of shorts and a sports top from her dresser and put them on in her bathroom, picked up her gym bag. She always took that with her when she traveled.

"Where are you going?" Nash asked out of the darkness when she walked into the living room.

He didn't startle her. She knew that he, too, was still awake. She'd heard him get up a couple of times since they'd gone to bed. She would have stayed put if he were sleeping, would have let him rest.

"Gym's open around the clock," she said.

"Hang on a sec." He went and got Dave up to take over and guard Greg, then grabbed his own bag, checked the hallway before letting her step outside.

Nothing but a small table lamp had been on inside the suite, but the lights were on in the hallway. Nash's short hair was mussed, but he didn't sport the same sleep-deprived look she knew must be evident on her face. His eyes were sharp and alert. His body...

She looked away. The flat-out best thing she could do for herself was not think about his body at all, especially when they were alone in the middle of the night. Temporarily alone. She hoped the hotel was full of insomniacs and the gym would be buzzing.

"Let's take the stairs." She walked toward the door at the end of the hall. The gym was only two floors above them.

He stood still, watching her. "The guy is dead. He can't hurt you anymore," he said softly.

She knew that. In the morning, she would take an elevator down, but tonight, the near crash was still too close. "Extra exercise," she told him.

Whether he believed her or not, he followed her. Their footsteps echoed off the bare walls of the staircase as they made the short trip up. He passed her, putting his body squarely in front of her like a shield.

Which left her with little to do but look at his butt. The man could sell jeans. No other marketing message was needed. She forced herself to look away. The physical attraction was insane. Made her nervous.

For the most part, she was in control of her life. It was

a wonderful feeling and fairly new. Before his death, her father had run the family and the business with an iron hand. Stepping up to the plate fully, making million-dollar decisions, taking on more responsibility and facing down difficult challenges had been scary for her at first. But she'd found that she liked it. She was her father's daughter after all. She did like to be in control.

Except that with Nash Wilder, she couldn't pretend that she had a prayer. He could take control of the growing sexual tension between them so fast it would leave her head spinning. Which meant her best bet was not to give him any sign, any clue at all that she was the least bit attracted to him.

"Good luck with that," she murmured under her breath as they arrived at last.

The gym was empty save for the two of them. For a second, she thought of turning right around. But she didn't want to explain why she had changed her mind suddenly. He turned on the overhead lights. She went straight to the treadmill. He seemed to be set on working with weights. She tried not to watch him.

That worked for about two minutes.

His movements were even, efficient and powerful. His body was a well-oiled machine. He went through the stations, pushing insane amounts of weight slowly, deliberately as he completed his repetitions. Long, fabulous muscles stretched and contracted, forming mesmerizing bulges.

It'd been a long time since she'd been in the presence of a man she was attracted to. And she'd never been as attracted to a man as she was to Nash. Even if she knew nothing about him beyond that he worked for a top-notch agency and was supposed to be a top-notch bodyguard.

"Do you have a girlfriend…or something? At home. Wherever that is." She was surprised by how much she hated that possibility.

He stopped doing bench presses and sat up, looked at her, an amused smile playing above his top lip. "When would I have time for that?"

Good point. Yet she couldn't picture a man like him remaining celibate either. She supposed there was downtime between assignments. She didn't want to think about what he did during those times and with whom he did it. Just too damn depressing. But there were plenty of other things she wanted to know about other areas of his life.

"What did you do before you became a bodyguard?"

"This and that."

Oh, for heaven's sake. He took the dark and mysterious act too far. "On the good side or on the bad? I'd like to know at least whether you were a soldier or an assassin."

A dark eyebrow slid up his forehead, his gaze steady on her and heating. "Started out as a marine."

Right. His *Semper Fi* tattoo was all but staring her in the face, but she didn't seem to be able to hold many coherent thoughts in her mind just now. The heart-rate monitor built into the handle of the treadmill beeped. She slowed a little. "And after that?"

"Why the sudden interest?" He let the weight slide back, got up and came closer.

Her feet slowed further on the treadmill. *Because I want to know more about the man who's making me blind with lust.* "I'm trusting you with my life."

"I'm going to save it or die trying. That's all you need to know." He was almost directly in front of her now, his gold whiskey eyes still holding her gaze.

The hotel was quiet around them. They were the only two people in the world. Energy and power radiated from him, a potent masculinity she clearly wasn't immune to. She shut the treadmill down before she tripped over her own feet.

"I'm—" God, it was hot in here. "I'm going to rinse off and swim a few laps." She stepped off and escaped his nearness. It was either that or step into his arms.

"Good idea." He followed.

Right into the women's dressing room.

She stopped and turned to face him. "I think I'll be safe in here."

"I have to rinse off, too, and I'm not leaving you alone." His voice was dangerously low.

They were going to shower together? Her throat went dry. Every nerve ending in her body came alive.

"You take that stall, I'll take one on the other side. Close the curtain. I won't peek." His eyes darkened even as he said it.

"I'm not comfortable with this."

He said nothing. He simply turned and walked away.

Embarrassment washed over her. Of course he could keep his hands off her. Girlfriend or not, a guy like him had to have a dozen women at his beck and call. She turned and marched off into her corner, waited until he disappeared around a dividing wall to go to his shower on the other side.

She undressed and rinsed off as quickly as possible,

much too aware of how little space separated their naked bodies. She paid a minimum of attention to the luxurious finishes, the marble tile on the wall and the fancy towels. She finished first. For another minute or so, she could still hear his shower running. She pulled on her swimsuit with superspeed, trying hard not to think of him naked, water sluicing over his wide shoulders.

"Ready?" he gave warning before coming around the corner.

"Good to go." She was walking toward the door already, but her steps faltered at the sight of him.

His shoulders *were* wide and massive; an impressive amount of muscle covered his torso. He hadn't bothered to dry off, so droplets of water glistened on his skin and on the smattering of hair that began around his belly button and disappeared below the waistline of his Bermuda-style swim shorts.

She swallowed hard and skipped that area, then swallowed again when her gaze dropped to his legs.

He always wore jeans with a black T-shirt, a pair of sweatpants in the gym. This was the first time she'd seen him in anything short. She eyed the extensive scars on his right leg warily.

He caught her looking.

"Land mine," he said. "There. Now you know something else about me."

"Where did that happen?"

"On the Korean border. I was looking for the damn thing. Missed it. Thank God for the protective suit. Still gave me a mother of a concussion."

"And nearly took off your leg."

"There was that," he said, his face tightening.

"I didn't know marines disarmed land mines."

"Marines do everything and then some. But by then I wasn't with the marines."

Where do you graduate to from the marines? Hadn't that job been dangerous enough for him? "Are you going to tell me who you were with?"

He gave a small smile. "Not a chance."

"You're not an easy man to get to know." And if she had any brains at all, she wouldn't try to get to know him better. She would let him do his job then forget him when he left.

She stopped and dropped her towel on a plastic chair, remembering the conversation she'd had with her mother after her first disastrous date when a guy had used her for a publicity stunt, getting her tipsy at a party then getting her up on a pool table to dance, flipping her skirt up for a photo that had made tabloid headlines all over the country.

She'd had such a crush on him. They'd been in the same accounting class all semester.

"I'm not ever going to trust a guy again," she'd told her mom. "And since I can't fall in love with someone I don't trust, I'm probably never getting married," she'd warned. "How did you ever trust Dad?"

Her father was partial owner of an up-and-coming business when he and her mother had met. Her mother came from one of the oldest Pennsylvania families, with plenty of old money and connections among the top tier. She'd had plenty of suitors who'd wanted a piece of that.

"When you really know a man with all your heart,

you'll know whether you can trust him. If you can, love comes after that," her mother had said.

She wondered if anyone had ever loved Nash. If he'd ever let anyone close enough to get to know him.

"Worried about tomorrow?"

She hadn't realized that he'd been watching her. She shook her head. "Thinking about my mother. How about your parents? Do you have any brothers or sisters?"

They were by the pool, at the deep end.

"Only child. Parents both dead," he said in a tone of voice that said that was the end of that conversation.

"You ever *really* talk to anyone?" she asked. How on earth did anyone ever get close to a man like this when he never shared anything about himself? Not that she wanted to get close to Nash. If she had any brains at all, she would stay far away from him.

"Not much to say." He shrugged.

"I doubt that."

"Women love a man of mystery," he said with a sudden, teasing smile. And then he jumped into the pool, splashing her.

She could do little else but go after him. Nash was beside her, they were trapped together in their own world. In that one moment, for the first time in a long time, she felt completely safe. Too bad she couldn't stay there forever. She pushed away, desperate for air.

He was still underwater when she broke the surface, but only a second or two passed before he came up next to her, shaking water from his hair. He had a leaf on his shoulder. Must have come from one of the dozen potted ficus trees that edged the pool.

She reached out to brush it off. His skin radiated heat. Their gazes held. The air disappeared from her lungs. Physical attraction drew her forward. Common sense held her in place.

She held her breath as time stopped.

"We should swim those laps," he said, breaking the spell.

And she threw herself into the task as if thrown a lifeline. She put every ounce of energy she had into slicing through the water. One lap, two, three…five, six. She was only vaguely aware that he passed her periodically, his powerful body outpacing hers almost two laps to one.

When she was gasping for air, her muscles burning, she stopped and hung on to the pool's edge, watched him finish.

He stopped next to her once again, just as close as before. Closer. Drops of water rolled off his wide shoulders. His eyes burned with desire. Her mouth went dry as primal need overtook her.

He shook his head. "It's not working. I still want you so much I can't see straight."

She couldn't breathe.

"It's about the stupidest thing we could do. Your call."

She had no idea where she got the temerity to slip into his arms. "I haven't done anything colossally stupid in at least a week," she murmured against his mouth.

The second their lips met, pleasure flooded her body. He pulled her to him tightly, leaving no doubt where he wanted her, how much he wanted her, every inch of them touching. And then he kissed her dizzy.

His lips were firm and warm on hers, tasting, teasing, cajoling. He was still the soldier. First he did a thorough recon, then he moved ahead and conquered. His large, masculine hands explored her body under the water. She wore very little, barely anything blocking his way. Her breasts grew full under his palms. Heat gathered low in her belly. She was about ready to wave the white flag and surrender everything when he pulled away.

He was breathing as erratically as she was. But he grabbed on to the side of the pool and pushed himself out of the water, his triceps bulging. Among other things. When he was out, he turned to offer a helping hand.

He pulled her out and up into his arms, carried her to the showers. This time, they showered together. And what little clothes they had on didn't leave much to the imagination.

Whatever was happening between them was progressing at the speed of light. They had to stop, but as his hands slid down the curve of her back, she found herself pressing even closer to him.

He kissed her, possessed her, tasted her mouth, her neck, her nipples. She wanted him, then and there, their bodies slick with water.

She had never in her life done anything as crazy as making love in a public place when she knew very well the paparazzi were always lurking. She had to be out of her mind to be doing this.

As if reading her thoughts, he pulled away, leaning his forehead against hers. "I'm sorry, princess. This is it."

Her body vibrated with frustration and need. She couldn't speak.

"I don't have any protection." His voice was thick with barely controlled desire.

"I'm not on the pill," she admitted.

He drew a few slow breaths, regained his composure faster than she did, pulled back to look into her eyes. "And even if we had… If we went any further, you'd regret it in the morning. You'd probably fire me, and there's no way in hell I'd leave while you were still in danger. Things could get real complicated."

He reached for a towel and wrapped her in it before he stepped away from her completely. For an endless moment he watched her, one emotion after the other flickering through his keen gaze. Then he said, "I crossed the line tonight. It's not going to happen again. My full focus has to be your safety. You're not safe yet. Not from the enemy, and as hard as I'm going to try, probably not from me," he said in a rueful tone.

She ignored that last bit for now, didn't know what to do with it. "But the man is dead."

She'd talked to the police. She and Nash had given statements. Thing was, the elevator crash did seem like a massive computer error, nothing more. The guy in the basement couldn't be linked to it in any way. He had no ID, so the police were still trying to find out who he was. Not an employee, although he wore an employee's uniform. The cops thought he might have stolen a uniform to get in free, maybe to see a show. He'd probably run from Nash only because he thought he was about to be caught by security.

"That guy wasn't here by accident. He was here for you." Nash clearly didn't agree with the police. "But you don't know him. Greg doesn't know him. Nobody on your team had ever seen the man before. It's unlikely that your whole family is being targeted by a random stranger. What's his angle? It's a lot more likely that he was a hired man, working for someone. And whoever hired him can hire another hit man just as easily."

"But he wasn't in my apartment when the picture was taken." She wasn't sure what that meant, only that she badly wanted her staff exonerated.

"Whoever wants to hurt you could have more than one person working for him." He went to grab his clothes.

She made sure she was dressed by the time he came back, not an easy task when her limbs were still weak with need.

Once again, he went first in the staircase, stopped at the bottom before they stepped out into the hallway on their floor.

His whiskey-gold gaze held hers. "My mother was a small-town diva, Miss Montgomery County, the beauty queen. Married my father then decided blue collar was too low for her. Couldn't forgive him that he got her pregnant and cost her a magazine-ad photo shoot, either. She kept leaving and coming back. He started drinking. She left when I was sixteen. By then the old man was pretty mean. I stuck around until I graduated from high school, then I joined the service. My old man drank himself into the grave before I was done with basic training."

Her worst fear was that she would lose all her family. Her worst fear, and he was living it. She moved toward him, but he opened the door and stepped out into the hallway, didn't turn to her again until they were inside her suite. He walked her to her bedroom and wished her good-night without so much as a chaste peck on the cheek. Which was probably for the best. She would have hated embarrassing herself by begging him to stay with her.

She dropped on top of the covers, not bothering with undressing. She wore a pair of clean shorts and a tank top. But despite all the running and swimming she had done, sleep didn't come easily.

She kept thinking of Nash.

And the more she thought, the more grateful she became that nothing had happened in that shower. As attractive as she found the man, she couldn't have an affair with her bodyguard. He didn't even like her. And he'd be gone in a couple of days.

If she weren't careful, she was going to end up like her fast-and-loose celebrity image. And that wasn't the direction she wanted to take her life. Some day, when the danger was over, she was going to have a serious image makeover. She was going to be a businesswoman to reckon with, one who was strong enough and respected enough to take over the company after Uncle Al retired.

Nash was a temporary distraction. She needed to stop thinking of him as a man and stick to business. She needed to focus on her future and her plans.

PART OF HIM was glad that she didn't get hurt, part of him was furious that the man he had paid had failed. He was a friend of a friend, someone he trusted.

She should have left things alone. But she kept pushing and pushing. And now that Wilder guy was on her team. What were they doing anyway, sneaking in and out of the suite together? He didn't like that.

The man made him uneasy. Wilder took charge. Wilder was investigating. But Wilder had been hired by her. When she was gone, Wilder would go away. He had to outsmart Wilder for only a little while longer. He would find someone else who could help him with Kayla. And then it would all be over.

NASH STARED at the ceiling. Kissing her had been incredibly stupid. Yet he couldn't regret it. He wanted her still. His body demanded that he walk into her bedroom, close the door behind him and finish what they'd started.

It had been a frustrating day all around. Someone had nearly gotten to Kayla. Fury whipped through him every time he thought about that. When he nearly had the bastard, the idiot had gone and got himself killed, so they were no closer to an answer now than at the very beginning.

And he'd even asked for Welkins's help. He'd taken the picture of the man who'd messed with the elevators and sent it on to the boss by cell phone. Maybe there'd be a hit in one of the databases Welkins had access to.

Other than that, his only lead was the photo taken inside Kayla's apartment. And that photo pointed to someone on staff. But he'd been unable to make any progress on that.

Tsini plodded out of Kayla's room and walked around the living room, checking the perimeter, sniffing around the front door. She looked at Nash as if to make sure he was awake and on guard, as well.

The dog looked as goofy as all get out with her fancy haircut, but she was growing on him. As if sensing the danger to Kayla, whenever she wasn't competing, Tsini stuck close to her.

"Nothing we can do tonight," he told her. "Might as well go to sleep."

He needed rest. He needed to be at one hundred percent tomorrow. The enemy had one man down. Which didn't mean she was safe. All depended on how fast the bastard who was behind all this could find a replacement.

Tsini made another round, then, seeming satisfied with the result of her inspection, moseyed back into Kayla's bedroom to settle at the foot of her bed.

Not that long ago, when he went to battle his teammates provided cover with rocket launchers. Now he had a poodle for backup, Nash thought, and shook his head.

He slept in fits and starts, waking bleary-eyed in the morning, not that he would let that affect him. He'd been trained to operate on little sleep.

Kayla looked as fit for the silver screen as always. Since she wouldn't meet his eyes when she came out of her room for breakfast, he figured he'd been right and she regretted everything that had happened between them during the night.

He shouldn't have felt disappointed. She was way out of his league. She was a celebrity heiress. He was a washed-up nobody.

She raced through her food then Elvis did full hair and makeup. Pretty early, he thought, considering that Tsini wasn't competing for the Best in Show title until that afternoon.

"I'm going down to see the agility competitions," she said before he had a chance to ask anything. "I don't want to sit around up here all morning."

"No." The word came out too loudly, too forcefully. In front of her whole staff.

Just the thing Welkins had told him not to do if he knew what was good for him.

He wasn't supposed to take over. He wasn't supposed to act the boss, especially in front of the client's employees and friends. He no longer cared.

Her lips, the same lips that he'd kissed senseless the night before, now tightened. Mike and Dave pulled themselves taller, ready to see him lose his authority, allowing them to get some back.

"It'd be safer to stay. I'm sure you would agree, considering all that's happened." He tried to backpedal, hating that he couldn't simply issue orders. He didn't much like operating in the civilian world. Dealing with military personnel was much easier.

On his team, he'd been the leader. And his men had followed rank. Here, Kayla outranked him, which, if he were honest, bugged him to hell.

"Agility is fun. I don't want to be locked up here. I deserve a normal life," she said. "We'll be careful."

He could have pushed. He was a tough son of a bitch, he could have probably browbeaten her, scared her into staying in her suite. But suddenly he found he didn't want to do that. Because she was right. She did deserve a normal life.

He was used to living under battle conditions. But she shouldn't have to live her life as if she were at war.

She was still in danger, he had no doubt in his mind about that. But maybe they'd get a little breather before her enemy, whoever the bastard was, regrouped.

He held her ocean-blue gaze. "Stick to me. Draw no attention. When I say we leave, we leave."

She surprised him with a smile and a mock salute.

And the tension leaked out of the room as everyone went about their business.

In the end, Tom stayed behind to beautify Tsini for the Best in Show competition. Greg stayed with him. Poor guy had another one of his headaches. Nash left Dave in the suite with them, and Mike joined him and Kayla. Elvis, Fisk and Ivan tagged along, but soon split off, going after their own interests.

The elevator ride was uneventful. If Kayla felt nervous, she didn't show it. He had to give it to her, she was one tough woman. She didn't crack easily.

The morning contest didn't turn out to be as boring as he'd expected. The working dogs were all right. They conquered the obstacle course like nobody's business. Although, now that he'd gotten to know Tsini better, he was beginning to think that Tsini could more than hold her own against them. Apparently, fanciness and toughness weren't mutually exclusive.

Agility was followed by Junior Showmanship. Since Kayla so obviously wanted to stay, he didn't push too hard to get her back upstairs. They didn't return to her suite until lunch, in fact.

After lunch, it was Tsini's turn again.

And Nash found himself leaning forward in his seat, rooting for her, hoping for another win.

The dogs were checked from head to toe as before. They had to run around the judge in a circle. Tsini pranced between a rottweiler and a St. Bernard. He had no idea how the judges could compare breeds that were so different from each other.

Kayla was nearly vibrating in her seat next to him.

The judge was ready to make his decision. "Would the standard poodle please step out? The beagle. The rottweiler."

The dogs ran another round, led by their handlers. And the judge nodded at last. "In that order," she said, and the audience broke out in a cheer.

Kayla had been cool toward Nash all morning, but now she jumped up and threw herself into his arms again. She had no idea what she was doing to him. She couldn't know that he was cross-eyed with lust if he as much as looked at her. She was pushing him closer and closer to the edge with all this touching. She gave him a brilliant smile as she drew back. Then she pushed away as fast as she had jumped him and ran toward the stage where Tom was accepting a large silver cup and a big blue ribbon on Tsini's behalf.

Nash swore and dashed after her. "You wait for me."

"Sure." She ran faster.

He had half a mind to throw her across his shoulder and carry her back to her room. Except that he was beginning not to trust himself if he needed to put his hands on her. Somewhat of a problem, seeing how he was her bodyguard. He needed to get his head on straight.

The rest of the afternoon was spent attending celebrations and giving interviews. Since Tsini had won

Best in Show, Kayla decided to attend the closing gala that evening, which signaled the end of the competition. And he didn't try to stop her. The gala was their last event at the show. The only thing left for the morning were some organizational meetings where the membership could vote on a number of issues. Kayla had already decided not to attend. They were flying out in the morning and would be home by noon.

Then his assignment would be over.

And Nash was no closer to catching the bastard who wanted to get to her. That thought practically killed him as he watched Kayla do the victory dance with Tsini again.

NASH LOOKED breathtaking in his rented tuxedo. He'd insisted on being her escort to the closing gala and Kayla didn't argue with him. She didn't want to. Truth was, she wanted to feel his strong arms around her.

He was tall, his dark hair gleaming in the candlelight, his dark gold eyes focused solely on her. Always on her. She tried to remind herself that he only watched her because she was paying him to do exactly that.

But she hadn't paid him to kiss her in that pool or do what they'd done in the shower the night before. His desire for her had been unmistakable.

What did he want? Experience showed that nobody wanted her just for herself. They wanted the lifestyle, the attention, the chance to come into the public eye. She'd been in relationships—not nearly as many as the tabloids suggested, but enough to have her heart broken over and over again. She didn't want to go there, not with Nash.

He was different from any other man she had ever

met. He was more real, tougher, larger than life. If she gave herself to him, he would consume her completely. There'd be nothing left of her when it was time for him to go. And he *would* go. On another assignment, or back to whatever team he'd joined after the marines.

She was glad that they hadn't gotten completely carried away the night before in the gym. Okay, part of her was glad. Another part of her would have loved to have finished, to have that memory. But without that, maybe, eventually she could forget him. Right. When rottweilers grew long tails with puffs on the end, got dressed up in pink tutus and danced the waltz around the show ring.

"Champagne?" Nash asked next to her.

The ballroom swirled with people, networking, dancing, celebrating the end of another successful show.

"Thank you, but no." Two glasses were her limit these days. She needed to keep a clear head, especially now, especially with Nash.

They were the only two people left at the table. She'd sent Mike off to chat up the brunette he'd been staring at through the whole show. Somebody deserved to have a little fun. Just because she was definitely reining in her hormones, it didn't mean everybody on her team had to be celibate.

He didn't go far, just one table over. And she felt safe with Nash, although his nearness, his masculine scent, his steady gaze had her ready to jump out of her skin every time he turned to her with yet another question.

"Let's dance," she said without thinking it through, just wanting to get moving.

"I don't dance." He blinked. "What are you grinning at?"

"First time you admitted you can't do something."

"I can't do a lot of things."

"Such as?"

"Sing."

"What else?"

"Can't play any musical instruments."

"That's all?"

"Pretty much," he said, deadpan.

She actually believed him. "What do you say we try widening your circle of competence tonight?"

He drew a slow breath as he considered her. And all of a sudden she itched to get him out onto the dance floor. He was tough and gruff and solid as a rock. She wanted to see what he would be like at a disadvantage, wouldn't have minded having the upper hand just once for a change.

He rose without a word and extended his hand to her.

And drew plenty of female attention from all around the room.

She put her hand in his and came to her feet, not one hundred percent sure that she was doing the smart thing here, but going with it anyway. Too late now to turn back.

Then they were on the dance floor. He put his arms around her, keeping a respectable distance. Around them, cameras flashed. She'd already posed with people for pictures and signed autographs when they'd first come down, but seeing her on the dance floor with a gorgeous mystery man drew everyone's attention again.

Some of those photos would be in next week's

tabloids. She tried not to let that bother her. She needed to take it as a fact of life and move beyond.

Nash was doing some kind of a bear shuffle.

She stifled a grin. "You kind of step like this, then step like this, then do a quarter turn and repeat it again."

"Hmm." He didn't look as though he thought that was going to make a difference, but gave it a try anyway. And kept trying until he got better.

"Not bad."

Although, once he didn't need to keep his full attention on his feet, he was giving all that attention to her. She was in his arms, their eyes—and lips—neatly lined up, thanks to her impossible heels. His amber gaze trapped her.

"Not bad," he echoed her words and gathered her a little closer.

They danced that dance, then the next. She was growing breathless and it had nothing to do with the beauty of the music. They were so close. The look in his eyes said that if they were in private, he'd be inside her already. Her knees trembled, every cell in her body needing him.

Then that song was over and the lights went out without warning.

Nash practically wrapped his body around hers in a protective gesture. He moved them forward immediately, out of the last position where they'd been seen. She felt him reach for his gun at his back.

"When I say *now,* get down," he whispered in her ear, his warm breath tickling the sensitive skin of her neck.

Her blood raced. Her heart pounded in her chest. She

stayed close to his solid bulk, scared, but trusting him to take care of her. With all the uncertainty around her, he had become the one steady thing she counted on, she realized now, and she wasn't sure how she felt about that.

But instead of danger, another song came next, one sung by the people in the far corner then spreading through the crowd.

"Happy birthday…"

Then she saw lights, too. Flickering candles on a giant cake that was rolled into the middle of the dance floor. White frosting, decorated with chocolate paw prints going all around the layers.

"Happy birthday to Laura Wolfson, our fabulous president," the show chair was saying.

A chorus of "Happy Birthday!" followed. People cheered.

Relief rushed through her.

Nash relaxed next to her and stashed his gun away. He didn't release his grip on her, though. The adrenaline rush that came with expecting an attack switched back to instant heat and awareness.

The birthday girl was giving a thank-you speech as she got ready to blow out her candles. Kayla couldn't process the words. All she could hear, think and feel was Nash.

"I forgot to tell you about this one other thing I can't do," he said close to her ear. "I can't seem to resist you."

And then he kissed her under cover of the darkness. His effect on her was instant and irresistible. She melted against him despite her best intentions. And got lost.

Her head reeled when he pulled back.

She blinked hard and forced herself to speak.

"Actually, um—I decided that whatever it is that's going on between us, we should just ignore it." Brave words, but her fingers were still curled around his biceps.

"Good luck with that," he said, then kissed her again.

Already, his firm lips on hers were as familiar as if they belonged there, his hands on her, welcome. Her body went into instant meltdown. She was weak with wanting him, and he'd barely even touched her yet. They fitted together as if they'd been made for each other. As different as they were in every other area of their lives, in passion they were a perfect match.

This was where the real danger lay. Here was a man she could lose her heart to. Five years ago, she would have. She would have already been a goner by now. But she'd learned a lot as she got her heart broken a couple of times, watched her friends lose inheritances to bad decisions, as they—along with she—had been dragged through the mud in the media.

Yes, she'd learned a lot. And the number-one thing she'd learned was that people in the public eye shouldn't give their hearts, they shouldn't believe in romance. Because every time they did, it ended in disaster.

But to resist this man would take a lot more than smart thinking.

Chapter Seven

"Congratulations on Tsini. I still can't believe she pulled that off," her uncle was saying on the phone, catching her just after she got in from the airport with her staff, her luggage still in a pile in the middle of the den. He'd been in Europe on business for the last two weeks. It was the first time they'd connected since before she'd left for Vegas. "We'll go out and celebrate when I get back."

"That would be nice. Everything's going well over there?" She rubbed her forehead. A low-grade headache pulsed back and forth across her head, from temple to temple.

"A couple of meetings left." He was negotiating a deal to use Landon's Popcorn exclusively in the largest movie-theater chain in the European Union, a major coup that would mark the company's most significant overseas deal to date.

Kayla's grandfather had started the company then left it to his two sons, Kayla's father, William, and her uncle, Albert. Those two took a flourishing small company and turned it into a multimillion-dollar global business.

Uncle Al had no children. William had been preparing his eldest son, Lance, to succeed him at the helm. But Lance had died a year after their father. And if they wanted to keep the company in family hands, the three remaining members had to step up to the plate.

"Pretty soon, our popcorn will be winning over movie audiences all over Europe." Her uncle sounded pleased with himself.

"And once people taste it at the movies, they'll want it at home," she responded. Movie-theater popcorn was their spearhead into new markets, but since seventy percent of popcorn was consumed at home, the real goal was to seduce that segment to their brand.

"But to get that, we need a bigger presence here. European headquarters. We'll need a VP of European Operations. I was thinking of you. Something else to talk about when I get back."

She was too stunned to respond. Vice President. The acknowledgment and responsibility her father hadn't been willing to give to her. In Europe, though. She'd have to move. She wasn't sure how Greg would take that. She would definitely have to give the idea a lot of thought before she made her decision.

"Can't wait for you to get back," she told her uncle.

"How is that new bodyguard working out?"

"Good." The less said about the subject, the less chance that she would betray her attraction toward the man.

"From what I hear, Welkins doesn't have bad people. You just pay attention to what his man says."

She hadn't mentioned the elevator incident. There'd be time for that when Al came back. No one but the police knew that she'd been in the elevator that had crashed. Nash had made sure they hadn't released that bit of news. She wanted to keep out of the spotlight as much as possible, and he did everything in his power to help her.

He'd saved her life by figuring out a way for her to get out of the elevator.

He'd nearly made love to her in that shower.

He was leaving.

"I only hired extra protection for the four days of the dog show. No one came near Tsini. His assignment is up tonight." Even saying those words hurt.

"Don't be foolish, Kayla. Those two bodyguards of yours… They're fine young men, but you need Welkins's guy."

In more ways than her uncle knew. In fact, she'd been thinking about extending Nash's assignment the whole plane ride home. She'd also reconsidered a brief, no-one-needs-to-know affair with him.

Now that they were back in Philly and not in the difficult-to-control environment of the Vegas Dog Show, she was sure Nash would relax at last. He'd probably make more of an effort to fit into her team. Life would be much calmer. And yet it would remain plenty interesting. In a manageable way. This was her home. She definitely had the upper hand here. He would understand that and wouldn't try to ride roughshod over her the way he'd done in Vegas.

She was still on leave from work for another week.

A week with Nash.

All she had to do was think that and her pitiful body buzzed with excitement.

"All right, sweetheart, I have to leave the hotel to get to my next meeting in time," her uncle was saying. "Hang in there. I'll be home in another day. Keep an eye on the company."

"I could do that better if I went back to the office." Uncle Al had been the one who had suggested she take a couple of weeks off after she'd gotten that package with the blue fur coat.

"You rest for a while," he told her. "You deserve it. I'll be back tomorrow. I can take care of whatever needs to be taken care of at work."

She hung up the phone just as Dave ambled in. "When's GI Joe leaving?"

Nash was checking her home security to make sure nothing had been tampered with while they were gone. He really did take his job seriously.

"I think I'm going to ask him to stay on for a little longer."

The look of disappointment on Dave's face was immediate and undisguised. "I don't like him," he said, in case she missed it. "Mike and I can handle everything." He pulled a piece of folded paper from his pocket.

She looked at the circle in the middle with a list of names inside.

"What's this?"

"The people closest to you who could be affected if there's any sort of attempt. These are the people who need to be protected." His index finger brushed over the names: Kayla, Greg, Uncle Al, Elvis, Ivan, Fisk and the rest of her staff, including her secretary.

Tom wasn't on the list. He'd already taken off as

soon as he'd brought up Tsini's crate. He was on staff only during shows and sometimes when Kayla traveled. Right on the circle, as if they were the protective circle themselves, were written two words: *Dave* and *Mike*.

She gave Dave a grateful smile, appreciating the sentiment.

"We don't need him." Dave gestured toward Nash with his head. "We're like family around here. Nobody except Nash thinks that the photo to your e-mail came from one of the staff. And none of us knew that dead guy in Vegas whose picture Nash was showing around. The cops said the whole elevator thing was an accident. You ask me, he came in with those wild accusations to bust up the team and take over."

"He'll make more of an effort to fit in to the team now that we're back here safely," she reassured Dave.

Nash walked by, hustling off to whatever task he was on to next and glanced at the list. "List of suspects?"

She looked up too fast and her headache intensified to a pulsing stream of pain behind her eyelids. He was gone by the time she could respond. She pushed off the couch and thanked Dave for the talk. "I'm going to lie down for a quick nap."

She took the paper with her without meaning to, just forgot to give it back, and looked at it again as she took some aspirin. She fell asleep with nothing but questions on her mind. Who was outside the circle? Who hunted her and her family?

She had strange dreams about Nash and her uncle, dreams that left her uneasy, although when she woke, she couldn't quite recall them. At least the headache was gone.

Nash was working on his laptop when she came out of her bedroom. His head came up. He was all graceful power as he sat there, a warrior at rest. Heat came into his gaze as he looked her over. Predictably, every cell in her body responded. *Maybe soon,* she promised herself. But first she needed to ask him to stay on. Should have done that before she'd said anything to Dave, but she hadn't been able to think, thanks to that damned headache.

"I'll call Welkins in a minute, but I want to tell you first. I'm going to extend your assignment. I mean, if you're willing to stay on longer." Wasn't exactly the way she'd meant to tell him, but she was too frazzled to do better. She just hoped he couldn't read her ulterior motives in her face.

A quick emotion flashed across his eyes, but it was gone before she could decipher it.

"Head of security. Carte blanche," he said, his attention focused completely on her.

So much for him "mellowing" now that the dog show was behind them and Tsini and Greg and she were safely back home.

She didn't want to talk strategy with him. She wanted his arms around her so badly that she ached with it. She was still fuzzy from sleep. She didn't have it in her to fight him, so she simply nodded.

She had a glass of juice in the kitchen then jumped off the barstool when she noticed the time. Her yoga instructor would arrive any minute. She washed her face and changed, and by the time she was coming out of the bedroom again, Ilona was there.

Nash checked her out thoroughly, including her bag. Then he insisted that they leave the door to the meditation room at the end of the long hall half-open.

"Everything okay?" Ilona asked as they were getting ready to start. "What's up with Mr. Hot-'n'-Protective out there?" She was twenty-two with the body of a— well, a yoga instructor. Dave and Mike got a lot of mileage out of flirting with her.

"Don't mind Nash. New security." Kayla stretched.

"Believe me, I don't mind him at all." Ilona's eyes twinkled as she gave a small laugh. "Sadly, I think he's only got eyes for you. All right, deep breath in," she started. And for the next hour, they went through their regular poses while Kayla wondered if Ilona could be right.

Was that pitiful? She did want Nash to have eyes only for her. But she was realistic enough to realize that at best he wanted only a quick, hot affair. And she wanted him so much that she'd take whatever he had to offer.

By the time Ilona left, Dave and Mike had gone off somewhere, and only Nash was left, sitting in the kitchen. Kayla was sweaty so she didn't stop to chat. She let Nash walk Ilona out while she hopped in the shower.

Then she was ready to see about dinner. When she was in residence, dinner was delivered from her favorite restaurant down the road every night at seven for her and her staff. She liked cooking, often put breakfast together for herself and Greg during the week and even lunch on the weekends. But during the week she usually ate lunch at company headquarters where she worked, more often than not having a lunchtime meeting. And her evenings were usually busy with social engagements. There was little time left for dinner preparations.

Dave usually called in how many people they had on any given night. TJ, the manager at the restaurant, knew what she liked and he kept the menu varied.

Except there was no sign of dinner tonight and no sign of Dave. Or Mike for that matter. Two strange men sat in her kitchen with Nash. She watched them for a second, staying in the cover of the potted palms. Friends of Nash, that was obvious from the familiar way they were talking, understanding each other from halfwords and looks. They were built like Nash, too, bringing some serious testosterone overload to the room. One had multiple scars crossing his left eyebrow. Another sported a nose that had been flattened pretty badly at one point.

In size alone, they were smaller than Mike and Dave, but looked ten times as tough and menacing. These were no gentlemen bodyguards who would put on a tux to take her to events. They looked like they'd been born in combat boots and were damned determined to die in them. She wasn't sure if she was comfortable with these two in her home. And frankly, she didn't think it terribly professional for Nash to bring his friends by for a visit while on the job.

She wanted fewer people in the apartment with them tonight, not more. She was going to ask him into her room after dinner to discuss his role on her team. And if he kissed her again… She didn't plan on putting up too much resistance.

Just thinking of him kissing her sent tingles through her body. She wanted him. He wanted her. For once, she wasn't going to overcomplicate things.

"Hi." She stepped into view at last.

Nobody seemed surprised by her sudden appearance, almost as if they'd known that she'd been standing back there. Creepy.

"Hey." Nash turned to her. "Meet you new body-guards. Mo and Joey."

It took her a minute to comprehend what he was saying. This was really bad. She'd known she was going to regret that "carte blanche" comment. Mike and Dave were absolutely going to hate this. *She* hated it. Lust gave way to outrage. Of all the underhanded…

Keep calm. There had to be some sort of an explanation, a compromise they could come to.

"Where are Mike and Dave?" She needed to prepare them before they met Nash's men.

"They're gone," Nash said easily. "I fired them."

NASH SAT calmly while Kayla yelled at him, completely flying off the handle. Pretty much what he'd expected.

"You can't fire them. They're my people! You had no right whatsoever." Her face was turning an interesting shade of red.

Couldn't say it made her less attractive. He didn't mind a bit of fire in a woman.

"They were clueless. They were looking for some phantom outside enemy. They were more of a liability than a help. I need people I can trust backing me up. Mo and Joey are up to the task."

Mike and Dave hadn't been bad. He'd especially appreciated Mike's help with that elevator. But they weren't Mo and Joey. And he needed Mo and Joey. For

Kayla, nothing less would do. He wasn't about to take any chances with her life.

For all he cared, Mike and Dave could have stayed on, but they'd already proven that they didn't take orders well. Getting used to him had taken them days. Nash didn't have days now. He didn't have the time to deal with friction and possible insubordination, not when the attacks on Kayla were intensifying.

Threatening her dog was one thing. But someone had been in her bedroom in Vegas. Then the John Doe the police still hadn't identified had tried to kill her in that elevator. And every instinct Nash had said it wasn't over yet.

"You—" She took a deep breath and narrowed her eyes, looking as though she was about to send him to hell. Then she changed her mind, spun on her heels, strode back to her bedroom and slammed the door behind her so hard it reverberated throughout the penthouse.

A moment of silence passed after that as the three men exchanged a look over the kitchen counter.

"She hates your guts," Joey remarked, not the least perturbed by this display of feminine emotion. He had a known weakness for temperamental women.

Nash shot him a warning, proprietary look.

Joey gave a lopsided smile. "You like the girl."

Mo's half-missing eyebrow went up. "You're so doomed, man."

Joey stood, playing off him. "We should go. He's going down. I don't want to be witness to that carnage."

"Sit down," Nash snapped at him. "I don't *like* her. Where are we? Kindergarten?"

Now Mo stood, and the barstool he'd been sitting on sighed with relief. The man was built like a tank. "Can't be working with you on a job if we're not going to be honest," he said, deadpan.

Nash raised a hand in capitulation. "Quit busting my chops. She's okay. I kinda like her. I guess."

At that, the two gave identical grins.

He itched to knock their heads together over the counter, but that would have led to a brawl and a destroyed penthouse apartment. Not the way to get back into Kayla's or Welkins's good graces, so, instead, he opened the folder that had been sitting in front of him on the counter. "Can we move on to business? We do have a killer to catch."

SHE WAS TIRED and furious and not entirely sure how to handle the situation. She called both Mike and Dave. They were mad beyond reason, but neither seemed inclined to come back and tackle the men in her kitchen. And after a couple of moments Kayla understood that once again she had overestimated her relationships. They weren't her best friends. They'd been her hired bodyguards. They would have given their life for her while they'd been on her payroll. But now that their employment had ended, they were moving on to their next assignment. One where they wouldn't have to fight three ex-commando human tanks just to get started.

On some level, she understood. But on another level she was hurt and felt betrayed by those men. She had thought they were part of her core team. The team she could trust through thick and thin.

Her father had been big on the whole *core-team* thing. To him, it had meant the family: his wife, his sons and his daughter. He was big on not trusting anyone beyond that, not even his own brother. He viewed Uncle Al more as competition. He hadn't been crazy about sharing the company's leadership with him. William Landon had been too much of an alpha male to share something like that.

Which meant that Uncle Al hadn't been a big part of Kayla's childhood. But they'd grown much closer since her father's death. He'd become a replacement father figure of sorts. He'd never remarried after his wife had run off with that bodyguard. Maybe he had his own trust issues, Kayla thought for the first time. Was her whole family struggling with that?

Her stomach growled. But she no longer felt like eating. It was past eight anyway. She would watch a movie in her room and go to bed. She couldn't face Nash Wilder again tonight or she might murder him.

Her dreams were dark and disjointed. In one of them, Nash loomed large and dark, scaring her spitless. He held a gun on Greg. Her uncle stood in the background.

She woke gasping for air in the middle of the night, turned on the light on the nightstand. She was alone in the room, save for Tsini, who raised her head for only a minute before going back to sleep.

Kayla took a drink from the water bottle she always kept by the bed, then leaned against the headboard. Her headache was back full-force and then some. She reached for the bottle of aspirin, her gaze falling on the piece of paper Dave had given her, the one with the protective circle. And immediately she was furious at Nash all over again. How dare he mess with her staff?

He'd considered her people suspects from the get-go. She should have fired him then and there. She should have trusted her staff more than she trusted him.

In her dream, he was going to kill Greg. And she just knew she would have been next.

But why would he be her enemy? What would he gain by that?

Her head pounded harder.

He could be someone's hired man. The hired-man theory had been his from the beginning. Maybe it was a situation he was more than familiar with?

Then she remembered how in the dream, her uncle had been there.

Her uncle had told her to hire someone from this particular agency. Then Nash had been sent.

Her uncle had told her to take a break from work.

Her father had never fully trusted Al. Had there been a reason for that? Her uncle was leading the corporation. But he didn't own enough shares to control it. Kayla and Greg were also major shareholders. The three of them were each other's beneficiaries. If Kayla and Greg were gone, Al would become majority shareholder with the ability to control the company.

She hated that those thoughts would even come into her head. Hated the fact that Nash had made her paranoid. Odd, though, that he would try to get her to be suspicious of everyone close to her, but never her uncle. Did that mean anything?

If her uncle wanted to take over everything, nobody

but Kayla could stand in his way. Certainly not Greg. Uncle Al already controlled Greg's trust fund.

Enough things clicked to make her sit up straight. But then she hesitated.

It couldn't be. No way it could be Al. What about the picture someone had sent to her? But if Al could buy Nash, he could buy someone on that camera crew to take the picture. Nash had been the only one who seemed to recall clearly that none of the camera crew had been in the den, thereby neatly transferring all suspicion to her people.

Al could have sent the threats to Tsini—he was a cat person, never cared for dogs in the first place—just so he could talk her into hiring extra help, someone who was his man.

Still, she could barely wrap her mind around the idea. Her brain cells were having a bongo-drum festival in her head. She was aware that it was the middle of the night, she'd just woken from a nightmare and she wasn't thinking straight. She was also aware that Al was out of the country, due back tomorrow. He lived in a historic brick townhouse just across the park. And she had a key and the code to the security system.

She had no one to ask for help. If she wanted to find out the truth, she needed to get over there and look around. Three murders and an attempted murder had to have left some kind of trail.

Tonight was her only chance to search through her uncle's place.

The first step was to find a way around Nash. The thought that they'd kissed, that she'd been in that shower with him, one irresponsible moment away from having sex… She'd made a few bad judgment calls in her youth, but she'd thought she'd become smarter since.

She would be this time.

"Don't trust anyone," Greg had told her before they left for Vegas. A lot of people thought Greg was dumb, but not her. Sometimes, Greg saw things nobody else did.

She poured her water on the nearest potted plant, then walked out of her bedroom with the empty bottle.

Mo was sitting in the darkest corner of her living room. Joey was in the kitchen, on the one barstool from which he had a clear view of the front door. They didn't look like the kind of men she would want to mess with.

And what did that say about how out of control her life was? She was surrounded by men she was scared of. That would have to change.

Her hands trembled. She made a point of steadying them. These men could have killed her and Greg twenty times by now. Nash could have, too, for that matter. What were they waiting for?

Maybe a chance to make it look like an accident.

But then how did the elevator crash fit into their plan? Nash had been on that elevator with her. Maybe he'd made a mistake. Or maybe getting off just in time was part of his plan. He could have set it up that way to make sure that later, when he did take her out, nobody could suspect him.

But then who was the guy Nash had chased? Maybe some poor innocent who'd gotten pushed to his death.

Her head pounded. She couldn't make heads or tails of the events of the last couple of days, but she couldn't get past the feeling that there was something here she wasn't seeing yet, that she was in danger.

She tossed the empty water bottle in the recycling bin and grabbed a full one from the pantry. "Where's Nash?" she asked on her way back, her mind buzzing with a thousand thoughts, each wilder than the one before.

"Checking on something," Joey said. His answer was pretty vague.

"When will he be back?"

The man shrugged.

Her heart picked up speed. *Nash is gone,* was all she could think. An advantage she needed to grab.

"Could I talk to both of you for a minute?" She remained standing as Mo lumbered out of the living room, giving her a what-now? look.

The two men loomed large in the dim light, beyond intimidating. She was well aware that either one of them could snap her like a twig without breaking a sweat. She inched toward the knife block and pulled her spine straight when she got there. She'd faced down rabid paparazzi, managed problem employees at work and successfully ran her part of the Landon empire. She couldn't back down now. She wouldn't.

"I thought about this. I'm sure you guys are great, but the fact is, Nash hired you without consulting with me first. I was happy with my own men. I was used to them. We worked together like a team. I'm going to ask them back. You're relieved of duty. You'll get your pay for the full week."

She stood strong and tall, just like her father always had. Wouldn't blink, wouldn't look away. That was the

Landon blood in her. William Landon had been a formidable man, and his only daughter had inherited more of that than he'd ever realized.

Mo and Joey exchanged an unreadable glance.

"I want you to leave."

"Not till Nash gets back," Mo said.

She gave him a strained smile. "See, that's kind of my problem with Nash. I am the boss here. When I say somebody is hired, they're hired. When I say they go, they go. This is my home." She paused for effect.

They still didn't seem impressed.

"Let me spell it out. I thank you for your hard work, but if you're not out of here in the next five minutes, I'll consider you trespassers and I'm calling the police."

Mo sat on the barstool next to Joey, tilted his head, gave her a look that might have been meant to seem patient. "Listen, Nash wouldn't like it if we left."

"I'm not terribly concerned over Nash's happiness. You can call him and explain later."

"He doesn't have his cell on when he's—" Joey started, but Mo fixed him with a glare, and he snapped his mouth shut without finishing.

"I really don't care. You need to leave."

"When Nash gets back," Mo said.

She stood there for another thirty seconds, trying to figure out what to do. She had to get them out of her home. No way was she going to leave them with Greg while she went across the park to her uncle's place. And she didn't want them following her either. She looked between the two men. Obviously, they didn't take her seriously.

"Okay. Time's up." She marched over to the security

system and pushed the silent alarm button. She was prepared to have the security company haul these guys out when they got here.

Mo stood, his half-mangled eyebrow up all the way to his hairline. "What did you do that for?" He clucked his tongue as he picked up his black duffel bag from the foyer, giving her a dirty look.

Joey was right behind him. "Nash isn't going to be happy about this."

She punched in the security code so she could open the door for them. She didn't want the full alarm going off and waking Greg. "I'll worry about that later when I have some time to spare. Right now, I'd like to get back to bed."

She closed the door behind them with a smile, locked it then called the security firm to call off the alarm. She dressed and checked in on Greg. She hated leaving him alone. But there had never been a single threat directed at him. And if she succeeded tonight in finding some proof against their uncle, solid proof that she could take to the police, then they would both be safe at last, safe for good. She had to take this chance.

"You watch him," she told Tsini, then set the alarm again and left the condo with her uncle's backup keys in her left pocket and a small bottle of pepper spray in her right. She lived in one of the best neighborhoods in the city, but she wasn't taking any chances.

Nobody in the hallway, nobody in the elevator. The lobby was empty, as well, except for the doorman.

She was a smidgen surprised at how easily she'd gotten rid of Nash's goons. But then again, what else could they have done? Wait for the police and go to jail for the night when she pressed charges for trespassing and harassment? She lifted her chin and smiled at the doorman. She'd handled this just right. She was pretty proud of herself.

"Going out late, Miss Landon. Should I call a cab?"

"Just stepping out to meet a friend for a second."

Stanislav, a Polish immigrant who was working to collect money to bring his fiancée over from Poznan, held the door open for her.

She walked up the sidewalk until she was out of his sight, then crossed the empty street and strode into the park.

Still no sign of Mo and Joey. Looked like they'd taken her seriously and cleared out for good. In the morning, she'd call a couple of friends, find a reputable security agency and hire her own men. Who would be right at her back when Nash showed up to demand an explanation, which she was sure he would. He was damned hardheaded. She wasn't looking forward to that confrontation. And Mike and Dave weren't the right men to stand up to Nash—she knew that now, as much as she liked those guys. To deal with Nash, she needed someone much tougher.

For a second she thought of him as he'd been with her nearly every second of the Vegas trip, and she wavered. Her uncle and Nash. God, that seemed so far-fetched. But nothing else made sense. And she'd fired Nash's men now. She was committed to seeing this to the end.

Where on earth was Nash anyway? For all she knew, he was off someplace even now, plotting against her.

She took the main path, the one edged with lights. She

lived in the best part of town, with the highest-priced con-dominiums, and the park reflected that. The city was quiet and the park even more so, the bushes and trees muffling the noise of the odd car that passed in the distance.

The sound of gravel crunching under her feet seemed deafening and made her head pound harder. The lights over the path were great, but they didn't reach far into the bushes. Darkness surrounded her.

The first rush of energy was beginning to wear off. And she slowed as she considered that there might be other issues here she hadn't yet considered. But if she'd waited to think every angle through, Nash would have returned. She wanted this over with, wanted proof in her hands either way before they met again.

She jumped when she heard a noise behind her, or thought she had. There was nothing there when she turned. Her heart beat faster. Okay, Nash or no Nash, it was probably pretty stupid to come out here in the middle of the night.

But it was too late to turn back.

If someone had followed her, without her noticing, and intended to harm her, she would be walking right into his arms. She had to keep going forward. She quick-ened her pace.

Light wind ruffled the bushes. A car passed on the street now and again. She reached the fountain at the halfway point. The water was shut off at night to save electricity. She didn't dare slow. She wanted to be out of the damned park. She grabbed the pepper spray in her pocket tighter. Just a little farther. She was almost there.

Then she did reach the end of the winding path,

bursting out onto the street and nearly stepping in front of a rushing cab. She pulled back, her heart racing a mile a minute. When she crossed the road at last, she looked in both directions.

Her uncle lived in one of a dozen historic redbrick townhouses that lined the street. They were small, cold and hideously expensive. And you couldn't ever do anything to them without obtaining a bucketload of permits from the Historical Council. She'd never understood why her uncle liked living here.

She stopped on the front stoop to catch her breath. All the lights were off. She didn't expect anybody to be here. Margaret Miller, his housekeeper, had gone to visit family in Minnesota, taking advantage of his absence.

She slid the key into the lock and got in without trouble. The alarm wasn't even on. Her first thought was that she needed to tell Al to be more careful, then she realized that she couldn't very well tell the man that she'd been breaking in while he'd been gone.

She shook her head at the absurdity of the situation. Then she couldn't move all of a sudden. The house was dark and quiet around her. Her uncle's house. Uncle Al's. What in the hell was she doing here?

She had no idea beyond that she was desperate. She needed to figure out what was going on, who was after her. It *couldn't* be Uncle Al. But she moved forward anyway, so frightened now that she was becoming unreasonable.

She padded up the stairs, didn't turn on the light. Doors stood open to the left and right, rooms that were too big with too many dark corners. If as much as a leaf fell off a houseplant, she was going to have a heart attack. She was so wound up she couldn't breathe. She would never have cut it as a cat burglar for sure.

Then she was at the office at last, at Al's desk. None of his drawers were locked, not even his filing cabinets. His laptop was gone. He had taken that on his trip.

She rifled through his in-box first, but didn't find anything unusual. Mostly his personal business, life-insurance papers, letters from charity boards he was on and the like. His drawers held more of the same. The file cabinets stored various receipts and tax documents.

The longer she searched the stupider she felt. What had she expected? A copy of a check with *Payment for Elevator Incident* stamped on the back?

A picture on the shelf caught her eye. Greg and Lance and herself when they were little with Uncle Al. The photo had been taken at a rare family get-together. Al was looking at the three kids in the picture with such love and maybe even longing in his eyes. Did he ever wish he'd had his own children?

For a moment, she sank onto the leather couch by the wall. And the next second, tears filled her eyes. She couldn't believe she was here. She couldn't imagine what her uncle would say. He had been on her side since her parents' death, had given nothing but love to her and Greg. Guilt filled her to the brim, and as she blinked back her tears she felt ashamed of herself.

She was the one breaking in. If someone was untrust-worthy in her family, it was her.

She pushed up and ran out the room, down the hallway. She wanted to be back with Greg and forget that she'd ever stooped this low, that she'd ever betrayed the trust between her and her uncle.

She locked the house back up behind her, but left the security off, the way she'd found it.

The wind had picked up while she'd been inside. The trees and bushes made more noise in the park. Every snapping branch made her jump. The path seemed twice as long as it had on her way here. She stumbled on a shoelace that had come untied. She didn't dare stop to tie it.

Especially not when she heard footsteps crunch on the gravel behind her. This time, the noise wasn't in her imagination. Definite footsteps. Gathering speed.

She was all alone, no one to hear her call for help. She broke into a run, shoelaces be damned. By the time she passed the fountain, she realized that someone was moving in the bushes, too, to her right. There were two of them after her. She ran faster.

Stumbled.

A hand shot out of the bushes before she could regain her balance. She was yanked off the path roughly, branches scraping against her face, her throat too tight to scream, her body too numb with shock to fight back.

Chapter Eight

She was frozen in shock for about a split second, which worked just fine for Nash. Then pepper spray hit him in the face before he knocked the spray can to the ground. He blinked furiously to let the tears flush his burning eyes even as he put his left hand over her mouth so she wouldn't scream. His right gripped his gun while holding her tight against him at the same time. Her heart beat wildly against his bicep.

"Nash," he said, giving his identity.

But, instead of calming, she fought harder. He had to put her in a full restraining hold. Just in time.

A second later a man dressed all in black came around the bend, moving forward at a good clip. Nash tried to get a good look at him, not an easy task with his eyes burning like hell. He didn't let Kayla go when the guy passed. He waited until Mo appeared, moving considerably more quietly than the bastard he followed. He nodded to Nash in the bushes without breaking his stride.

And Nash bit down, gave a small shake of his head. Anything Mo didn't notice didn't exist. He'd spent most of his life in the worst of the world's jungles and was an expert in guerilla warfare.

Nash waited a minute or two after they disappeared before dragging Kayla deeper into the bushes, taking them out of hearing distance of anyone else who might walk the path this late at night. Then he wiped his eyes as best he could and blew his nose a couple of times. Cleared his throat as quietly as he could and spat some of the pepper spray into the bushes.

"What are you doing here?" To her credit, she kept her voice at a whisper as she pulled away from him, shaking.

"Keeping you alive," he snapped, halfway to a heart attack from thinking of all the trouble she could have gotten into. If he hadn't been inside her uncle's house, doing his own recon when she'd arrived, she would most likely be dead by now. "What in the hell were you doing going through your uncle's papers in the middle of the night?"

She bolted.

He grabbed her by the wrist and hauled her hard against him. "I want an answer. Now."

She looked as though she was ready to break down.

He didn't care. "When I was told I'd be working for you, I thought you were nothing but an empty-headed beauty who lived off her parents' money. But somewhere along the way, I managed to convince myself that you were more. That you actually had a brain." He knew he was being too tough on her, but he could have strangled her. She'd gotten rid of the men he'd brought in to protect her, then sneaked out in the middle of the night. Was she completely crazy?

She opened her mouth, but a gunshot interrupted whatever she was about to say.

She almost jumped out of her skin. "Why are *you* here? Do you work for my uncle? I don't know if I can trust you." Her words were as desperate as the look on her face.

"Yeah, I got that from Mo and Joey." He'd turned on his phone and called them the second Kayla had stepped out of her uncle's house. Sure didn't expect to see her there. He'd been surprised at first, then angry as hell that she would risk her life like that.

He let her go and gave her a little room, but not so much that he couldn't grab her again if necessary.

"Who's shooting? Who was the guy in black?" She wrapped her arms around herself as she glanced furtively at the ground.

Better not be looking for the damned pepper spray. He still couldn't see straight. His throat burned as if he'd drunk liquid fire. "He followed you from the moment you stepped outside your uncle's house. Mo will know more when he gets back."

"Where's Joey?"

"Stayed behind to guard Greg while Mo followed you across the park to make sure nothing happened to you."

His vision was clearing enough now that he caught her look of surprise, mixed with guilt. "I fired them."

"And in a couple of minutes you can thank them for being good sports about it and not taking you seriously." He took her hand and pulled her back toward the path, keeping in front of her as he heard Mo coming their way. They'd worked together in the past enough for him to recognize his gait. He came alone.

But the news was worse than that.

"Bastard shot me." Mo pressed his palm against the side of his leg.

Kayla made a strangled noise behind Nash.

Mo paid her little attention. "Damn scratch." He gave a disgusted huff. "Ducked it just fine but it ricocheted off a rock and hit me. Not my night. Threw me off stride for a second. Bastard got away. Someone in an old Jeep picked him up. No license plate."

Nash swore under his breath, but regrouped fast. "Don't let her go anywhere." He walked to the fountain, ducked his head under the surface of the water and swooshed it around a couple of times before coming up to shake droplets out of his hair. His eyes burned a little less. "Let's get her home. Keep your eyes open."

Mo's bushy eyebrow went up as he took in Nash's appearance, but he didn't ask any questions. He was a man of few words. Right now, Nash appreciated that about the man more than ever.

They were back at her place in twenty minutes.

"Everything okay, Miss Landon?" the doorman asked as he came out from behind the desk.

Mo moved so the blood on his leg would be out of the doorman's view. Nash gave the guy a bleary grin. "Great party." He pointed at his head. "I'd better go before I drip beer on your carpet."

The doorman didn't comment, but his expression said, *crazy Americans.*

They made it up in the elevator without running into anyone else. Kayla went straight to her bedroom once they were inside her apartment. Nash walked in after her.

"I want you to leave." She looked out of sorts and exhausted, still scared.

She could be dead, he thought, and squelched any sympathy that might have influenced him. "We need to talk." He turned and locked the door behind them.

The way her eyes went wide with fear hit him like a sledge hammer in the middle of his chest. He didn't usually mind if people were scared of him. It was a plus in his line of work, in fact. But he wanted something else from Kayla. He pulled his gun. She stepped back, her eyes darting from side to side.

"Take it easy." He grabbed the Beretta by the barrel and held it out toward her. "Here. You take this if it makes you feel better." He had to be losing his mind here. She had him tied up in knots. Did he need her trust this badly?

The answer was fast and simple: yes, he did.

After a moment of hesitation, she stepped forward and watched him carefully as she grabbed the gun. "How about others?"

"Other what?"

"Weapons. I don't think you'd go around without a backup."

Sharp as anything. Definitely. He reached for the ankle holster and the smaller handgun he kept there. He put it on the nightstand.

She sighed, sounding and looking tired. "You probably have a knife, too, don't you?"

For a moment he thought about denying it. But this whole exercise was about getting her to trust him, so he pulled the switchblade from his pocket and set that down, too.

"Is that everything?" she asked.

"Want to strip-search me?" he countered. He could have warmed to the idea in a hurry.

She shook her head, decidedly not looking as if she was up to the task.

Too bad.

He stepped back. "Mind if I use your bathroom for a sec?"

"Go ahead."

He walked in there, without any sudden movements, and washed his face again, rinsed his mouth and eyes a couple of times.

"How are you doing?" he asked her when he came back.

"I don't know what to think anymore," she admitted as she sank onto her bed.

He sat on her reading chaise to make himself look smaller, less threatening. He leaned back. If he looked relaxed, maybe she'd relax a little, too. "You lost your parents and your brother and now someone is out to kill you. That's a lot to deal with."

She nodded, holding his gun in a white-knuckled grip.

Thank God Welkins couldn't see him now. He needed to stop going around arming clients. Especially ones who were likely to shoot him.

Not that he really thought she would. She was smart and reasonable. She was just scared.

But even though he was pretty sure she wasn't going to shoot him, he still hated staring down the business end of a gun. And he hated even more the idea of her thinking that he would harm her.

"Good job with the pepper spray," he said.

She flinched. "Sorry about that."

"If you really think I'm out to get you, you shouldn't be. But if you're having second thoughts and you're ready to hear me out, you could put the gun down for a while. Just to be polite and all that."

She hesitated way too long before she laid the Beretta on her lap.

"Want to walk me through your thought process here?"

She tucked her hair behind her ears, bit her full lower lip. She looked lost and fragile for the first time since he met her. It took effort to stay still instead of crossing the room and scooping her into his arms. In which case, she probably would have shot him.

"You kept saying that the killer was someone close to me," she began. "Then Dave gave me that list of everyone in my inner circle. And I had this flash of paranoia. My uncle just called. And I thought how he'd be majority shareholder of the company if Greg and I were out of the picture. And you were recommended by him. What better way to get his man inside the house?"

"Brian Welkins picked me. Your uncle doesn't know me from Adam. He liked the agency because he heard good things about it from another client."

"But I didn't know all that."

He wasn't going to give her any flack. She couldn't have known. "When people are out to kill you, it's smart not to trust anyone," he told her.

"But it's driving me crazy." She sounded desperate.

"On the other hand, if you could find a way to trust

me," he went on, "it would make my job of protecting you a lot easier. We can't be working against each other."

She didn't say anything, but he could practically hear her thinking from across the room.

"I've had about a hundred opportunities by now if I wanted to hurt you."

She stiffened. "Maybe you wanted to do it without witnesses."

"I could have done that at the park just now."

The truth was, he could protect her no matter how she felt about him. He'd protected all kinds of people with success. People who looked down on him, people who considered him a servant, people who resented having to be protected. It was all part of the job and he'd learned to work around it. But he wanted Kayla's trust. How important that was to him took him by surprise.

"Sorry," she said in a thin voice and hung her head. "I learned not to trust outsiders the hard way. But I could always trust my family. It hadn't been the warmest and most supportive place growing up, my father was a tough man, but my family and the immediate staff always had my back. He always said not to trust outsiders. And by outsiders he meant anyone but the core team—him, Mom, Lance, Greg and me. Then in the last two years, my staff became my core team. And Uncle Al. I don't know how to live if I have to start questioning that."

"Give me a little more time. I'll have this figured out," he promised her.

For a second or two, they sat in silence.

"I guess you know firsthand about betrayal." Some of

the media articles he'd read about her came up as suspect all of a sudden. Everything he knew about her now said that she didn't court paparazzi attention on purpose. "How did you become a media sensation to start with?" He knew a lot about her past from her files, but there were some areas he still didn't fully understand.

He told himself anything he learned about her might help him figure out who was after her family. But the truth was his interest in her went beyond that. It was personal.

"Slow news day." She gave a pained smile. "Penny Holiday, heiress to the department-store chain, was propelling herself into the limelight just when I started college. Then she got that DUI and laid low for a couple of months. The tabloids needed a replacement. Anyway, some sleazy photographer tracked me down on campus and ambushed me, took my picture as I was doing laundry. The headline read, Penny Holiday Out of Control while Popcorn Cinderella Learns to Survive without a Maid."

He didn't say anything. He wanted to wring the bastard's neck, but he figured it wouldn't change anything now. Still, the sheer satisfaction… Maybe he'd look into it when she was safe and his assignment was over.

He ignored the heavy feeling that thought brought to his chest.

"And you know the rest," she said, resigned. "Soon I went from Popcorn Cinderella to Popcorn Princess. I suppose it sold more copies." She shrugged. "Do you know what the worst part is? I actually became the person they made me out to be. At the end I became a bimbo so Greg and I would be safe. I didn't want anyone to think that I was a threat." Tears came into her eyes.

"I should have pushed harder to have those accidents more thoroughly investigated."

"You faced an impossible choice. Nothing will bring back your parents. Nothing will bring back Lance. But you could still save Greg." He understood. "Life is full of hellish decisions. We make them, then all we can do is live with the consequences."

"Except I never make a mistake just once." She leaned against the headboard. "My mistakes are forever. Every time they catch me on camera, they drag out all the old stuff again and again. And if they have nothing on me, they make something up."

She closed her eyes for a moment, then opened them again, but wouldn't look at him. "My last boyfriend posted pictures of me online after he talked me into skinny-dipping off the Landon yacht in the Mediterranean, calling me every kind of prude and chicken if I didn't go along with him."

He'd seen those pictures when he'd done research on her, had had a couple of restless nights because of them.

"And when he decided he liked the taste of being a media sensation, he gave an interview about me being narcissistic and whatever."

A lifeless doll in bed, had been the exact words, something Nash pretty much doubted. She'd come alive in his arms in the pool and in that shower afterwards. Her passion was alive and more than well. He'd never been more turned on by a woman.

He watched her as she sat on her bed, her shoulders slumping. The fight seemed to have gone out of her. He hated to see her broken.

And it went way beyond wanting to protect a client. *Man, oh man.*

He was a straightforward guy. He recognized a brick wall when he slammed into it. He knew damn well that Kayla was different from any other woman who'd click-clicked through his life in four-inch stilettos. She was smart and caring. She was fun to be around even when they were fighting. She was the most loyal person he knew. Everything about her made him want her until he was cross-eyed from trying to resist.

But he would. She was heiress to an empire worth obscene amounts of money. She was almost ten years younger than he and—despite her tabloid record—in some ways, infinitely more innocent. He would never fit into her life and she would never fit into his.

She needed a guy who would wear a tux close to every night of his life and go to highbrow charity events with her, someone who played golf with business executives, someone who'd gone to the right university and knew the right people, fitted in with her social circle. Someone who would have children with her.

That last thought hit him harder than the others. Made him ache deep inside his chest. She would be a good mother. She was protective and loving.

He could see her happy. He just couldn't see himself as part of that picture.

His past was too dark. He was used to living in the shadows. He could never follow her into the limelight. He had too many secrets. Any guy who got involved with her would be taken apart by the media. He'd been a secret soldier. A commando. His whole life was about keeping a low profile.

"Hey," he said, his gut twisting when the moonlight glinted off moisture on her face and he realized that she was silently crying.

He went to her, kneeled in front of the bed and took the gun from her, laid her back and covered her with a blanket. "Try to get a couple of hours of sleep. Everything will look better in the morning. We'll talk then. We'll come up with a plan." Then he backed away before he could do anything stupid. Like kiss her.

The key was to get out fast.

Five more feet.

Two.

He was at the door, about to congratulate himself on his self-restraint, when he heard her ask the question he both dreaded and desired hearing.

"Could you please stay?"

SHE WOKE midmorning, surprised that nobody had gotten her up before that. She had to have gotten a half dozen calls by now. But her phone wasn't on her nightstand, and Kayla could guess why. Nash was keeping the world at bay.

He'd spent the night on her reading chaise, watching over her. And somehow in the night, a tenuous trust did build between them. Now, with sun pouring in the window, her suspicions and fears of the night before seemed exaggerated.

She'd sprayed Nash with pepper spray. And Mo had gotten hurt. All because of her.

She sat up and buried her face in her hands. She allowed herself one full minute of wallowing and hating what her life was becoming.

By the time she'd showered and was coming out of the bathroom, Nash was standing in the bedroom doorway. He extended his hand toward her with her cell phone in his palm.

"Your uncle called a couple of times."

A pang of guilt shot through her. She called back immediately, not completely surprised when Nash stayed where he was instead of walking away.

"Did you have a good flight back?"

"Worked the whole time. I have some good news for you on the European projects. Come to dinner tonight?"

Nash shook his head. Her uncle's voice was strong enough that he could hear it standing next to her.

She wanted to go. She wanted to tell Al everything, wanted him to forgive her, wanted to forget that she'd ever doubted him.

"Tonight would be—"

Nash glared, shaking his head vehemently now.

"Tonight would be tight for me. Can we do tomorrow?" she corrected.

Nash gave her an approving nod. She didn't care about his approval. She just wanted her normal life back.

"You're not mad at me about anything, are you? You sounded strange on the phone yesterday. I know I said what I said about that last boyfriend of yours, but I only wanted the best for you."

"You were right."

"I don't want you to get hurt. I know I'm not your

father. But I do love you as if you were my daughter. And I tend to forget that you're a grown woman and a very capable one at that. You have to forgive me if I overstep my boundaries now and then."

"We're good. Really. I promise." God knew, she'd overstepped some serious boundaries last night herself. She only hoped that her uncle would understand and forgive her.

Because her father hadn't considered Al "core team," it had taken too long for Kayla to do so. Time wasted. And her father's attitude of mistrust had come back when she'd thought Al would want the company more than he wanted the family.

They needed to start fresh. Tomorrow she would make sure that her uncle knew that she loved him. They talked for another minute or two before hanging up on a positive note that made Kayla feel better.

Nash was still there, considering her, the look in his eyes unreadable as usual.

"I'm going tomorrow," she said to preempt him. "He loves me. He's like a second father to me. You fired Mike and Dave. But don't think you're going to stand between me and my family. Back off, Nash. Al has nothing to do with anything."

"I don't think he does," he said mildly.

"Then why can't I see him tonight?"

"A friend is running a full background check on him for me, and that won't be in until tomorrow morning."

"He's my uncle. I'm not going to have him investigated. Do you hear me, Nash? I'm serious. I forbid you to do that. This is important to me. When I went over there, I betrayed his trust. I'm not going to do that again."

Her emotions were tied up in knots. She was scared of whatever attack might come next, felt guilty for doubting her uncle, was thoroughly confused by an elemental attraction to Nash that she no longer knew what to do with. If she ever had. Deep down she knew a quick affair was not the right solution. But she didn't believe anything more than that was possible.

She went back to the thing that lay most heavily on her mind. "You're not to harass my uncle. Promise me, Nash."

"Fine. I'm not going to harass him," he said.

NASH CHECKED the front of the house first, walking along the sidewalk a couple of times, noting which windows were dark. Then he went around to the back alley and surveyed the situation there.

He loved Kayla's loyalty, but nothing, absolutely nothing, was going to stop him from keeping her safe. If she trusted her uncle blindly, good for her. But he didn't trust anyone to be near her until he figured out what was going on and who wanted her dead.

He didn't expect to find anything here tonight. Hell, he was *hoping* not to find anything. If her uncle was involved, it would break Kayla's heart. Nash stepped up on a garbage can to reach the lowest window. Al Landon's bedroom. He hadn't been in there yet. He'd searched the man's office when he'd been here before, along with the kitchen, living room and the basement. Then Kayla had interrupted him. And he'd followed her home. Thank God.

So the bedroom might hide some secrets yet. The bedside light was on. A laptop lay on the nightstand. A half-open closet door revealed a small built-in safe. Nobody in there.

He got his pocketknife out and inserted the blade into the infinitesimal space between the window and the frame. Then pulled it back and ducked as Al came in.

"It is exceedingly good to be home, I tell you that."

Nash couldn't see who he was talking to.

Could his visitor be the guy who had followed Kayla across the park the night before?

Nash chanced a look, and found himself eye to belly button with a naked woman whose barefooted steps he hadn't heard on the plush carpet as she'd walked over to the window. An expanse of pink skin and a ruby belly-button ring. He was pretty much prepared for a lot of things, but not that. Caught him off guard for a second.

He looked up, wanting to know who the hell that was. She could be a clue to all this mess.

She looked down at the exact same second. For a heartbeat, Nash hoped she hadn't seen him. He was dressed all in black. But then she screamed and she was no slouch. He could swear the windowpane rattled.

He made no sound as he jumped off the garbage can and disappeared into the darkest corner of the alley, out of her sight, within a flat second. And swore. There'd be no getting into that bedroom tonight, not with the two of them in there and alert.

His plan had been to go in there before Al did. He hadn't expected the man to retire before 9:00 p.m., and he hadn't wanted to come before that, needed the cover of darkness. Kayla had said her uncle had no girlfriend. If worse came to worst, Nash could have gotten in after Al was asleep. But not now. There were two of them. And having seen a peeper at the window, they'd probably sleep with one eye open.

Or, depending on how paranoid the man and his sweetheart were, they might even call out the cops. That would be the perfect ending to an already annoying day. While Kayla had been taking care of business with her agent, he'd been following leads and working his tail off only to come up with no usable information.

Nash sped his steps and moved out of the alley, onto the street, disappearing into the park a few seconds later.

He watched the front of the house from the cover of the bushes. No cops came. He considered again whether he should try to get inside, but came to the same conclusion as before. Too risky. But he *would* come back another time, regardless of the background report. Even if Al hadn't committed any crimes in the past, it didn't mean he wasn't doing so now. He still had the strongest motive of anyone on Nash's list. Not something he was going to discount easily.

He wanted Kayla safe, even if she would strangle him if she knew that he was here. She thought he was out in the parking garage checking her and Greg's cars for signs of tampering.

He wanted Kayla, period.

All the time. Even at this moment, which was all the reason he needed to stick to his stakeout a little longer. Until he could be sure Kayla was in bed and asleep. Because if she asked him to stay the night in her room again, he wasn't sure he could keep to the chaise and keep his distance.

He shook his head. The year was barely half over and he'd managed to do a great number of stupid things already. But the stupidest by far would be falling for Kayla Landon.

He made up his mind then and there that he wasn't going to do it.

It was close to midnight by the time he returned to her penthouse. She was already asleep. He looked in on her, standing in the door too long, wishing he could shrug off his clothes and climb into bed with her. Even if it was just to hold her.

Man, he was pitiful.

He pulled back, talked to Mo and Joey. They made a battle plan for the next day. He'd tell Kayla to recommend a restaurant for dinner with her uncle. Joey would go and shadow her the whole time. Mo would stick with Greg. His leg was all patched up, but he could use a day of rest. Nash would check the uncle's bedroom, the only room he hadn't searched in the house the last time, while the man was out. He wanted to be done with that and be able to fully focus on other possible suspects.

He took second watch, midnight to 3:00 a.m., then went to get some shuteye in one of the guest bedrooms while Mo took over the kitchen until six. Joey would be up by then. Nash expected to sleep in until seven and still be up before Kayla. It didn't work out that way. He was woken by Joey at six-thirty.

"Yo. Cops are here."

Nash blinked the sleep from his eyes, rubbed a hand over his face as he sat up in bed. "What the hell for?"

"They want Kayla."

That got him up fast. But she beat him to the door, Mo standing protectively beside her. To his credit, he didn't ogle the cream silk robe that did little to disguise her curves.

"Margaret Miller said we could find you here, Miss Landon," the older of the two cops said, while the other one, who didn't look old enough to be out of high school, nervously shifted from one foot to the other. He definitely did notice the robe.

Nash disliked him already, but the cold feeling in the pit of his stomach was distracting him from a full-blown fit of jealousy. Still, just to make things clear, he came up behind Kayla and put a hand at the small of her back.

"Did something happen with Peggy?" she was asking, her voice sleep heavy.

"Miss Miller is fine." But they definitely had bad news. The look of sympathy in the man's eyes was unmistakable. He was black, late fifties, probably near retirement. Probably had a niece like Kayla somewhere.

"My uncle?" That came out in a higher, more worried note. She was definitely awake now.

"I'm sorry to have to give you this news. Your uncle was murdered last night."

Her legs folded.

Nash was there to catch her. He glared at the cops and carried her into the living room. The two officers followed. The younger one kept looking at him. He elbowed his partner. Then that one began scrutinizing Nash.

"And you would be?" the man asked at last.

"Miss Landon's security." Nash handed her the glass of water Mo brought from the kitchen.

"How?" she asked weakly, her eyes brimming with tears.

"Knife wound to the chest," the young one put in.

Her sharp intake of breath echoed in the momentary silence.

Then the older cop pulled a sheet of paper from his pocket, unfolded it and held it out for Kayla. "Margaret Miller, the housekeeper, said she'd seen someone earlier in the evening lurking at your uncle's bedroom window. I was going to ask you if you know this man, but I don't think that will be necessary."

Nash silently swore up a blue streak as he looked at his own image on the paper. Al's mystery lover was apparently his housekeeper. And the woman had a damn good memory. She hadn't missed a detail on Nash's face.

"Your name is?" the cop asked him, holding the paper in his left, leaving his right hand free and near his weapon.

"Nash Wilder."

"Were you at Mr. Landon's residence last night?"

Nash's jaw muscles tightened. The doorman saw him go out and come back a few hours later. The times would match. He hadn't done anything. He weighed the situation and decided that the easiest thing was to go with the truth. "Yes."

Kayla's eyes went wide, then she looked away from him as if not able to bear the sight of him.

"Listen, it's not—" Nash began, but the cop cut him off.

"I'm going to have to ask you to come down to the station with us, sir. We need you to answer a couple of questions."

Chapter Nine

"Were you outside Mr. Landon's bedroom around 9:00 p.m. last night as stated by his housekeeper?" the younger cop asked. He held a pen in his right hand, poised over his pristine notepad. He had a large cup of coffee in his left. He wasn't drinking.

Nash inhaled the aroma of freshly brewed java, his mouth watering for a sip. They probably only had the damned thing to torture him.

"Did you go to Mr. Landon's house last night?" the cop repeated his question.

Since they'd already done the whole line-up business and Al Landon's naughty housekeeper had probably already identified him, Nash said, "Yes."

"Did you go there to kill Al Landon?"

"If I did, I sure as hell wouldn't have left a witness," he snapped.

From the way the guy's eyes narrowed, it hadn't been the right answer.

"No, I didn't," Nash corrected, tapping his foot under the table. He hated wasting time here when Kayla was in danger. He needed to get back to her. God knew what she thought of him now. He hadn't "harassed" her uncle, but he'd known she'd meant more than that when she'd extracted that promise from him. And he'd gone anyway, because he refused to stop at anything to protect her.

He desperately wanted to know what she was thinking. The look she'd given him as he'd left with the police was cold enough to give him frostbite. He hoped she didn't think he had something to do with her uncle's death.

It all came down to how much she trusted him. He wanted her trust, he wanted her loyalty. He didn't dare go beyond that and admit that he also wanted something more from her. She was the Popcorn Princess. He was a temporary bodyguard. What he wanted was impossible.

"Why were you outside Al Landon's bedroom window in the dark?"

"I'm responsible for protecting Miss Landon." That was as good a place to start as any, and true. "Her parents and brother died under suspicious circumstances. Her dog received a number of death threats. She just came back from Vegas where she'd nearly died in an elevator incident. I was checking the people closest to her, doing my job."

The guy took notes. "Why would you think that Mr. Landon would be a danger to his niece?"

"Al Landon, Greg Landon and Kayla Landon together are majority stock owners of Landon enterprises. They are also each other's beneficiaries in the event that any of them should pass away." He'd learned that while searching Al's files two nights ago—apparently, those three felt very strongly about keeping the business in the family.

Luckily, the officer didn't ask where Nash had gotten

his information. "Do you have a sexual relationship with Miss Landon?" he asked Nash instead.

"None of your damned business." His blood pressure ticked up a notch.

The young man glanced nervously back at the two-way mirror behind him as if to remind himself that he wasn't alone with the suspect. Others watched, ready to help. He turned to Nash and pulled his spine straight, put on his tough face. "I ask the questions, you answer. Are you sleeping with Miss Landon?"

Nash leaned forward, paused a second, dropped his voice as he answered. "You ask that question one more time and I'm going to cram that pen down your throat, followed by the notepad, and I'll send the table after them."

The guy's Adam's apple bobbed. Nash leaned back in his chair. The man needed a couple of years of experience, but he wasn't bad. He was probably still in training. They let him have a go at the suspect, but likely his partner and his supervisor were behind that mirror, evaluating him. Nash didn't want to be too hard on the poor bastard, but he wasn't in the mood for a leisurely chat, either. And his private business was his private business.

"Where were you between 10:00 p.m. and midnight last night?" The man fully recovered at last.

Nash considered the time spread. The time of the murder. "Memorial Park."

"Stargazing?" Buddy boy tried for humor.

But Nash wasn't in a lighthearted mood. "Watching the front of the house." While someone went in through the back and stabbed Kayla's uncle to death.

"Why?"

"As I said, I thought Mr. Landon might be behind the trouble Miss Landon was having. I was just covering my bases."

"Anyone see you in the park?"

"Not being seen was the point."

The officer looked down at his notes then back at Nash, trying to conceal his frustration, but failing. He took a sip of his coffee at last. Got up, picked up all his stuff. "I'll be back in a minute."

He was gone for two hours. Nash was just about frothing from impatience by then, considering a breakout. He could have done it, hell, he could have done it with one hand tied behind his back. The only thing that held him back was that it would complicate things and, for Kayla's sake, he was determined to avoid complications. He needed to be able to fully focus on keeping her safe.

"We're going to let you go for now, Mr. Wilder. Don't leave town." Nash was already at the door when the man called after him. "Any ideas who might have wanted to harm Al Landon?"

He almost didn't respond. The cop wasn't on his favorite-people list. Then he reconsidered. "Might want to check the housekeeper. Landon was doing her. Knife in the heart… Could be a crime of passion," he said as he let the door swing closed behind him.

But he didn't believe that for a minute.

SHE HAD her secretary cancel all her social appointments for the next week or so. But as Kayla sat in the living room, she was beginning to consider whether that was a mistake. She might go crazy with nothing to do.

She was responsible for her uncle's death.

If she'd been there last night for dinner, her bodyguards with her, nobody would have been able to get near Al.

He'd died thinking she was mad at him. That clawed at her heart.

Her eyes burned. She'd cried all her tears. All that remained now was that numb, cold shock that had overtaken her after her parents' deaths and after Lance's. Somebody was murdering her family one by one and she was powerless to stop the man.

It had to do with the money that had disappeared, she was sure of that. And it had to do with her. Everyone she'd told was dead now, everyone but Nash.

Thank God she had never said anything to Greg. She couldn't bear it if anything happened to him.

"Are you okay?"

She looked up as her brother came in from the kitchen. He came over with that slow, meandering gait of his and gave her a hug, and she melted into his embrace. Greg was the baby brother she had raised because their parents had been too busy with the business.

She held him tight, but he held her tighter. Too tight. She wiggled to loosen his arms after a while. Greg wasn't always good with hugs. At times he seemed almost incapable of showing affection, other times he overdid it. But Kayla loved him as he was, loved him and swore to protect him.

"I'm fine. Don't worry about me. You okay?"

He nodded, looking puzzled. While Kayla's distress disturbed him, he had taken the news of Uncle Al's death with little upset.

"Want some cheesecake?" Margaret, Al's house-keeper, had baked up a storm to keep herself busy, needing Stanislav's help to get all the boxes up to the penthouse apartment when she'd come by to visit Kayla earlier.

They didn't talk much. She'd been a mess. Both of them were.

"I want popcorn," Greg said.

"You don't have to do that now," Kayla told him gently. Greg didn't like popcorn, but he'd figured out back when he'd been a toddler that the way to gain his father's approval was to pretend that it was his favorite. "I'll get you cheesecake."

"Okay. With chocolate drizzle?"

"With chocolate drizzle."

She walked to the pantry and brought the box out, placed it on the kitchen table and was putting a slice on a plate for Greg when Nash walked through the door.

He looked annoyed and tense. "I'll take a slice of that," he said and went straight for the coffeepot.

"How was it?"

He faced her, cup in hand. "Aren't you going to ask me if I did it?"

"I don't need to. I trust you, Nash."

His masculine lips stretched into a thin smile and his gaze softened, his shoulders relaxing. He drew a slow breath, then, still holding her gaze, took a gulp of coffee.

Her heart turned over in her chest. The plate wobbled in her hand as the realization hit her: she trusted him because she knew him with her heart.

Part of her wanted to rush into Nash's arms, part of

her wanted to escape. For now, self-preservation won. She took a step back. "I need to take this to Greg," she said, and fled.

SHE WAS killing him. Nash watched from across the room as Kayla pretended to go through some company paperwork. In the past three days, since her uncle's death, she had become a different woman. Gone were her sassy attitude and the spark in her eyes. He wanted to pick her up and carry her to her bedroom, comfort her, do whatever it took to erase the bottomless sadness from her eyes.

He wanted to make love to her.

He was a guy. In times of crisis, his thoughts were decidedly primal. Fighting any enemy for her and making her his were as primal as thoughts could get.

He picked up a tray of cheesesteaks he'd had delivered. On second thought, he chose just one—best not to overwhelm her—slid it onto a plate and grabbed a bottle of mineral water to go with it.

He crossed the room. "You should have a bite."

She hadn't eaten anything today, and it was past noon. She'd lost weight in the last couple of days. Her silk shirt hung on her slim shoulders.

She glanced at the plate, then looked away. "I need to get this done. I might be too tired later."

Or too upset. Her uncle's funeral was called for 4:00 p.m.

"One bite." He pushed the food toward her, until she had to take it to keep the plate from toppling over her paperwork.

She moved to put the plate down.

"One bite." Nash stopped her.

She gave him an annoyed look.

"Let's talk about security measures for this afternoon." He waited while she took the first bite, then went on talking to distract her from realizing that she kept on eating. "You, your brother, Joey and I'll go together and stay together. Joey will be Greg's detail and I'll be yours." Mo was in the hospital. His leg wound had gotten infected and they had him on an antibiotic drip. He wouldn't be back before tonight. "There'll be some cops there, too."

Her gaze went wide.

"In case the murderer shows up."

She swallowed hard. Pushed the plate away.

He put it back into her hands. "Don't worry. I'll be there. And even if the bastard comes to gloat, he'll be keeping a low profile. He wouldn't dare attack at a public affair."

She'd somehow gotten a streak of ink on her cheekbone from her pen. He reached up to rub it off with the pad of his thumb.

She went completely still.

Joey was out with Greg, taking Tsini for a walk. Nash had asked Joey to stick as close to him as possible. Not only to protect him, but also to figure out where his money was going. Now that they were back in Philly, he was determined to solve that puzzle.

Although, at the moment the only thing Nash was interested in was the lovely puzzle right in front of him.

They were alone in the apartment.

And now that he'd touched her velvet skin, he didn't want to let go.

He leaned forward.

She jumped up so fast that she nearly upended her leftover sandwich over his head.

"I have to start getting ready. I'll be taking a shower."

The exact wrong thing to say.

He hadn't been able to forget their shower at that Vegas hotel yet. Just hearing her say the word caused a riot in his pants.

He leaned against the back of the sofa and let her go. And hated watching her walk away.

He never had trouble with letting women walk away from him. Hell, he preferred it. They saved him the trouble. But watching Kayla practically run from him twisted something inside his chest.

He pulled out his cell to make a couple of calls.

"Nothing in Landon's e-mail," Nick Tarasov said. Nash had asked him to hack into Al's account back when he'd thought the man might have had something to do with Kayla's Vegas accident. "Mostly business, with some quick notes to Kayla, and a few dozen hot-and-heavy love letters to a woman named Margaret. I checked his deleted files, too. Couldn't find anything."

And if Nick Tarasov couldn't get dirt off someone's computer, it wasn't there.

"No hint why someone would want him dead?"

"Not unless Margaret had a husband."

Nash had already investigated that angle and come up with nothing. Margaret Miller had no other boyfriend, no family. For the past ten years, she had lived for Al Landon and was now devastated by his death.

"I've been meaning to call you, actually," Nick said. "About that seed money."

Oh, hell. "Lost it all, didn't you?" There went his life savings. He drew a deep breath. It'd been the right thing to do. Nick and Carly were good people. They were raising a family. He'd shown his support. They could have just as easily succeeded. "That's okay." He probably wasn't ever going to retire anyway. In his line of work, people didn't figure on a long life expectancy.

"We got the patents, actually," Nick said.

He didn't want a lengthy explanation now. "It's fine, Nick. Really. Tell that gorgeous wife of yours that she can cook me a couple of dinners and we're even."

Nick laughed on the other end. "You should be cooking for her. She put the final deal together with a big Mexican telecom company. Your cut should come to a little over two million."

His pulse kicked up a notch even as his mind struggled with processing the words. "Say it's not in pesos."

"American dollars it is."

"I'll be damned."

"Possibly. But first, you'll be stinking filthy rich. There'll be more money coming in. You own major stock in the company."

They talked for another few minutes, until Nash's head was swimming. Then he put all that out of his mind and focused back on the task at hand. Money was nice, but Kayla was still in danger. And Kayla meant more than a couple of million dollars to him. In fact, Kayla meant more to him than anything else.

Hell of a realization to deal with just now. Not that

he could think of a better time for dealing with something like that. He'd thought he was prepared for anything. But he hadn't been prepared for falling in love with Kayla Landon.

Now what?

Ignore it and keep going. No way someone like her would ever fall for someone like him.

He called Joey next. "Let's take two cars this afternoon. If there's a problem with one, I want backup."

"Sure."

He was counting on having only Kayla and Greg to deal with, but it suddenly occurred to him that they might need to give someone else a ride to the cemetery, like Margaret or even the priest.

"Hey," he got up to ask Kayla through the closed bathroom door, just as something crashed inside.

He was through that door in a split second.

She was sitting on the floor in the shower, her legs pulled up in front of her, her arms folded tight around her knees. Tears rolled down her face.

The handheld showerhead lay next to her. She must have dropped it to the tile when she'd folded.

"You okay?" He shut off the water and grabbed a towel, pulled her up and wrapped her in it.

Then he took her into his arms, and she looked up at him with those big blue eyes, tear-soaked this time, and it was just like in Vegas. He didn't have any pretty words for her. He didn't know how to do that. So he put all the comfort he wanted to give her into his kiss.

Her slim body was flush against his and still not close enough. He dragged his lips over hers, savoring the taste.

She let him in with a small sigh as her arms went around his neck. This was what he wanted, this was what he needed. But was it what Kayla needed? From the way she kissed him back, apparently yes.

Forget what he couldn't have from her. Right now, in this moment, being able to touch her was enough. Whatever she needed from him, she would have it.

He got lost in her completely, until she stepped back.

And dropped the towel.

He'd never been so grateful for anything in his life.

Water from her hair ran down her shoulders, rivulets circled her amazing breasts, a perfect drop forming on one of the peaks.

Who knew water could be this sexy? He'd been a marine. He was more than familiar with water. He'd fought in it, nearly died in it on a couple of occasions. But Kayla and water seemed to make their own new element. For the rest of his life, he was going to think of her every time he saw water. Think of her and want her. These two would go together for as long as he was alive and kicking.

He reached for her, bent to catch that drop of water with his tongue, looked up into her red-rimmed eyes, which were darkening with desire.

He wanted her. She wanted him. Simple.

Except that it wasn't.

SHE WAS NAKED in front of him, and completely vulnerable. Kayla wanted him to enfold her in his strength. She wanted him to make her forget everything for a few minutes. Even the fact that she was stupidly falling in love with him.

The thought took her breath away. He was surefire heartbreak. She didn't care. No, that wasn't true. She did care. She just didn't seem to be able to help herself.

She took a step toward him.

But he took a step back. "You're not thinking clearly. You're upset."

His rejection was like a slap in the face. She reeled. Her throat tightened. Her eyes burned all of a sudden.

How stupid she'd been. She'd thought all he wanted her for was a brief affair. But he didn't even want her for that.

Her towel was on the floor, but she gathered the last shreds of her dignity around her. "Could you please leave my room?"

She was careful not to let a single tear drop as she watched his retreating back. Not until her bedroom door closed with a click behind him did she allow her tears to flow again.

She loved him, and he wanted nothing to do with her.

Truth was sometimes the hardest thing to accept.

Her mother had said that someday Kayla would meet a man she'd know with her heart and she would fall in love. Her mother's advice said nothing about what Kayla should do if that man didn't love her back.

She dried her tears first, then her hair. She'd taken so many losses over the last couple of years, she would deal with this, too, somehow. She dressed carefully, slowly, taking as much time as she needed. She didn't come out of the bedroom until she was sure she could face Nash.

She planted her feet firmly on the floor, drew herself straight. "This is not working," she told him. "It's just—"

she closed her eyes for a second "—weird." She looked away, then forced herself to meet his gaze again as she said, "After the funeral, I'm going to request another man from the agency. I appreciate everything you've done for me. I really do. Mo and Joey can stay, but I'd like you to leave."

"Like hell," Nash said, springing to his feet.

"We're a distraction to each other." He had to admit at least that much.

"I'm not leaving as long as you're in danger."

"I have money. Lots of it. There'll always be people who want it. I could be in danger for the rest of my life."

"That's the duration of my assignment, then," he said without hesitation.

Her heart gave a painful thud. The thought of a lifetime spent with Nash stole her breath for a second. Except that it wouldn't be a life with him the way she would want it. He would never let down his guard. He would always stay out of reach.

Maybe he still thought her empty-headed fluff, not woman enough to tempt him.

"We'd end up hurting each other. You'd hurt me," she confessed.

His gaze burned with intensity. "I'd never do anything to hurt you."

"You already have," she quietly told him.

Her words stood in the air between them.

"I'm trying to do the right thing here. And it's killing me. Don't make this harder than it has to be," he said after a moment.

"I can't live like this." She blinked furiously, not wanting to cry in front of him.

He swore softly under his breath. "And I'm not sure I can live without you." He crossed the distance between them. "I should never have touched you. I definitely shouldn't do it again." He pulled her to him slowly, giving her time to move away.

She didn't.

"I should never have kissed you," he murmured as he lowered his lips to hers.

By the time he was done kissing her, she was dizzy from the heat between them.

"I've broken every rule of conduct," he said ruefully as he put his hands under her buttocks and lifted her up, backed her up against the media console.

She wrapped her legs around his waist. Her skirt slid up to the top of her thighs from the movement. She wasn't wearing pantyhose.

He worked the buttons of her shirt with a deft hand until it hung open, revealing her black lace bra. Gave a growling sound deep in his throat as he went after that.

When her breasts were free, he took his mouth to them, freeing his hand for her matching panties. Pleasure spiraled through her. He was intent and flushed with desire, focused on her, strong and male and completely absorbed in her body.

Then his pants were open and a condom appeared from the direction of his back pocket. He kissed her again. Then pushed deep inside her just as she began to melt.

THE SEX had been mind-blowing.

The guilt was staggering.

Too bad the sudden release of sexual tension hadn't resolved anything between them.

The mood in the car on the way to the cemetery couldn't have been more awkward. Thank God it was over.

He was her bodyguard for heaven's sake. He wasn't supposed to take her against the wall like a rutting animal. For the second time. Not that the first had been more civilized.

He should have given her time, seduced her slowly. But all that talk about her letting him go had sent Nash over the edge.

"We must remember him as the man he was. He isn't gone. We just can't see him. But he is smiling down at his family from heaven." The priest paused then started praying.

Nash's attention wasn't on him. He was scanning the crowd as he had been since they'd gotten here. He could pick out the plainclothes cops, knew most of the others from Kayla's introductions at the beginning. Of course, Elvis, Ivan and Fisk were there in a protective circle around her and Greg. Tom, too. And her secretary. Al Landon's housekeeper sobbed in the back.

Not one suspicious person who didn't look like he belonged here, no one who didn't appear genuinely grief-stricken.

Nash hummed with frustration. Half the clues he had were erratic. The other half made no sense. He was either facing a criminal mastermind or someone who had no idea what he was doing. But if he showed up today...

There had to be over two hundred people in the

sprawling cemetery. Al Landon had been well-loved in life and was widely mourned in death.

Nash moved his gaze to the very edge of the crowd, determined to examine each face one more time as the people broke into a hymn. Frustration warred with disappointment. He had pitifully few clues, and what he had was more than confusing. He'd hoped he would gain some insight here, but that didn't seem likely. The funeral was almost over.

Then a second cousin bent to pick up a small child and Nash spotted a hunched man behind her. A familiar shape.

The man from the park the other night.

He cleared his throat.

Joey looked at him.

"At two o'clock," Nash said under his breath. "You take them home. I'm going to check this guy out."

Easier said than done. The hymn ended and everyone moved toward Kayla and Greg to offer their condolences.

No time to talk to the plainclothes officers who stood at the other end. Nash pushed through the crowd. The man must have caught sight of Nash because he was edging away.

Nash pushed harder, eliciting some comments about rudeness. He didn't care.

The guy had a good head start, got to his car first. But Nash drove down a walking path and caught up with him by the time they made it to the cemetery's ten-foot-tall cast-iron gate.

Once an affluent area, Queensland Avenue had since fallen into disrepair, the once-splendid mansions cut up into duplexes with a warren of narrow connecting roads between them. All one-way. The bastard disappeared down one of those.

Nash stayed as close to the small green Honda as he could, but his black Navigator was a tight fit for the sharp corners.

They came out somewhere in Philly's old industrial quarter, empty factories and not much else. Other areas of the city had seen a revival over the last decade, developers taking over old industrial buildings and making them into high-priced condominiums. But not here.

The man went off the road, crossing from parking lot to parking lot, probably hoping to disappear among the jumble of buildings. And for a short while he did.

Then Nash found the man's car parked under a lopsided overhang.

He parked behind it, blocking it in, then slipped out, kept low, his gun in front of him. Weeds grew in the cracked cement. Graffiti decorated almost every available surface, including the two steel doors on the side of the building. One of them had a lock on it. The other's cheap padlock had been smashed off.

Nash ducked inside, immediately going for cover, and waited until his eyes adjusted to the darkness. Some broken windows sat high up on the factory's north side. Most were boarded up, but the boards had rotted and fallen from a couple, so the place wasn't completely dark. He spotted a light switch on the other side of the door, but didn't go for it. The less light, the better.

Abandoned assembly stations littered the room, covered with dust. The only thing that indicated recent occupation of the place was a giant Mummers' float in the middle, complete with palm trees and a thatch-roofed hut. The empty space was probably rented by one of the brigades—the Mummers—that paraded through the city on New Year's Day each year.

On the one hand, he hated that he couldn't survey the place at a glance. On the other, the workstations and the float did provide him with cover.

He moved forward, keeping low, his weapon ready. His rubber-soled shoes made no sound on the cement. But no matter how much ground he gained, no matter which way he turned, he didn't see or hear the man. He began to wonder if the guy might have sneaked out another door at the far end.

He was moving that way when a soft creak behind him made him spin around and dive for cover. A shot rang out. He swore at the bite of a bullet in his shoulder, shooting back at the flash of movement behind the float, hitting nothing but a fake palm tree that snapped in half.

He kept in cover as he stole forward, ignoring the sharp pain in his shoulder. A minute passed, then another. No sign of the bastard. Nash's shoulder began to burn. He stopped for a second to take a look. No exit wound. The bullet was still in there. At least it didn't hit the bone.

He took off his belt and tied off the blood flow, grateful that he was hit on the left. He'd been shot worse more times than he cared to count. The most important thing was that he had his man and Kayla was safe. By now, Joey had her and Greg back at the apartment.

And Nash wasn't leaving here until this bastard

was incapacitated and told him who the hell was behind the attacks.

"That was stupid. Coming to the funeral," he said to keep the guy distracted and maybe goad him into making a mistake. "Did you really think you could get to her with all those people around?"

A moment of silence passed before the response came in a voice of derision. "I wasn't there to take the bitch out. I went to get you away from her."

Chapter Ten

The whole way home from the funeral, Kayla kept looking back for Nash, but he'd completely disappeared.

"Do you know who he went after?"

"Young guy, dark hair, shifty eyes," Joey said.

He parked under the building, in the secure lot, and they all went up in the elevator. For security reasons, the parking elevator only went to the lobby where they had to get off and cross to the other elevator bank to go up. This ensured that everyone who went up to the residences would be seen by the doorman. She'd chosen this building especially for the security features. She'd be safe here, she told herself. She and Greg would be fine with Joey until Nash got back.

Kayla took her brother's hand. He let her. He didn't always. Most of the time, he didn't like to be touched. He'd been silent and depressed all day, but now he gave her a strained, distracted smile.

"I'm sorry for your loss. If there's anything I can do, Miss Landon, you just let me know," Stanislav said.

"Thank you, Stan."

Greg let her hold on to him all the way up, not pulling

away until they were inside. She disarmed the alarm. Joey went to check every room. They weren't to leave the entryway until the all clear was given, standing orders from Nash.

"Everything looks good," Joey said as he made his way back to Kayla.

"Anyone hungry?" She moved toward the kitchen, Tsini following closely.

The dog had been sticking to her like Velcro since they'd returned from Vegas. She whined every time Kayla left the apartment, and came into her bedroom to check on her a couple of times a night.

"I'll change first." Greg walked to his room.

She pulled a tray of sandwiches from the fridge as Joey came back in. "Anything for you?" She tossed Tsini a slice of bologna.

"Later."

"Can you call Nash?"

"He'll call. I don't want to distract him if he's in the middle of something."

Like a shootout, she thought, and her stomach constricted. She put down her sandwich.

Greg was coming into the kitchen.

She gave a double take when she saw the gun in his hand.

Joey must have read her expression because his hand went to the weapon at his side, but he didn't get a chance to turn.

The gun went off.

"Greg!" she screamed when her mouth would work at last.

Joey crashed to the floor, taking a barstool with him, making a terrible racket.

She dove behind the counter.

"Put that down!" Where on earth did he find a gun? It wasn't like Nash to leave something like that carelessly lying around. Had Mo or Joey? "Put it down before it goes off again. Are you okay, Joey?" She peeked out from behind the counter and saw Greg standing still, his face white, the gun at his side as he stared at Joey on the floor.

Blood was everywhere. She acted on instinct.

"Put it down, Greg." She rushed over to Joey and tried to plug the hole in his chest with her bare hands, knowing it was futile. "Call an ambulance." She thought to check for a pulse at last. Faint. He was bleeding out fast. Too much blood. The hole was too big, the damage too extensive.

Greg still wasn't moving. Probably in shock.

"It was an accident. Everything will be fine," she said, her body shaking. *Nothing would be fine.* But she couldn't afford to let Greg go into one of his fits. Sometimes he would completely lose it if he got too overwhelmed. She needed to keep him calm. She needed to calm down herself.

She let go of Joey at last and went to the phone. Her hands were covered with blood, and soon so was the receiver. She had to wipe the tears from her eyes so she could see the numbers. She dialed nine, then one.

Then Greg was there and he took the phone from her with his left hand while his right hand brought the gun back up to chest level.

"What are you doing? I need to call for help." She tugged at the phone, but Greg wouldn't let go.

Thoughts too crazy to comprehend jammed her mind. Her blood ran cold.

Tsini was growling next to her.

"I have to finish what I started," Greg said.

NASH EASED some pressure off the belt to let circulation return to his injured arm. Fresh blood ran down on his shirt immediately. He waited a second or two, then tightened the belt again.

He needed to get the hell out of the abandoned factory and get back to Kayla. But first he had to take care of the bastard who'd shot him. Had to be somewhere close by.

Then he caught movement again. Not the man, but his shadow, a dark spot on the floor that wasn't as still as the rest. The guy was hiding behind a piece of plywood leaning against an assembly station.

Nash aimed and fired. The bullet went through the wood with ease, the sound echoing in the empty space.

The man uttered an expletive and dove to better cover, leaving behind drops of blood on the cement. He was muttering and swearing. "Kid's not payin' me for this." He rushed across the next gap, moving back toward the door where they'd come in.

Nash was gaining ground. "Who hired you?"

The guy dove across another opening without answering.

Nash took a shot, but missed. *Kid.* Then everything fell into place. Dammit. He pulled out his phone and dialed Joey to warn him just as the guy made a run for the door.

Nash dropped the phone to hold the butt of the gun with his other hand and steady his aim. Squeezed off a shot.

The guy dropped to his knees right in the door, then slumped against the door frame.

It was over. Nash rushed forward, ready to fly to Kayla. He wasn't going to be late. He couldn't bear thinking of the alternative. He was going to get to her in time.

But the bastard turned back, lifted his arm and fired.

"YOU DON'T want to do this, Greg." She'd been keeping him talking for the last twenty minutes, hoping someone would come to her rescue. But one of the perks of luxury penthouse living was super-soundproofed walls.

If anyone had heard the gunshot and realized it had been a gunshot, they would have been here by now.

"You don't know what you're doing," Kayla pleaded.

Greg's mouth tightened. "I'm not stupid."

"That's not what I meant. You know I never thought that about you."

"Everybody else does. I was never going to get my share of the company."

Her heart sank at the cold way he spoke those words.

"I had to steal my own money."

Puzzle pieces fell into place. "The missing million?"

"Then you told Dad and he was going to fire me. He yelled at me."

Greg hated yelling.

"You didn't do anything to them, did you? Mom and Dad? Please, Greg?" she pleaded with him.

"He was mad when they drove off. He was going to tell Mom. I wished he would die."

"But you didn't do anything?"

"I wished it. And it came true."

A small part of the tension inside her eased. "That wasn't your fault. He could have driven slower even if he was angry."

A moment passed in silence.

"Then you told Lance about the money," Greg said quietly.

"Oh, Greg. You didn't."

"Lance yelled at me just like Dad. I wished he'd go away, too, but it didn't work. I wished it for a long time."

Tears rolled down her cheeks, blurring Greg's face.

"What did you do?"

"Yancy helped."

An insolent security guard who'd befriended Greg and gotten him into betting on street races. He'd been fired when their father found out, although Greg had begged and bargained for the man's job for days and was as angry as she'd ever seen him when their father wouldn't listen.

"You still see Yancy." She should have known. Why didn't she? She should have paid more attention to his friends.

"He protected me from people who made fun of me."

"Did Yancy do something to Lance?"

"His cousin works at the ski lodge. He has lots of cousins."

She understood at last. Greg had a problem with their father. And when their father died, the problem went away. Then he had a problem with Lance. And he applied the same solution. Then with Uncle Al. And now with Kayla.

Simple logic.

He was doing what worked in the past. It all made sense to his linear brain.

"Was that man who died in Vegas Yancy's cousin, too?"

Greg's face darkened as he nodded.

"And Uncle Al?"

"Yancy did that."

Her brain was paralyzed. Think. Gain time. "Don't you love me?"

Joey's cell phone rang in his pocket. Again. Probably Nash. She forced her limbs to move, toward Joey and the gun at his hip, half out of the holster. She could only get one thing, the gun or the phone. Instinct told her it was too late to send out an SOS at this stage.

"I do."

"Then please don't do this. Joey is hurt. Let me help him."

"I started. I have to finish."

They'd learned that from their father. *You always finish what you start. Always,* he used to say. Greg had wanted the man's love so desperately, everything their father said was gospel to him.

She kneeled next to Joey. "Wake up." She touched the man's shoulders, knowing Joey wouldn't wake up, not ever. Then went lower as if checking the wound. And grabbed the gun, came up with it in her hand.

Shock and dismay reflected on her brother's face. "You tricked me." He sounded hurt and betrayed.

Exactly the way she felt. "I'm sorry, Greg. Please put the gun down."

"The police will take me away if I don't finish it. Yancy told me the police will do bad things to me and nobody can protect me."

"I'll protect you."

But he shook his head stubbornly.

Just pointing the gun at him hurt. "Greg? Don't do this. Please, don't do this."

"I have to finish what I started." His finger moved on the trigger.

The counter was too far. She was out in the open. No place to hide. No time to run.

Then Tsini attacked Greg.

A shot went off. Didn't hit the dog. The bullet went into the marble-tile kitchen floor.

"Tsini!"

But the dog wouldn't come to her. She was growling and holding on to Greg's leg, pulling him away from Kayla. Greg took aim again.

The front door crashed open, Nash barreling through it like a speed train. A football player couldn't have done a better job at plowing forward and leaping, tackling Greg to the ground.

And still Tsini was holding on to him.

"Go wash your hands," Nash growled at Kayla. He couldn't stand the sight of her all bloody.

His heart had stopped when he'd broken down that door and saw her standing there, her hands and her face covered in blood, Greg pointing the gun at her. That goofy dog of hers was doing everything to distract him, Greg kicking her away.

She had a gun, but didn't look like she could use it, not on her own brother. Hell, Nash couldn't even take out the kid knowing what he meant to Kayla. He would have been willing to take another bullet to spare her that pain.

So he took the path of least violence. Welkins would have been damned proud of him.

"We're done in there for now." A cop was coming out of her bedroom.

The police were all over her apartment.

Nash nudged her forward. "Go change." He watched her go, wanting to go with her. He never wanted to let her out of his sight again. Tsini followed her, nudging her leg.

"She'd be better off with a rottweiler. What's a cotton ball like that gonna do when you're in trouble?" The younger cop smirked to one of the paramedics.

And something inside Nash snapped. "Her name is Tsini." He turned to the guy and gave him a narrow-eyed look. "She saved Miss Landon's life today. She's as fine a dog as they come. You could probably learn a thing or two from her."

The two were smart enough to hear the warning in his tone and simply nodded, slinking away from him.

He drew a deep breath and walked back into the kitchen, to the body bag two men were lifting onto the stretcher. He reached for Joey's shoulder and squeezed it through the black plastic. "I'm sorry, Joey. I'm sorry, man."

"The job is what the job is," the older cop he knew from the other morning said, coming up behind him, his voice full of understanding.

Nash watched as the men carried Joey out, stood there until the door closed behind them.

The job was what the job was. This was what they'd signed up for. They all knew that at any moment a bullet could be coming. He wished he'd been here. He wished he could have done something. Joey had taken the job because of him.

"You need to come in to have that bullet taken out, sir." One of the paramedics came back to bug him.

They'd come for Joey, but there hadn't been anything anyone could have done to help. Determined to save someone as long as they were on location, they took turns trying to browbeat Nash into going down to the ambulance with them. Fat chance.

"You want to torture me, you're going to have to do it here."

"I can't do that, sir. I'd lose my job. A doctor will have to see you at the hospital."

"Give me that kit. I'll take the damn bullet out."

The man took a step back. "You can't do that, sir."

"Wanna bet?" But he wasn't in the mood to push it. Joey was dead. Another good man gone. Another good friend. And Nash took it hard.

The job was what the job was.

But he wasn't sure he wanted the job anymore.

Not that long ago, he'd thought he was nothing without the agency and the guys. His heart had been black and dead. He needed that one connection to normal life. Then Kayla brought a change he'd been slow to recognize.

He wondered for a moment if Welkins's connections

were powerful enough to engineer a whole new past for him. One that would pass media muster.

Truth was, he wanted to go to more dog shows with Kayla. He'd be damned if he knew where that left them. If she were half as smart as she looked, she should refuse to do anything with him.

He should make sure she was okay, then walk away without embarrassing himself. But no, didn't look like he had that much sense. Because before the day was out, he was determined to tell her how he felt about her. He was a warrior, after all. He wasn't going out without one last battle.

BY THE TIME they made it back home from the police station and the hospital, Kayla was drained emotionally and physically. The police had identified the man Nash had shot at some abandoned factory. *Yancy.* He'd been the one fleecing her brother and putting ideas into his head. Yancy had known that to get to serious money, he had to remove the family from around Greg. And Greg had been only too easily led. She'd gotten the best lawyers money could buy for Greg, but they still couldn't get him released on bail. She would keep trying. He needed to be someplace where doctors could help him, not in jail.

His actions had just about killed her inside. But she couldn't hate her brother. She'd loved him too much for too long for that. She wanted to help.

She collapsed on a barstool, looked to the front door that miraculously worked again. She would have to thank Stanislav. He must have pulled some strings to get help up here in a hurry. Nash had done a number on the frame when he'd kicked it in.

He was at the phone, ordering food—minestrone soup and fettuccini Alfredo for two. And a steak. "That's for Tsini," he said, then opened a bottle of red wine and poured her a glass. "Drink."

"You're going to spoil her rotten. How is the arm?"

"How are you?"

"I'm still having trouble taking it all in. I should have known."

"How could you? *I* should have known. I looked at everyone but him. He was a kid. He loves you."

"In his mind, there's no conflict with that." She hung her head and sniffed.

"Hey. We'll figure this out."

We? She looked up in time to see him cross the kitchen, favoring his bad leg. "Did you hurt your leg, too?"

"It's fine."

It wasn't. He'd probably pulled it when he'd leaped on Greg, crashing to the floor with him. "Why didn't you say anything at the hospital?"

"I had all the prodding I could take."

She thought of the new scar that would be added to his old ones. "You were lucky with that land mine," she observed. She hoped that old injury wasn't aggravated.

"Unlike Pounder," he said under his breath, his face darkening.

She didn't expect him to tell her more, but he said, "Bobby Smith—Pounder—and I were on the Korean border finishing up an op, tying up loose ends. Then all of a sudden Melena Milo shows up with a camera crew in the middle of nowhere. Big celebrity, thinks she can do anything she wants. Daughter of Milan Milo, the famous producer."

She nodded. She knew both of them.

"Her godfather is a four-star general."

She didn't know that.

"So, next thing we know, we're ordered to help her with her pet project, filming the locals and the troubles they face. And she insists on filming in this patch of woods that was full of craters. The week before, a couple of kids were blown to pieces there. And I tried to talk her out of it, but she got to me."

Probably seduced him, Kayla thought and burned with jealousy. Melena was famous for always getting what she wanted, one way or the other. She would have gone after Nash, big-time.

"She got to Bobby, too. We'd kind of had a rough morning. So there we are, readying the place for her. And one of us made one bad move. And one second later, my leg was cut to shreds. Bobby was dead."

"And Melena got an award." She remembered the documentary. Neither Bobby nor Nash were mentioned.

"It was a long time ago." He came up behind her and put his arms around her. Held her without a word until the food arrived. Then he fed her. And while Tsini was gulping down her steak, Nash carried Kayla to bed.

"I don't even have the strength to wash my face." And she definitely didn't have the strength to watch him walk away. Her family had been decimated. Her core team had all but disappeared.

But instead of leaving her, he lay next to her on top

of the covers and pulled her into his arms. "Give yourself a break. You'll shower in the morning."

That sounded good. His arms felt wonderful around her. She might not want to move, ever. He'd faced as many losses as she had, if not more. He had his own issues with trust. Had made his own mistakes. She felt that he understood her. She could be Kayla Landon, the person, with him, not her celebrity persona the rest of the world knew.

She snuggled against him. "You saved my life. Again."

"That was the job. Have to earn my keep. And you saved mine back in Vegas. So I owed you one, anyway."

"I love you." God, why did she have to say that? The words just slipped out. She had no control over her emotions tonight.

Nash's arms tightened around her. "I love you, too. I've been waiting all evening to tell you that. Just so you know, I'll probably be fired for getting personally involved here. And if not, I'm going to quit. I'm ready for a new start. Maybe we could start a new team, the two of us."

"Wait. You love me? You love me back and you're just telling me now? Casually?" Her heart raced as she turned to him, disbelief mixing with utter pleasure.

He gave a slow grin, his eyes fast on her face, his gaze heating. His hand stole up her arm, caressing her skin, infusing her with warmth. "Women love a man of mystery," he said.

Epilogue

CELEBRITY FLASH JOURNAL
Software Millionaire Marries Popcorn Princess

In the ongoing saga of the Landon family, Landon Enterprises CEO Kayla Landon married software millionaire Nash Wilder in a small private ceremony yesterday. Sources in the know suggest that before his rise to fame and fortune, Wilder might have worked for Miss Landon in a bodyguard capacity. However, this tabloid scooped them all by obtaining legal documents of Mr. Wilder's past, which seems a tad more boring than that.

That's right. Mr. Wilder was apparently nothing more glamorous than a computer geek, working at the same no-name company since college. That would certainly explain his acumen for picking tech investments.

Again, some people suggested that the reason for no media photos of the wedding is that Mr. Wilder's ex-commando friends ran the event like a veritable black op. However, our publication would never endorse that sort of sensationalist, make-it-up-as-we-go journalism.

And we predict that piece of reporting will be withdrawn by next week, this time with an apology.

One tidbit had been correctly reported, however. The bride's brother, Greg Landon, was released from a treatment facility to attend the wedding.

And, last but not least, the strangest rumor of all… A guest apparently let it slip that the groom even danced with the bride's dog at the wedding?! Too much champagne? Go to our Web page and let us know what you think.

* * * * *

CAVANAUGH
REUNION

BY
MARIE FERRARELLA

All the characters in this book have no existence outside the imagination of
the author, and have no relation whatsoever to anyone bearing the same name
or names. They are not even distantly inspired by any individual known or
unknown to the author, and all the incidents are pure invention.

First published in Great Britain 2011
Harlequin Mills & Boon Limited,
Eton House, 18-24 Paradise Road, Richmond, Surrey TW9 ISR

© Marie Rydzynski-Ferrarella 2010

ISBN: 978 0 263 88501 9

46-0111

Harlequin Mills & Boon policy is to use papers that are natural, renewable
and recyclable products and made from wood grown in sustainable forests.
The logging and manufacturing processes conform to the legal environmental
regulations of the country of origin.

Printed and bound in Spain
by Litografia Rosés S.A., Barcelona

Dear Reader,

So here we are with another Cavanaugh story. By all rights, this is also the last one. And if you believe that, you don't know me. I have a great deal of trouble letting go, except for a truly awful experience. In essence, I am an emotional pack rat.

Case in point: when I was a teenager in New York City, every year we had a real Christmas tree. I would plead for our tree to stay well into January and once actually into February (Valentine bush, anyone?). As with everything else, it had been a source of joy once and I didn't want to let it go. So how could I possibly say goodbye to a family I have come to love?

Sidebar: this is my two hundredth book. Not bad for a person who thought she had only one, possibly two books in her when she started out. I have loved every nail-biting minute and hope to write another two hundred! As ever, thank you for reading my books, and from the bottom of my heart I wish you someone to love who loves you back.

Marie Ferrarella

To the wonderful Intrigue family, and especially
Patience Smith, who more than lives up to her name.
I thank you all for making my dreams come true.
Also, to Pat Teal, who started it all by asking,
"Would you like to write a romance?"
Thank God I said, "Yes." And last, but by no means
least, to you, beloved readers, thank you!
I wouldn't be here without you.

USA TODAY bestselling and RITA® Award-winning author **Marie Ferrarella** has written two hundred books, some under the name of Marie Nicole. Her romances are beloved by fans worldwide. Visit her website at www. marieferrarella.com.

Chapter 1

He smelled it before he saw it.

His mind elsewhere, Detective Ethan O'Brien's attention was immediately captured by the distinct, soul-disturbing smell that swept in, riding the evening breeze. Without warning, it maliciously announced that someone's dreams were being dashed even as they were being burnt to cinders.

Or, at the very least, they were damaged enough to generate a feeling of overwhelming sorrow and hopelessness.

Summers in California meant fires, they always had. Natives and transplants would joke that fires, earthquakes and mudslides were the dues they paid for having the best, most temperate overall weather in the country. But they only joked when nothing was burning, shaking or sliding away. Because during these catastrophic events, life proved to be all too tenuous, and there was no time for humor, only action. Humor was a salve at best, before and after the fact. Action was a way to hopefully curtail the amount of damage, if at all humanly possible.

But it wasn't summer. It was spring, and ordinarily, devastating fires should have still been many headlines away from becoming a very real threat.

Except that they were a real threat.

There were fires blazing all over the southern section of Aurora. Not the spontaneous fires that arose from spurts of bone-melting heat, or because a capricious wind had seized a not-quite-dead ember and turned it into something lethal by carrying it off and depositing it into the brush. These fires, ten so far and counting in the last two months, were man-made, the work of some bedeviled soul for reasons that Ethan had yet to understand.

But he swore to himself that he would.

He'd been assigned to his very first task force by Brian Cavanaugh, the Aurora Police Department's chief of detectives, and, as he'd come to learn in the last nine months, also his paternal uncle.

Knowledge of the latter tie had jolted him, Kyle and Greer the way nothing ever had before. He could state that for a fact, seeing as how, since they were triplets, there were times when he could swear that they functioned as one, single-minded unit.

The three of them received the news at the same time. It had come from their mother in the form of a deathbed confession so that she could meet her maker with a clear conscience. She'd died within hours of telling them, having absolutely no idea what kind of turmoil her revelation had caused for him and his siblings.

Initially, finding out that he, Kyle and Greer were actually part of the sprawling Cavanaugh family had shaken the very foundations of their world. But in the end, once they'd gotten used to it and accepted the truth, the information had proven not to be life-shattering after all.

He had to admit, at least for him, that it was nice to be part of something larger than a breadbox. Back when his mother's death was still imminent, he'd anticipated life being pared down to it being just the three of them once she was gone. Three united against the world, so to speak.

Instead, the three of them were suddenly part of a network, part of something that at times seemed even greater than the sum of its parts.

Just like that, they were Cavanaughs.

There were some on the police force who were quick to cry "Nepotism!" when he, Kyle and Greer advanced, rising above the legions of patrol officers to become detectives in the department. But as he was quick to point out when confronted, it was merit that brought them to where they were, not favoritism.

Merit riding on the shoulders of abilities and quick thinking.

Like now.

On his way home after an extraordinarily long day that had wound up slipping its way into the even longer evening, Ethan had rolled his windows down in an attempt to just clear his head.

Instead, it had done just the opposite.

It felt as if smoke were leeching its way into his lungs and body through every available pore. The starless sky had rendered the black smoke all but invisible until he was practically on top of it.

But nothing could cover up the acrid smell.

In the time that it took for the presence of smoke from the fire to register, Ethan was able to make out where the telltale smell was emanating from. The building to his right on the next block was on fire. Big-time.

Ethan brought his lovingly restored 1964 Thunderbird sports car to a stop, parking it a block away so he didn't block whatever fire trucks were coming in. And truth be told, it was also to safeguard against anything happening to it. After his siblings, he loved the car, which he'd secretly named Annette, the most.

"I'll be right back, Annette," he promised the vehicle as he shut down the engine and leaped out. Despite the urgency of the situation, Ethan made sure that he locked the car before leaving it.

Where was everyone?

There were no fire trucks, not even a department car. People from the neighborhood were gathering around, drawn by the drama, but there was no indication of any firefighters on the scene.

But there was screaming. The sound of women and children screaming.

And then he saw why.

The building that was on fire was a shelter, specifically a shelter for battered women and their children.

Protocol, since there was no sign of a responding firehouse, would have him calling 911 before he did anything else. But protocol didn't have a child's screams

ringing in its ears, and calling in the fire would be
stealing precious seconds away from finding that child,
seconds that could very well amount to the difference
between life and death.

Out of the corner of his eye, Ethan saw several
people gathering closer, tightening the perimeter of the
so-called spectacle.

Voyeurs.

Disasters attracted audiences. This one time he used
that to his advantage. Or rather the shelter's advantage.

"Call 911," he yelled to the man closest to him. "Tell
them that the Katella Street Shelter's on fire." He had to
shout the end of his sentence, as he was already running
toward the building.

Turning his head to see if the man had complied,
Ethan saw that he was just staring openmouthed at the
building. Disgusted, Ethan reached into his pocket and
pulled out his cell phone.

The fire couldn't be called an inferno yet, but he
knew how little it took to achieve the transformation. It
could literally happen in a heartbeat.

Raising the windbreaker he was wearing up over his
head as a meager protective barrier against the flames,
Ethan ran into the building even as he pressed 911.

The next moment, he stumbled backward, losing his
footing as someone came charging out of the building.
Springing up to his feet, Ethan saw that he'd just been
knocked down by a woman. A small one at that. The
blonde was holding an infant tucked against her chest
with one arm while she held a toddler on her hip on
the other side. A third child, just slightly older than the

toddler, was desperately trying to keep up with her gait. He was holding tightly on to the bottom of her shirt and screaming in fear.

Trying to catch his breath, Ethan was torn between asking the woman if she was all right and his initial intent of making sure that everyone was out of the building.

The once run-down building was spewing smoke and women in almost equal proportions. In the background, Ethan heard the sound of approaching sirens. It was too soon for a response to the call he'd made. It was obvious to him that someone else must have already called this fire in. There were two firehouses in Aurora, one to take care of the fires in the southern portion, the other to handle the ones in the northern section. Even given the close proximity of the southern-section fire station, the trucks had to have already been on their way when he'd first spotted the fire.

The woman who had all but run over him now passed him going in the opposite direction. To his amazement, she seemed to be running back into the burning building.

Was she crazy?

He lost no time heading her off. "Hey, wait, what about your kids?" he called out. She didn't turn around to acknowledge that she'd heard him. Ethan sped up and got in front of her, blocking her path. "Have you got another one in there?" Ethan grabbed the woman's arm, pulling her away from the entrance as two more women, propping each other up, emerged. "Stay with your children," he ordered. "I'll find your other kid," he promised. "Just tell me where."

"I don't know where," she snapped as she pulled her arm free.

The next moment, holding her arm up against her nose and mouth in a futile attempt to keep at least some of the smoke at bay, the woman darted around him and ran back into the burning building.

Ethan bit off a curse. He had a choice of either remaining outside and letting the approaching fire-fighters go in after her or doing it himself. Seeing as how they had yet to pull up in front of the building, by the time they could get into the building, it might be too late. His conscience dictated his course for him. He had no choice but to run after her.

Ethan fully intended to drag the woman out once he caught up to her. If she was trying to find another one of her children, he had the sinking feeling that it was too late. In his opinion, no one could survive this, and she had three children huddled together on the sidewalk to think about.

Mentally cursing the fate that had him embroiled in all this, Ethan ran in. He made his way through the jaws of the fire, its flames flaring like sharp yellow teeth threatening to take a chunk out of his flesh. Miraculously, Ethan saw the woman just up ahead of him.

"Hey!" he shouted angrily. "Stop!"

But the woman kept moving. Ethan could see her frantically looking around. He could also see what she couldn't, that a beam just above her head was about to give way. Dashing over, his lungs beginning to feel as if they were bursting, Ethan pulled the woman back just as the beam came crashing down. It missed hitting her by a matter of inches.

Still she resisted, trying to pull free of his grasp again. "There might be more," she shouted above the fire's loud moan. She turned away but got nowhere. Frustrated fury was in her reddened eyes as she demanded, "Hey! Hey, what are you doing?"

"Saving your kids' mother," Ethan snapped back. He threw the obstinate woman over his shoulder, appropriately enough emulating fireman style.

She was saying something, no doubt protesting or cursing him, but he couldn't hear her voice above the sounds of the fire. As far as he was concerned, it was better that way.

His eyes burned and his lungs felt as if they were coming apart. The way out of the building felt as if it were twice as far as the way in had been.

Finally making it across the threshold, he stumbled out, passing several firefighters as they raced into the building.

One of the firefighters stopped long enough to address him and point out the paramedic truck that was just pulling up.

"You can get medical attention for her over there," were the words that the man tossed in his direction as he hurried off.

"Let go of me!" the woman yelled angrily. When he didn't respond fast enough, she began to pound on his back with her fists.

For a woman supposedly almost overcome with smoke, Ethan thought, she packed quite a wallop. He was having trouble hanging on to her. When he finally set her down near the ambulance, Ethan instinctively stepped back to avoid contact with her swinging fists.

She all but fell over from the momentum of the last missed swing. Her eyes blazed as she demanded, "What the hell do you think you were doing?"

He hadn't expected a profusion of gratitude, but neither had he expected a display of anger. "Off the top of my head, I'd have to say saving your life."

"Saving my life?" she echoed incredulously, staring at him as if he'd just declared that he thought she were a zebra.

"You're welcome," Ethan fired back. He gestured toward the curb where two of the three children were sitting. The third was in another woman's arms. The woman was crying. "Now go see to your kids."

She stared at him as if he'd lost his mind. What the hell was he babbling about? "What kids?" she cried, her temper flaring.

"Your kids." Annoyed when she continued staring at him, Ethan pointed to the three children she'd had hanging off her as if she were some mother possum. "Those."

She glanced in the direction he was pointing. "You think—" Stunned and fighting off a cough that threatened to completely overwhelm her, Kansas Beckett found that she just couldn't finish her thought for a moment. "Those aren't my kids," she finally managed to tell him.

"They're not?" They'd certainly seemed as if they were hers when she'd ushered them out. He looked back at the children. They were crying again, this time clinging to a woman who was equally as teary. "Whose are they?"

Kansas shrugged. "I don't know. Hers, I imagine." She nodded toward the woman holding the baby and gathering the other two to her as best she could. "I was just driving by when I smelled the smoke and heard the screams." Why was she even bothering to explain her actions to this take-charge Neanderthal? "I called it in and then tried to do what I could."

Kansas felt gritty and dirty, not to mention that she was probably going to have to throw out what had been, until tonight, her favorite suit because she sincerely doubted that even the world's best dry cleaner could get the smell of smoke out of it.

Ethan gaped at what amounted to a little bit of a woman. "You just ran in."

She looked at him as if she didn't understand what his problem was. "Yeah."

Didn't this woman have a working brain? "What are you, crazy?" he demanded.

"No, are you?" Kansas shot back in the same tone. She gestured toward the building that was now a hive of activity with firemen fighting to gain the upper hand over the blazing enemy. "From the looks of it, you did the same thing."

Was she trying to put them on the same footing? He was a trained professional and she was a woman with streaks of soot across her face and clothes. Albeit a beautiful woman, but beauty in this case had nothing to do with what mattered.

"It's different," he retorted.

Kansas fisted her hands on her hips, going toe-to-

toe with her so-called rescuer. She absolutely hated chauvinists, and this man was shaping up to be a card-carrying member of the club.

"Why?" she wanted to know. "Were you planning on using a secret weapon to put the fire out? Maybe huff and puff until you blew it all out? Or did you have something else in mind?" she asked, her eyes dipping down so that they took in the lower half of his frame. Her meaning was clear.

He didn't have time for this, Ethan thought in exasperation. He didn't have time to argue with a bull-headed woman who was obviously braver than she was smart. His guess was that she probably had a firefighter in the family. Maybe her father or a brother she was attempting to emulate for some unknown reason.

Ethan frowned. Why was it always the pretty ones who were insane? he wondered. Maybe it was just nature's way of leveling the playing field.

In any case, he needed to start asking questions, to start interviewing the survivors to find out if they'd seen or heard anything suspicious just before the fire broke out.

And he needed, he thought, to have the rest of his team out here. While his captain applauded initiative, he frowned on lone-ranger behavior.

Moving away from the woman who was giving him the evil eye, Ethan reached into his pocket to take out his cell phone—only to find that his pocket was empty.

"Damn," he muttered under his breath.

He remembered shoving the phone into his pocket and feeling it against his thigh as he started to run into the burning shelter. He slanted a look back at the woman.

He must have dropped it when she knocked him down at the building's entrance.

Kansas frowned. "What?"

Ethan saw that she'd bitten off the word as if it had been yanked out of her throat against her will. For a second, he thought about just ignoring her, but he needed to get his team out here, which meant that he needed a cell phone.

"I lost my cell phone," he told her, then added, "I think I must have lost it when you ran into me and knocked me down."

Ethan looked over in the general direction of the entrance, but the area was now covered with firefighters running hoses, weaving in and out of the building, conferring with other firemen. Two were trying to get the swelling crowd to stay behind the designated lines that had been put up to control the area. If his phone had been lost there, it was most likely long gone, another casualty of the flames.

"You ran into me," she corrected him tersely.

Was it his imagination, or was the woman looking at him suspiciously?

"Why do you want your cell phone?" Kansas asked him. "Do you want to take pictures of the fire?"

He stared at her. Why the hell would he want to do that? The woman really was a nut job. "What would anyone want their phone for?" he responded in annoyance. "I want to make a call."

Her frown deepened. She made a small, disparaging noise, then began to dig through her pockets. Finding her own phone, she grudgingly held it out to him.

"Here, you can borrow mine," she offered. "Just don't forget to give it back."

"Oh damn, there go my plans for selling it on eBay," he retorted. "Thanks," he said as he took the cell phone from her.

Ethan started to press a single key, then stopped himself. He was operating on automatic pilot and had just gone for the key that would have immediately hooked him up to the precinct. He vaguely wondered what pressing the number three on the woman's phone would connect him to. Probably her anger-management coach, he thought darkly. Too bad the classes weren't taking.

It took Ethan a few seconds to remember the number to his department. It had been at least six months since he'd had to dial the number directly.

He let it ring four times, then, when it was about to go to voice mail, he terminated the call and tried another number. All the while he was aware that this woman—with soot streaked across her face like war paint—was standing only a few feet away, watching him intently.

Why wasn't she getting herself checked out? he wondered. And why was she scrutinizing him so closely? Did she expect him to do something strange? Or was she afraid he was going to make off with her phone?

No one was picking up. Sighing, he ended the second call. Punching in yet another number, he began to mentally count off the number of rings.

The woman moved a little closer to him. "Nobody home?" she asked.

"Doesn't look that way."

But just as he said it, Ethan heard the phone on the other end being picked up. He held his hand up because she'd begun to say something. He hoped she'd pick up on his silent way of telling her to keep quiet while he was trying to hear.

"Cavanaugh," a deep voice on the other end of the line announced.

Great, like that was supposed to narrow things down. There were currently seventeen Cavanaughs on the police force—if he, Greer and Kyle were included in the count.

He thought for a moment, trying to remember the first name of the Cavanaugh who had been appointed head of this task force. Dax, that was it. Dax.

Ethan launched into the crux of his message. "Dax, this is Ethan O'Brien. I'm calling because there's just been another fire."

The terse statement immediately got the attention of the man he was calling—as well as the interest of the woman whose phone he was using.

Chapter 2

"Give me your location," Dax Cavanaugh instructed. Then, before Ethan had a chance to give him the street coordinates, he offered, "I'll round up the rest of the team. You just do what you have to do until we get there."

The chief had appointed Dax to head up the team. Calling them was an assignment he could have easily passed on if he'd been filled with his own importance. But Ethan had come to learn that none of the Cavanaughs ever pulled rank, even when they could.

Ethan paused for a moment as he tried to recall the name of the intersection. When he did, he recited the street names, acutely aware that the woman to his right was staring at him as if she were expecting to witness some kind of a rare magic trick. Either that or she was afraid that he was going to run off with her cell phone.

"You want to call the chief, or should I?" Dax was asking, giving him the option.

Ethan thought it just a wee bit strange that Dax was referring to his own father by his official title, but he supposed that just verified the stories that the Cavanaughs went out of their way not to seem as if they were showing any favoritism toward one of their own.

"You can do it," Ethan told him. "The chief's most likely home by now, and you have his private number."

Ethan shifted to get out of the way. The area was getting more and more crowded with survivors from the shelter and the firemen were still fighting the good fight, trying to contain the blaze and save at least part of the building.

"And you don't?" Dax asked in surprise.

Out of the corner of his eye, Ethan saw the woman moving in closer to him. Apparently, she had no space issues. "No, why should I?"

"Because you're family," Dax said, as if Ethan should have known that. "My father lets everyone in the family have his home number." To back up his claim, Dax asked, "Do you want it?"

Dax began to rattle off the numbers, but Ethan stopped him before he was even halfway through. "That's okay, I'm going to have my hands full here until the rest of the team comes. You can do the honors and call him."

The truth of it was, Ethan didn't want to presume, no matter what Dax said to the contrary, that he was part of the Cavanaugh inner circle. Granted, he had Cavanaugh blood running through his veins, but the way he came to have it could easily be seen as a source of embarrassment, even in this day and age. Until he felt completely comfortable about it, he didn't want to assume too much. Right now, he was still feeling his way around this whole new scenario he found himself in and wanted to make sure he didn't antagonize either Andrew or Brian Cavanaugh.

Not that he would mind becoming a real part of the family. He wasn't like Kyle, who initially had viewed every interaction with their newfound family with suspicion, anticipating hostile rejection around every corner. He and his sister, Greer, secretly welcomed being part of a large, respected family after all the years they'd spent on the other side of the spectrum, poor and isolated—and usually two steps in front of the bill collector.

But he wanted to force nothing, take nothing for granted. If Brian Cavanaugh wanted him to have his private number, then it was going to have to come from Brian Cavanaugh, not his son.

"Will do," Dax was saying, and then he broke the connection.

The moment Ethan ended the call and handed the phone back to her, the blonde was openly studying him. "You a reporter?" she asked.

Damn, she was nosey. Just what was it that she was angling for? "No."

The quick, terse answer didn't seem to satisfy her curiosity. She came in from another angle. "Why all this interest in the fires?"

He answered her question with a question of his own. "Why the interest in my interest in the fires?" he countered.

Kansas lifted her chin. She was not about to allow herself to get sidetracked. "I asked first."

Instead of answering, Ethan reached out toward her hair. Annoyed, she began to jerk her head back, but he stopped her with, "You've got black flakes in your hair. I was just going to remove them. Unless you want them there," he speculated, raising a quizzical eyebrow and waiting for a response.

Something had just happened. Something completely uncalled-for. She'd felt a very definite wave of heat as his fingers made contact with her hair and scalp. Her imagination?

Kansas took a step back and did the honors herself, carelessly brushing her fingers through her long blond hair to get rid of any kind of soot or burnt debris she might have picked up while she was hustling the children out of the building. She supposed she should count herself lucky that it hadn't caught fire while she was getting the children out.

"There," she declared, her throat feeling tight for reasons that were completely beyond her. She tossed her head as a final sign of defiance. And then her eyes narrowed as she looked at him. "Now, why are you so interested in the fires, and who did you just call?"

She was no longer being just nosey, he thought. There was something else at work here. But what? Maybe she was a reporter and that was why she seemed to resent his being one, as per her last guess.

If that was what she was, then she was out of luck. Nothing he disliked more than reporters. "Lady, just because I borrowed your phone doesn't entitle you to my life story."

She squared her shoulders as if she were about to go into battle. He braced himself. "I don't want your life story. I just want an answer to my question, and it's Kansas, not 'lady.'"

Ethan's eyebrows lifted in confusion. What the hell was she talking about? "What's Kansas?"

Was she dealing with a village idiot, or was he just slow? "My name," she emphasized.

Ethan cocked his head, trying to absorb this meandering conversation. "Your last name's Kansas?"

She sighed. She was fairly certain he was doing this on purpose just to annoy her. "No, my *first* name is Kansas, and no matter how long you attempt to engage in this verbal shell game of yours, I'm not going to get sidetracked. Now, who did you call, and why are you so taken with this fire?" Before he could say anything, she asked him another question. "And what did you mean by 'there's been another one'?"

"The phrase 'another one' means that there's been more than one." He was deliberately goading her now. And enjoying it.

She said something under her breath that he couldn't quite make out, but he gathered it wasn't very favorable toward him.

"I know what the phrase means," she retorted through gritted teeth. "I'll ask you one more time—why are you so interested in the fires?"

"What happens after one more time?" Ethan wanted to know, amused by the woman despite himself. Irritating women usually annoyed the hell out of him—but there was something different about this one.

She drew herself up to her full height. "After one more time, I have you arrested."

That surprised him. "You're a cop?" He thought he knew most of the people on the force, by sight if not by name. He'd never seen her before.

"No. I'm a fire investigator," she informed him archly. "But I can still have you arrested. Clapped in irons would be my choice," Kansas added, savoring the image.

"Kinky," he commented. Damn, they were making fire investigators a hell of a lot prettier these days. *If* she was telling the truth. "Mind if I ask to see some identification?"

"And just so I know, who's asking?" she pressed, still trying to get a handle on his part in all this.

It was a known fact that pyromaniacs liked to stick around and watch their handiwork until the object of their interest burnt down to the ground and there was nothing left to watch. Since she'd begun her investigations and discovered that the fires had been set, Kansas had entertained several theories as to who or what was behind all these infernos. She was still sorting through them, looking for something that would rule out the others.

"Ethan O'Brien," he told her. She was still looking at him skeptically. He inclined his head. "I guess since you showed me yours, I'll show you mine." He took out his ID and his badge. "Detective Ethan O'Brien," he elaborated.

Like his siblings, he was still debating whether he was going to change his last name the way Brian and his brother Andrew, the former chief of police and reigning family patriarch, had told them they were welcome to do.

He knew that Greer was leaning toward it, as were Brian's four stepchildren who'd become part of the family when he married his widowed former partner. Kyle was the last holdout if he, Ethan, decided to go with the others. But he, Greer and Kyle had agreed that it would be an all-or-nothing decision for the three of them.

As for himself, he was giving the matter careful consideration.

"*You're* a cop," she concluded, quickly scanning the ID he held up.

"That I am," Ethan confirmed, slipping his wallet back into his pocket. "I'm on the task force investigating the recent crop of fires that have broken out in Aurora."

"They didn't just 'break out,'" she corrected him. "Those fires were all orchestrated, all set ahead of time."

"Yes, I know," Ethan allowed. He regarded her for a moment, wondering how much she might have by way of information. "How long have you been investigating this?"

There was only one way to answer that. "Longer than you," she promised.

She seemed awfully cocky. He found himself itching to take her down a peg. Take her down a peg and at the same time clean the soot off her bottom lip with his own.

Careful, O'Brien, he warned himself. *If anything, this is a professional relationship. Don't get personally involved, not even for a minute.*

"And you would know this how?" he challenged her. How would she know what was going on in his squad room?

"Simple. The fire department investigates every fire to make sure that it wasn't deliberately set," she answered him without missing a beat. "That would be something you should know heading into *your* investigation."

He'd never been one of those guys who felt superior to the softer of the species simply because he was a man. In his opinion, especially after growing up with Greer, women were every bit as capable and intelligent as men. More so sometimes. But he'd never had any use for people—male or female—who felt themselves to be above the law. Especially when they came across as haughty.

"Tell me," he said, lowering his voice as if he were about to share a secret thought. "How do you manage to stand up with that huge chip on your shoulder?"

Her eyes hardened, but to his surprise, no choice names were attached to his personage. Instead, using the same tone as he just had, she informed him, "I manage just fine, thanks."

"Kansas!" The fire chief, at least a decade older than his men and the young woman he called out to, hurried over to join them. Concern was etched into his features. "Are you all right?"

She flashed the older man a wide smile. "I'm fine, Chief," she assured him.

The expression on the older man's face said that he wasn't all that sure. "Someone said you ran into the burning building." He gestured toward the blazing building even as he leaned over to get a closer look at her face. "They weren't kidding, were they?"

She shrugged, not wanting to call any more undue attention to herself or her actions. "I heard kids screaming—"

Chief John Lawrence cut her off as he shook his head more in concern than disapproval. "You're not a firefighter anymore, Kansas," he pointed out. "And you should know better than to run into a burning building with no protective gear on."

She smiled and Ethan noted that it transformed her, softening her features and in general lighting up the immediate area around her. She was one of those people, he realized, who could light up a room with her smile. And frost it over with her frown.

It was never a good idea to argue with the fire chief. "Yes, I do, and I promise to do better next time," she told him, raising her hand as if she were taking an oath. "Hopefully, there won't be a next time."

"Amen to that," the chief agreed wholeheartedly. He had to get back to his men. The fire wasn't fully contained yet. "You stay put here until things are cool enough for you to conduct your initial investigation," he instructed.

The smile had turned into a grin and she rendered a mock salute in response to the man's attempt at admonishing her. "Yes, sir."

"Father?" Ethan asked the moment the chief had returned to his truck and his men.

Kansas turned toward him. He'd clearly lost her. "What?"

"Is the chief your father?" The older man certainly acted as if she were his daughter, Ethan thought.

Kansas laughed as she shook her head. "Don't let his wife hear you say that. No, Captain Lawrence is just a very good friend," she answered. "He helped train me, and when I wanted to get into investigative work, he backed me all the way. He's not my dad, but I wouldn't have minded it if he were."

At least, Kansas thought, that way she would have known who her father was.

His curiosity aroused, Ethan tried to read between the lines. Was there more to this "friend" thing than met the eye? Lawrence was certainly old enough to be her father, but that didn't stop some men. Or some women, especially if they wanted to get ahead.

"Friend," Ethan echoed. "As in boyfriend?" He raised an eyebrow, waiting to see how she'd react.

She lifted her chin. "Unless you're writing my biography, you don't have the right to ask that kind of question," she snapped.

Ethan's smile never wavered. He had a hunch that this woman's biography did *not* make for boring reading. "I'm not writing your biography," he clarified. "But there are some things I need to know—just for the record."

She bet he could talk the skin off a snake. "All right. For the 'record' I was the first one on the scene when the shelter began to burn—"

He'd already figured that part out. "Which is why I want to question you—at length," he added before she could brush the request aside. "I need to know if you saw anyone or anything that might have aroused your suspicions."

"Yes," she deadpanned, "I saw the flames—and I instantly knew it was a fire."

He had nothing against an occasional joke, but he resented like hell having his chain yanked. "Hey, 'Kansas,' in case it's escaped you, we're both on the same team. It seems to me that means we should be sharing information."

She was sure that he was more than eager for her to "share" and doubted very much that it would be a two-way street as far as he was concerned. Until he brought something to the table other than words, she was not about to share anything with him.

"Sorry." With that, she pushed past him.

"I bet the box that said 'works and plays well with others' always had 'needs improvement' checked on it," he said, raising his voice as she walked away.

She looked at him over her shoulder. "But the box labeled 'pummels annoying cop senseless' was also checked every time."

Ethan shook his head. Working together was just going to have to wait a couple of days. He had a definite hunch that she'd be coming around by then.

"Your loss," he called after her and turned just as he saw Dax Cavanaugh coming toward him.

Right behind him were Richard Ortiz and Alan Youngman, two other veteran detectives on the force who now found themselves part of the arson task force. Remarkably, none of the men seemed to resent his presence despite the fact that they were all veterans with several years to their credit, while this was his very first assignment as a detective.

There were times he could have sworn that his shield was still warm in his wallet.

"What have you got?" Ortiz asked him, looking more than a little disgruntled. "And it better be worth it because I was just about to get lucky with this hot little number."

"He doesn't want to hear about your rubber doll collection," Youngman deadpanned to his partner.

Ortiz looked insulted. "Hey, just because you're in a rut doesn't mean that I am," the younger man protested.

"Guys," Dax admonished in a low voice. "Playtime is over."

Youngman frowned as he shook his head. "You're no fun since they put you in charge."

"We'll have fun after we catch this arsonist and confiscate his matches," Dax replied.

Overhearing, Kansas couldn't help crossing back to the men and correcting this new detective. "He's not an arsonist."

Dax turned to her. His eyes, Ethan noticed, swept over the woman as if he were taking inventory. What was conspicuously missing was any indication of attraction. Brenda must be one hell of a woman, Ethan couldn't help thinking about the man's wife.

"And you would know this how?" Dax asked the self-proclaimed fire investigator.

"An angel whispered in her ear," Ethan quipped. "Dax, this is Kansas Beckett. She says she's the fire department's investigator. Kansas, this is Dax Cavanaugh, Alan Youngman and Richard Ortiz." Three heads bobbed in order of the introductions.

It was more information than she wanted, but she nodded at each man, then looked at the man conducting the introductions. "I didn't *say* I was the fire investigator. I *am* the fire investigator. And how did you know my last name?" she wanted to know. "I didn't give it to you."

"But remarkably, I can read," Ethan answered with an enigmatic smile. "And it was in on the ID you showed me"

"How do you know it's not an arsonist?" Dax persisted, more emphatically this time.

She patiently recited the standard differentiation. "Arsonists do it for profit," she told him, moving out of the way of several firefighters as they raced by, heading straight for the building's perimeter. "Their own or someone else's. The buildings that were torched, as far as we can ascertain, have no common thread drawing them together. For instance, there's no one who stands to profit from getting rid of a battered-women's shelter."

Ethan turned the thought over in his head. "Maybe there's a developer in the wings, looking to buy up land cheap in order to build a residential community or a king-sized mall or some vast hotel, something along those lines."

But she shook her head. "Too spread apart, too far-fetched," she pointed out. "It would have to be the biggest such undertaking in the country," she emphasized. "And I don't really think that's what's going on here."

Dax was open to any kind of a guess at this point. "So who or what do you think is behind these fires?" he asked her.

She was silent for a moment. Almost against her will, she glanced in Ethan's direction before answering. "My guess is that it's either a pyromaniac who's doing it for the sheer thrill of it, or we're up against someone with a vendetta who's trying to hide his crime in plain sight with a lot of camouflage activity."

"In which case, we have to find which is the intentional fire and which were set for show," Ethan theorized.

Kansas looked at him. "I'm impressed. Chalk one up for the pretty boy."

He couldn't tell if she was being sarcastic or actually giving him his due. With Kansas, he had a hunch that it was a little bit of both.

Chapter 3

In all, twelve children and nineteen adults were saved. Because the firefighters had responded so quickly to Kansas's call—and despite the fact that several women and children wound up being taken to the hospital for treatment—not a single life was lost.

Tired, seriously bordering on being punchy, Ethan nonetheless remained at the scene with the other detectives, interviewing anyone who'd been in the building just before the fire broke out. It was a long shot, but he kept hoping that someone might have witnessed even the slightest thing that seemed out of the ordinary at the time.

Because she wanted to spare the victims any more unnecessary trauma, and since the nature of the questions that the police were asking were along the lines of what she wanted to ask, Kansas decided it was best to temporarily join forces with the Neanderthal who had slung her over his shoulder.

The women and children who'd been in the fire had her complete sympathy. She knew the horror they'd gone through. Knew, firsthand, how vulnerable and helpless they'd all felt. And how they'd all thought, at one point or another, that they were going to die.

Because she'd been trapped in just such a fire herself once.

When she was twelve years old, she'd been caught in a burning building. It occurred in the group home where she'd always managed to return. She came to regard it as a holding zone, a place to stay in between being placed in various foster homes. But in that case, there'd been no mystery as to how the fire had gotten started. Eric Johnson had disobeyed the woman who was in charge and not only played with matches but deliberately had set the draperies in the common room on fire.

Seeing what he'd done, Kansas had run toward the draperies and tried to put the fire out using a blanket that someone had left behind. All that had done was spread the flames. Eric had been sent to juvenile hall right after that.

Kansas couldn't help wondering what had happened to Eric after all these years. Was he out there somewhere, perpetuating his love affair with fire?

She made a mental note to see if she could find out where he was these days.

Kansas glanced at O'Brien. He looked tired, she noted, but he continued pushing on. For the most part, he was asking all the right questions. And for a good-looking man, he seemed to display a vein of sensitivity, as well. In her experience, most good-looking men didn't. They were usually one-dimensional and shallow, too enamored with the image in their mirror to even think about anyone else.

More than an hour of questioning yielded the consensus that the fire had "just come out nowhere." Most of the women questioned seemed to think it had started in the recreation room, although no one had actually seen it being started or even knew *how* it had started. When questioned further, they all more or less said the same thing. That they were just suddenly *aware* of the fire being there.

Panic had ensued as mothers frantically began searching for their children. The ones who hadn't been separated from their children to begin with herded them out into the moonless night amid screaming and accelerated pandemonium.

The chaos slowly abated as mother after mother was reunited with her children. But there was still one woman left searching. Looking bedraggled and utterly shell-shocked, the woman went from one person to another, asking if anyone had seen her daughter. No one had.

Unable to stand it any longer, Kansas caught O'Brien by the arm and pulled him around. She pointed to the hysterical woman. "She shouldn't have to look for her daughter on her own."

Busy comparing his findings with Dax and all but running on empty, Ethan nodded. "Fine, why don't you go help her." More than any of them, this impetuous, pushy woman seemed to have a relationship with the women at the shelter. At the very least, she seemed to be able to relate to them. Maybe she could pick up on something that he and the others on the task force couldn't—and more important, she could bring to the table what he felt was a woman's natural tendency to empathize. That would probably go a long way in giving the other woman some measure of comfort until they were able to hopefully locate her missing daughter.

Kansas pressed her lips together, biting back a stinging retort. She couldn't help thinking she'd just been brushed off.

Not damn likely, Detective.

Detective Ethan O'Brien, she silently promised herself, was about to discover that she didn't brush aside easily.

The moment she approached the distraught woman, the latter grabbed her by the arm. "Have you seen her? Can you help me find my Jennifer?"

"We're going to do everything we can to find her," Kansas told the woman as she gently escorted her over to one of the firemen. "Conway, I need your help."

"Anytime, Kansas. I'm all yours," the blond-haired fireman told her as he flashed a quick, toothy grin.

"This woman can't find her daughter. She might have been one of the kids taken to the hospital. See what you can do to reunite them," Kansas requested.

The fireman looked disappointed for a moment, then with a resigned shrug did as he was asked and took charge of the woman. "Don't worry, we'll find her," he said in a soothing, baritone voice.

Kansas flashed a smile at Conway before returning to O'Brien to listen in on his latest interview.

"Buck passing?" Ethan asked when she made her way

back to his circle. Curious to see what she did with the woman, he'd been watching her out of the corner of his eye.

"No," she answered tersely. "Choosing the most efficient path to get things done. Conway was part of the first team that made it inside. If there was anyone left to save, he would have found them." She crossed her arms. "He's also got a photographic memory and was there, helping to put the injured kids into the ambulances. If anyone can help find this woman's daughter, he can."

Ethan nodded, taking the information in. "You seem to know a lot about this Conway guy. You worked with him before?"

"For five years."

He was tempted to ask if she'd done more than just work with the man. The fact that the question even occurred to him caught him off guard. The woman was a barracuda. A gorgeous barracuda, but still a barracuda, and he knew better than to swim in the water near one. So it shouldn't matter whether their relationship went any deeper than just work.

But it did.

"How does someone get into that line of work?" he wanted to know.

He was prejudiced. It figured… "You mean how does a woman get into that line of work?"

Ethan knew what the sexy force of nature was doing, and he refused to get embroiled in a discussion that revolved around stereotypes. He had a more basic question than that. "How do you make yourself rush into burning buildings when everyone else is running in the opposite direction?"

It was something she'd never thought twice about. She'd just done it. It was the right thing to do. "Because you want to help, to save people. You did the very same thing," she pointed out, "and no one's even paying you to do it. It's not your job." She looked back toward Conway and the woman she'd entrusted to him. He was on the phone, most likely calling the hospital to find out if her daughter was there. Mentally, Kansas crossed her fingers for the woman.

"It's all part of 'protect and serve,'" she heard O'Brien telling her.

Kansas turned her attention back to the irritating detective with the sexy mouth. "If you understand that, then you have your answer."

Greer blustered through life, but Ethan's mother had been meek. He'd always thought that more women were like his mother than his sister. "Aren't you afraid of getting hurt? Of getting permanently scarred?"

Those thoughts had crossed her mind, but only fleetingly. She shook her head. "I'm more afraid of spending night after night with a nagging conscience that won't let me forget that I *didn't* do all I could to save someone. That because I hesitated or wasn't there to save them, someone died. There are enough things to feel guilty about in this world without adding to the sum total."

She didn't want to continue focusing on herself or her reaction to things. There was a more important topic to pursue. "So, did you find out anything useful?" she pressed.

What did she think she missed? "You were only gone a few minutes," he reminded her. The rest of the time, she'd been with him every step of the way—not that he really minded it. Even with soot on her face, the woman was extremely easy on the eyes.

"Crucial things can be said in less than a minute," she observed. Was he deliberately being evasive? *Had* he learned something?

"Sorry to disappoint you," Ethan said. "But nothing noteworthy was ascertained." He looked back at the building. The firemen had contained the blaze and only a section of the building had been destroyed. But it was still going to have to be evacuated for a good chunk of time while reconstruction was undertaken. "We'll know more when the ashes cool off and we can conduct a thorough search."

"That's my department," Kansas reminded him, taking pleasure in the fact that—as a fire investigator— her work took priority over his.

"Not tonight." He saw her eyes narrow, like someone getting ready for a fight. "Look, I don't want to have to go over your head," he warned her. He and the task force had dibs and that was that.

"And I don't want to have to take yours off," she fired back with feeling. "So back off. This is *my* investigation, O'Brien. Someone is burning down buildings in Aurora."

"And running the risk of killing people while he's doing it," Ethan concluded. "Dead people fall under my jurisdiction." And that, he felt, terminated the argument.

"And investigating man-made fires comes under mine," she insisted.

She didn't give an inch. Why didn't that surprise him?

"So you work together."

They turned in unison to see who had made the simple declaration. It had come from Brian Cavanaugh, the chief of police. When Dax had called him, Brian had lost no time getting to the site of the latest unexplained fire.

Brian looked from his new nephew to the woman Ethan was having a difference of opinion with. He saw not just a clash of temperaments as they fought over jurisdiction, but something more.

Something that, of late, he'd found himself privy to more than a few times. There had to be something in the air lately.

These two mixed like oil and water, he thought. And they'd be together for quite a while, he was willing to bet a month's salary on it.

His intense blue eyes, eyes that were identical in hue to those of the young man his late brother had sired, swept over Ethan and the investigator whose name he'd been told was Kansas. He perceived resistance to his instruction in both of them.

"Have I made myself clear?" Brian asked evenly.

"Perfectly," Ethan responded, coming to attention and standing soldier-straight.

Rather than mumble an agreement the way he'd expected her to, the young woman looked at him skeptically. "Did you clear this with the chief and my captain?"

"It was cleared the minute I suggested it," Brian said with no conceit attached to his words. "The bottom line is that we all want to find whoever's responsible for all this."

The expression was kind, the tone firm. This was a man, she sensed, people didn't argue with. And neither would she.

Unless it was for a good cause.

Kansas stayed long after the police task force had recorded and photographed their data, folded their tents and disappeared into what was left of the night. She liked conducting her investigation without having to trip over people, well intentioned or not. Gregarious and outgoing, Kansas still felt there was a time for silence and she processed things much better when there as a minimum of noise to distract her.

She'd found that obnoxious Detective O'Brien and his annoying smile most distracting of all.

Contrary to the fledgling opinion that had been formed—most likely to soothe the nerves of the shelter's residents—the fire hadn't been an accident. It had been started intentionally. She'd discovered an incendiary device hidden right off the kitchen, set for a time when the area was presumably empty. So whoever had done this hadn't wanted to isolate anyone or cut them off from making an escape. A fire in the kitchen when there was no one in the kitchen meant that the goal was destruction of property, not lives.

Too bad things didn't always go according to plan, she silently mourned. One of the shelter volunteers had gotten cut off from the others and hadn't made it out of the building. She'd been found on the floor, unconscious. The paramedics worked over the young woman for close to half an hour before she finally came around. She was one of the lucky.

Frowning, Kansas rocked back on her heels and shook her head.

This psychopath needed to be found and brought to justice quickly, before he did any more damage.

And she needed to get some sleep before she fell on her face.

She wondered where the displaced residents of the shelter would be sleeping tonight. She took comfort in the knowledge that they'd be returning in a few weeks even if the construction wasn't yet completed.

With a weary sigh, Kansas stood up and headed for the front entrance.

Just before she crossed the charred threshold, she kicked something. Curious, thinking it might just possibly have something to do with the identity of whoever started the fire, she stooped down to pick it up.

It turned out to be a cell phone—in pretty awful condition, from what she could tell. Flipping it open, she found that the battery was still active. She could just barely make out the wallpaper. It was a picture of three people. Squinting, she realized that the obnoxious detective who thought she needed to be carried out of the building fireman-style was in the photo.

There were two more people with him, both of whom looked identical to him. Now there was a curse, she mused, closing the phone again. Three Detective O'Briens. Kansas shivered at the thought.

"Tough night, huh?" the captain said, coming up to her. It wasn't really a question.

"That it was. On the heels of a tough day," she added. She hated not being able to come up with an answer, to have unsolved cases pile up on top of one another like some kind of uneven pyramid.

Captain John Lawrence looked at her with compassion. "Why don't you go home, Kansas?"

"I'm almost done," she told him.

His eyes swept over her and he shook his head. "Looks to me like you're almost done *in*." Lawrence nodded toward the building they'd just walked out of. "This'll all still be here tomorrow morning, Kansas. And you'll be a lot fresher. Maybe it'll make more sense to you then."

Kansas paused to look back at the building and sighed. "Burning buildings will never make any sense to me," she contradicted. "But maybe you're right about needing to look at this with fresh eyes."

"I'm always right," Lawrence told her with a chuckle. "That's why they made me the captain."

Kansas grinned. "That, and don't forget your overwhelming modesty."

"You've been paying attention." His eyes crinkled, all but disappearing when he smiled.

"Right from the beginning, Captain Lawrence," she assured him.

Captain Lawrence had been more than fair to her, and she appreciated that. She'd heard horror stories about other houses and how life became so intolerable that female firefighters wound up quitting. Not that she ever would. It wasn't in her nature to quit. But she appreciated not having to make that choice.

Looking down, she realized that she was even more covered with dust and soot than before. She attempted to dust herself off, but it seemed like an almost impossible task.

"I'll have a preliminary report on your desk in the morning," she promised.

Lawrence tapped her on the shoulder, and when she looked at him quizzically, he pointed up toward the sky. "It already is morning."

"Then I'd better go home and start typing," she quipped.

"Type later," Lawrence ordered. "Sleep now."

"Anyone ever tell you that you're a nag, Captain Lawrence?"

"My wife," he answered without skipping a beat. "But then, what does she know? Besides, compared to Martha, I'm a novice. You ever want to hear a pro, just stop by the house. I'll drop some socks on the floor and have her go at it for you." He looked at her. "I don't want to see you until at least midday."

"'O, Captain! my Captain!'" Throwing her wrist against her forehead in a melodramatic fashion, Kansas quoted a line out of a classic poem by Walt Whitman that seemed to fit here. "You've hurt my feelings."

He gave her a knowing look. "Can't hurt what you don't have."

"Right," she murmured.

She'd deliberately gone out of her way to come across like a militant fire investigator, more macho than the men she worked with. There was a reason for that. She didn't want to allow *anything* to tap into her feelings. By her reckoning, there had to be an entire reservoir of tears and emotions she had never allowed herself to access because she was sincerely afraid that if she ever did, she wouldn't be able to shut off the valve. It was far better never to access it in the first place.

Heading to her car, she put her hand into her pocket for the key…and touched the cell phone she'd discovered instead. She took it out and glanced down at it. She supposed that she could just drop it off at O'Brien's precinct. But he *had* looked concerned about losing the phone, and if she hadn't plowed into him like that, he wouldn't have lost the device.

Kansas frowned. She supposed she owed O'Brien for that.

She looked around and saw that there was still one person with the police department on the premises. Not pausing to debate the wisdom of her actions, she hurried over to the man. She was fairly certain that the chief of detectives would know where she could find the incorrigible Detective O'Brien.

"I could drop it off for you," Brian Cavanaugh volunteered after the pretty fire investigator had approached him to say that she'd found Ethan's cell phone.

She looked down at the smoke-streaked device and gave the chief's suggestion some thought. She *was* bone-tired, and she knew that the chief would get the phone to O'Brien.

Still, she had to admit that personally handing the cell phone to O'Brien would bring about some small sense of closure for her. And closure was a very rare thing in her life.

"No, that's all right. I'll do it," she told him. "If you could just tell me where to find him, I'd appreciate it."

"Of course, no problem. I have the address right here," he told her.

Brian suppressed a smile as he reached into his inside pocket for a pen and a piece of paper. Finding both, he took them out and began writing the address in large, block letters.

Not for a second had he doubted that that was going to be her answer.

"Here you go," he said, handing her the paper.

This, he thought, was going to be the start of something lasting.

Chapter 4

Ethan wasn't a morning person, not by any stretch of the imagination. He never had been. Not even under the best of circumstances, coming off an actual full night's sleep, something that eluded him these days. Having less than four hours in which to recharge had left him feeling surly, less than communicative and only half-human.

So when he heard the doorbell to his garden apartment ring, Ethan's first impulse was to just ignore it. No one he knew had said anything about coming by at a little after six that morning. and it was either someone trying to save his soul—a religious sect had been making the rounds lately, scattering pamphlets about a better life to come in their wake—or the neighbor in the apartment catty-corner to his who had been pestering him with everything from a clogged drain to a key stuck in the ignition of her car, all of which he finally realized were just flimsy pretexts to see him. The woman, a very chatty brunette who wore too much makeup and too little clothing, had invited him over more than a dozen times, and each time he'd politely but firmly turned her down. By the time the woman had turned up on his doorstep a fifth time, his inner radar had screamed, "Run!" Two invitations were hospitable. Five, a bit pushy. More than a dozen was downright creepy.

When he didn't answer the first two rings, whoever was on his doorstep started knocking.

Pounding was actually a more accurate description of what was happening on the other side of his door.

Okay, he thought, no more Mr. Nice Guy. Whoever was banging on his door was going to get more than just a piece of his mind. He wasn't in the mood for this.

Swinging the door open, Ethan snapped, "What the hell do you want?" before he saw that it wasn't someone looking to guide him to the Promised Land, nor was it the pushy neighbor who wouldn't take no for an answer. It was the woman he'd met at the fire. The one, he'd thought, whose parents had a warped sense of humor and named her after a state best known for a little girl who'd gone traveling with her house and a dog named Toto.

"To give you back your cell phone," Kansas snapped back in the same tone he'd just used. "Here." She thrust the near-fried object at him.

As he took it, Kansas turned on her heel and started to walk away. *March away* was actually more of an accurate description.

It took Ethan a second to come to. "Wait, I'm sorry," he called out, hurrying after her to stop her from leaving. "I'm not my best in the morning," he apologized.

Now there was a news flash. "No kidding," she quipped, whirling around to face him. "I've seen friendlier grizzlies terrorizing a campsite on the Discovery Channel."

With a sigh, he dragged his hand through his unruly hair. "I thought you were someone else."

She laughed shortly. "My condolences to 'someone else.'" Obviously, it was true: no good deed really did go unpunished, Kansas thought.

But as she started to leave again, her short mission of reuniting O'Brien with his missing cell phone completed, the detective moved swiftly to get in front of her.

"You want to come in?" he asked, gesturing toward his apartment behind him.

Kansas glanced at it, and then at him. She was bone-weary and in no mood for a verbal sparring match. "Not really. I just wanted to deliver that in person, since, according to you, I was the reason you lost it in the first place."

Ethan winced slightly. Looking down at the charred device, he asked, "Where did you find it?"

"It was lying on the floor just inside the building." Because he seemed to want specifics, she took a guess how it had gotten there. "Someone must have accidentally kicked it in." She looked down at the phone. It did look pretty damaged. "I don't think it can be saved, but maybe the information that's stored on it can be transferred to another phone or something." She punctuated her statement with a shrug.

She'd done all she could on her end. The rest was up to him. In any case, all she wanted to do was get home, not stand here talking to a man wearing pajama bottoms precariously perched on a set of pretty damn terrific-looking hips. Their initial encounter last night had given her no idea that he had abs that would make the average woman weak in the knees.

The average woman, but not her, of course. She wasn't that shallow. Just very, very observant.

With effort, she raised her eyes to his face.

Ethan frowned at the bit of charred phone in his hand. They had a tech at the precinct who was very close to a magician when it came to electronic devices. If anyone could extract something from his fried phone, it was Albert.

"That's very thoughtful of you," he told her.

"That's me, thoughtful," Kansas retorted. It was too early for him to process sarcasm, so he just let her response pass. "Well, I'll see you—"

Ethan suddenly came to life. Shifting again so that he was once more blocking her path, he asked, "Have you had breakfast yet?"

Kansas blinked. "Breakfast?" she echoed. "I haven't had *dinner* yet." She'd been at the site of the women's shelter fire this entire time. And then she replayed his question in her head—and looked at him, stunned. "Are you offering to cook for me, Detective O'Brien?"

"Me?" he asked incredulously. "Hell, no." Ethan shook his head with feeling. "That wouldn't exactly be paying you back for being nice enough to bring this over to me. No, I was just thinking of taking someone up on a standing invitation."

And just what did that have to do with her? Kansas wondered. The man really wasn't kidding about mornings not being his best time. His thought process seemed to be leapfrogging all over the place.

"Well, you go ahead and take somebody up on that standing invitation," she told him, patting his shoulder. "And I'll—"

He cut her off, realizing he hadn't been clear. "The invitation isn't just for me. It applies to anyone I want to bring with me."

She looked at him. Suspicion crept in and got a toehold. Ethan O'Brien was more than mildly good-looking. Tall, dark, with movie-star-chiseled features and electric-blue eyes, he was the type of man who made otherwise reasonable, intelligent women become monosyllabic, slack-jawed idiots when he entered a room. But she'd had her shots against those kinds of men. She'd been married to one and swiftly divorced from him, as well. The upshot of that experience was that she only made a mistake once, and then she learned enough not to repeat it.

Her eyes narrowed. "Excuse me?"

"It's easier to show you. Wait here," Ethan told her, backing into the apartment. "I've just got to get dressed and get my gun."

"Now there's a line that any woman would find irresistible," she murmured to herself, then raised her voice as she called after him, "If it's all the same to you, Detective—" not that she cared if it was or not "—I'll just be on my way."

Ethan turned from his doorway, still very much underdressed. It was getting harder and harder for her to focus only on his face. "The invitation's for breakfast at my uncle's house," he told her. "Dozens of chairs, no waiting." The quote belonged to Andrew.

She had to admit that O'Brien had made her mildly curious. "What's he run, a diner?"

He had a feeling Andrew would have gotten a kick out of the question. "Very nearly. I've only been a couple of times," he confessed. "But the man's legend doesn't do him justice."

"I'm sure," she murmured. Ethan had the distinct feeling he was being brushed off. Her next words confirmed it. "But all I want to do right now is crawl into bed. If it's all the same to you, I'll just take a rain check."

Where this tinge of disappointment had come from was a complete mystery to him. He was only trying to thank her for reuniting him with his phone, nothing more. Ethan chalked it up to having his morning shaken up. "If I tell him that, he'll hold you to it. He'll expect you to come for breakfast sometime soon," Ethan added when she made no comment.

Like she believed that.

Kansas knew she should just let the matter drop, but it annoyed her that this walking stud of a detective thought she was naive enough to believe him. She deliberately pointed out the obvious.

"Your uncle has no idea who I am." And it was mutual, since she had no idea who this "Uncle Andrew" and his so-called legend were.

"Uncle Andrew's the former chief of police," O'Brien informed her. "He makes a point of knowing who *everyone* is when it comes to the police and fire departments."

This was something she was going to look into, if for no other reason than to be prepared in case she ever bumped into Detective Stud again.

"I consider myself duly warned," she replied. "Now, unless you want me falling asleep on your doorstep, I'm going to have to go."

Maybe not the doorstep, Ethan thought, but he certainly wouldn't mind finding her—awake or asleep—in his bed. He had a hunch, though, that she wouldn't exactly appreciate him vocalizing that right now.

"Sure. I understand. Thanks again," he said, holding up the phone she'd brought to him.

Kansas merely nodded and then turned and walked quickly away before O'Brien found something else he wanted to talk about. She headed toward the vehicle she'd left in guest parking.

Closing his hand over the charred phone, Ethan watched the sway of the fire investigator's hips as she moved. It was only when he became aware of the door of the apartment cattycorner to his opening that he quickly beat a hasty retreat before his neighbor stepped out and tried to entice him with yet another invitation. Last time she'd come to the door wearing a see-through nightgown. The woman spelled trouble any way you looked at it.

Andrew smiled to himself when he looked up to the oven door and saw the reflection of the man entering his state-of-the-art kitchen through the back door.

"C'mon in, little brother." Andrew turned from the tray of French toast he'd just drizzled a layer of powdered sugar on. His smile widened. He knew better than anyone how hectic and busy the life of a chief could be. "It's been a long time since you dropped by for breakfast." Maybe he was taking something for granted he shouldn't. "You *are* dropping by for breakfast, aren't you?"

Brian moved his shoulders vaguely, trying to appear indifferent despite the fact that the aroma rising up from his brother's handiwork had already begun making him salivate—and food had never been all that important to him.

"I could eat," he answered.

"If breakfast isn't your primary motive, what brings you here?" Andrew asked, placing two thick pieces of toasted French bread—coated and baked with egg batter, a drop of rum and nutmeg—onto a plate on the counter and moving it until it was in front of his brother.

Brian took the knife and fork Andrew silently offered. "I wanted to see if you'd gotten over it."

Andrew slid onto the counter stool next to his younger brother. "'It'?" he repeated in confusion. "Someone say I was sick?"

"Not sick," Brian answered, trying not to sigh and sound like a man who'd died and gone to heaven. His wife, Lila, was a good cook, but not like this. "Just indifferent."

Rather than being clarified, the issue had just gotten more muddied. "What the hell are you talking about, Brian?"

Brian's answer came between mouthfuls of French toast. He knew it was impossible, but each bite seemed to be better than the last.

"About not answering when someone calls to you."

He paused to look at his older brother. The brother he'd idolized as a boy. "Now, my guess is that you're either going deaf, or something's wrong."

Andrew frowned slightly. None of this was making any sense to him. "My hearing's just as good as it ever was, and if there's something wrong, it's with this so-called story of yours."

Putting down his fork, Brian looked around to make sure that his sister-in-law wasn't anywhere within earshot. He got down to the real reason he'd come. Lowering his voice, he said, "I came here to tell you to get your act together before it's too late."

This was just getting more and more convoluted. "Explain this to me slowly," he instructed his brother. "From the top."

Brian sighed, pushing the empty plate away. "I saw you with that woman."

"Woman?" Andrew repeated, saying the word as if Brian had just accused him of being with a Martian. "What woman? Where?" Before Brian could elaborate, Andrew cut in, concerned. He knew how hard Brian worked. "Brian, maybe it's time to start considering early retirement. We both know that this job can eat you alive if you let it. You have a lot to live for. Lila, your kids, Lila's kids—"

This time Brian cut Andrew off. "This has nothing to do with the job, and I'm well aware of my blessings. I'm just concerned that maybe you're taking yours for granted." He hated being his brother's keeper. Andrew was always the moral standard for the rest of them. But after the other day, he knew he had to say something. "I know what I saw."

Andrew sighed. "And what is it that you *think* you saw?"

He's actually going to make me say it, Brian thought, upset about having been put in this position. "You, walking into the Crystal Penguin, with another woman."

"The Crystal Penguin?" Andrew repeated incredulously. The Crystal Penguin was an overpriced restaurant that didn't always deliver on its promises of exquisite dining experiences. "Why would I go to a restaurant? And if I did go to one, it certainly wouldn't be a restaurant that overcharges and undercooks."

That's what he would have thought if someone had come to him with this story. But he'd been a witness to this. "I saw you, Andrew."

Andrew didn't waste his breath protesting that it wasn't possible. "And just when did this 'sighting' occur?"

Brian had been sitting on this for several days now, and it was killing him. "Last Friday evening. At about seven-thirty."

"I see." His expression was unreadable. "Why didn't you come up and talk to me?"

He almost had, then decided to restrain himself. "Because you're my older brother and I didn't want to embarrass you."

And then Brian delivered what in his estimation was the knockout blow.

"Some of the others have mentioned seeing you around the city with this woman. I told them they were crazy, but then on Friday I saw you myself, and now I'm begging you," he entreated, putting his hand on

Andrew's arm, "break it off before Rose gets hurt. You spent all that time looking for Rose when everyone else, including me, thought she was dead. Don't throw all that away because of some middle-aged itch you want to scratch."

"You done?" Andrew wanted to know.

"Yes," Brian said quietly. "Just promise me you'll break if off with her."

"It would seem like the thing to do." To Brian's surprise, his brother got off the stool, walked to the doorway between the kitchen and the living room and called out, "Rose? Would you mind coming here?"

Brian hurried over to him. "What are you doing?" he whispered into Andrew's ear. He knew that for some, the need to confess was almost an overpowering reaction, but he would have never thought it of Andrew. This had all the makings of a disaster. "Don't dump this on Rose. Don't tell her you've been cheating on her just to clear your conscience."

"Good advice," Andrew quipped.

Before Brian could ask if he'd lost his mind, Rose walked in. "Hello, Brian. Nice to see you." She turned toward her husband. There was no missing the love in her eyes. "You wanted me, honey?"

"Only every minute of every day," Andrew said, a gentle smile curving the corners of his mouth. He slipped his arm around her waist. "Rose, could you tell Brian where we were last Friday?"

Rose sighed, shaking her head. "Don't see why you would even want to admit to it."

He laughed, giving her a quick hug. "Humor me, my love."

"Okay." Rose turned toward her brother-in-law. "We saw the most god-awful movie. *Heaven Around the Corner*. Quite honestly, I still can't figure out how the people behind that silly thing managed to get funding to produce it." Her eyes crinkled as she slanted a glance and a grin in her husband's direction. "Even Andrew could have written a better story."

"Thank you, dear," Andrew deadpanned. "I can always count on you to extol my many talents."

She laughed. Standing on her toes, she brushed a kiss against his cheek. "Don't worry, dear. No one can touch your cooking."

Still holding his wife to him, Andrew turned his attention back to his younger brother and Brian's allegations. "Satisfied?"

Rose looked from one man to the other, a curious expression filling her eyes. "Satisfied about what? What's this all about, Andrew? Brian?" She waited for one of them to enlighten her.

"Brian thought he saw me clear across town last Friday. At the Crystal Penguin. With another woman. I don't know which is more absurd, the restaurant part or the other woman part." He caught the look on Rose's face. "The other woman part. Definitely the other woman part," he assured her.

Amused, Rose laughed. "Not unless Andrew's suddenly gotten superpowers and found a way to be in two places at the same time."

Brian sighed with relief. "You don't know how glad it makes me to hear that." But then he frowned slightly. There was still a mystery to be unraveled. "But whoever I saw looked just like you, Andrew."

"Maybe it was one of the boys," Andrew suggested.

But Brian shook his head. He'd already thought of that. "Too old."

Andrew gave him a quick jab in the arm. "Thanks a lot."

He hadn't meant it as an insult. "You know what I mean. Around our age, not younger."

"Someone else out there with those handsome features?" Rose teased, brushing her hand across her husband's cheek.

"I know. Lucky dog," Andrew deadpanned. He grew a little more serious as he asked Brian, "And you're saying this isn't the first time this doppelgänger's been spotted?"

Brian nodded. "Jared's mentioned seeing 'you,'" he told Andrew, referring to one of his sons. "Said you ignored him when he called out to you. And Zack said he thought he saw you walking into the Federal Building about a month ago. Same scenario. He called out and was ignored."

Listening to this, Rose glanced at her husband. He'd become quietly thoughtful. "I know that look," she said. "You're working something out in your head."

"What's on your mind?" Brian probed.

Andrew raised his eyes to look at Brian. "That maybe Mom wasn't imagining things all those years ago."

Chapter 5

Still completely in the dark, Brian and Rose exchanged quizzical glances.

Brian was the first to speak. "Mom wasn't wrong about what?"

Andrew looked up as if he'd suddenly become aware that he wasn't alone and talking to himself. "That the hospital had given her the wrong baby." He doled out the words slowly, thoughtfully, as he continued sorting things out in his mind.

"The wrong baby?" Brian echoed, staring at Andrew as if his brother had just sprouted another head. This was making less sense now, not more. "Which one of us is supposed to have been this 'wrong baby'? Mike or me?"

Andrew took a deep breath before answering. It had been a very long time since the name he was about to say had been uttered. An entire lifetime had gone by. It had become a family secret, known to only his late parents and him. Maybe it was time to air out the closet.

"Sean."

"Sean?" Brian repeated, more mystified than ever. "Andrew, maybe you've been standing in the kitchen too long and the heat's gotten to you. I know that there are a lot of Cavanaughs to be tallied these days, but there is no Sean in our family."

"I know." Andrew's eyes met Brian's. "That's because he died."

Brian shook his head as if to clear it. It didn't help. "Andrew, what are you *talking* about?"

In for a penny, in for a pound. He needed to get this whole thing out. It was long overdue.

"Something Mother and Dad never wanted to talk about." He looked from his brother to his wife. "Sit down, Brian. You, too, Rose."

Rose dropped onto the counter stool beside her husband. "I think I'd better. Is this where you tell me I'm married to someone who's descended from the Romanovs?" she asked, clearly trying very hard to lighten the somber mood that was encompassing them.

Maybe he should have done this years ago, after their parents were both gone. But he'd always felt it wasn't his secret to share. And he'd been so young when it was all going down. There were times he had almost talked himself into believing it had all been just a dream.

"No, love." He felt her slip her fingers through his, as if silently offering him her support, no matter what was ahead. God, he loved this woman. "This is where I tell Brian that there were actually four Cavanaugh boys, not three."

None of this was making any sense to Brian, and it was only getting murkier. And if this Sean person was supposedly dead, who was it that he had seen walking into the Crystal Penguin on Friday?

"So where is this Sean?" he asked, struggling with a wave of angry confusion that was totally foreign to him. "Did Mom and Dad decide they could only afford to keep three of us and made us draw straws to see who'd stay and who'd go? And why haven't I heard anything about this before?"

Andrew chose his words very carefully. "Because Sean died before he was a year old." He backtracked a little to give Brian a more concise picture. "He was born between Mike and you." Andrew closed his eyes, remembering the anguish on his mother's face. Everything about the day had left an indelible impression on his young mind. "One morning, Mom got up all sunny because Sean had slept through the night for the first time. She went into the nursery to get him and then I heard her start screaming." As he spoke, it all came back to him in vivid color. "I remember Dad rushing in and then coming out with the baby in his arms, trying desperately to revive him. But it was too late to save him. He was blue. Sean'd died somewhere in the middle of the night." He felt Rose tighten her grasp on his hand. "They called it crib death back then."

"SIDS," Rose murmured. "Sudden infant death syndrome."

Andrew nodded. He noted that Brian still looked confused, and unconvinced.

"So this is what?" Brian pressed. "Sean's ghost walking the earth?"

"No," Andrew answered patiently. "But when she first brought Sean home from the hospital, I'd see Mom staring at him, shaking her head. Saying that she felt there'd been a mix-up in the hospital. That this baby didn't *feel* like *her* baby." He took a deep breath. "After Sean died, Dad told me that maybe some inherent, unconscious defense mechanism had made Mom find reasons not to get close to Sean. He said it was as if she'd subconsciously known that Sean wasn't going to live long.

"The very thought of losing Sean upset her so much, Dad told everyone at the time, including me, that we weren't to talk about Sean anymore." He looked at his youngest brother. "You were born less than a year after that. She went a little overboard and completely doted on you," he reminded Brian.

Brian shrugged, trying to lighten the moment for both his brother and himself. "I always thought it was because I was so adorable."

Andrew laughed shortly and snorted. "Not damn likely."

"So now what?" Rose prodded gently, looking from her husband to her brother-in-law and back again.

"Now," Andrew answered, "we go and find out who this guy who looks like me is—"

"And more important, exactly where and when he was born," Brian interjected. "That includes the name of the hospital."

Rose sighed. Shaking her head, she rose from the stool. "I've got a very strong feeling that I'm going to have to be buying more dishes soon." She looked at the table in the next room. "Not to mention more chairs."

Andrew laughed and gave her a one-arm hug while planting a quick kiss against her temple. "This is one of the reasons why I love you so much, Rose. You're always one step ahead of me."

"Only to keep from being trampled by the Cavanaugh brothers," she quipped just before she left the kitchen.

Since Andrew had dropped this bombshell on his unsuspecting brother, he knew that his wife had made a graceful exit so the two could talk in private. However, he had no doubt that she would ask her own questions later.

With almost five hours of sleep under her belt, Kansas was back at the shelter. Bypassing the yellow crime-scene tape that encircled the entire outer perimeter of what was left of the building, she made her way inside. Once there she began sifting through the rubble in an effort to piece together as much information as she could about what had gone on here less than a day ago.

She'd managed to find the fire's point of origin and also to rule out that the fire had been an accident. She discovered what was left of the incendiary device. It had a timer on it, which could only mean that the fire had been deliberately set, and whoever had done it had a definite time in mind. To kill someone specific? she wondered. If so, whoever had set it had miscalculated. No one had died last night.

The device wasn't a match for the MO of any of the known arsonists or pyromaniacs in the area. There was an outside chance that it could still be the work of someone belonging to one group or the other, someone who had managed to go undetected.

Until now.

It was frustrating, she thought. There *had* to be some kind of a connection, no matter how minor, if she was to believe that these weren't just random fires haphazardly set. But what connection? And why? Why these structures and not the ones down the block or somewhere else? What did these particular buildings that had been torched have in common—assuming, of course, that they actually *had* something in common?

Rocking back on her heels, Kansas ran her hand through her hair and sighed. It was like banging her head against a concrete wall. There were no answers to be found here.

"Penny for your thoughts."

Caught completely off guard, Kansas swallowed a gasp as she jumped to her feet. When she swung around, she found O'Brien watching her from a few feet away. She's been so preoccupied, she hadn't heard anyone come in. She was going to have to work on that, she told herself.

"A penny?" Kansas hooted. "Is that all it's worth to you? I take it I'm in the presence of the last of the big-time spenders."

"I don't believe in throwing my money away," he told her matter-of-factly. "I also didn't expect to find you here."

"Oh?" She looked at him, perplexed. "Tell me, just where would you expect to find a fire investigator, Detective?"

He shrugged, joining her. He looked down at the

rubble she'd been sifting through. "I just thought you'd gotten everything you needed last night."

Maybe he was a little slow on the uptake, she thought. The good-looking ones usually were.

"If I had," she pointed out patiently, crouching down again, "I'd know who did it. Or at least why. Right now, I'm still trying to find all the pieces of that puzzle," she said under her breath.

Crouching down beside her, Ethan looked at what she was doing with interest. "Find anything new?"

Amusement curved her mouth as she glanced up for a moment. "Are you asking me to do your work for you, Detective?"

"No, I'm asking you to share," he corrected. He thought the point of all this was to find who was responsible, not participate in a competition. "We're both part of the same team."

He *couldn't* be that naive. "Detective, not even different divisions of the same department are on the same team, and in case you haven't noticed, you're with the police department and I belong to the fire department. Big difference," she concluded.

He followed her statement to its logical conclusion. "So to you, this is a competition?" He wouldn't have thought that of her, but then, he reminded himself, he really didn't know this woman. Chemistry—and there was plenty of that—was not a substitute for knowledge.

It wasn't a matter of competition, Kansas thought defensively, it was a matter of sharing information with someone she trusted. Right now, she had no basis for that. Moreover, she didn't trust this man any further than she could throw him.

"To me, Detective, you're basically a stranger—"

He finished the statement for her. "And your mother taught you never to speak to strangers, right?"

One would think, after all these years, the word *mother* wouldn't create such a feeling of emptiness and loss within her. But it did.

"I'm sure she would have if I'd had one," Kansas answered, her voice distant. He looked as if he was going to say something apologetic, so she quickly went on. "What I'm saying is that you're an unknown quantity and I haven't got time to waste, wondering if you have some kind of ulterior motive…or if I can confide in you because you're really one of those pure-hearted souls who believes in truth, justice and the American way."

"I think a red cape and blue tights would go with that," he responded dryly. "Me, I'm not that noble. I just want to put this son of a bitch away before he hurts someone else—and if I have to work with the devil or share the stage with him to do it, I will."

There was only one conclusion to be drawn from that. For the second time, Kansas rose to her feet, her hands on her hips. "So now I'm the devil?" she demanded.

He looked surprised that she would come to that conclusion. "No, I didn't say that. You really are something," he freely admitted, "but *devil* isn't the word that readily comes to mind when thinking of you." He flashed a grin at her that shimmied up and down her spine and was totally out of place here. "I was just trying to let you know how far I'd be willing to go to catch this guy if I had to."

His grin, she caught herself thinking, had turned utterly sexy. And he undoubtedly knew that. She'd never met a handsome man who was unaware of the kind of charisma he wielded.

"So," Ethan was saying, "why don't we pool our resources and see what we can accomplish together? Bring your team over to the precinct," he encouraged.

It pained her to admit what she was about to say. "I *am* the team."

"Then you won't need to find a large car to drive over." Ethan put his hand out to seal the bargain. "What do you say?"

She looked down at the hand he held out to her. While she preferred working on her own, the point here was to catch whoever was setting these fires and keep him—or possibly her—from doing it again. The firebug needed to be caught as quickly as possible…before actual lives were lost.

She slipped her hand into his and shook it firmly. "Okay."

"Attagirl." He saw a look come into her eyes he couldn't fathom. Had she just taken that in a condescending manner? "Sorry, I didn't mean it the way it might have sounded. Just expressing relief that I got you to come around so quickly."

Okay, she needed to set him straight right from the beginning. "You didn't get me to 'come around so quickly,' Detective. It's just common sense. You have an entire task force devoted to tracking down this firebug." There was a safe expression, she thought. It didn't espouse any particular theory other than this unbalanced person felt a kinship to flames. "That means you have more resources available to you than I do. We can hopefully move forward more quickly and put an end to this sick reign of fire before someone *is* actually killed."

Ethan nodded in agreement. "A woman after my own heart."

She paused to pin him with a look that spoke volumes. Mostly it issued a warning. "Not even in your wildest dreams, Detective."

Ethan smiled to himself. Nothing goaded him on like a challenge. Maybe, he thought, he'd get this strong-principled, "get the hell out of my way" woman to eat her words. He had a feeling that she could be a hell of a wildcat in bed.

"If you're through here," he said, "you're welcome to come back to the precinct with me now and take a look at the information we've got."

It was probably more than she had compiled. They had only recently been entertaining the idea that the fires were connected and the work of just one person or possibly one team.

Kansas nodded. "Okay, I just might take you up on that, Detective."

"I do have a first name, you know."

Kansas looked at him with the most innocent expression she could muster. "You mean it's not 'Detective'?"

"It's Ethan."

Like he was telling her something she didn't already know. She made it a point to access all the information she could about the people whose paths she crossed.

"Yes, I know. What floor are you on, Detective?" She deliberately used his title.

Ethan laughed softly under his breath. She'd come around in her own time. And if she didn't, well, he could live with that. She wasn't the last beautiful woman he'd ever encounter.

"Third," he answered. "Why?"

She packed up some of the tools she'd been using to collect evidence. "Well, here's a wild thought—so I know where I'm going."

He looked at her quizzically. "I thought I'd take you."

"Yes, I know," she told him. "I'd rather take myself if it's all the same to you. Besides, there's something I need to do first before going to the precinct."

He made an educated guess as to what that was. "You don't have to run this past your captain. The chief of D's has already cleared it with him."

She didn't like being second-guessed. It made her feel hemmed in. "That's all well and good, but that's not what I need to do first."

She still wasn't elaborating. "You always this vague about things?" he wondered.

Her smile widened. "Keeps people guessing." *And me safe,* she added silently. Slipping the recorder she'd been using to tape her thoughts into her case, she snapped the locks into place and picked up the case. "I'll see you in a bit."

He had no idea if she intended to make good on that or if she was just saying it to humor him. All he knew was that he fully intended to see her again, fire or no fire.

* * *

Dax paced back and forth before the bulletin boards in the front of the room.

"There's *got* to be some kind of pattern here," he insisted, staring at the three bulletin boards he'd had brought into the task force's makeshift squad room.

Each fire had its own column with as much information as they could find listed directly beneath it. All the fires had all broken out in the last six months in and around Aurora. Other than that, there was nothing uniform and no attention-grabbing similarities about them.

And yet, he had a gut feeling that there had to be. What was he missing?

"If there is," Ortiz commented in a lackluster tone, "I can't see it." Rocking in his seat, Ortiz slowly sipped his extra-large container of chai tea. He drank the beverage religiously at least once a day, claiming it gave him mental clarity.

The others knew better. Especially after Ethan had pointed out that Ortiz liked to flirt with the cute dark-haired girl behind the counter who filled the detective's order as well as his less-than-anemic imagination.

"Maybe we're including too many fires," Ethan speculated, gesturing at the bulletin boards with its news clippings.

"Isn't that the point?" Youngman questioned. "These are all the fires that've taken place in and around Aurora in the last six months. If we don't include all of them, we might come up with the *wrong* pattern."

He knew he was playing devil's advocate here, but they had to explore all the avenues before they found the one that would lead them to the right answer. To the man or men responsible for all that destruction.

"But maybe they weren't all set by the same guy," Ethan insisted.

"But they *were* all set."

Ethan, Dax, Youngman and Ortiz all turned to see Kansas walking into the small, cluttered room that the task force was temporarily using to cut down on any distractions from the other detectives.

She walked as if she owned the room.

"And we won't come up with the wrong answer," she assured them with feeling. "If we just keep talking all this out long enough, we're going to either find the answer, which has been right in front of us all along, or stumble across something that'll eventually lead us to the right answer.

"But one way or the other," Kansas concluded, "we *are* going to get to the bottom of this."

Her eyes swept over the four detectives. There was no mistaking the confidence in her voice.

Ethan couldn't help wondering if she meant it, or if she was just saying that for their benefit, giving them a glimpse of her own version of whistling in the dark to keep the demons at bay.

It wouldn't be the first time that he'd encountered female bravado. Because of his sister, Greer, he'd been raised with it. He had a gut feeling that the two women were very much alike.

Chapter 6

Ethan was the first to break the silence.

"My money's still on an arsonist doing this," he said even though he knew that the new, adjunct member of the team vehemently disagreed with this theory.

Kansas thought about holding her tongue. She was, after all, the outsider here, and arguing was not the way to become part of the team. She'd stated her point of view and should just let it go at that.

But she'd never been one to merely go with the flow. It just wasn't part of her nature. The words seemed to come out almost of their own accord.

"Where's the profit to be gained from burning down a church and an abused-women's shelter that's already pretty run-down?" she challenged.

"Real estate," Ethan argued. "The places aren't worth anything as they are, and there might be little or no insurance on the structures, so there's definitely not enough money to rebuild. That would make whoever owns the property willing and maybe eager to sell." He shrugged. "Maybe they feel that they can start somewhere else with the money they get from selling the land the property stands on."

Kansas rolled her eyes at his explanation. "So, in your opinion, some big, bad CEO is paying someone to run around and burn down buildings in and around Aurora in order to put together a colossal shopping mall or something to that effect?"

Ethan scowled. He didn't care for her dismissive tone. "It sounds stupid when you say it that way," he accused.

"That's because it *is* stupid—no matter which way you say it," Kansas pointed out, happy that he got the point.

Dax literally got in between his cousin and the woman his father felt they needed to work with.

"Children, children, play nice," he instructed, looking from one to the other to make sure that his words sank in. "And in the meantime," he said, turning to another detective, "Ortiz, see if you can check with Records down at the civic center to see if anyone has put in for permits to start building anything of any consequence."

"If Ortiz doesn't find anything, it doesn't mean the theory doesn't hold up," Ethan interjected.

Dax crossed his arms before his chest, striking a pose that said he was waiting for more. "Go ahead. I'm listening."

"It just means that whoever it is who's doing this hasn't had time to properly file his intent to build whatever it is that he's going to build," Ethan explained. "The destroyed properties are far from desirable, so maybe he figures he has time. And the longer he takes to get to 'step two,' the less likely it'll be that someone will make the connection between the arson and the motive behind it."

Kansas supposed that O'Brien had a point. She wasn't so married to her theory that she would stubbornly shut her eyes to exclude everything else.

"Maybe we should check out whether anyone's bought any of the properties previously destroyed by the fires," she suggested.

"Then you're on board with this theory?" O'Brien asked. There was a touch of triumph in his voice that irritated her. It had her reverting to her original theory.

"No, I just want to put it to rest once and for all." Her eyes narrowed ever so slightly as she continued. "I'd stake my job that this isn't a fire-for-hire situation." She could feel it in her bones, but she wasn't about to say that out loud. She didn't know these people well enough to allow them to laugh at her, even good-naturedly. "It's some pyromaniac getting his high out of watching everyone scramble, trying to keep the fire from destroying another piece of real estate. Another person's hopes and dreams."

Dax was still open to all possibilities until something started to gel. "Okay, why don't you and Youngman go check it out," he instructed her. "Begin with the first fire on the list and work your way up."

But Youngman shook his head. "No can do, Dax. I've got that dental appointment to go to. Doc says it's going to take the better part of two hours to do the root canal." He cupped his right cheek to underscore his situation. "I'd cancel, but I already did that once, and this thing is just *killing* me."

Dax nodded. Youngman had already told him about the appointment this morning. Things were getting so hectic, he'd just forgotten. "Go. Get it seen to." Without missing a beat, Dax turned to his cousin. "Take his place, Ethan."

"In the dental chair?" Ethan asked hopefully.

"Very funny. You, her, go," Dax said, nodding toward the door. "See what you can come up with that might get your theory to float."

"An anchor comes to mind," Kansas muttered under her breath.

Grabbing his jacket and slipping it on, Ethan shot her an annoyed look. He was going to enjoy putting her in her place. And then, once the shrew was tamed, other possibilities might open up, he mused.

"I'll drive," he announced as they left the squad room. He punched the down button for the elevator.

The statement was met with a careless shrug. "If it's that important to you, I wouldn't dream of fighting with you about it," she murmured.

The elevator car arrived and she stepped in. He was quick to get in with her, then pressed the button for the first floor.

"It's not important to me," he informed her, his irritation growing. Supposedly, the woman was agreeing with him. But it was the manner in which she was agreeing that he found annoying. "It's just that—"

She turned the most innocent expression he'd ever seen in his direction. "Yes?"

The woman was playing him. The second the steel doors parted, he all but shot out of the elevator, heading for the precinct entrance. "Never mind," he ground out. "You want to drive? Because if you do, we'll take your car."

She preceded him outside. There was a soft spring breeze rustling through everything, quietly reminding them that at any moment, it could pick up and fan any flames it encountered.

"You don't trust me with your car?" she asked. *Typical male*, she thought.

"I don't trust *anybody* with my car," he told her. "I spent too much time, effort and money restoring her to just hand the keys over to someone else."

Sounded like the man was obsessed with his car, she thought. The smile she raised to her lips was the embodiment of serenity. "You can drive," she told him. "It's okay."

She was yanking his chain—and a few other things, as well. He led the way to his car, parked over in the third row. "Why do I get the feeling that you're laughing at me?"

The woman looked as if she were seriously considering the question. "My first guess would be insecurity," she said brightly.

"Your first guess would be wrong," he retorted.

She paused before the cream-colored two-seater. She wasn't really up on cars, but she recognized it as a classic. "It really is a beauty," she told him.

The compliment instantly softened him. "Thanks."

He pressed the security button on his key chain and released the locks. "You have the list of sites where the fires took place?" he asked. Since she'd already gotten in on her side, he slid in behind the steering wheel—and saw that instead of buckling up, she was holding up several sheets of paper. He presumed they were the list he'd referred to. "Okay, where to first?"

"How about MacArthur and Main?" she suggested after a beat. "That's the church," she explained, shifting as she buckled her seat belt. "That was the second fire," she added in case he'd forgotten.

He hadn't. "Where that firefighter rescued the visiting priest from Spain. The priest was sleeping in Father Colm's room," he recalled.

She vividly remembered all the details of that one. Daring, last-minute rescues like that always tugged on her heartstrings. "There was footage of the old priest being carried out of the burning building."

The media, always hungry for something to sink its teeth into, carried the story for days, and the morning talk shows vied for the exclusive rights to being the first to interview both the firefighter and the priest, sitting in the studio side by side.

He thought of the theory that he'd espoused. It seemed rather shaky here. "I really doubt that the church is being put up for sale."

"I doubt it, too," she agreed. Since he'd backed off, she could afford to be magnanimous. "But we can still ask if anyone made any offers on the property since the fire." She shrugged again. "At any rate, it's better than nothing."

As he drove, he slanted a glance at her, looking for

confirmation in her expression. "You're humoring me, aren't you?"

"No," she said honestly, sitting back in her seat, "what I'm trying to do is prove or disprove your theory once and for all so we can move on."

He knew which side of the argument she was on, and he didn't care for being summarily dismissed. "What if it turns out that I'm right?"

"Then, most likely," she recited, "you'll be impossible to live with and I'll be happy that I'm not part of the police department, because I won't have to put up with it. But even if hell does freeze over and you're right, the upshot will be that we've caught the person or persons responsible for all this destruction, and that'll be a very good thing." And then the corners of her mouth curved in a forced smile. "But you won't be right, so there's no point in anticipating it."

The woman was being downright smug, he thought. Since when did he find smug so arousing? "You're that sure?"

She lifted her chin ever so slightly, making it a good target, he couldn't help thinking. Damn, his feelings were bouncing all over the place today. "I'm that sure."

The light up ahead turned yellow. In any other car he would have stepped on the gas and flown through. But this was his baby, and he eased into a stop at the intersection several beats before the light turned red.

"Tell me," he said, turning toward her, "do you walk on water all the time, or just on Sundays?"

"Mainly Sundays," she answered with a straight face. There wasn't even a hint of a smile. "There's the church." She pointed to the building in the distance on the right. "Looks like it's being rebuilt."

The light turned green. Ethan drove over to the church and said nothing as he pulled the vehicle into the parking lot. He brought his vehicle to a stop in front of the partially demolished building.

Kansas was out of the car before he had a chance to pull up the handbrake. For a woman who was wearing rather high heels, she moved inordinately quickly, he thought.

Kansas was more than several strides ahead of him by the time he got out.

"Father," she called out to the cleric, waving her hand to get his attention.

A white-haired man in jeans and a sweatshirt, its sleeves pushed all the way back beyond his elbows, turned around in response to her call. He was holding on to the base of a ladder that was up against the side of the church, keeping it steady while a much younger man stood close to the top, trying to spread an even layer of stucco.

Kansas flipped her wallet open to her ID and held it up for the priest to see as she approached. "I'm Investigator Kansas Beckett—with the fire department." Putting her ID away, she nodded toward Ethan. "This is Detective Ethan O'Brien with the Aurora PD. We're looking into this awful fire that almost took down your church, Father."

"*Almost* being the key word," the priest responded with a pleased smile. He turned back to look at the church. His smile told her that he was seeing beyond what was currently standing before them.

"I see that you're rebuilding," Ethan observed.

"Not me," the priest answered modestly. "I'm just holding the ladder, stirring paint, that sort of thing. St. Angela's is blessed to have such a talented congregation." He beamed, looking up the ladder he was holding steady. "Mr. Wicks is a general contractor who, luckily for us, is temporarily in between assignments, and he kindly volunteered to give us the benefit of his expertise."

The man Father Colm was referring to climbed down the ladder. Once his feet were on the ground, he shook hands with Ethan and Kansas, holding on to her hand, she noted, a beat longer than necessary. But she did like the appreciative smile on his lips as he looked at her.

Flattery without any possibility of entanglement. The best of all worlds, she thought.

"By 'in between,' Father Colm means unemployed." Wicks regarded the older man with affection. "I'm just glad to help. It keeps me active and allows me to practice my trade so I don't forget what to do. It's been a *long* dry spell," he confessed.

"With so many of the parishioners volunteering their time and talent, it won't be long before we have the church whole and functional again," the priest informed them with no small amount of pride.

It was as good an opening as any, Kansas thought. "Father, right after the fire—"

"Terrible, terrible time," the priest murmured, shaking his head. His bright blue eyes shone with tears as he recalled. "I was afraid that the Vatican wouldn't approve of our being here any longer and would just authorize everyone to attend Our Lady of Angels Church on the other end of Aurora."

Kansas waited politely for the priest to finish unloading the sentiments that were weighing down on him. When he stopped, she continued her line of questioning. "Did anyone come with an offer to take the property off your hands? Or, more aptly I guess, off the Church's hands?"

"The only ones who approached me," Father Colm told her and O'Brien, "were Mr. Wick and some of the other parishioners. Everyone's been so generous, donating either their time, or money, or sometimes even both, to rebuild St. Angela's." He sighed deeply. "I am a very, very blessed man." There was a hitch in his voice and he stopped to clear it.

Ethan rephrased the question, asking it again, just to be perfectly clear about the events. "So, you're sure that no one offered to give you money for the property, saying you'd be better off starting over somewhere else from the ground up?"

"No, Detective O'Brien," the priest assured him. "I might be old, but I would have remembered that. Because I would have said no. I've been here for thirty-six years. I'm too old to start at a new location." And then he paused, looking from one to the other, before exchanging puzzled looks with the general contractor. "Why do you ask?"

O'Brien hesitated. Kansas saw no reason for secrecy, not with the priest. So she was the one who answered the man. "We're investigating the rash of recent fires in Aurora. Yours was among the first. We're attempting to find a common motive."

Father Colm looked horrified. "You seriously think

that someone *deliberately* tried to burn down St. Angela's?"

"All evidence points to the fact that the fire here wasn't just an accident. It was set," Ethan told the priest.

"You're kidding," Wicks said, looking as if he'd been broadsided.

Father Colm shook his head, his expression adamant. "No, I refuse to think of this as a hate crime, Detective O'Brien. That's just too terrible a thought to entertain."

"I don't believe that it was a hate crime, either," Kansas assured him. Although, she supposed that would be another avenue they could explore if they ran out of options. "This is the only church that was burned down. If it were a hate crime, there would have been at least a few more places of worship, more churches targeted. Instead, the range of structures that were torched is quite wide and diverse."

The priest looked as if he were struggling to absorb the theory. "But the fires were all deliberately set?"

O'Brien looked as if he were searching for a diplomatic way to phrase his answer. Kansas took the straightforward path. "Yes."

The old man, a priest for fifty-one years, appeared shell-shocked. "Why?" The question came out in a hoarse whisper.

"That, Father, is what we're trying to find out," Ethan told him, thinking that they had just come full circle. He was quick to launch into basic questions of his own.

Again the priest, and this time Wicks, were asked if there was anything unusual about that day, anything out of the ordinary that either of them could remember seeing or hearing, no matter how minor.

Nothing came to either of the men's minds.

Kansas nodded. She really hadn't expected any earthshaking revelations. Hoped, but hadn't expected.

She dug into her pocket and retrieved two of her cards. "If either of you *do* think of anything," Kansas told the men as she held out her business cards, offering one to each of them, "please call me."

Ethan gave the priest and Wicks his own card. "Please call us," he amended, glancing in Kansas's direction and silently reprimanding her for what he took to be her attempt to edge him out.

"Right, us," Kansas corrected with a quirk of a smile that came and left her lips in less than a heartbeat. "I forgot I'm temporarily assigned to Detective O'Brien's task force," she confided to the priest.

Father Colm nodded, apparently giving his whole-hearted approval to the venture. "The more minds working on this, the faster this terrible situation will be resolved."

She'd never gone to any house of worship. There'd been no one to urge her to choose one religion over the other, no one to care if she prayed or not. But if she were to choose a single place, she thought, it would be one whose pastor was loving and kind. A pastor like Father Colm.

Kansas flashed a grin at the cleric. "From your lips to God's ears," she said, reciting a phrase she'd once heard one of the social workers say to one of the other children in the group home.

Father Colm laughed warmly in response. Kansas

found the sound strangely reassuring. "I'll be back," she promised.

The bright blue eyes met hers. "Feel free to stop by anytime," the priest urged. "God's house is always open to you."

Kansas merely nodded as she left.

O'Brien and she made no headway of any kind at site of the second fire. The charred remains of the building were still there, abandoned by one and all and presently neglected by the city. Kansas made a mental note to look up the current status of the property and see who owned it.

The site of the third fire, a movie triplex that had gone up in flames long after the last show had let out, appeared to be suffering the same fate as the second site. Except that someone had put in a bid for it.

In front of the burnt-out shell that had once contained three movie theaters was a relatively new sign announcing that several stores were coming soon to that area. The name of the developer was printed in block letters on the bottom right-hand side of the sign. Brad McCormack and Sons.

Kansas wrote the name down in her small, battered notepad. "What do you say to paying Mr. McCormack a visit?" she asked when she finished.

"Sure," Ethan agreed. He glanced at his watch. "How about right after lunch?"

"It's too early for lunch," she protested. She wanted to keep going until they actually had something to work with.

"It's almost noon," he pointed out. "What time do you eat lunch?"

It couldn't be that late. Kansas glanced at her watch, ready to prove him wrong. Except that she couldn't. "You're right," she muttered.

"I know. I had to learn how to tell time before they'd let me join the police force," he told her dryly.

She sighed, walking back to his car. "Did you have to learn sarcasm, as well? Or was that something you brought to the table on your own?"

"The latter." He waited until she got in. Because she'd leaned her hand on the car's hood for a moment, Ethan doubled back and wiped way the print with a handkerchief before finally getting in on his side. He didn't have to look at her to know that Kansas had rolled her eyes. "And speaking of table, where would you like to go for lunch?"

He wasn't going to stop until she gave in, she thought. That could start a dangerous precedent. *Where the hell had that come from?* she wondered, caught off guard by her own thoughts.

Out loud she asked, "What is it with you and food?"

"I like having it. Keeps me from being grumpy." He looked at her pointedly as he started up the vehicle. "You might want to think about trying it sometime. Might do wonders for your personality."

She let the comment pass. "All right, since you have to eat, how about a drive-through?"

He was thinking more in terms of sitting back and recharging for an hour. "How about a sit-down restaurant with table and chairs?" he countered.

She merely looked at him. "Takes less than twenty minutes to start a fire."

Yeah, he thought, his eyes washing over the woman sitting next to him in the vehicle. *Tell me something I didn't already know.*

And then he sighed. "Drive-through it is."

Chapter 7

"Is it okay to pull over somewhere and eat this, or do we have to ingest lunch while en route to the next destination?" Ethan asked dryly, driving away from the fast-food restaurant's take-out window.

The bag with their lunches was resting precariously against his thigh while the two containers of economy-sized sodas were nestled in the vehicle's cup holders. The plastic lids that covered the containers looked far from secure.

Amused rather than annoyed by the detective's sarcasm, Kansas answered, "It's okay to pull over. I just meant that going inside a restaurant is usually a full-hour proposition, especially at this time of day. And if we're going to spend time together, I'd rather it was at one of the sites where the fires took place."

Driving to a relatively empty corner of the parking lot that accommodated seven different fast-food establishments, Ethan pulled up the parking brake. He rolled down his window and shut off the engine. Glancing inside the oversized paper bag he'd been awarded at the drive-through window, he pulled out a long, tubular, green-wrapped item and held it out to her.

"This is yours, I believe. I ordered the cheeseburger."

"I know. Not exactly very imaginative," Kansas commented, taking the meat-and-cheese wrap from him.

She tried not to notice how infectious his grin was. "Sue me. I like basic things. I'm a very uncomplicated guy."

Uncomplicated? Kansas raised her eyes to his. *Who does he think he's kidding?*

Drop-dead gorgeous men with their own agendas were generally as difficult to figure out as a Rubik's Cube. Definitely *not* uncomplicated.

"Yeah, I'll bet," she muttered audibly just before taking her first bite.

With a cheeseburger in one hand, he reached into the bag with the other and pulled out several French fries. He held them out to her. "Want some of my fries?" he offered.

She shook her head, swallowing another bite. She hadn't realized until she'd started eating just how hungry she actually was. If she didn't know better, she would have said her stomach was celebrating. "No, I'm good, thanks."

A hint of a smile curved his mouth. "I'm sure you are."

The low, sultry tone he'd used had her looking at him again, but she kept silent. She had a feeling that she was better off not knowing the explanation behind his words. No doubt, the path to seduction, or what he perceived as the path to seduction, was mixed in there somewhere.

Giving her full attention to eating the turkey-and-pastrami wrap she'd ordered, Kansas was in no way prepared for what came next.

"You never knew your mother?"

The bite she'd just taken went down her windpipe instead of her esophagus. She started coughing until there were tears in her eyes. Abandoning his lunch, Ethan twisted her in her seat and began pounding on her back until she held her hand up in surrender.

"It's okay. I'm okay," she protested, trying to catch her breath. When she finally did, her eyes still somewhat watery, she looked at O'Brien. "Where did that come from?"

He slid back into his seat. "From what you said earlier."

Her mind a blank, she shook her head. "I don't recall."

He had a feeling that she remembered but was dismissing the subject outright. "When I made that crack about your mother teaching you not to talk to strangers and you answered that you were sure she would have if you'd had one."

Kansas placed what was left of the wrap down on the paper it had come in and looked at him. "Where is this going?"

There was a dangerous note in her voice that warned

him to tread lightly. Or better yet, back off. "I was just curious if your mother died when you were very young."

Her expression was stony as she told him, "I have no idea if she's dead or alive. Now could we drop this?" she asked in the coldest tone she'd ever summoned.

It wasn't cold enough. "You didn't know her." It didn't take much of a stretch for him to guess that.

The first reply that came to her lips was to tell him to damn well mind his own business, but she had a feeling that the retort would fall on deaf ears. He didn't strike her as the type to back off unless he wanted to. The best way to be done with this was just to answer his question as directly and precisely as possible.

"No, I didn't know her." She addressed her answer to the windshield as she stared straight ahead. "All I know is that she left me on the steps of a hospital when I was a few days old."

Sympathy and pity as well as a wave of empathy stirred within him. There'd been times, when he was much younger, when he'd felt the sting of missing a parent, but his mother had always been there for all of them. What must it have been like for her, not having either in her life?

"You're an orphan?"

He saw her jawline harden. "That's one of the terms for it. 'Throwaway' was another one someone once used," she recalled, her voice distant, devoid of any feeling.

She wasn't fooling him. Something like that came wrapped in pain that lasted a lifetime. "No one ever adopted you?"

She finally turned toward him. Her mouth quirked in a smile that didn't reach her eyes. "Hard to believe that no one wanted me, seeing as how I have this sweet personality and all?" One of the social workers had called her unadoptable after a third set of foster parents had brought her back.

He knew what she was doing, and he hadn't meant to make her feel self-conscious or bring back any painful memories. "I'm sorry."

Her back was up even as she carelessly shrugged away his apology. "Hey, things happen."

"Do you ever wonder—"

She knew what he was going to ask. If she ever wondered about who her parents had been. Or maybe if she wondered what it would have been like if at least her mother had kept her. She had, in both cases, but she wasn't about to talk to him about it. That was something she kept locked away.

"No," she said sharply, cutting him off. "Never." Balling up the remainder of her lunch, she tossed it and the wrapper into the bag. "Now, unless you've secretly been commissioned to write my biography, I'd appreciate it if you'd stop asking me questions that aren't going to further this investigation." She nodded at the burger he was still holding. "Finish your lunch."

Not until he evened the playing field for her, he thought. He didn't want her thinking he was trying to be superior or put her down in any manner. That was not the way he operated.

"I never knew my father."

Oh no, they weren't going to sit here, swapping deep-down secrets that he hoped would ultimately disarm her so that he could get into her bed. It wasn't going to work that way. It had once, but she'd been very young and vulnerable then. And stupid. She'd grown up a lot since she'd made that awful mistake and married a man she thought could be her shelter from the cruelties of life. Grown up enough to know that there would never be anyone out there to love her the way she needed to be loved.

The way she so desperately wanted to be loved.

Like it or not, she'd made her peace with that and she wasn't about to suddenly grow stupid because the guy sitting across from her with the chiseled profile and the soulfully beautiful blue eyes was doing his best to sound "nice."

Kansas looked at him and said flatly, "I don't want to know this."

Ethan didn't seem to hear her. Or, if he did, it didn't deter him. He went on as if she hadn't said anything.

"My mother told us he died on the battlefield, saving his friends. That he was a hero." For a moment, a faraway look came into his eyes as bits and pieces of that time came back to him. "She told us a lot of things about our father, always emphasizing that we had a lot to be proud of."

She had no idea why he was telling her this. Did he think that sharing this was going to somehow bring them closer? "Okay, so you had a legend for a father and I didn't. How does this—"

She didn't get to finish framing her question. His eyes met hers and he said very simply, without emotion, "She lied."

That brought what she was about to say to a screeching halt. Kansas stared at him. "Excuse me?"

"She lied," he repeated and then, for emphasis, said again, "My mother lied."

Despite her initial resolve, Kansas could feel herself being drawn in ever so slowly. It was the look in his eyes that did it. She supposed, since O'Brien seemed so bent on talking, that she might as well try to gain a measure of control over the conversation. "About his being a hero?"

If only, Ethan thought. If it had just been that, he could have easily made his peace with it. But it went far beyond a mere white lie. And it made him slow to trust anyone other than Kyle and Greer, the only two people in the world who had been as affected as him by this revelation.

"About all of it. Everything she'd told us was just a lie."

Kansas felt for him. She would have been devastated in his place. *If* what he said was true. "How did you find out?"

"From her. On her deathbed." *God, that sounded so melodramatic,* he thought. But it was the truth. Had his mother not been dying, he was certain that the lie would have continued indefinitely. "She knew she didn't have much longer, and apparently she wanted to die with a clear conscience."

Kansas took a guess as to what was behind the initial lie. "She didn't know who your father was?"

"Oh, she knew, all right." An edge entered Ethan's voice. "He was the man who abandoned her when she told him she was pregnant. The man who bullied her into not telling anyone about the relationship they'd had. If she did, according to what she told us, he promised that he would make her life a living hell."

Kansas didn't know what to say. Going by her own feelings in this sort of a situation, she instinctively knew he wouldn't want her pity. She shook her head, commiserating. "Sounds like a winner."

"Yeah, well, not every Cavanaugh turned out to be sterling—although, so far, my 'father' seems to be the only one in the family who dropped the ball."

The last name made her sit up and take notice. Her eyes widened. "Are you telling me that Brian Cavanaugh is your father?"

He realized that he hadn't been specific. "No, it's not Brian—"

"Andrew?" she interjected. She'd never met the man, but the detective had mentioned him and she knew the man by reputation. The very thought that Andrew Cavanaugh would have a love child he refused to publicly acknowledge sounded completely preposterous, especially since he was known for throwing open his doors to *everyone*.

But then, she thought, reconsidering, did anyone really ever know anyone else? When she'd gotten married, she would have sworn that Grant would never hurt her—and she'd been incredibly wrong about that.

"No, not Andrew, either." He would have been proud to call either man his father, but life hardly ever arranged itself perfectly.

She frowned. *Was* he pulling her leg? "All the other Cavanaughs are too young," she retorted. The oldest was possibly ten or twelve years older than O'Brien. Maybe less.

"It was Mike Cavanaugh," he said flatly.

Mike. Michael. Kansas shook her head. "I'm afraid I don't know who that is."

"Was," he corrected her. "Mike Cavanaugh died in the line of duty a number of years ago. Patience and Patrick are his legitimate kids—"

She stopped him cold. He was treading on terrain that encompassed one of her pet peeves.

"Every kid is 'legitimate,'" she said with feeling. "It's the parents who aren't always legitimate, not thinking beyond the moment or weighing any of the consequences of their actions. Allowing themselves to get careless and carried away without any regard for who they might wind up hurting—"

Ethan held up his hand to get her to stop. "I'm not trying to get into an argument with you," he told her. "I'm trying to make you see that we have more in common than you think."

Not really, she thought.

"At least you *had* a mother, a mother who tried to shield you from her mistake, however badly she might have done it. A mother who tried to give you something to believe in. Mine couldn't be bothered to do anything except to literally pin a name on me that would always make me the butt of jokes." She saw him looking at her quizzically and elaborated. "She pinned a piece of paper to my blanket that said, 'Her name is Kansas. I can't raise her.' That's it. Eight words. My entire legacy, eight words."

"At least she did give you a chance to live," he pointed

out. "I've seen newborn babies thrown out in garbage cans, discarded by the wayside, like spoiled meat." He recalled one specific case that had taken him months to get out of his head.

Kansas sat silent in the car, studying him for a long moment. Just as the silence began to seem as if it was going on too long, she said, "You're a silver-lining kind of guy, aren't you?"

Kyle had been the last one to accuse him of that, except that the terminology his brother had used wasn't quite as squeaky-clean as what Kansas had just said.

"Once in a while," he allowed. "It does help sometimes."

Kansas didn't agree. Optimists tended to be stomped on. She'd been down that route and learned her lesson early on.

"Being a realist helps," she countered. "That way, you don't wind up being disappointed." Her mouth feeling exceptionally dry, she stopped to drain the last of her soft drink. "What do you say we get this show on the road and go talk to Mr. Silver, the owner of that discount store that burned down?" In case he'd forgotten, she prompted, "It was the fourth fire."

He nodded, recalling the notes he'd written beneath the photos on the bulletin board. "That was the fire that led the chief of D's to believe that there was just one person setting all of them."

"Right." Captain Lawrence had mentioned that to her in passing.

O'Brien turned the key in the ignition and started the car. Just as he was about to shift out of Park, she put her hand on top of his, stopping him. He could have sworn he felt something akin to electricity pass through him just then. Masking it, he looked at Kansas quizzically.

"This all stays here, right?" she questioned sharply. "What we just talked about, my background, it stays here, between us. It goes no further. Right?" This time it sounded more like an order than a question. Or, at the very least, like a sharply voiced request for a confirmation.

"Absolutely," he assured her immediately. Pulling out of the spot and then merging onto the street, he slanted a glance in her direction. "But if you find you ever want to just talk about it—"

She cut him off before he could complete his offer. "I won't."

The lady doth protest too much, he thought. "Okay," he allowed. "But should hell begin to freeze over and you find that you've changed your mind, you know where to find me."

"Don't worry," Kansas assured him. "I won't be looking."

She bottled things up too much, he thought. He'd had one of his friends, a firefighter at another house, discreetly ask around about this woman. She didn't go out of her way to socialize and definitely didn't hang out with the firefighters after hours. She was, for all intents and purposes, a loner. Loners tended to be lonely people, and while he had no illusions or desires to change the course of her life, he did want to offer her his friendship, for whatever that was worth to her.

"Ever heard that poem about no man being an island?" he asked.

She could feel her back going up even as she tried to tell herself that O'Brien didn't mean anything by this. That he wasn't trying to demean her.

"Yeah," she acknowledged with a dismissive tone. "It was about men. Women have a different set of rules."

He doubted that she really believed that. She was just being defensive. She did that a lot, he realized. "Underneath it all, we're just human beings."

"Stop trying to get into my head, O'Brien," she warned. "You'll find it's very inhospitable territory."

He debated letting this drop and saying nothing. The debate was short. "You're trying too hard, Kansas."

God, she hated her name. It always sounded as if the person addressing her were being sarcastic. "Excuse me?"

"I said you're trying too hard," he repeated, knowing that she'd heard him the first time. "You don't have to be so macho. This isn't strictly a man's field anymore. Trust me, just be yourself and you'll have the men around here jumping through hoops every time you crook your little finger."

Was he serious? Did he actually think she was going to fall for that? "I don't know if that's insulting me or you. Or both."

"Wasn't meant to do either," he said easily, making a right turn to the next corner. He slowed down as he did so and gave her a quick glance. "You really are a beautiful woman, you know."

She straightened, doing her best to look indignant even as a warmth insisted on spreading through her. "I'd rather be thought of as an intelligent, sharp woman, not a beautiful one."

He saw no conflict in that. "You can be both," he answered matter-of-factly, then added more softly, "You are both."

Kansas frowned. Oh, he was a charmer, this temporary partner of hers. He was probably accustomed to women dropping like flies whenever he decided to lay it on. Well, he was in for a surprise. She wasn't going to let herself believe a word coming out of his mouth, no matter how tempting that was or how guileless he sounded as he delivered those words. She'd had the infection and gotten the cure. She was never going to allow herself to be led astray again. Ever.

"Don't you know that ingesting too much sugar can lead to diabetes?" she asked sarcastically.

"I'll keep that in mind," he promised, not bothering to keep a straight face. "Were the cross streets for that discount house Culver and Bryan?"

"Culver and Trabuco," she corrected.

As soon as she said it, he remembered. "That's right." He laughed shortly. "After a while, all the names and descriptions start running together."

"Not to me," she informed him crisply. "Each and every one of the buildings are different. Like people," she added.

The way she said it, he knew she wasn't trying to sound high-handed or find fault with him. She meant it. It was almost as if every fire had a separate meaning for her.

Ethan had a feeling that the fire inspector he'd initially felt that he'd been saddled with had more than one outstanding secret in her closet. He meant to find out how many and what they were, although, for the life of

him, he couldn't clearly state *why* he was so determined
to do this. Why he wanted to unravel the mystery that
was Kansas Beckett.

But he did.

Chapter 8

They were getting nowhere.

Five days of diligently combing through ashes, testimonies and the arrest records of felons who had a penchant for playing with fire hadn't brought them to any new conclusions, other than to reinforce what they already knew: that there were some very strange sociopaths walking the earth.

Their lack of headway wasn't for lack of tips. What they did lack for, however, were tips that didn't take them on elaborate wild-goose chases.

With a frustrated sigh, Ethan leaned back in his chair. He rocked slightly as he stared off into space. The lack of progress was getting to him. The latest "person of interest" he was looking into turned out to have been in jail when the fire spree initially started. Which brought them back to square one.

Again.

"I'm beginning to feel like a dog chasing his own tail," he said out loud, not bothering to hide his disgust.

Kansas looked up from the computer screen she'd been reading. "I'd pay to see that," she volunteered.

Closing her eyes, Kansas passed her hand over her forehead. There was a headache building there, and she felt as if she were going cross-eyed. She'd lost track of the number of hours she'd been sitting here, at the desk that had been temporarily assigned to her, going through databases that tracked recent fires throughout the western states in hopes of finding something that might lead to the firebug's identity. Every single possibility had led to a dead end.

There had to be something they were missing, she thought in exasperation. Fires that could be traced to accelerants just didn't start themselves. Who the hell was doing this, and when was he finally going to slip up?

Noting the way Kansas was rubbing her forehead, Ethan opened his bottom drawer and dug out the container with his supply of extra-strength aspirin in it. In the interest of efficiency, he always bought the economy size. He rounded his desk and placed the container on top of hers.

The sound of pills jostling against one another as he set the bottle down had Kansas opening her eyes again. She saw the bottle, then raised her eyes to his. "What's that?"

"Modern science calls it aspirin. You can call it whatever you want," Ethan told her, sitting down at his desk again. Because she was looking at the oversized bottle as if she wasn't sure what it might really hold, he said, "You look like you have a headache. I thought a few aspirins might help."

Picking the bottle up, Kansas shook her head in wonder. "This has *got* to be the biggest supply of aspirin I've ever seen."

"We get it by the truckload around here," Dax told her as he walked into the room, catching the tail end of the conversation. He raised his voice slightly to catch the rest of the task force's attention. "I suggest you all take a few with you."

Kansas swung her chair around to face Dax. A leaden feeling descended on her chest. There could be only one reason why he was saying that. "Another one?"

"Another one," Dax confirmed grimly. "Just got the call."

Ethan was on his feet, grabbing his jacket and slipping it on. "Where?"

"Down on Sand Canyon," he answered. "The place is called Meadow Hills."

Kansas stopped dead. She recognized the name instantly. "That's a nursing home," she said to Dax, but even as she said it, she was hoping that somehow she was wrong.

She wasn't.

Dax nodded, holding a tight rein on his thoughts. He was not about to let his imagination run away with him. "Yeah."

Kansas shuddered, trying to curtail the wave of horror that washed over her. She couldn't get the image of terrified senior citizens out of her head.

"What a monster," she muttered.

"It's still in progress," Dax told them as they all

hurried out the door. "Luckily, the firefighters got there quickly again. They've been a regular godsend. They had a lot of people to clear out, and I'd hate to think of what might have happened if they'd delayed their response even by a few minutes."

Kansas said nothing. She didn't even want to think about it, about how helpless and frightened some of those older residents of the convalescent home had to feel, their bodies immobilized in beds as they smelled smoke and then having that smoke fill their fragile lungs.

Another wave of frustration assaulted her, intensifying the pain in her head.

"Why can't we find this bastard?" she cried, directing the question more to herself than to any of the men who were hurrying down the hall along with her.

"Because he's good," Ethan answered plainly. "He's damn good."

"But he's not perfect," she shot back angrily.

"That's what we're all counting on," Dax told her.

Reaching the elevator first, Kansas jabbed the down button. When it failed to arrive immediately, she turned on her heel and hurried over to the door that led to the stairwell.

Ethan was quick to follow her. "Running down the stairs really isn't going to make that much of a difference," he told her, watching the rhythmic way her hips swayed as she made her way to the door. "In the long run, it won't get you there any faster."

Kansas didn't slow down. Entering the stairwell, she started down the stairs, her heels clicking on the metal steps.

"I know," she tossed over her shoulder. "I just need to be moving." She hadn't really meant to share that. What was it about this man that seemed to draw the words out of her? That seemed to draw out other things, too? "It makes me feel as if I'm getting something accomplished."

"We're going to catch him," Ethan told her with quiet affirmation once he reached the bottom step and was next to her.

She looked at him sharply, expecting to see that he was laughing at her and being condescending. But he wasn't. He looked sincere. Which either meant that he was or that he was a better actor than she'd initially given him credit for.

Kansas went on the offensive. "You don't really believe that."

"Actually," he told her, "I do." They went down another flight, moving even faster this time. "I just don't know how long it's going to take. The more fires there are, the more likely it is that he's going to trip up, show his hand, have someone catch him in the act. *Something,*" he underscored, "is going to go wrong for him—and right for us."

Reaching the first floor, Kansas hurried to the front entrance. Not waiting for the others, she pushed it open with the flat of her hand.

"Meanwhile, the bastard's turning Aurora into a pile of ashes."

"Not yet," Ethan countered. They were outside, but she was still moving fast. Heading toward his car. He kept up with her. "I take it that you don't want to wait for the others."

"They'll meet us there," she said, reaching his vehicle.

His keys in his hand, he hit the remote button that disarmed the security device. Getting in, he shook his head. "Ever have a partner before?" he asked Kansas.

She got in and buckled up, tension racing through her body. She was anxious to get to the site of the fire, as if her presence there would somehow curtail any further harm the fire might render.

"I don't have one now," she pointed out glibly. As far as she was concerned, "temporary" didn't count.

The look Ethan gave her did something strange to her stomach. It felt as if she'd just endured an accelerated fifty-foot drop on a roller-coaster ride.

"Yeah," Ethan corrected, "you do. Better adjust," he advised mildly.

Mild or not, that got her back up. "And if I don't?" she challenged, unconsciously raising her chin as if silently daring him to take a swing.

"It'd just be easier on everyone all around if you did. We're all after the same thing," he reminded her not for the first time. "Nailing this creep's hide to the wall."

She began to retort, then thought better of it. The man was right. This was her frustration talking, not her. Taking a deep breath, she forced out the words that needed to be said. "You're right, I'm sorry."

He gave her a long glance. Had she just apologized to him? That wasn't like her. "Don't throw me a curve like that," he told her, and she couldn't tell if he was serious or not. "I'm liable to jump the divider and crash this beautiful car."

She noticed that he put the car first. The man really

was enamored with this cream-colored machine, wasn't he?

"Very funny," she cracked. "I admit I have a tendency to go off on my own, but it's just that I'm so damn frustrated right now," she told him. Then she elaborated: "We should have been able to find him by now. *I* should have been able to find him by now."

"No, you had it right the first time," he said quietly. "*We* should have been able to find this sicko by now."

She was out of ideas and her brain felt as dry as the Mojave Desert. "What are we doing wrong?"

"I don't know," he admitted.

There was a long moment of silence, and then he became aware of Kansas suddenly straightening in her seat. He was beginning to be able to read her. And she'd just thought of something. He'd bet money on it.

"Talk," he told her. "What just suddenly occurred to you?"

So excited by what she was thinking, she could hardly sit still. But she answered Ethan's question with one of her own. "Do we have any footage of the crowds that gathered around to see the outcome of these fires?"

"*We* don't, but I'm sure the local news stations do. This is the kind of story that they live for." With each fire, the coverage became that much more intense, lasting that much longer. He'd never known that so much could be said about any given topic. The media were in a class by themselves.

She didn't care about the press. Reporters who earned a living focusing on people in possibly the worst moments of their lives had always struck her as annoying at best. At worst they were vultures. But right now, they could unwittingly provide a useful service.

"Do you think we can get our hands on some of that footage?"

He personally couldn't, but he figured Dax could. Or, if not him, then certainly the chief of D's could. "Don't see why not." It didn't take much to figure out where she was going with this. "You think our firebug's in the crowd?"

She never liked committing herself, even though her answer was yes. "Worth a look."

Ethan nodded. "I'll ask Dax to requisition as much footage from each fire as is available. If he can't, the chief can. I'll tell him it's your idea," he added, just in case she thought he might be tempted to steal her thunder.

Because O'Brien was being magnanimous, she could return the favor, all the while reminding herself not to let her guard down. That would be a mistake.

"*Our* idea," she corrected. "We were brainstorming. Kind of."

Ethan grinned. "You just might make it as a team member yet, Kansas."

"Something to shoot for," she allowed. Although she damn well knew that by the time she'd adjusted to being "one of the guys," or whatever O'Brien wanted to call it, she'd be back at the firehouse, working on her own again.

It might, she couldn't help thinking as she stole a side glance at Ethan, actually take a little adjusting on her part to make the transition back.

Who would have ever thought it?

When they arrived at the site of the newest fire some fifteen minutes later, chaos had settled in. The rather small front lawn before the nursing home was completely littered with vintage citizens, many of whom, despite the hour, were in their pajamas and robes. A number were confined to wheelchairs.

She saw several of the latter apparently on their own, deposited haphazardly away from the fire. One resident looked absolutely terrified. There weren't nearly enough aides and orderlies, let alone nurses, to care for or reassure them.

As she started toward the terrified, wild-eyed old woman, Kansas's attention was drawn away to the almost skeletal-looking old man who was lying on the grass. There was a large and burly firefighter leaning over the unconscious resident, and she could tell from the fireman's frantic motions that the old man's life hung in the balance.

Kansas held her breath as the firefighter, his protective helmet and gloves on the ground, administered CPR. He was doing compressions on the frail chest and blowing into the all-but-lifeless mouth.

A distressed nurse was hovering beside the firefighter like an anemic cheerleader, hoarsely giving instructions as he worked over the senior citizen.

"Now that's really odd," Kansas muttered under her breath.

Before Ethan could ask her what she meant, Kansas was already working her way through the crowd and over to the scene. By the time she reached them, the firefighter had risen unsteadily to his feet. His wide face was drawn and he was clearly shaken.

"I lost him," he lamented in disbelief. The anguished words weren't addressed to anyone in particular, but more to the world in general. It was obvious that the towering firefighter was berating himself for not being able to save the old man. "I lost him," he cried again, his voice catching. "Oh God, I lost him."

With effort, the nurse dropped to her knees. Steadying herself, she pressed her fingers against the elderly man's throat, searching for any sign of a pulse. She didn't find it.

The nurse sighed, shaking her head. Her next words confirmed what had already been said. "Mr. Walters is gone." Looking up at the fireman, in her next breath she absolved him of any blame. "You did everything you possibly could."

"I didn't do enough," the firefighter protested. He looked defeated and almost lost.

"Yes, you did," the nurse said with feeling. She held her hand up to him and the distraught firefighter helped her to her feet. "Don't beat yourself up about it. It was Mr. Walters's time."

The next moment, a reporter with one of the local stations came running over to the firefighter and the nurse. His cameraman was directly behind him. Thrusting his microphone at the duo, the reporter began firing questions at them, ready and willing to turn this tragedy into a human-interest sound bite in a blatant attempt to be the lead story of the hour tonight.

Kansas noted that the firefighter looked even more anguished than he had a few moments earlier as he began to answer the reporter's questions.

She glanced over toward Ethan, who had caught up to

her again. "What do you make of that?" she murmured in as discreet a voice as she could manage and still be heard above the din.

Ethan wasn't sure where she was trying to go with this. "He's obviously someone who takes his job to heart." He saw the number on the engine and knew that she'd come from that fire station. "I take it that you don't know him."

Kansas shook her head. "He came to the house just when I got promoted to investigator. I hang out at the firehouse, but I have my own office, do my own thing. They answer the calls, I only go if arson's suspected." She pressed her lips together. "I'm really not part of that whole firefighting thing anymore."

Ethan detected something in her voice. "Do you miss it?"

He had a feeling he knew the answer to that no matter what she said. He was prepared for her to say something dismissive in response. He'd come to learn that she was nothing if not a private person. Ordinarily, that would be a signal for him to back off.

But she intrigued him.

"Sometimes," she murmured in a low voice, surprising him. "Other times, I feel I'm doing more good as an investigator. Or at least I was before this lunatic showed up, setting fire to everything in his path and driving me crazy. Us," Kansas amended quickly. "Driving us crazy."

Thinking in the plural was harder than she'd realized. It was really going to take practice.

Ethan grinned, appreciating the effort she was making. He couldn't help wondering if she was just turning over a new leaf or if she was doing this solely because of what he'd said earlier.

"You're coming along, Kansas. You're coming along."

She had no idea why his approval didn't incense her. Why it had, oddly enough, the exact opposite effect. Maybe she'd been breathing in too much smoke these last few years, she theorized.

About to say something flippant about his comment, Kansas stopped as she became aware that the rest of the task force had just joined her and Ethan.

The moment they had, Ethan went to Dax and she knew without having to listen in that he was making the request for the available footage of the last dozen fires. She couldn't help smiling to herself as she made her way over to the two men.

They looked alike, she caught herself thinking. Both dark, both good-looking. On a scale of 1 to 10, they were both 10s. With Ethan possibly being a 10.5.

And what did *that* have to do with the price of tea in China? she upbraided herself. She needed to stay focused and not let her mind wander like this.

When she was within earshot, she heard Dax ask her partner, "You think he stuck around to watch the fire department try to save the buildings?"

"The minute Kansas said it, it made sense. I'm sure of it," Ethan told Dax vehemently. "He wouldn't be able to resist. This is like an opiate to him. It's too much of a draw for him to pass up."

"Okay," Dax agreed. "I've got a few connections. I'll see what I can do."

"I've got a smartphone," Ethan suddenly remembered as Dax began to walk to his car.

Youngman looked at him oddly. "As opposed to what, a stupid phone?"

"No, you idiot," Ortiz, years younger than the veteran detective, berated his partner in disgust. "He means he's got a video camera in it."

Ethan was already putting his phone to use, panning the surrounding area and committing the image to film. It was a very simple act. He sincerely hoped it would help in capturing what was turning out to seem like a very complex perp.

"I believe this comes under the heading of 'be careful what you wish for,'" Dax announced the following morning as he walked up to Kansas's desk and deposited a huge carton. The carton was filled to the brim with videotapes.

She had to rise from her chair in order to see inside the box. "What's all this?" she asked.

"These are the tapes you asked for," he reminded her. "This is all footage from the fires."

"All these?" she asked incredulously, having trouble processing the information. There was an incredible amount of footage to review, she thought with a sinking feeling.

"No. That's only a third. Youngman and Ortiz are bringing the other two boxes."

She groaned as she took out the first tape. It looked as if her eyes were about to become tread-worn.

Chapter 9

"What are you doing?" Kansas asked in surprise.

On her feet, she'd picked up the first box of tapes that Dax had gotten for her to review. Braced for hours of incredible boredom, she was about to head to the small, windowless room where a monitor, coupled with a VCR, was housed. Her question, and the surprise that had prompted it, was directed toward Ethan, who had just picked up one of the other boxes and was walking behind her.

"Following you," he said simply.

She immediately took that to mean that he thought she needed help transporting the tapes. It was inherently against her nature to allow anyone to think she wasn't capable of taking care of herself in any fashion.

Kansas lifted her chin. He was beginning to recognize that as one of her defensive moves. He really needed to find a way to get her to be more trusting, Ethan thought.

"I can carry them."

"I'm sure you can," he told her in an easygoing voice, but he couldn't help adding, "Probably with one hand tied behind your back." He gave her a weary look. "For once, why don't you just accept help in the spirit it's offered? This isn't any kind of a covert statement about your capabilities. I just thought I'd help you with them, that's all."

Kansas felt a flush of embarrassment. She supposed she was being a little paranoid. She was far more accustomed to put-downs than help. It hadn't been easy, even in this day and age, getting accepted in her chosen field. It was still, for all intents and purposes, mostly an all-boys club. Female firefighters and female arson investigators were a very small group, their authority and capabilities challenged almost at every turn.

"Sorry," she murmured in a small voice as she resumed walking. "Thank you."

Ethan nodded. "Better." Grinning, he fell into place beside her as they went down the hall. "I thought I'd give you a hand viewing them. There're two monitors in the room and two sets of eyes are better than one."

She hadn't realized that there were two monitors, but even if she had, she wouldn't have expected anyone else to volunteer for the tedious job of looking for the same face to pop up somewhere within every crowd shot of the various fires.

She stopped walking and looked at him in astonishment. "You're actually volunteering, of your own free will, to help me go over the tapes?"

Arriving at the room, he shifted the box to one side, balancing it on his hip in order to open the door for her. He stepped back and allowed her to go in first. "I think if you play back the conversation, that's what I just said."

Walking in, she deposited the box on the long, metal-top table that served as a desk. Both monitors with their VCRs were on it.

"Why?" she asked, turning to face him.

He put down his box next to hers. "Because that's what partners do, and like I said, for better or for worse, we're temporary partners." He pulled out his chair and sat down. "The sooner we get done with these, the sooner we can move on to something else. Maybe even catching this guy," he added.

Considering the way she'd treated him, O'Brien was being incredibly nice. She wondered if it were a mistake, letting her guard down just a little. She didn't like leaving herself open. But verbally sparring with him after his offer of help didn't seem right, either.

"Thank you," she finally said. "That's very nice of you."

He took out the first tape. The writing on the label was exceptionally neat—and small. An ant would need glasses to read it, he thought.

Ethan gave her a glance. "Remember that the next time you want to take my head off."

She supposed she had that coming. She hadn't exactly been the most easygoing, even-tempered person to work with.

"It's not your fault, you know," she murmured, sitting down. "The way I react."

"Never thought it was," he answered glibly. Ethan paused, waiting. But she didn't say anything further. So he did. "Okay, whose fault is it?"

Again, Kansas didn't answer right away. Instead, she seemed to be preoccupied with taking tapes out of the box and arranging them in some preordained order on the long, narrow table that they were using. It was a balancing act at best. Most of the space was taken up by the monitors. She remained silent for so long, Ethan decided she wasn't going to answer him.

And then she did.

"My husband's," she replied quietly. "It's my husband's fault."

Ethan stared at her. To say he was stunned would have been a vast understatement. His eyes instantly darted to Kansas's left hand. There was no ring there, which caused another host of questions to pop up in his head. Men didn't always wear a wedding ring. Women, however, usually did. But she didn't have one.

"You're married?" he asked, the words echoing in the small room.

"Was," Kansas corrected him. "I *was* married. A long time ago." She took a breath, because this wasn't easy to admit, even to herself, much less to someone else. But he was still a stranger, which in an odd way made it somewhat easier. "Biggest mistake of my life."

The statement instantly prompted another thought. "He abused you?"

The moment the words were out of his mouth, Ethan felt himself growing angry. Growing protective of her. The only other time he'd ever felt that way was when his mother had told them about their father. About being abandoned by the only man she'd ever loved, which to him represented abuse of the highest degree.

"Not physically," Kansas was quick to answer. Which only led him to another conclusion.

"Emotionally?"

She laughed shortly, but there was no humor in the sound. "If you call bedding the hotel receptionist on our honeymoon emotional abuse, then yes, Grant abused me emotionally." And broke her heart, but she wasn't about to say that part out loud. That was only for her to know, no one else.

She knew that kind of thing couldn't just happen out of the blue. A guy didn't become worthless scum after he pledged to love, honor and cherish. The seeds had to have been there to begin with.

"You didn't have a clue what he was like before that?"

Yes, she supposed, in hindsight, she had. But she was so desperate to have someone love her that she'd disregarded any nagging doubts she had, telling herself that it would be different once they were married.

Except that it wasn't. It just got worse. So she'd ended it. Quickly.

Kansas shrugged carelessly. "I was in love and I made excuses for him."

Ethan looked at her for a long moment. She didn't strike him as the type who would do that. Obviously he was wrong. His interest as well as his curiosity was piqued a little more.

"If he came back into your life right now," Ethan asked, selecting his words carefully as he continued unpacking tapes and lining them up in front of him, "and said he was sorry, would you take him back?"

Kansas regretted having said anything. He was asking a question that was way too personal, but she couldn't blame him. This was all her fault. She'd opened the door to this and O'Brien was doing what came naturally to him—prying. And besides, the man *was* being helpful to her. She supposed she owed him the courtesy of an answer.

"That depends," she said tentatively.

He raised a quizzical brow. Definitely not what he would have expected her to say. He decided to push it a little further. "On what?"

And that was when he saw the lightning flash in her eyes. "On whether or not I could find a big enough barbecue skewer to use so that I could roast him alive."

Now *that* he would have expected to hear, Ethan thought, doing his best to keep a straight face. "I had no idea you were so bloodthirsty."

"I'm not," she admitted after a beat, "but he wouldn't know that—and I'd want him to sweat bullets for at least a while."

Ethan didn't even try to hold the laughter back. "How long did you stay married?" he asked once he finally sobered a little.

Kansas didn't answer him immediately. She hadn't talked about her short stint as a married woman to anyone. In a way, it almost felt good to finally get all this out. "Just long enough to file for a divorce."

That, he thought, explained a lot. "Is that what has

you so dead set against the male species?" he asked, voicing his thoughts out loud.

"Not all of it," she corrected. "Only the drop-dead handsome section of the species." Her eyes narrowed as she looked at him. "Because drop-dead handsome guys think they can get away with anything."

She was looking at him as if she included him in that small, exclusive club. But there was no way to ask her without sounding as if he had a swelled head. Ethan opted for leaving it alone, but he couldn't resist pointing out the obvious. "You can't convict a section of the population because one guy acted like a supreme jerk and didn't know what he had."

"And what is it that you think he had?" The question came out before she could think to bank it down. Damn it, he was going to think she was fishing for a compliment. Or worse, fishing for his validation. Which she didn't need, she thought fiercely. The only person's validation she needed was her own.

"A woman of substance," Ethan told her, his voice low, his eyes on hers. "You don't just make a commitment to someone and then fool around."

No, he's just trying to suck you in. He doesn't mean a word of it.

"And you, if you make a commitment, you stick to it?" she asked, watching his eyes. She could always tell when a man was lying.

"I've never made a commitment," he told her honestly. "It wouldn't be fair to have a woman clutching to strings if there weren't any."

Why was her breath catching in her throat like that? This was just talk, nothing more. There was absolutely no reason for her to feel like this, as if her pulse were just about to be launched all the way to the space station.

Shifting, trying to regain her bearings, her elbow hit one of the tapes and sent it falling to the floor. She exhaled, and bent down to pick it up. So did Ethan. They very narrowly avoided bumping heads.

But other body parts were not nearly so lucky. Stooping, their bodies brushed against one another, sending electric shock waves zipping through both of them at the same time. Kansas sensed this because just as she sucked in her breath, she thought she heard him do the same, except more softly.

When their eyes locked, the circuit seemed absolutely complete. Rising up, his hands on either side of her shoulders as he brought her up to her feet, Ethan didn't think his next move through, which was highly unlike him. What he did was go with instincts that refused to be silenced.

Ethan bent his head, lightly brushing his lips against hers. And then he savored a second, stronger wave of electricity that went jolting through his system the moment he made contact.

He would have gone on to deepen the kiss, except that was exactly the moment that Dax chose to walk in with the third box of tapes.

Dax looked from his cousin to the fire department loan-out. It didn't take a Rhodes Scholar to pick up the vibes that were ricocheting through the small room. The vibes that had absolutely nothing to do with the apprehension of a firebug.

Clearing his throat, Dax asked a nebulous question.

"Either of you two need a break?" His tone was deliberately mild.

Ethan glanced at her, then shook his head. "No, we're good," he assured Dax.

Yes, he certainly is, Kansas couldn't help thinking. Even a mere fleeting press of his lips to hers had told her that.

She was definitely going to have to stay alert at all times with this one, she thought. If she wasn't careful, he was going to wear away all of her defenses in the blink of an eye without really trying.

This was not good.

And she didn't know if she believed him about not making any false promises. He sounded convincing, but it could all be for show, to leave her defenseless and open. After all, she didn't really know the man.

But she knew herself.

It wasn't in her to play fast and loose no matter how much she wanted to. She wasn't the kind who went from man to man, having a good time with no thought of commitment. If she succumbed to this man, it would be a forever thing, at least on her part. And she already knew that there was no such word as *forever* in O'Brien's vocabulary.

"Good." She seconded Ethan's response when Dax turned his gaze in her direction.

"I'd send you a third pair of eyes." He addressed his remark to both of them, then waved at the equipment they were going to be using. "But there are only two monitors to be had."

"That's okay, Dax," Ethan answered for both of them. "We'll manage somehow."

"I'll hold you to that," Dax promised. Then, with a nod toward Kansas, he left the room, closing the door behind him. The lighting in the windowless room went from soft to inky.

It felt to Kansas that she'd been holding her breath the entire time. She stared at the door as if she expected it to open at any moment.

"Do you think that he saw us?" she asked Ethan uneasily.

"If he had, he would have said as much." There was no question in his mind about that. "Dax doesn't play games. None of the Cavanaughs do. They're all straight shooters."

She laughed softly, shaking her head. "That puts the lot of them right up there with unicorns, mermaids—and you."

He grinned at her. "Always room for more."

What did that even mean? she wondered. Was O'Brien just bantering, trying to tease her? Or was there some kind of hidden meaning to his words? What if he was saying that he and she could—

Stop it. Don't be an idiot. That's just wishful thinking on your part. How many Grants do you need in your life before you finally learn? We come into this world alone and we leave it alone. And most of us spend the time in between alone, as well.

"I'll have to get back to you on that," she told Ethan.

"Fair enough," he commented. And then he looked back at the piles of tapes. "We'd better get to work before Dax assigns us a keeper."

She merely nodded and applied herself to the task at hand.

And tried very, very hard not to think about the firm, quick press of velvet lips against hers.

"So?" Dax asked when Ethan and Kansas finally returned to their desks two days later and sank down in their chairs. They had brought in the boxes of tapes with them and deposited them on the floor next to their desks.

Ethan groaned, passing a hand over his eyes for dramatic effect. "I may never look at another TV monitor again."

There was only one way to take that comment. Disappointment instantly permeated the room. "Then you found nothing?"

"Nothing," Ethan confirmed. "Except that a lot of people could stand to have complete makeovers," he quipped.

Dax looked over toward the fire investigator. "Kansas, have you got anything more informative than that for me?"

She really wished she did. After all, looking through the crowd footage had been her idea. "No, I'm afraid not. Neither one of us saw anyone who turned up at all the fires—or even half of them," she added with an impatient sigh. "Because a lot of the fires took place in close proximity, there were some overlaps, the same people turning up at more than one blaze, but they definitely didn't pop up at enough fires for us to look for them and ask questions."

Dax didn't look as if he agreed with her. "How many overlaps?" he pressed.

"One guy turned up four times," Ethan interjected. Dax looked at him, listening. "Another guy, five. But five was the limit," he added. "Nobody showed up more than that."

Ethan opened his bottom drawer, looking for the giant bottle of aspirin. Finding it, he took it out. Then, holding it up, he raised an inquiring eyebrow in Kansas's direction.

Kansas nodded, the motion relatively restrained because of the headache that was taking over. Shaking out two pills, Ethan leaned over and placed them on her desk, along with an unopened bottle of water that seemed to materialize in his hands. She didn't know until then that he usually kept several such bottles on hand in his desk.

"So here we are again, back to square one," Ortiz complained, looking exceedingly frustrated. "No viable suspects amid the known arsonists and pyromaniacs, no firebug hanging around in the crowd, bent on watching his handiwork, secretly laughing at us."

Youngman added in his two cents. "Only good thing is that, except for that old man the other day, there haven't been any casualties at these fires."

Dax pointed out the simple reason for that piece of luck. "That's because the fire department always turns up quickly each and every time. Don't know how long that lucky streak's going to continue."

"Yeah, lucky for the people involved," Youngman commented, picking up on the key word. "Otherwise they'd most likely be being referred to in the past tense right about now."

Kansas began to nod, then stopped as Youngman's words as well as Dax's words replayed in her head. When they did and the thought occurred to her, she all but bolted ramrod straight in her chair.

Ethan noted the shift in her posture immediately. She'd thought of something, something they hadn't covered before. It surprised him how quickly he'd become in tune to her body language.

He told himself he was just being a good detective. "What?" he pressed, looking at Kansas.

She in turn looked around at the other three men on the task force. "Doesn't that strike anyone else as strange?" she wanted to know.

"What, that the fire department turned up at a fire?" Ortiz asked, not following her. "It's what they do." His puzzled expression seemed to want to know why she was even asking this question. "You of all people—"

But Ortiz didn't get a chance to finish.

"No," she interrupted, "the fire department turning up early. Each and every time. Doesn't that seem a little odd to anyone? It's the same firehouse that answers the call each and every time, as well." And it was her firehouse, which made her pursuing this line of questioning even worse.

"There're only two firehouses in Aurora," Dax pointed out. "These fires are taking place in the southern section."

She was well aware of that fact. And aware that in many towns, there *were* no fire departments with firefighters who were paid by the city. Instead, what the townships had were dedicated volunteers who responded to the call whenever it went out, no matter where they were and what they were doing. Aurora was lucky to have not one but two firehouses charged with nothing more than looking out for their citizens.

But these early responses were definitely a lot more than just happy coincidences. Something was off here.

"I know that. But getting there in time to save everyone, the odds start to rise against you when the number of occurrences goes up. And yet, each and every time, the fire department is practically there just as the fire starts."

Dax looked at her sharply. "What are you getting at, Kansas?"

She took a deep breath before saying it. And then she forced the words out. "That maybe whoever is setting these fires is one of the firefighters."

Chapter 10

Her statement had gotten all four detectives to sit up and stare at her. Frustration and exhaustion were temporarily ousted.

"Do you know what you're saying?" Dax asked her incredulously.

Kansas nodded grimly. "I know *exactly* what I'm saying. But what other avenues are open to us?" She didn't want to think this way, but it had been a process of elimination. "The way I see it, it *has* to be one of the firefighters."

What she was suggesting was something no one wanted to think about or seriously consider.

"This is your own house you're pointing a finger at," Dax reminded her, clearly trying to wrap his mind around what she was saying.

The anguish was evident in her voice as she answered

him. "Don't you think I know that? Don't you think that I wish there was some other answer?"

"What makes you think *this* is the answer?" Dax persisted.

Telling him it was a feeling in her gut would only have the detectives quickly dismissing the idea. As far as they were concerned, she was the "new kid." And the new kid wasn't allowed to have gut feelings for at least a couple of years. So she cited the clinical reference she'd read about the condition.

"It's the hero syndrome," she replied simply.

Scratching the eight or nine hairs that still populated the top of his head, Youngman looked at his partner, who offered no insight. Youngman then looked at her.

"And the hero syndrome is?" he wanted to know.

To her surprise, Ethan took over just as she was about to explain. "That's when someone arranges events in order to come running to the rescue and have people regard him—or her—as a hero," he told the others. "Or like a nurse might fiddle with a patient's medication, making them code so that she can rush in with defibrillator paddles to bring them back from the brink of death. People like that get off playing the hero. It makes them feel important, like they matter." Finished, Ethan looked at Kansas. "That's what you mean, right?"

He explained it better than she could, she thought. Had he come across this before? "Right."

Dax seemed to be turning his cousin's words over in his head before asking his next question. "And just which of these firefighters do you think is capable of something like that?"

She wished it was none of them, but she simply couldn't shake the feeling that it had to be.

"I don't know," she told Dax honestly. She was aware that all four pairs of eyes were on her, with perhaps Ethan's being the kindest. "Look, I hope I'm wrong, but if I am, then we're back to that damn square one again."

That suggestion was obviously more to Ortiz's liking. "It could still be a pyromaniac who just hasn't made the grid yet," he pointed out.

Ethan shot down his theory. "That's why Kansas and I just spent all those hours going over the news footage, looking for a face that might keep cropping up in the crowd shots. There wasn't any. The most hits we got were five." He repeated the information he'd already delivered once.

"So maybe these actually *were* just accidental, random fires," Ortiz suggested hopefully. "That kind of thing *does* happen around here."

"Then how do you explain the accelerants I found?" Kansas asked quietly.

"I forgot about that." Ortiz's shoulder slumped and he seemed to slide down a little farther in his chair. "I can't."

"You know those firefighters better than any of us," Dax pointed out, turning toward her again. Crossing his arms before him, pausing for a long moment, he finally asked, "How do you suggest we get started?"

When in doubt, go the simple route. Someone had once said that to her, she couldn't remember who. But she did remember that she'd taken it to heart and it had helped her see things through.

"Same way we'd get started with any suspects we're trying to rule out," she told the prime detective on the case. "Call them in and interview each of them one at a time."

Ortiz shook his head. "They're not going to cooperate," he predicted.

"They might," Ethan theorized. The others looked at him curiously. "If we ask the right questions, we should be able to get some idea of what's going on."

"Right questions," Ortiz echoed. "Such as?"

She'd already started forming them in her head. "Such as if they remember seeing anyone suspicious in the vicinity when they arrived. Or if they saw anything suspicious at all—coming, going, while they were there. Anything." She took a breath. This was the million-dollar question. "And if they thought that any of the other firefighters behaved with undue valor."

"You're going to question their bravery?" Ortiz asked in astonishment.

"Exactly," she answered.

Youngman shook his head, evidently foreseeing problems. "That'll make their radar go up immediately."

"We've got five interview rooms." Dax volunteered a fact they all already knew—with the exception of the fire investigator. "We divide and conquer and keep this under wraps."

"For as long as it takes to interview the first five firemen," Ortiz pointed out glumly. "After that, all hell's going to break loose. They'll talk."

Broad shoulders rose and fell. "Still better than nothing," Dax commented.

"I don't like this," Youngman protested. "Those guys risk their lives, running into a burning building when any sane person would run in the opposite direction as fast as they could—and now we're pointing fingers at them? Accusing them of actually *starting* the fire?"

"Not at *them,* at *one* of them," Kansas insisted.

Youngman frowned, clearly not won over. "I can't believe you just said that. You know how united those guys are. You focus on one of them, the rest close ranks around him, forming an impenetrable wall that's next to impossible to crack."

She pressed her lips together and nodded. "Yes, I know."

The older detective shifted in his seat, making direct eye contact with her. "And when they find out this is your idea," he predicted, "they're not going to be very happy."

She knew that, too. But she refused to let that dictate how she did her job. "Nothing I haven't encountered before," she replied quietly, bracing herself for what was to come.

Ethan was perched against her desk, leaning a hip against the corner. He had been observing her for a few minutes and now finally commented: "You know, if you shrug your shoulders just the right way, that big chip you're carrying around could very possibly fall off."

If there was something she hated more than criticism, she couldn't remember what it was. "I don't *have* a big chip," she insisted.

Ethan lifted his right shoulder in a timeless, careless shrug. "Then it's got to be the biggest dandruff flake I've ever encountered," he assessed.

Swallowing an exasperated sigh, she ignored him and instead looked at Dax. "I don't *want* to be right about this."

He could see by the look on her face that she was telling the truth.

"I know you don't," Dax commiserated. "For the time being, why don't you and Ethan re-canvass the areas of the last few fires, knock on the same doors, see if any of the stories have been altered this time around."

She saw through the suggestion. "I appreciate what you're trying to do, Detective Cavanaugh, but I really don't need to be shielded. I don't break. It's my suggestion, so I can handle my end of it."

Dax couldn't hide his concern. "I'm thinking about when this is all over and you have to go back."

So was she...for about a second. Why borrow trouble? It would be there waiting for her once this was over.

"I appreciate that, Detective, but I really can handle myself. Captain Lawrence is a fair man, and I don't really interact with the men on any sort of a regular basis anymore anyway." Kansas didn't realize at first that she was smiling as she looked around the squad room. "Not like I do here."

Dax allowed himself a small smile as he nodded. "All right, then. Since this involves possibly getting on the fire department's bad side, let me just run this by the chief of D's and see what he has to say about it." He looked around at the task force. "When he gives his okay, who wants to inform Captain Lawrence?"

She began to say that she would, but she wasn't fast enough. Ethan raised his hand and beat her to it. "I will."

"Hope you're up on your self-defense classes," Ortiz murmured.

Kansas swung around to look at her partner. "It's my idea. I'll do it." He began to say something, but she held up her hand to silence him. "They won't hit me. You, they just might."

Dax laughed. "She's got a point," he said to his cousin.

Ethan wasn't going to argue with him—and he knew better than to argue outright with her.

"Fine," Ethan compromised. "We'll both go."

He was adamant on that point. There was no way he was going to let her walk into the firehouse with this new twist like some lamb to the slaughter. Whether she liked it or not, he was her partner for the time being, and that meant he intended to have her back at all times.

Kansas waited until Dax left to talk to his father. "I don't need a keeper," she informed Ethan indignantly, keeping her voice low.

"Yeah, you do, but that's an argument for another day," he retorted. "Besides, we send you alone, we look like a bunch of chickens hiding behind a woman." He shook his head. "Ain't gonna happen."

She inclined her head. Much as she wanted to argue with him, she could see his point. "I didn't think of it that way."

And neither had he—until just now.

But Ethan merely nodded in response and kept his satisfied grin to himself.

Brian looked at his son thoughtfully. Dax had laid out the theory that Kansas had come up with and that

Ethan had backed as succinctly as possible. Finished, his son waited for a comment.

Instead, Brian gestured for him to take a seat. Once Dax did, he asked for his opinion. "So what do you think of this idea?"

Dax knew that this was a giant step they were taking, one that didn't allow for any backtracking. And if they were wrong, there was going to be hell to pay. There might be hell to pay even if they were right. No one took being a suspect well, and this would cause at least a temporary rift between the police and the fire departments.

All that considered, Dax said, "I think they might be onto something. We've followed up all the so-called tips that have been coming in from the public hotlines, and all we've done is go around in circles." He sighed. "And meanwhile, buildings keep being burned. After each fire, we haul out all the usual suspects, all the firebugs out on parole and the known pyromaniac wannabes and come up with nothing. They all make sure that they've always got an alibi."

"And the media footage?" Brian asked. It had taken a bit of persuading on his part to secure that from the various local stations. "Did that show up anything?"

Dax shook his head. "Different faces at different fires. If this firebug's doing it to get a rush, he's got some remote hook-up going to view the sites, because he's not showing up in the crowds."

They had no choice but to pursue this new avenue, Brian thought. They were out of options. "I'll talk to Captain Lawrence. Go ahead and question the firefighters. Just try to do it as delicately as possible," he cautioned, though he was fairly confident he didn't really have to. Dax had a good head on his shoulders. All the younger Cavanaughs did. "I don't want some yahoo getting it into his head to turn this into a feud between the Aurora Police Department and the fire department."

Dax was already on his feet and crossing to the door. "Don't worry, we'll do our best to be discreet," he promised.

"Oh, and, Dax?" Brian called out just as his son was about to walk out.

Stopping, Dax looked at his father over his shoulder. "Yes?"

"How's Ethan coming along?" This was the first time that Dax was working with the other detective, and Brian was curious about the way things were going between them. As a family, the three O'Briens and the Cavanaughs were all still getting accustomed to one another.

And that didn't even begin to take in the curveball that Andrew had thrown him the other week. That, Brian knew, was still under wraps as far as the rest of the family was concerned.

Dax grinned. "Just like you'd expect, Chief. Like a born Cavanaugh."

Brian nodded his head. "Good to hear." He had equally good reports on Kyle and Greer. At this point, it seemed as if the only one of them who had ever disappointed the family had been Mike, who'd ultimately never managed to conquer the demons he lived with. "Keep me apprised of the way the questioning is going," he requested. "And give me a holler if you need me," he added, raising his voice just before his son went down the hall.

Dax raised his hand over his head as he kept going. "Absolutely."

Brian crossed to the door and closed it. He knew that Dax wouldn't be coming to him with any problems. He'd raised them all to know that family was always there for them if the need arose but that they were expected to stand independently on their own two feet if at all possible. None of his sons, nor his daughter, had ever disappointed him.

And neither, he thought now, had Lila's four kids, whom he'd regarded as his own even before he and Lila had exchanged vows.

All in all, he mused, getting back to the report he'd been reading just before Dax came in, he was one hell of a lucky man.

Arms crossed before his barrel chest, covering the small drop of ketchup that recalled lunch and the fries he'd had, Captain John Lawrence was one frown line short of a glare as he regarded the young woman who'd spent the last four years assigned to his firehouse.

"What do you want to talk to them for?" he asked suspiciously, grinding out the words.

The smile on his lips as he'd greeted her and the detective she'd walked in with had quickly dissolved when she'd made her request to interview each of his men. Eyes the color of black olives shifted from Kansas to the man standing beside her and then back again, waiting.

Kansas tried again. She'd been the object of Lawrence's displeasure before, when she'd first been assigned to him. In time, she'd won him over. It looked now as if all her hard work and dedication had just been unraveled in the last couple of minutes.

"We're hitting a dead end," she explained patiently, "and we're hoping that one of them might have seen something that we didn't."

"They were kind of busy at the time," he pointed out. Lawrence didn't bother trying to mask the sarcasm in his voice.

"We appreciate that, Captain Lawrence," Ethan said respectfully but firmly. "But you never know what might help break a case. Sometimes the smallest, most inconsequential thing—"

Impatient, Lawrence waved a hand at him, dismissing the explanation. "Yeah, yeah, I know the drill—and the drivel," he added pointedly. He looked far from pleased. Just as it seemed that he was going to be stubbornly uncooperative, the captain grudgingly said, "If you really think it can help the investigation, I'll send them over to talk to you." He looked at Kansas and his expression softened, but only slightly. Ethan could see that she had fallen out of favor. With any luck, it was only temporary. "You want everybody?"

She gave him a little leeway. "Everybody who was on call for the fires."

The disgruntled expression intensified. "That's everybody."

"Wasn't it just one shift?" Ethan asked innocently. Most of the fires had taken place under the cover of twilight or later.

"They overlapped," the captain answered coldly. His

attention was back to Kansas. "Okay with you if I send just three at a time—barring a fire, of course," he added cynically.

Ethan ran interference for her, determined to take the brunt of the captain's displeasure. "Of course," he said. "Goes without saying. The fires always take precedent."

There was something akin to contempt in the captain's dark eyes as they swept over him. "Glad you agree," Lawrence finally commented. And then he asked Kansas, "Tomorrow okay with you? Most of the guys you want to talk to are off right now. It's been a rough few days."

In Ethan's opinion, it had been a rough few months. And besides, it was getting late anyway. He and Kansas were both off the clock and had been for the last half hour. Lawrence had kept them waiting almost an hour before he "found" the time to see them.

"Tomorrow's fine," Ethan answered. Leaning forward, he shook Lawrence's hand. "Thanks for your cooperation." He managed to say the words with a straight face.

"Hey, we're all on the same team, right?" It was hard to tell whether Lawrence was being serious or sarcastic, but Ethan was leaning toward the latter.

"Right," Kansas agreed.

It had earned her a less than warm look from the captain. She was in the doghouse and she knew it. It was obvious that the man was annoyed with her because she hadn't been able to somehow spare him what she was sure Lawrence saw as a major inconvenience.

She was equally sure that he didn't realize that his

men were under suspicion at the moment. Because if he had known, he would have said as much. Most likely at the top of his lungs while liberally sprinkling more than a few choice words throughout his statement. Lawrence wasn't the kind to keep things bottled up and to himself. If he was angry, *everyone* knew he was angry. They also knew about what and at whom. The man didn't believe in sparing feelings.

Taking their leave, Kansas and Ethan walked out of the fire station. Once outside, she turned to him and said, "You should have let me do the talking."

He'd done the brunt of it for a very simple reason. "You've got to come back here. I don't. I wanted Lawrence to think of me as the messenger in all this. When he realizes what's going on, he's not going to be a happy camper," Ethan predicted. "I don't want him taking it out on you."

Kansas looked at him, curbing her natural impulse to shrug off any offers of help and declare that she could take care of herself. If pressed, she would have to admit, if only to herself, that it was rather nice to have someone looking out for her. It was something she'd really never experienced before.

Her lips curved in a half smile as she said, "I guess chivalry isn't dead."

Smiling in response, Ethan lead the way across the parking lot to his car.

The fact that she'd accepted his help had him deciding to venture out a little further. He watched as she got in, then got in himself. His key in the ignition, he left it dormant for a moment and turned toward her.

"Feel like getting some dinner?" he asked her, then added, "We're off the clock."

A couple of weeks ago, she would have turned him down without a moment's hesitation. A couple of weeks ago, she *had* turned him down, she recalled.

But that was then, and this was now. And she really didn't feel like going home and being by herself. Not after the captain had just looked at her as if she were a leper.

"Sure, why not?"

He'd learned not to declare victory with her until he was completely certain of it. "You realize I don't mean a drive-through, right?"

Her smile widened. "I realize."

He found he had to force himself to look away. Her mouth could look very enticing when it wasn't moving. "Good. We're on the same page."

Not yet, she thought, a warmth slipping over her. But she had a feeling that they were getting there.

Chapter 11

"You look like you could use a friend," Ethan commented as he sank down into his chair across from Kansas.

It was the end of yet another grueling day of interviews. For the last two days, he and Kansas had been questioning the firefighters who had been the first responders to each and every fire under investigation. The firefighters who, for the most part, she had once worked with side by side.

The interviews, as she'd expected, had not been a walk in the park. At best, the men were resentful and growing steadily more begrudging in their answers. At worst, the responses bordered on being insulting, hostile and verbally abusive. And Kansas, because she was considered one of them—or had been until now—had caught the worst of it.

It took her a moment now to realize that O'Brien was

talking to her. And then another moment to replay in her head what he'd just said.

"I could use a drink," she countered, closing her eyes and leaning back in her chair. Every muscle in her shoulders felt welded to the one next to it, forming knots the size of boulders. "And a friend," she added after a beat.

If he was surprised by the latter admission, he didn't show it. "I might have a solution for both," Ethan proposed. The comment had her opening her eyes again. "We're off duty." Technically, they'd been off for the last twenty minutes. "What do you say to stopping by Malone's?"

"I still have these reports to finish," she protested, indicating the daunting pile of files sitting in front of her on the desk.

Getting up, Ethan leaned over their joint desks and shoved the files over to the far corner.

"We're off duty," he repeated. Then, to make his point, he rounded their desks, got behind her chair and pulled it back so that she was actually sitting in the aisle rather than at her desk.

She looked over her shoulder at him. "What's Malone's?" she wanted to know.

Ethan took her hand, urging her to her feet. She had no choice but to acquiesce. "A haven," Ethan answered simply.

"A haven that serves drinks," Kansas amended in amusement.

"That's what makes it a *good* haven," he explained, a whimsical smile playing along his lips.

He'd become acquainted with Malone's the day he

became a detective. One of the other detectives invited him along for a celebratory drink in honor of his newly bestowed position. Malone's was a local gathering place, more tavern than bar. Detectives of the Aurora police force as well as various members of their family gravitated there for no other reason than to just be among friends who understood what it meant to be a police detective or part of a detective's family.

On any given evening, a healthy representation of the Cavanaughs could be found within the ninety-year-old establishment's four walls. He, Kyle and Greer had discovered that shortly after they'd discovered their new identities. Coming to Malone's helped bolster a sense of camaraderie as well as a sense of belonging.

"Are you up for it?" he prodded.

"If I say no, you won't give me any peace until I surrender." It wasn't a question, it was an assumption. O'Brien had definite pit bull tendencies. She could relate to that. "So I guess I might as well save us both some grief and say yes."

Ethan grinned, looking exceeding boyish. He didn't come across like someone to be reckoned with—but she knew he was.

"Good conclusion," he told her. He watched her close down her computer. "I can take you," he volunteered. "And then later I can bring you back to your car."

The last interview had gone exceptionally badly. Tom Williams, a man she had once regarded as a friend, had all but called her a traitor. She was feeling very vulnerable right now, and the last thing she wanted was to be in a car with Ethan when she felt like that. Major mistakes were built on missteps taken in vulnerable moments. If she hadn't felt so alone, she wouldn't have fallen for Grant like that.

"Why don't I just follow you and save you the trouble of doubling back," she countered.

"No trouble," he assured her, spreading his hands wide. The look on her face didn't change. "Have it your way," he declared, raising his hands up in mock surrender. "I'll lead the way." She had her purse, and her computer was powered down. He looked at her expectantly. "You ready?"

Kansas caught her bottom lip between her teeth. She supposed that one drink couldn't hurt. But one, she promised herself, was going to be her limit.

"Ready," she echoed.

It was a good plan, and had she stuck to it she would have been home at around the time she'd initially planned. In addition, there would have been plenty of time to get a good night's sleep. But she strayed from the path within the first fifteen minutes of arrival.

Because she'd felt as stiff as a rapier and really wanted to loosen up a little and fit in, she'd downed the first drink placed in front of her instead of sipping it. Ethan's cautionary words to go slow—something that surprised her—were ringing in her ears as she ordered a second drink. Maybe she'd ordered it *because* he'd warned her to go slow and she was feeling combative.

After facing what amounted to blatant hostility all day, being here, amid the laughter of friendly people in a warm atmosphere, was the difference between night and day. Reveling in it, she consequently let her guard down as she absorbed the warm vibrations of the people around her.

An hour into it, as more and more people filled the tavern, she turned to Ethan and whispered, "I can't feel my knees."

He hadn't left her side the entire time and had warned her against the last two of the three drinks she'd had. He looked down now, as if to verify what he was about to say. "They're still there," he assured her.

"I'm serious," she hissed. She didn't like this vague, winking-in-and-out feeling that had come over her. "What does that mean?"

This time he looked at her incredulously. She was serious. Who would have thought? "You've never been drunk before?"

"I'm drunk?" Kansas echoed, stunned. "You sure?" she questioned.

Suppressing his grin, Ethan held up his hand, folding down two fingers. "How many fingers am I holding up right now?"

Kansas squinted, trying her best to focus. Her best was not quite good enough. "How many chances do I get?"

He had his answer. "Okay, Cinderella, time for you to go."

Kansas tried to take a deep breath and began to cough instead. She was feeling very wobbly. "I don't think I can drive."

"No one was going to let you," he assured her. His tone was friendly but firm. He would have wrestled the keys away from her if he'd had to. "C'mon, let's go outside for some fresh air," he urged, slowly guiding her through the crowd.

She found that she had to concentrate very hard to put one foot in front of the other without allowing her knees to buckle. "I'd rather go somewhere more private. With you." Those were the words in her head. How they'd managed to reach her tongue and emerge, she really wasn't sure.

He nodded toward the room behind them teeming with people. "Right now, outside *is* more private. And I'll be coming with you. I'll be the one holding you up," he told her.

"Good," she said, "because I'm not altogether sure I can manage to do that on my own," she confessed. The second the words registered with her brain, she asked, "What did you put in my drink?"

"I didn't put anything into your drink," he told her, shouldering a path for her as he kept his arm around her waist. He caught Kyle looking his way—and smiling. "Could be that having three of them in a row might have had something to do with your knees dissolving on you."

Having made it to the front door, he pushed it open and guided her over the threshold. Once outside, he moved over to the side and leaned her against the wall in an effort to keep her upright and steady. He had the feeling that if he stepped back, she'd slide right down to the ground.

He was close to her. So close that his proximity worked its way into her system, undermining every single resolution she'd ever made.

God, he was handsome, she thought. Jarringly handsome.

"You know, you're just too damn good-looking for my own good."

She would have never said that sober, he thought. Ethan couldn't help the grin that came to his lips. "I'll remember you said that. You probably won't want me to, but I will." He put his arm up to hold her in place as she began to sink a little. "Take a deep breath," he instructed. "It'll help."

She did as he told her, which was when Ethan realized that his supporting arm was way too close to her chest. As she inhaled, her breasts rose, making contact with his forearm.

All sorts of responses went ricocheting through Ethan.

"Maybe not quite so deep," he suggested.

She was very aware of the contact. And equally aware of what it was doing to her.

"Why?" she asked, cocking her head as she looked at him, her blond hair spilling out onto his arm like soft fairy dust. "Am I getting to you, Detective O'Brien?"

She has no idea, does she? he thought. "You need to sleep this off," he informed her.

Her eyes were bright as she asked, "You're taking me home?"

"Yes." And then, to make sure that there wasn't any confusion about this, he added, "Your home."

Kansas sucked in another deep, deep breath. "'K," she agreed glibly.

Weaving one arm around her waist again, Ethan began to usher her to his car. While trying to maneuver,

Kansas got the heel of her shoe caught in a crack in the asphalt. She kept moving, but the shoe didn't, and she wound up dipping forward. Sensing she was about to fall, Ethan tightened his hold around her waist, dragging her closer against him.

For one second, their faces were less than a measurable inch away from one another.

And the next second, even that was gone.

Giving in to the moment and her weakened state of resistance, Kansas kissed him. Not lightly as she had in the kiss they'd previously shared, but with all the feeling that Ethan had stirred up within her. The alcohol she'd consumed had eroded her defenses and melted the distance she'd been determined to keep between herself and any viable candidate for her affections. Kansas wrapped her arms around his neck as she leaned into his very hard body. Leaned into the kiss that was swallowing them both up.

For a single isolated moment in time, Ethan let himself enjoy what was happening. Enjoy it and savor it because almost from the beginning, he'd wondered what it would be like to *really* kiss this vibrant woman who had for reasons that were far beyond him been thrust into his world.

Now he had his answer.

The kiss packed a wallop that left him breathless… and wanting more. Definitely more.

Which was when the warning flares went up.

This wasn't just something to enjoy and move on. This was something that created intense cravings that would inevitably demand to be filled.

As heat engulfed his body, he knew he had to tear

himself free—or else there very likely would be no turning back. And if he was going to make love with this woman, it was *not* going to be because her ability to reason had been diluted by something that came out of a bottle marked 90 proof.

Expending more self-control and effort than he ever had before, Ethan forcibly removed her arms from around his neck, broke contact and took a less than steady step back.

Bewilderment crossed her face. How could she have been so wrong? It was only because she was still inebriated that she had the nerve to ask, "You don't want me?"

He heard the confusion and hurt in her voice. "Not on my conscience, no."

His keys already in his hand, he pointed them toward his car, pressed the button and released the locks a second before he gingerly turned her toward his vehicle. Ethan opened the door and then very carefully lowered her onto the passenger seat. When she merely sat there, he ushered in her legs, shifting her so that she faced forward.

Hurrying around the back of the car, Ethan got in on the driver's side.

"You don't want me," she repeated in a soft, incredulous voice that was barely above a whisper. "God, I'm such an idiot," she upbraided herself.

Sticking the key in the ignition, he left it there and turned toward her. Maybe it was safer to have her think that, but the hurt in her voice was more than he could live with.

"Look, on a scale of one to ten, wanting you comes

in at fifteen," he told her. "But I want you because *you* made the decision to be with me. I don't want you making love with me because the decision was made for you by your alcohol consumption."

She stopped listening after the first part. "Fifteen?" she questioned as he started the engine.

"Yeah," he bit off, frustration eating away at him. There were times he wished he wasn't such a damn Boy Scout—even if his reasoning was dead on. "Fifteen."

Kansas took a deep breath, smiling from ear to ear with deep satisfaction. Sliding down in her seat, she stretched like a cat waking from a long, invigorating nap in the sun.

She had the grace of a feline as well, Ethan thought, trying—and failing—to ignore her.

She slanted a coy glance at him. "I can live with that."

He only wished he could.

But he was going to have to, he lectured himself. He had no other choice.

The most intense part of her buzz had worn off by the time Ethan made the turn that brought them into her garden apartment complex.

Her knees, she noted, were back, as were some of her inhibitions. But there was something new in the mix as well: surprise steeped in respect.

Ethan could have easily taken advantage of her temporary mindless condition. She'd all but thrown herself at him. Had he been anyone else, he could have very easily taken her to the backseat of his car and had sex with her, then crowed about it later to his friends.

That he didn't left her feeling grateful—and feeling something more than just simple attraction.

There was nothing simple about what was going on inside her.

The emotion was vaguely familiar, yet at the same time it was as new as the next sunrise. And she had no idea what to make of it, what to do about it or where to go from here. It was all just one great big question mark for her.

That, and an itch that all but begged to be scratched.

"Where can I park the car?" he asked her as they drove past a trove of daisies, their heads bowed for the night.

"Guest parking is over there." She pointed to a row of spaces, some filled, some not, that ran parallel to the rental office just up ahead.

Ethan took the first empty spot he came to. After pulling up the hand brake, he put the car into Park and turned off the engine. Getting out, he rounded the rear of the vehicle and came around to her side. He opened the door and took her hand to help her out.

She placed her hand in his automatically. The semi-fog around her brain was lifting, enabling her to focus better, physically and mentally. When she did, she had to squelch her initial impulse to just get out on her own and she took his hand, allowing him to help her. She knew she needed it.

There was something comforting about the contact, about having someone there with her, that she couldn't deny. That she *had* been denying herself, she thought, ever since she'd run from her disastrous, abbreviated marriage.

She raised her eyes to his as she got out. "Thanks," she murmured.

His smile was slow, sensual and instantly got under her skin. "Don't mention it."

Instead of getting into the car again as she'd expected, Ethan remained at her side. Nodding toward the array of apartments, he asked, "Which one is yours?"

"Number eighty-three," she told him, pointing toward the second grouping of apartments.

As he began walking in that direction, Ethan took her arm and held on to it lightly. He was probably worried that she was going to sink again, she thought. Kansas took no offense. How could she? Her limbs had been the consistency of wet cotton less than half an hour before. He was being thoughtful.

And getting to her more than she cared to admit.

Reaching her door, he waited until she took out her key and unlocked it.

"You going to be all right?" he asked.

The words "of course" hovered on her lips, straining to be released. It was the right thing to say. What she would have normally said.

But instead, what came out was, "Maybe you should walk me in, just in case."

Her eyes met his and there was a long moment that stretched out between them. A moment with things being said without words.

And then he inclined his head.

"All right."

Chapter 12

The second Kansas stepped across her threshold into her apartment, she felt her adrenaline instantly kicking in. It raced madly to all parts of her at once, sounding a multitude of alarms like so many tiny Paul Reveres riding in the night. Her whole body went on alert—not in waves, but simultaneously.

The feeling intensified when she heard the lock click into place as Ethan closed the door behind him.

This is it, she thought. *Time to fish or cut bait, Beckett.*

She wanted to fish. Desperately.

Damn it, Ethan thought as a warmth undulated through his body, why was he doing this to himself? Why was he testing himself this way? He should have just ushered Kansas in, politely said good-night and then gotten out of there.

For every moment he hesitated, every moment that

he *didn't* do the right thing, it became that much harder for him to walk away.

But as much as he wanted her—and until this very moment he had no idea that he could possibly *ever* want a woman this much—he couldn't allow himself to act on that desire. He had a sister. If someone had taken advantage of her in this kind of a situation, he would have cut the guy's heart out and served it to him for lunch. Just because he was on the other side of this scenario didn't make it any more excusable for him to take advantage of the woman.

"So, if you're okay, I'll be going," he said, fully expecting his feet to engage and begin moving back to the door.

But they didn't move. They seemed to remain glued in place.

Kansas looked up at him. How could she be getting more beautiful, more desirable by the second? It wasn't possible.

And yet...

"But I'm not okay," she said.

The drinks she'd had at Malone's were probably getting to her stomach, Ethan guessed. "What's wrong? You feel sick?" He should have never brought her there, he upbraided himself.

"That wouldn't be the word I'd use," she answered, moving closer to him, dissolving the tiny distance between them until there wasn't space enough for a heartbeat.

As she began to put her arms around his neck, Ethan stopped her, catching her wrists and bringing her arms down again. He saw confused frustration crease Kansas's brow.

"In case you haven't noticed, Detective," she told him, "I'm throwing myself at you."

"Oh, I've noticed, all right." He'd been acutely aware of everything about her from the first moment. "And at any other time, I'd be more than happy to do the catching."

Her eyes narrowed as she struggled to understand. She took his words at face value. "What's wrong with Thursdays?"

He laughed softly, shaking his head. "There's nothing wrong with Thursdays. There's something wrong with taking advantage of a woman." He appealed to her because he really needed help if he was going to do the right thing. He couldn't do it on his own. He was only human. "Kansas, you're not thinking clearly. You're probably not thinking at all," he amended.

Otherwise, he reasoned, she wouldn't be acting this way. The Kansas he'd come to know wouldn't have thrown herself at a man. She would have skewered him if he even attempted anything.

Kansas took a breath, absorbing this. Men like O'Brien weren't supposed to exist. Everything she'd ever learned pointed to the fact that they didn't. And yet, here he was, sounding as noble as if he'd just ridden in on a charger with Lancelot.

No, with Galahad, she silently corrected herself, because Lancelot lusted after the queen, but Galahad was purity personified.

Looking Ethan squarely in the eye, she said, "Give me a calculus problem."

Just how hard had those three drinks hit her? "What?"

"A calculus problem," she repeated. "If I solve it, will that prove to you that my brain is functioning? That it isn't in a fog and neither am I? I admit the drinks hit me hard at first," she said before he could bring it up, "but the effect didn't last, and believe me, that 'I can touch the sky' feeling is long gone." Although, she thought, it had served its purpose. "While it lasted, it let me say what I couldn't say stone-cold sober. That I want to make love with you."

Pausing for a moment, she looked up at him. Every breath she took registered against his body, against his skin.

"Don't you want to make love with me?" she asked as the silence stretched out between them.

Oh God, did he ever. "You have no idea," he told her, feeling as if the effort to restrain himself was all but strangling him.

The smile that slipped over her lips in almost slow motion drew him in an inch at a time. Trapping him so that he couldn't turn back, couldn't cut loose. Couldn't tear his eyes away.

She rose up on her toes. "Then educate me," she whispered, her lips all but brushing against his as she spoke.

He was just barely holding on to his self-control. The next second, as the promise of her mouth whispered along his, his self-control snapped in two, leaving him without any resources to use in the fight against his reactions.

Instead of doing the noble thing and protesting, or

saying anything about the way she was going to regret this, Ethan pressed his lips against hers and kissed her. *Really* kissed her.

Kissed her so deeply and with such feeling that he was instantly lost.

All he could think of was having her. Having her in the most complete, satisfying sense of the word and steeping himself in her until he wouldn't be able to tell where he ended and she began.

The kiss went deeper.

Yes!

The single, triumphant word echoed over and over again in Kansas's brain even as she felt her body melting in the flames that his mouth had created within her. This, this was the connection she'd missed, the part of herself she had struggled to pretend didn't exist, the part of her that hadn't been allowed to see the light of day. It broke free and filled every single space within her.

Everything within Kansas hummed with a happiness she hadn't known was achievable.

But as that feeling of happiness, of absolute joy, progressed, all but consuming her, Kansas swiftly came to realize that this really *wasn't* the feeling she'd hoped for.

This was more.

So very much more.

Before this, any kind of happiness she'd experienced with Grant amounted to little more than a thimbleful in comparison. This "thing" she was feeling was like an ocean. An all-encompassing, huge ocean. And she was swimming madly through it as the current kept sweeping her away, taking absolutely all control out of her hands.

She was at its mercy.

And she loved it!

She felt Ethan's breath on her neck, making her skin sizzle.

Making her want more.

And all the while the very core of her kept quickening in anticipation of what was to be. What she *hoped* was to be.

She struggled to hold herself at bay, struggled to savor this for as long as she could. For as long as it went on. Because something told her that these conditions would never be met again. This was a one-of-a-kind, one-time-only thing. Like the sighting of a comet.

And then, just like that, Ethan was no longer kissing her. His lips were no longer grazing the side of her neck, rendering her all but mindless. Ethan had drawn back, cupping her face in his hands as he silently declared a "time-out."

Confused, with shafts of disappointment weaving through her, she looked at Ethan quizzically. "What?" she asked breathlessly. Had she done something wrong? Turned him off somehow?

"Last chance," he offered.

She shook her head, not understanding. "Last chance for what?"

"For you to back out." He held his breath, waiting for her answer. Praying she'd say what he wanted her to say.

It came in the form of a soft laugh. The sound all but

ricocheted around her small living room. "Not on your life."

He couldn't begin to describe the urge he felt just then.

"Okay, just remember, I gave you a chance. You asked for this," he told her, his voice gruff.

"I know," she managed to say before her lips became otherwise engaged.

The next moment, his mouth was back on hers, kissing her senseless as his fingers got busy removing the layers of her clothing that were between them.

He began with her jacket, sliding it down her arms. The garment was followed by her cherry-red tank top and her white skirt. With each piece of clothing he removed from her, the heat encircling her intensified. And his breathing grew shorter, she noted, as a haze began to descend over her brain.

Refusing to be passive, even if she was being reduced to a mass of fiery yearning, Kansas started to remove his clothes, as well. As she worked buttons free, took down zippers, she felt as if her fingers were clumsier at this process than his were. But then, it wasn't as if she was altogether clear-headed right now. Or experienced at doing this kind of thing.

They achieved their goal at the same time.

Clothes commingling in a pile on the floor, their bodies primed and aching, he swept her into his arms as if she weighed no more than one of the reports that she'd left abandoned on the desk at the precinct.

"Where's your bedroom?" he asked in between pleasuring her mouth with bone-melting kisses.

"At the end of the hall," she answered with effort.

Because her lips had been separated from his during this short verbal exchange, Kansas framed his face with her hands, held his head in place as she raised up her mouth to cover his.

He almost dropped her. But that was because she was so effectively weakening his limbs.

Bringing her into her bedroom, he placed her on the bed, joining her without breaking rhythm. Ethan began kissing her with even more passion.

He made her forget absolutely everything, especially the glaring looks and thinly veiled derogatory remarks she'd received from this afternoon's collection of firefighters.

Nothing else mattered. Not her past, not the lonely isolation of her childhood, nor the emptiness of her short-lived marriage to a narcissist. All that mattered was sustaining this incredible feeling that was crescendoing through her.

Because of him.

In response to him, her own kisses became more passionate, more intense. Each place that Ethan touched, she mirrored the gesture, sweeping soft, questing fingertips over his tantalizingly hard body. Glorying in the way he responded to her, the way he moved. The sound of his moan drove her crazy.

She saw that she could arouse him even more with just a touch—just the way he could her. The thought of exercising that kind of control over him was mind-blowing. She felt like an equal, not just like a receptive vessel. That was the moment that this completely transcended anything she'd ever experienced before.

Thinking that she was at the highest level she could

reach short of the final one, she discovered in the next moment that she was wrong.

She all but lost the ability to snatch a thought out of the air when Ethan began to trace a hot, moist path to her very core, first with his hands and then, very swiftly, with his lips.

Suppressing a surprised gasp, Kansas was barely able to breathe as she rode the crest of the all-consuming climax Ethan had just produced within her.

She arched and bucked, desperate to absorb the sensation and keep it alive for even so much as a heartbeat longer. But when it left, leaving her convinced that she'd experienced the best that there was, Ethan's clever mouth brought another wave to fruition.

And then another. Until she cried out something unintelligible. Whether she was asking for mercy or for more, neither one of them knew.

But suddenly, there he was, over her, pressing her deep into her bed as he slid his hard body along hers, activating yet another host of sensations until she was completely convinced that she had somehow just vibrated into an alternative universe where pleasure was king and nothing else mattered. Ever.

Breathing hard now, trying vainly to draw in enough air to sustain herself, Kansas parted her legs and opened for him.

And cried out his name as she felt him enter.

The music suddenly materialized in her head, coming from nowhere.

The dance began slowly, building quickly.

A waltz developed into a samba, then the tempo went faster and faster until the final moment with its satisfying dispersion of mind-numbing sensations echoed within them both.

It was like New Year's Eve when the clock struck midnight and confetti came raining down, accompanied by cries of good wishes and happiness.

Gradually, she became aware of clinging to Ethan, became aware that her arms were still wrapped tightly around his back and that her body was still arching into his even though he was on top.

She became aware as well that his breathing was just as short as hers.

And aware, most of all, that she didn't want this very special moment to end. Didn't want to exchange what she was feeling for reality, where guilt and vulnerability and, most of all, disappointment resided, ready to rain on her parade.

But the moment linked itself to another and then another until finally, the descent came, slowly rather than rapidly, but it came. And it brought her down with it.

She felt Ethan shift his weight off her and realized that he'd been propping himself on his elbows the entire time they'd made love to spare her being oppressed by his weight.

That was when she recalled having trouble breathing when Grant made love with her. Grant always allowed his full weight to press against her, against her lungs, after he'd satisfied himself. Once he'd actually fallen asleep and had gotten angry at her for waking him up. He claimed not to remember the incident when he was awake the next day. And because she loved him, because she wanted him to love her, she'd believed him.

Or said she had.

They weren't the same kind of men at all, he and Ethan, she realized. Maybe there really were two different kinds of men. The good ones and the bad ones.

No, don't do that. Don't go there, she warned herself sternly. *You're just going to start hoping and setting yourself up for a fall. You fell once, crashing and burning, remember? That should be enough for anyone, including you.*

She felt Ethan's smile before she saw it.

Turning her head to look at him, Kansas saw that she was right. He was smiling. Grinning, really. Was he laughing at her, enjoying some private joke at her expense?

She could feel herself withdrawing. "What?" she demanded.

His smile seem to soften, or maybe that was wishful thinking on her part, a way for her to save face in her own eyes.

"You, Kansas," he told her, "are just full of surprises."

She could feel her defenses going up, and just like that, she was ready for a fight. "Meaning?"

"Meaning I don't think I've ever actually been blown away before." He stopped as if he was thinking, trying to remember. But there was no need to think, really. Because he already knew. "No, never blown away. Until now." He combed his fingers through her hair, looking into her eyes. Despite everything, all those defenses she thought she'd just hastily thrown up, she felt herself melting. "You really can make the earth move, can't you?"

What she wanted to do was lean into his touch. But she knew the danger in that. Instead, she rebuffed his words. "You don't have to flatter me, O'Brien. We already made love," she pointed out.

"I don't *have* to do anything at all," he told her. "I tend not to, as a matter of fact. Kyle's the family rebel, but that doesn't mean that Greer and I just fall docilely into step, doing whatever we're told, following all the rules just because they're rules." His smile deepened as he looked at her, thoughts cropping up in his head that he was not willing to share yet—if ever. "You, Beckett, are a force to be reckoned with. But I already kind of figured you would be."

He was doing it again, she thought, he was breaching her soul. But somehow the sense of alarm that should have accompanied that realization was missing. "Oh, you did, did you?"

He traced a light, circular pattern along the back of her neck and managed to send shivers down her spine. "Yup."

"Is that because you think you're such a red-hot lover?" she asked, doing her best to sound sarcastic. But her heart just wasn't in it. Her heart was elsewhere. Hoping…

"No," he answered seriously, his eyes holding hers. "It's because I'm a pretty good judge of people."

"And does this ability to correctly judge people help you guess what's going to come next?"

"Sometimes," he allowed.

"Okay," she challenged, "what's going to come next now?"

She could feel his smile getting under her skin as it spread over his lips. "Surprise me," he whispered.

Funny how a whisper could send such shock waves through her system, she thought. "That," she informed him as a sexy smile curved her lips, "is a downright dangerous challenge."

"Oh God, I certainly hope so."

Then, before she could comment on his response, Ethan pulled her to him, his mouth covering hers. Silencing her the best way he knew how.

It was the best way she knew how…as well.

Chapter 13

There had to be something. *Something,* Kansas insisted silently as she sat at the desk that, after more than a month of being here, she'd begun to regard as her own. She felt as if she'd been reexamining files forever.

It was late and everyone on the task force had gone home long ago. She'd even sent away Ethan, who had remained after the others—including the two extra detectives the chief had given them—had left, trying to do what he could to make the tedious process go faster. But another case he'd been working on had required his attention as well, and consequently he'd gotten next to no sleep in over two days.

He was beginning to resemble death walking, she'd told him, insisting that he go home. Ethan had finally given in about ninety minutes ago, leaving the precinct after making her promise that she'd only remain another few minutes.

A "few minutes" had knitted themselves into an hour, and then more. She was still here.

But there was nothing waiting for her at home, and she felt far too wired to actually get any sleep, so she reasoned that she might as well stay and work. At least if she was working, she wouldn't be tempted to call Ethan, suggesting a really late dinner. That was, at best, thinly veiled code for what she knew would happen.

It wasn't the thought of dinner that aroused her. It was the thought of sitting opposite Ethan in a setting where she didn't have to remain the consummate professional. Where, mentally, she would count off the minutes before he would reach for her and they would make love again.

After that first night together, there had been several more evenings that had ended with their clothes being left in a heap on the floor and their bodies gloriously entwined.

And with each time that they made love, she found that instead of finally becoming sated, she just wanted more.

Always more.

At least if she was here, embroiled in what was beginning to look like a futile hunt, she couldn't do anything about getting together with Ethan. Superman or not, the man did need his sleep.

As for her, Kansas thought, she needed to be vindicated, to prove to herself that she hadn't all but destroyed her hard-won career with the fire department on a baseless hunch.

She was right, Kansas silently insisted. She could feel it in her bones. She just needed to find something, that one elusive, tiny trace of something or other that would finally lead her to the person who was responsible for setting the fires.

But so far, it didn't look as if she was going to get anywhere. All the firefighters who had responded to the various alarms seemed to be above reproach. There were no citations, no disciplinary actions of any kind in their personal files.

The only unusual notation that she'd come across was the one in Nathan Bonner's folder. He was the firefighter who had come on the job after she was no longer an active member of the team. The captain had inserted a handwritten note that said the man was almost too eager, too ready to give 110 percent each and every time. The captain was afraid he was going to burn himself out before his time. Otherwise, he was excellent.

She sighed, leaning back in her chair, staring at the screen and the database that she'd been using. Her methodical review had been eliminating suspects one by one until, instead of at least a few left standing, there was no one. From all indications, this was a sterling group of men.

They probably didn't even cheat on their taxes, she thought, disgruntled. Too bad. When all else failed, the authorities caught racketeers and career criminals by scrutinizing their taxes. Income tax evasion was the way the FBI had brought down the infamous Al Capone. Her mouth curved at the irony in that. When in doubt, check out their tax forms.

She sat up, straight as an arrow, as the thought registered.

Why not?

She'd tried every other avenue. Maybe she *could* find something in their income tax forms that she could use. At this point, Kansas was desperate enough to try anything.

Pressing her lips together, she stared at the screen, thinking. Trying her best to remember. When she was in college, before she'd thought that the world began and ended with Grant, she'd gone out with a Joe Balanchine. Joe had an ingrained knack for making computers do whatever he needed them to do. Trying to impress her, he'd taught her a few things, like how easy it was to hack into files that were supposedly beyond hacking.

"Here's hoping I can remember what you taught me, Joe," she murmured.

It took her several unsuccessful tries before she finally managed to scale the electronic cyberspace walls and hack into the system. When it finally opened up, allowing her to access federal and state income tax data, Kansas felt almost giddy with triumph.

She realized that she should have taken that as a sign that maybe it was time for her to go home and get some sleep, approaching this from a fresh perspective tomorrow morning. But again, she was far too wired to even contemplate going to bed. If she went home now, she'd spend the night staring at the ceiling.

Or calling Ethan.

The latter thought had her chewing on her lower lip. When had that become the norm for her? When had sharing moments large and small with Ethan become something she looked forward to? This was dangerous ground she was traversing, and she knew it.

But right now, she was far too happy with this latest success to care.

With the firefighters' Social Security numbers at her fingertips, she arranged them in ascending numerical order. That done, she quickly went from one file to another, using the seven-year window that had once been the standard number of years an audit could go back and hold the taxpayer culpable for any errors, unintentional or not.

Employing a general overview, she went from one firefighter's file to another.

And one by one, she struck out.

She couldn't find a single suspicious notation, a single red flag that an auditor had questioned. There weren't even any random audits.

The euphoria she'd previously experienced faded as dejection took hold. Her eyes swept over the tax forms of the second-to-last firefighter, the numbers hardly penetrating.

This had been her last hope. Her last…

"Hello," she murmured to herself, sitting up. "What's this?"

Blinking a few times to make sure she wasn't seeing something that wasn't there—or rather, not seeing something that was, she focused on Nathan Bonner's file.

"So you *do* have a skeleton in your closet," she said to the screen, addressing it as if she were talking to Bonner. The likeable firefighter's returns went back only three years. The same amount of time he'd been with the Aurora Fire Department.

According to the form he'd filled out when he joined

the department, he had transferred from a firehouse in Providence, Rhode Island. She recalled seeing copies of glowing letters of recommendation in his file. But if that were the case, he would have had to have worked at the firehouse there. And earned a living. Which necessitated filing a tax form.

And he hadn't.

Kansas went through the records a second time. And then a third. There were no returns filed from that period.

Maybe it wasn't Rhode Island. Maybe it was somewhere else. She did a search, using just his name and inputting it into each state, one by one. A Nathan Bonner, with his Social Security number, finally turned up in New York City. With a death certificate.

She sat back, staring at the information. Nathan Bonner died in a car accident in January of 2001. He was seventy-five years old at the time. The Social Security number and month and date of birth all matched the ones that Bonner had claimed were his.

Wow.

"Nathan Bonner" was a fraud, she thought, her heart launching into double time. This was it, this was what she was looking for. Bonner was their firebug. He had to be. She didn't know why he'd gone through this elaborate charade or what else he was up to, but he was their man. She was sure of it.

Excited, she grabbed the phone receiver and was inputting Ethan's cell-phone number. He had to hear this.

The phone on the other end rang four times and then Kansas heard it being picked up. She was almost breathless as she started talking. "Ethan, it's Kansas. Listen, I think that—"

"You've reached Ethan O'Brien's cell phone. I can't talk right now, but if you leave your—"

"Damn it!" Impatience ate away at Kansas. Was he sound asleep? She heard the tone ring in her ear. "Ethan, it's Kansas. If you get this message, call me. I think I found our man." Why hadn't she gotten the number of his landline? At least when she left a message, if he was anywhere in the area, she stood a good chance of waking him up by talking loudly.

Biting off an oath, she hung up.

She contemplated her next move. Everyone liked Bonner. He was friendly and outgoing and appeared to take an interest in everyone around him. He was always willing to listen, always willing to go catch a beer at the end of the day—or lend money to tide a brother firefighter over to the next paycheck.

If she suggested that he was behind the fires, the rest of the house would demand her head on a platter. There was no way anyone was going to believe her without proof.

Okay, if it's proof they wanted, proof they were going to get. She hit the print button, printing everything she'd just read. She'd need it to back her up.

Once that was done and she had collected the pages from the mouth of the printer, she tried calling Ethan again. With the same results. She hung up just before his voice mail picked up.

Frustrated, she deposited the papers she'd just printed into a folder. She wanted Ethan to see this. The sooner the better. He was, as he'd claimed, her partner, and he needed to see proof that she was right. That he hadn't just backed her up only to have her take a dive off a cliff.

Humming, she got her things together and left the squad room.

She barely remembered the trip to Ethan's apartment. She'd been there only twice before. Once to return his cell phone that first night—and once when he'd brought her to his place after taking her out for dinner and a movie.

Her mouth curved. Just like two normal people. That night they'd made love until they fell asleep, exhausted, in each other's arms.

Excitement raced through her veins, and it was hard to say what was more responsible for her getting to that state—the fact that she was convinced that she'd found their firebug or that she was going to Ethan's apartment to see him.

By her calculation, Ethan had gotten about two hours' sleep if he'd gone right home and straight to bed. A person could go far on two hours if he had to, she reasoned. God knew she had. More than once.

And she *knew* Ethan wouldn't want her to wait until morning with this.

Pulling up directly in front of his apartment, taking a slot that she knew had to belong to someone else who, conveniently, was gone at the moment, she jumped out of her car. She didn't even bother locking the doors. She'd move the car later, but right now she had to see him.

Kansas headed straight for his door. It took everything she had to keep from pounding on it. Instead, she just knocked on his door as if this were nothing more than just a social visit instead of one that ultimately was a matter of life and death. They needed to catch Bonner before he set off another device.

When no one answered her knock, she knocked again, harder this time. Hard enough to hurt her knuckles.

"C'mon, c'mon. Wake up, Ethan," she called, raising her voice and hoping that it carried through the door. Just as she was about to try to call him on her cell again, thinking that the combination of pounding and ringing phone would finally wake him, the door to his apartment opened.

"Well, it's about time that yo—"

The rest of the sentence froze on her tongue. She wasn't looking at Ethan. She was looking at a woman. A gorgeous blonde with hypnotic eyes.

She felt as if someone had punched her in the stomach. Just the way she'd felt when she'd walked in on Grant and the hotel receptionist.

Stunned speechless, Kansas took a step back. "I'm sorry, I must have made—"

That was when she saw Ethan approaching from the rear of the apartment. Where the bedroom was located. He was barefoot and wearing the bottom half of a pair of navy blue pajamas. The ones he kept at the foot of his bed in case he had to throw something on to answer the door at night, he'd told her.

"—a mistake," she concluded. "I've made a terrible mistake. I'm sorry to have bothered you," she told the woman coldly. Kansas turned on her heel and hurried away, leaving the woman in the doorway looking after her, confused.

She heard Ethan call her name, but she refused to stop, refused to turn around. She was too angry. At him. At herself.

And too full of pain.

Damn it, it had happened again. She'd *let* it happen again. How could she have been naive enough, stupid enough to think that Ethan was different? That he could actually be someone who was faithful? It was inherently against a man's religion to be faithful, and she should have her head examined for thinking it was remotely possible.

Getting into the car, she didn't even bother securing her seat belt. She just started the car and put it into Drive.

Kansas felt her eyes stinging and she blinked several times, trying to push back her tears, fiercely telling herself that she wasn't going to cry. He wasn't worth tears.

No strings, remember? You promised yourself no strings. Strings just trip you up, she told herself. *What the hell happened?*

"Kansas, stop!" Ethan called after her.

She deliberately shut his voice out. All she wanted to do was get away.

Now.

She should have never come here—no, she amended, she *should* have. Otherwise, how would she have ever found out that he was just like all the rest? Deceitful and a cheat. Better now than later when she—

Kansas swallowed a scream. Keen reflexes had her swerving to the left at the last minute to avoid hitting him. Ethan had raced after her and had managed, via some shortcut he must have taken, to get right in front of her. He had his hand on her hood in an instant, using himself as a human roadblock.

Her heart pounded so wildly it was hurting her chest. Had she gone an instant quicker, been driving an instant faster, she wouldn't have been able to swerve away in time.

Angry as she was at him, she didn't want to think about that.

Had it not been so late, she would have leaned on her horn. Instead, she rolled down her window and shouted, "Get out of the way."

"Not until you tell me what's wrong with you," he ground out between teeth that were clenched together to keep from giving her a piece of his mind.

"Nothing anymore," she declared, lifting her chin in what he'd come to know as sheer defiance. "Now get the hell out of the way or I'll run you over. I swear I will," she threatened.

A movement in her rearview mirror caught her eye. The woman who'd opened the door was hurrying toward them. Great, that was all she needed. To see the two of them together.

"Your girlfriend's coming," she informed him, icicles clinging to every syllable. "Go and talk to her."

"What the hell are you talking about?" Ethan demanded. "What girlfriend?"

Did he think that if he denied any involvement, she'd fall into his arms like a newly returned puppy? "The one who opened the door."

He looked at her as if he was trying to decide if she'd

lost her mind—or he had. Glancing behind the car for confirmation, he told her, "That's Greer."

Was that supposed to make her feel as if they were all friends? "I don't care what her name is. Just go to her and get out of my way." She gripped the steering wheel as if she intended to go, one way or another.

The woman he'd just referred to as Greer peered into the passenger-side window. In contrast to Ethan, she looked calm and serene. And she had the audacity to smile at her.

The next moment, she was extending her hand to her through the opened window. "Hi, we haven't met yet. I'm Greer. Ethan's sister."

Had her whole body not been rigid with tension, her jaw would have dropped in her lap. "His what?"

"Sister," Ethan repeated for her benefit. "I told you I had one."

A sense of embarrassment was beginning to shimmer just on the perimeter of her consciousness. She valiantly held it at bay, but the feeling of having acted like a fool was blowing holes in her shield.

"You said you were triplets," Kansas protested. "She's a blonde. She doesn't look like you—"

"And I thank God every day for that," Greer interjected with a very wide grin. A grin that made her resemble Ethan, Kansas thought, chagrined. "I'm going to go, Ethan. Thanks for the pep talk, I really appreciate it." She looked from the woman behind the wheel to her barefoot brother. "I didn't mean to wake you," she apologized. About to walk away, she stopped and added, "By the way, you're right," she told her brother, amusement in her eyes. "She really is something."

And then she nodded at her. "Hope to see you again, Kansas."

For a second, Kansas was silent, watching the other woman walk to her car. "She knows my name?" she asked Ethan.

"Yeah." His expression gave nothing away.

There was only one reason for that as far as Kansas knew. "You told her about me."

Ethan shrugged carelessly. "Your name might have come up." And then a smattering of anger returned. "What the hell is all this about?" he wanted to know.

As embarrassing and revealing as it was, Kansas told him the truth. She owed him that much for having acted the way she had. But it wasn't easy. Baring her soul never was.

"For a minute, I thought I was reliving a scene from my past," she confessed.

His eyes narrowed. "Involving your husband, the idiot?"

Kansas pressed her lips together before nodding. "Yes."

"I'm not him, Kansas." He wondered if he would ever get that through to her. And what it would do to their relationship if he couldn't.

It wasn't in her nature to say she was sorry. For the first time, she caught herself wishing that it was. But the words wouldn't come no matter how much she willed them to. Saying "I know" was the best she could do.

"Good. Now go park your car and come back inside." He looked down at the pajama bottoms. "I'm going to go in before someone calls the police to complain about a half-naked man running around in the parking lot, playing dodgeball with a car."

The moon was out and rays of moonlight seemed to highlight the definition of his muscles. The term "magnificent beast" came to mind. "I don't think they'd be complaining if they actually saw you," she told him.

His eyes met hers. Again, she couldn't tell what he was thinking—or feeling. "It's going to take more than a few words of flattery to make up for this."

"Maybe when you hear why I came in the first place, you'll find it in your heart to forgive me." Mentally, she crossed her fingers.

"We'll see," he told her, making no promises one way or another.

Turning away, Ethan hiked up the pajama bottoms that were resting precariously on his hip bone, threatening to slip, and started back to his apartment.

Kansas sat in her car, watching him walk away, appreciating the view and trying not to let her imagination carry her away.

It was a couple of minutes before Kansas started up her car engine again. Her other engine was already revving.

Chapter 14

"Do you really think that little of me?" Ethan demanded, his voice controlled, the second she walked in. "So little that you just assume that if I'm with another woman, it has to be something sexual? That I have to be cheating on you?"

"No, I don't think that little of you," she answered, raising her voice to get him to stop talking for a moment and listen. "I think that little of *me*." He looked at her, confused, so she elaborated. "I'm not exactly the greatest judge of character when it comes to the men in my personal life. I try not to have a personal life because… because…" The words stuck in her throat and her voice trailed off.

"Because you're afraid of making a mistake?" he guessed.

She shrugged dismissively, wanting to be done with

this line of discussion, and looked away. "Something like that."

Ethan threaded his fingers through her hair, framing her face with his palms and gently forcing her to look at him. When she did, he brought his mouth down to hers and kissed her with bone-melting intensity.

After a very long moment, he drew back and asked her, "Does that feel like a mistake?"

Kansas's adrenaline had already launched into double time, threatening to go into triple. Everything else was put on hold, or temporarily forgotten.

The only thing that mattered was experiencing heaven one more time.

At least one more time, she silently pleaded with whoever might be listening. Because tomorrow would come and it might not be kind. But she had today, she had right now, and she desperately wanted to make the most of it.

"Ask me again later," she breathed. "I'm too busy now."

And with that, she recaptured his lips with her own and slipped off for another dip in paradise's sun-kissed waters.

He lost no time in joining her.

It wasn't until dawn the next morning, as Kansas woke up by degrees in his arms and slowly started removing the cobwebs from her brain, that she began thinking clearly again.

"What was it that you came here to tell me?" Ethan wanted to know, bringing everything back into focus for her.

Kansas raised herself up on her elbow to look at this man who, however unintentionally, kept rocking her world. From his expression, he'd been watching her sleep again. The fact that he hadn't woken her up with this question, that he'd waited until she'd opened her eyes on her own, just reinforced what she already knew to be true—the man was completely devoid of any curiosity.

Unlike her.

She needed to know everything. Public things, private things, it made absolutely no difference. She had always had this incredibly insatiable desire to know everything.

As for him, if the information wouldn't help him crack a case, he could wait it out—or even have it just fade away. It appeared to be all one and the same to Ethan.

"It's about Nathan Bonner—" She saw that there was no immediate recognition evident in his expression when she said the name. "The firefighter who was giving that old man from the nursing home CPR. The old man who died," she added.

It was the last piece that had the light dawning in his eyes.

"Oh him, right."

Playing with a strand of her hair, he was completely amazed that he could be so fiercely drawn to a woman. In the past, his usual MO was to make love with someone a couple of times—three, tops—and then move on, deliberately shunning any strings. But he didn't want to move on this time. He wanted to dig in for the long haul.

That had never happened to him before.

"What about him?" Ethan asked, whispering the question into her hair.

His breath warmed her scalp and sent ripples throughout her being. If this wasn't so important, she would have just given in to the feeling and made love with him. It was a hell of a good way to start the day.

But this had to be said. Ethan needed to know what she had discovered. "He doesn't exist."

Ethan looked at her, somewhat confused. "Come again?"

"Nathan Bonner doesn't exist," Kansas told him, enunciating each word slowly—then quickly explaining how she'd come to her conclusion. "He didn't even exist seven years ago. There're no federal income tax forms filed except for the last three years. If you go back four, there's nothing. No driver's license, no tax forms, no credit cards. Nothing," she emphasized.

Ethan stopped curling her hair around his finger and straightened, as if put on some kind of alert. Kansas had managed to get his undivided attention. "Hold it. Just how did you get hold of his tax records?"

A protective feeling nudged forward within her. Kansas shook her head, even though she knew her response frustrated him. She couldn't tell him how she'd gotten the information.

"If I don't tell you, the chief can't blame you," she told him. "Or kill you." Then, because he was staring at her intently, obviously not pleased with her answer, she sighed. It wasn't that she didn't trust him. She didn't want him blamed. But he had to know that her information was on the level. "I hacked into his files. His and a few others," she confessed.

For a second, she looked away and heard him ask in a quiet voice, "How many are a few?"

She thought of hedging, then decided against it. "All of them," she said quietly.

He'd never been this close to speechless before. "Kansas—"

"I was looking for something we could use," she explained, afraid he was going to launch into a lecture. "I didn't expect to find that Bonner was just an alias this guy was using." The moment he disappeared off the grid, she started hunting through old tax returns, trying to match the Social Security number. Her dogged efforts brought success. "He got his identity off a dead man."

That kind of thing happened in the movies, not real life. Ethan cast about for a reasonable explanation. "Maybe he's in the witness protection program."

The suggestion took some of the wind out of her sails.

"I suppose that could be one possibility." She rolled the idea over in her mind. Her gut told her it was wrong, but she knew she was going to need more than her gut to nail this down. "Do you know anyone in the marshal's office?" she asked him. "Someone who could check this out for us?"

Ethan grinned in response. She was obviously forgetting who she was talking to. "I'm a Cavanaugh by proxy. If I can't find out, someone within the family unit can."

There were definite advantages to having a large family beyond the very obvious, she thought with a mild touch of envy. "You're going to need a search warrant," she added.

"*We* are going to need a search warrant," he corrected.

"No," she contradicted him in a deceptively mild voice that made him decidedly uneasy. "Technically I can search his place, warrant or no warrant. Some people might see that as breaking and entering, but if I find anything incriminating, it *can* be used against him."

Ethan knew that look by now. It was the one that all but screamed "reckless." He had a feeling that it was probably useless, but he had to say this anyway. "Don't do anything stupid, Kansas."

The expression she gave him was innocence personified. "I never do anything stupid."

It took all he had not to laugh. "I wouldn't put that up for a vote if I were you." Throwing back the covers, he got up and then held his hand out to her. "C'mon, let's shower."

Taking it, she swung her legs out to the side and rose. "Together?"

Ethan paused for a second just to drink in the sight. Damn, he wanted her more each time he was with her. "It'll save time," he promised.

But it didn't.

Within an hour, they were at the firehouse. Together they confronted the captain with their request.

The veneer on the spirit of cooperation had worn thin and there was definite hostility in Captain Lawrence's eyes as he regarded them. The brunt of it was directed at Kansas.

"Bonner? You've already questioned everyone here once. Why do you want to talk to him again?" Lawrence demanded impatiently. The question was underscored with a glare. Before either could answer, the captain said, "He's one of the best firefighters I've ever had the privilege of working with. I don't want you harassing him."

Ethan took the lead, trying once again to divert the captain's anger onto him instead of Kansas. After all, she had to come back here and work with the man as well as the other firefighters. A situation, he thought, that was looking more and more bleak as time wore on.

"We just want to ask him a few more questions, Captain. Like why there's no record of him before he came to the firehouse. And why he has the same Social Security number as a guy who died in 2001."

If this new information stunned him, the captain gave no such indication. He merely shrugged it off. "That's gotta be a mistake of some sort," he replied firmly. "You know what record keeping is like with the government."

"Maybe," Ethan allowed. "But that's why we want to talk to Bonner, to clear up any misunderstanding."

"Well, you're out of luck." Lawrence began to walk to his small, cluttered office. "I insisted he take the day off. He'd been on duty for close to three weeks straight. The man's like a machine. We've been short-handed this last month, and he's been filling in for one guy after another."

"Isn't that unusual?" Ethan challenged. "To have a firefighter on duty for that long?"

"That's just the kind of guy he is," the captain pointed out proudly. "I wish I had a firehouse full of Bonners."

"No, you don't," Kansas said under her breath as Ethan asked the man for Bonner's home address.

The look that the older man slanted toward her told Kansas that her voice hadn't been as quiet as she'd initially thought.

Less than twenty minutes later they were walking up to Bonner's door. The man without an identity lived in a residential area located not too far from the firehouse where he worked. The ride to work probably took him a matter of minutes.

Ethan rang the doorbell. It took several attempts to get Bonner to answer his front door.

When the firefighter saw who was on his doorstep, the warm, friendly smile on his lips only grew more so. Kansas would have wavered in her convictions had she not read the files herself. The man looked like the personification of geniality.

"Sorry," he apologized. "I was just catching up on some Z's. I like to do that on my day off. It recharges my batteries," he explained. "Come on in." Opening the door all the way to admit them, he stepped to the side. "Sorry about the place being such a mess, but I've been kind of busy, doing double shifts at the firehouse. We're short a couple of guys, and since I really don't have anything special on my agenda, I volunteered to pick up the slack. The pay's good," he confided, "but it leaves my house looking like a tornado hit it."

"I've seen worse," Kansas told him as she looked around.

Actually, she thought, she'd lived in worse. One of the foster mothers who had taken her in, Mrs. Novak, had an obsessive-compulsive disorder that wouldn't allow her to throw anything out. Eventually, social services came to remove her from the home because of the health hazards that living there presented.

But for all her quirkiness, Mrs. Novak had been kinder to her than most of the other foster mothers she had lived with. Those women had taken her in strictly because she represented monthly checks from social services. Mrs. Novak was lonely and wanted someone to talk to.

"What can I do for you?" the firefighter asked cheerfully.

"You can tell us why you're using a dead man's Social Security number," Kansas demanded, beating Ethan to the punch. She slanted a quick glance in his direction and saw him shaking his head. At any other time, she might have thought that her partner looked displeased because she had stolen his thunder. But not in this case. Ethan wasn't like that. He wasn't, she had to admit, like any of the other men she'd worked with. Maybe he thought she should have worded her statement more carefully.

Too late now.

"Oh." The firefighter cleared his throat, looking just a tad uncomfortable. "That."

The response surprised Kansas. Her eyes widened

as she exchanged a glance with Ethan. Was Bonner, or whatever his name was, actually admitting to his deception? It couldn't be this easy.

"Do you care to explain?'" Ethan prodded, giving him a chance to state his side.

The firefighter took a breath before starting. "All my life I wanted to be a fireman. I was afraid if they saw my record, they wouldn't let me join."

"Record?" Ethan asked. Just what kind of a record was the man talking about? Was he a wanted criminal?

"Oh, nothing serious," the firefighter quickly reassured them. "I just got into trouble a couple of time as a teenager." In his next breath, he dismissed the infractions. "Typical kid pranks. One of my friends took his uncle's car for a joyride. I went along with a couple of other guys. But he didn't tell his uncle he was taking it, so his uncle reported the car stolen and, you guessed it, we were all picked up.

"I tried to explain that I hadn't known that Alvin was driving without his uncle's blessings, and the policeman I was talking to thought I was giving him attitude." He shrugged. "He tried to use his nightstick, and I wouldn't let him hit me with it. I was defending myself, but the judge in juvenile court called it assaulting an officer of the law." And then he raised his hand as if he were taking a solemn oath. "But that's the sum total of my record, I swear on my mother's eyes."

Ethan supposed that could be true, but then, since it could all be explained away, why had he gone through this elaborate charade?

"That doesn't exactly make you sound like a hardened criminal," Ethan pointed out.

Bonner looked chagrined. "I know, I know, but I was afraid to risk it. I didn't want to throw away the dream."

"Of rushing into burning buildings," Ethan concluded incredulously. Most people he knew didn't dream about taking risks like that.

"Of saving lives," the other man countered, his voice and demeanor solemn.

That seemed to do it for Ethan. He rose to his feet and shook the firefighter's hand. "Sorry to have bothered you, Mr. Bonner."

Ethan glanced at Kansas. She had no choice but to rise to her feet as well, no matter what her gut was currently screaming.

A bright smile flashed across the firefighter's lips. "No bother at all," Nathan assured him. He walked them to the front door. "I understand. It's your job to check these things out. In your place, I would have done the same thing. That's why this city gets such high marks for safety year after year," he said, opening the door for them.

The minute they were alone, as they walked to his car, Ethan said to Kansas, "It all sounds plausible." Before she had a chance to comment, his cell phone began ringing. Taking it out of his pocket, he flipped it open. "O'Brien. Oh, hi, Janelle. How's that search warrant coming?" He frowned. "It's not? Why?" He said the word just as Kansas fired it at him in frustrated bewilderment. His response was to turn away from her so he wouldn't be distracted. "Uh-huh. I see. Okay. Well, you tried. I appreciate it, Janelle. Thanks anyway." With that, he terminated the call.

Kansas was filling in the blanks. "No search warrant?"

He nodded, shoving the phone back into his pocket. They were at the curb and he released the locks on the car's doors. "That's what the lady said. Turns out the judge that Janelle approached for the search warrant had his house saved from burning to the ground last year by guess who."

Kansas sighed. "Bonner."

He gestured like a game show host toward the winning contestant after the right answer had been given. "Give the lady a cigar."

She opened the passenger-side door and got in. "The lady would rather have a search warrant."

"Maybe we can find another way to get it," he told her, although he didn't hold out much hope for that. "But maybe," Ethan continued, knowing she didn't want to hear this, "it's as simple as what Bonner or whoever he really is said. He didn't want to risk not being allowed to become a firefighter because he was a stupid kid who went joyriding with the wrong people."

Kansas stared off into space. "Maybe," she repeated. But he knew that she didn't believe that for a moment.

The rest of the day was mired in the same sort of frustrating tedium. Every avenue they followed led nowhere. By the end of the day Kansas was far more exhausted mentally than physically. So much so that she felt as if she were going to self-combust, she told Ethan as he parked his car in her apartment complex.

Ethan grinned seductively. Getting out of his beloved

Thunderbird, he came around to her side of the car and opened the door.

"I have just the remedy for that," he promised, taking her hand and drawing her toward the door.

She hardly heard him. "Maybe if I just go over—"

He cut her off. "You've gone over everything at least twice if not three times. Anything you come up with now can keep until morning. Right now," he whispered into her ear, "I just want to get you into your apartment and get you naked."

That did have promise, she mused, her blood already heating. "I take it your girlfriend canceled on you," she deadpanned.

"Don't have a girlfriend," he told her, and then added, "Other than you," so seriously that it took her breath away.

"Is that what I am?" she heard herself asking, her throat suddenly extra dry. All the while a little voice kept warning her not to get carried away, not to let down all her barriers because that left her far too vulnerable. And she knew what happened when she was too vulnerable. Her heart suffered for it.

"Well, you're certainly not my boyfriend," he answered, his eyes washing over her warmly.

"I don't think they really use that word anymore," she told him. "Girlfriend," she repeated in case he didn't understand which word she was referring to.

"I don't really plan to use any words, either—once I get you behind closed doors."

He saw what he took to be hesitation in her eyes and gave it his own interpretation. She was thinking about the case, he guessed. It was going to consume her if he didn't do something about it.

"It's the best way I know of to unwind," Ethan assured her. "Do it for the job," he coaxed. When she looked at him in confusion, he explained, "This way, you'll be able to start fresh in the morning. Maybe even find that angle you've been looking for."

The man could sell hair dryers to a colony of bald people. "Well, if you put it that way…you talked me into it."

Slipping his arm around her waist, he pulled her to him. "I had a hunch I would."

Chapter 15

Kansas couldn't let go of the idea that she was right, that Bonner, or whatever his real name was, was the one who was behind the fires.

For a while, as Ethan made love to her, she hadn't a thought in her head—other than she loved being with this man and making love with him.

But now that he was lying beside her, sound asleep, she'd begun to think again.

And focus.

And maybe, she silently admitted, to obsess.

She just couldn't let go of the idea that she was dead-on about Nathan Bonner. Furthermore, she was afraid that he had a large, packed suitcase somewhere, one he could grab at a moment's notice and flee.

If he hadn't already.

She desperately wanted to look around his house, and, more important, to look around his garage. If she were part of the police force, the way Ethan was, her hands would be tied until that search warrant materialized—and that might never happen.

But she wasn't part of the police force, she thought, becoming steadily more motivated to take action. She was part of the fire department—a situation she had more than a sneaking suspicion might not be the case very soon. But right now she was still a fire investigator. And as such, she could very easily look around, turning things over to the police if she found anything the least bit incriminating. It was her job to prevent fires from starting.

Granted, entering Bonner's garage was technically, as she'd said to Ethan, breaking and entering, but if she found what she thought she would find, she sincerely doubted that she'd be charged with anything.

Even if she was, it would be worth it if she could stop this man from setting even one more fire.

Very slowly, moving an inch at a time so as not to wake Ethan, she slipped out of bed. Once her feet were finally on the floor, she quickly gathered up her scattered clothes and snuck out of the room.

Entering the living room, she left the light off and hurried into her clothing. With her purse in one hand and her shoes in another, she quietly opened the front door and eased herself out. Closing the door behind her took an equally long amount of time. The last thing she wanted to do was wake Ethan up. She knew that he would immediately ask where she was going.

She couldn't tell him the truth because he would stop her, and she didn't want to lie to him. Sneaking out like this allowed her to avoid either scenario.

Kansas quickly put together a course of action in her head while driving to the house of the man she now regarded as the firebug. She couldn't very well knock on his door and ask to see his garage. He was within his rights to refuse.

Her only option was not to give him that opportunity.

She'd noticed, as she and Ethan had left the man's house, that the garage had a side entrance as well as the standard garage doors that opened and closed by remote control.

Her way in was the side door.

More than likely, the door was locked, but that didn't pose a deterrent. Picking a lock was exceedingly simple if you knew what you were doing. And she, thanks to one of the foster kids whose path had crossed hers, did.

Because there was no traffic in the middle of the night, she arrived at her destination fairly quickly. Parking her vehicle more than half a block away from Bonner's house, Kansas made her way over to the one-story stucco building, keeping well to the shadows whenever possible.

Bonner, she noted, wasn't one of those people who left his front porch lights on all night. The lights were off. That worked in her favor, she thought, relieved.

Within a minute and a half of accessing the garage's side door, she'd picked the padlock and was inside the structure.

Taking out a pencil-thin, high-powered flashlight, Kansas illuminated the area directly in front of her.

She was extra careful not to trip over anything or send something clattering to the finished stone floor.

There was no car inside the garage, no car outside in the driveway, either. Maybe he was gone, or on call, she thought. Either way, she still wasn't going to take any chances and turn on the lights.

That, however, did slow down any kind of progress to a crawl. It wasn't easy restraining herself this way, considering the impatience drumming through her veins and the fact that the garage was easily a packrat's idea of heaven. There were boxes and things haphazardly piled up everywhere. Looking around, she sincerely doubted that any vehicle larger than a Smartcar could actually fit in the garage.

Rather than go through the preponderance of boxes, she decided to start with the shelves that lined opposite sides of the structure, methodically going from one floor-to-ceiling array to another.

Twenty minutes in, she got lucky.

Hidden beneath a tarp and tucked away on a bottom shelf situated all the way in the rear of the garage, conveniently behind a tower of boxes, she discovered some very sophisticated incendiary devices.

Several of them.

"Oh my God," she whispered, feeling her insides begin to shake. He wasn't planning on stopping. There were enough devices here for him to go on indefinitely, she realized.

Setting down her flashlight, she angled it for maximum illumination on her find and took out her camera. Holding her breath, Kansas took one photograph after another. This was definitely the proof she needed to convince the captain that he had a rogue firefighter on his hands.

"I'm really sorry you found those, Kansas."

Surprised, she bit down on her lower lip to keep from screaming. She shoved the camera quickly into her pocket before she turned around. When she did, she found herself looking up at Nathan Bonner. His genial expression was gone and he looked far from happy to discover her here.

"You can't do this," she told him. "You can't use these devices. You're liable to kill someone."

He waved away her protest. "No, I won't. I'm an expert on handling these things. Nobody's going to get hurt."

He couldn't believe that, she thought. But, looking into his eyes, she realized that all the dots were not connecting. He had no idea of the kind of havoc that he could bring down on a neighborhood if things went awry. He was too focused on what these fires would accomplish for *him*.

"Like no one was supposed to get hurt at the nursing home?" she challenged.

The firefighter looked genuinely stricken that she should think that he had somehow failed the deceased man. "That was his heart, not the fire."

Was the man that obtuse? "But the fire brought on the heart attack," Kansas cried.

The firefighter didn't seem to hear her. Instead, he grabbed her in what amounted to a bear hug, pinning her arms against her sides. Caught off guard, she desperately tried to get free, doing her best to kick him as hard as she could. But, although she made contact several times, he gave no indication that any of her blows hurt.

"You're going to tire yourself out," he warned. And then he shrugged as he carried her over to an old, dilapidated office chair. It had rusted wheels and its green upholstery was ripped in several places. Each rip bled discolored stuffing. "Maybe it'll be better that way for you."

A cold chill ran down her back. "Why?" Kansas demanded.

"If the fight goes out of you—" he slammed her down onto the chair, and the impact vibrated all the way up through the top of her skull "—you'll go that much quicker."

She thought she picked up a note of regret in his voice, as if he didn't want to do what he was about to do. "You're not talking about letting me go, are you?"

"No, I'm not."

She struggled, straining against the rope that he was wrapping around her as tightly as if it were a cocoon. Using the rope, he secured her to the chair. "I thought you said you planned these things so that no one would get hurt."

"I do. But all those fires have to do with my coming to the rescue. I can't come to your rescue. You made it so I can't come," he told her with a flash of anger just before he applied duct tape over her mouth. "This isn't my fault, you know. It's yours. If you hadn't come around the firehouse, snooping like that—if you hadn't accused me—" his voice grew in volume "—you could have gone on living. And I could have gone on fighting fires. Rescuing people. It's what I'm good at, what I *need* to do." His eyes glinted dangerously. "But you want to spoil everything. I can't let you go now."

For a moment, he stood over her, a towering hulk shaking his head. "You women, you always spoil everything. My mother was like that, always telling me I'd never amount to anything. That I was just some invisible guy that people looked right through. She said no one would ever notice me."

The angry look changed instantly and he beamed. "Well, she was wrong. They notice me, the camera people, they notice me." His hand fisted, he hit the center of his chest proudly. "People are grateful to me. To *me*." And then he sighed, looking down at her. "But I really am sorry it has to be like this."

And then, as she stared, wide-eyed, he was gone, using the side door. She heard him put the padlock back on the door.

He was locking her in.

She'd deal with getting out later, Kansas told herself. Right now, she needed to get untied from this chair. Somewhere along the line, the unbalanced firefighter had learned how to execute some pretty sophisticated knots.

Maybe there was something she could use to cut the ropes on the workbench.

But when she tried to move her chair over, she discovered that the wheels didn't roll. The rust had frozen them in place. She wasn't going anywhere.

Desperate, Kansas began to rock back and forth, increasing the momentum with each pass until she finally got the chair to tip over. The crash jolted through her entire body right down into her teeth. But it also did what she'd hoped. It loosened the ties around her just the slightest bit, giving her enough slack to try to work herself free.

But as she struggled and strained against the ropes, she realized that she smelled something very familiar.

Smoke.

It registered at the same time as the crackling sound of fire eating its way through wood. The entire garage was unfinished, with exposed wood on all four sides. A feast for the fire.

Panic slashed through her.

Kansas forced herself to remain calm. Panic would only have her using up her supply of oxygen faster. Filling her lungs with smoke faster.

The ropes are loosening, she told herself. *Stick with the program, Kansas.*

Straining against the ropes, she kept at them relentlessly. The rope cut into her wrists, making them bleed. She couldn't stop, even though she was getting very light-headed and dizzy. Even though her lungs felt as if they were about to burst.

Finally, her eyes stinging, she managed to get one hand partially free. Hunching forward, she bent her head as far as she could. At the same time, she stretched her fingers to the breaking point until she managed to get a little of the duct tape between two of her fingertips. The awkward angle didn't let her pull as hard as she wanted to. But she did what she could.

It seemed as if it was taking forever, but she finally got the tape off her mouth.

She could have cried. Instead, she screamed for help, hoping that someone would hear her. She screamed again, then stopped, afraid that she would wind up swallowing too much smoke if she continued. Using her teeth, she pulled and yanked at the ropes until she got them loose enough to pull her wrist free.

But all this struggling was getting to be too much of an effort for her, all but stealing the oxygen out of her lungs. She was losing ground and she knew it.

Damn it, she wasn't ready to die. Not now, not when it looked as if things might really be going right for her for the first time.

Why had she sneaked out? Why hadn't she told Ethan where she was going? Left him a note, woken him up, something? Anything.

She was going to die and he was never going to know how she felt about him. How she…

Kansas was winking in and out of her head. In and out of consciousness.

The smoke was winning.

She was hallucinating. She thought a car had just come crashing through the garage doors. But that was only wishful thinking. Just like thinking that she heard Ethan's voice, calling her name.

If only…

Her eyes drifted shut.

"Goddamn it, woman, you are a hard person to love," Ethan cried, trying to keep his fears banked down as he raced to her from his beloved Thunderbird, which he'd just embedded in the garage door in an effort to create an opening. He got to her chair-bound body on the floor. There wasn't time to undo her ropes so he lifted her, chair and all, and carried her and it out onto the front lawn.

Just in time.

The next moment, the shingled roof over the garage collapsed, burying the two-car garage in a shower of debris and flames.

Focused only on her, Ethan began cutting her free. Her eyelashes fluttered and then her eyes opened for just a second. His heart leaped into his throat. She was alive!

"Kansas, Kansas, talk to me. Say something. Anything. Please!"

He thought he heard her murmur, "Hi," before she passed out.

When she came around again, she was no longer bound to a chair. Instead, she was strapped to gurney. The gurney was inside an ambulance.

Its back doors gaping open, she could see what was left of Bonner's house. The fire was pretty much out, the embers winking and dying. The fire truck had arrived with its warriors in full regalia, ready to fight yet another fire. It wasn't much of a fight. The fire won before finally retreating into embers.

"Idiot."

Kansas smiled. She could recognize Ethan's voice anywhere.

Turning her head, she saw him sitting beside the gurney. She let the single word pass. "He did it, Ethan. He did it for the attention. He wanted to play the big hero and have everyone say how wonderful he was."

"You were right."

"I was right." She let out a long sigh, exhausted. If

Ethan hadn't come when he had… "How did you know where to find me?"

"Because I know how you think," he told her, torn between being angry at her and just holding her to him to reassure himself that he'd been in time, that she was alive and was going to remain that way. "Like some damn pit bull. Once you get an idea in your head, you don't let go. When I woke up to find you gone, I just *knew* you were at Bonner's house, trying to find something on him any way you could." He looked over at the ashes that had once been a house. "Looks like if there was any evidence, it's gone."

It all came back to her. The fear, the fire and everything that had come before.

"Not necessarily," Kansas told him. He looked at her quizzically. "I took pictures." She touched her pocket to reassure herself that the camera she'd used was still there. It was. "You find him, Ethan, we can convict him. He won't burn anything down anymore." Her voice cracked as it swelled in intensity.

He began to nod his head in agreement, but then he shook it instead. "Never mind about Bonner. I don't care about Bonner." Everything she'd just put him through— the concern, the fear, the horror when he first heard her scream and realized that she was inside the burning garage and he couldn't find a way to get in—came back to him in spades. He could have lost her.

"What the hell were you thinking, coming out here in the middle of the night, poking around an insane man's garage?"

Her throat felt exceedingly dry, but she had to answer him, had to make him understand. "That he had to be stopped. That you couldn't do this because the evidence wouldn't be admissible, but I could because I wasn't bound by the same rules as you were." She stopped for breath. Each word was an effort to get out. Her lungs ached.

He looked at her incredulously, still wanting to shake her even as he wanted to kiss her. "And getting killed never entered you head?"

She smiled that smile of hers, the one that always made him feel as if his kneecaps were made of liquid gelatin. "You know me. I don't think that far ahead."

Meaning she gave no thought to her own safety. He thought of the first night he met her. She'd run into a burning building to rescue children.

Ethan shook his head. "What am I supposed to do with you?"

The kneecap-melting smile turned sexy. "That, Detective, is entirely up to you."

He already had a solution. One he'd been contemplating for the last week. "I suppose I could always put you in protective custody—for the rest of your life."

Had to be the smoke. He couldn't be saying what she thought he was saying. "And just how long do you figure that'll be?"

He took her hand in his, still reassuring himself that she was alive, that he'd gotten to her in time. "Well, if I make sure to watch your every move, maybe the next fifty years."

Okay, it wasn't getting any clearer. "Are you saying what I think you're saying?"

"The way your mind works, I never know," he

admitted. "What is it you think I'm saying?" When she shook her head, unwilling or unable to elaborate, Ethan decided it was time to finally go the whole nine yards and put his feeling into words.

"Okay, maybe I'm not being very clear," he admitted. Leaning in closer so that only she could hear, he said, "I'm asking you to marry me."

A whole host of emotions charged through her like patrons in a theater where someone had just yelled "Fire!" Joy was prominently featured among the emotions, but joy was capped off by fear. Fear because she'd thought herself safe and happy once before, only to watch her world crumble to nothing right in front of her eyes.

She never wanted to be in that position again. "How about we move in together for a while and see how that goes?"

That wasn't the answer he was hoping for. "You don't want to marry me?"

Her first reaction was to shrug away his words, but she owed it to him to be honest more than she owed it to herself to protect herself. "I don't want another broken heart."

"That's not going to happen," he told her with feeling. "You have my word." He held her hand between both of his. "Do you trust me?"

She thought of how he came riding to her rescue—literally. A weak smile curved her mouth. "I guess if I can't trust the word of the man who just messed up the car he loves to save my life, who can I trust? You really sacrificed your car for me," she marveled.

"It doesn't kiss as well as you do," he told her with a straight face.

"Lucky for me."

"Hey, O'Brien." Ortiz stuck his head in, then saw that Kansas was conscious. "How you feeling?" he asked her.

"Like a truck ran over me, but I'll live," she answered.

The detective grinned and nodded his approval. "Good." Then he got back to what he wanted to say to Ethan. "We caught him," he announced triumphantly. "Dispatch just called to say that Bonner was picked up at the Amtrak station, trying to buy a ticket to Sedona. Seems that the machine rejected his credit card." He was looking directly at Ethan when he said the last part.

By the look on Ethan's face, Kansas knew he had to have something to do with the credit card being rejected. "Just how long was I out?"

Ortiz withdrew and Ethan turned his attention back to her. "Long enough for me to get really worried."

"You were worried about me?" She couldn't remember the last time anyone cared enough to be worried about her. It was a good feeling.

This was going to take some time, he thought. But that was all right. He had time. Plenty of time. As long as he could spend it with her. "I tend to worry about the people I love."

She struggled to sit up, leaning on her elbows. "Wait, say that again."

"Which part?" he asked innocently. "'I tend'?"

"No, the other part."

"'…to worry about'?"

She had enough leverage available to be able to hit his arm. "The last part."

"Oh, you mean 'love'?" he asked, watching her face.

"The people I love," she repeated, her teeth gritted together.

"Oh?" He looked at her as if this were all new to him. "And who are these people that you love?"

Why was he toying with her? "Not me. You!" she cried, exasperated.

"You love me?" Ethan asked, looking at her in surprise and amazement.

"Of course I love you—I mean—" And then it hit her. "Wait, you tricked me."

He saw no point in carrying on the little performance any longer. His grin went from ear to ear. "Whatever it takes to get the job done."

She was feeling better. *Much* better. "Oh, just shut up and kiss me."

This he could do. Easily. Taking hold of her shoulders to steady her, he said, "Your wish is my command."

And it was.

Epilogue

Andrew Cavanaugh's house was teeming with family members. All his family members. The former chief of police hadn't merely extended an invitation this time, as was his habit—he had *instructed* everyone to come, telling them to do whatever they had to in order to change their schedule and make themselves available for a family gathering.

When his oldest son had pressed him why it was so important to have everyone there, Andrew had said that he would understand when the time came.

"Anyone know what this is about?" Patrick Cavanaugh asked, scanning the faces of his cousins, or as many as he could see from his position in his uncle's expanded family room. There seemed to be family as far as the eye could see, spilling into the kitchen and parts beyond.

Callie, standing closest to her cousin, shook her head. "Not a clue."

Rayne moved closer to her oldest sister, not an easy feat these days given her condition. Rayne was carrying twins whom she referred to as miniature gypsies, given their continuous restless state.

"Maybe he's decided, since there're so many of us, that we're forming our own country and seceding from the union," she quipped. Rayne laced her fingers through her husband's as she added, "You never know with Dad."

Kansas looked at Ethan and briefly entertained the idea—knowing that the Cavanaugh patriarch celebrated each family occasion with a party—that this might be because she and Ethan were engaged. So far, it was a secret. Or was it?

"You didn't tell him, did you?" she whispered to Ethan.

Ethan shook his head, but the same thought had crossed his mind, as well. If not for the way the "invitation" had been worded, he wouldn't have ruled out the possibility.

"From what I hear," he whispered back, "there's never a need to tell the man anything. He always just seems to know things."

They heard Brian laugh and realized that the chief of detectives had somehow gotten directly behind them. "Despite the rumors, my older brother's not a psychic," Brian told them, highly amused.

This was the first opportunity Kansas had had to see the man since Bonner's capture. In all the ensuing action, she hadn't had a chance to tell him how grateful she was that he had come to her aid. Rescuing obviously ran in the family, she mused.

Turning around to face Brian, Kansas said, "I really want to thank you, Chief, for putting in a good word for me with the Crime Scene Investigation Unit."

"All I was doing was rubber-stamping a very good idea," he told her, brushing off her thanks.

Brian had been instrumental in bringing up her name to the head of the unit. He'd done it to save her the discomfort of going back to the firehouse and trying to work with people who regarded her with hostility because she'd turned in one of their own.

Seeing her smile of relief was payment enough for him. "Thank *you* for agreeing to join the CSI unit. They're damn lucky to have you," he told her with feeling. "Hopefully, you'll decide to stay with the department after Captain Lawrence comes to his senses and asks you to reconsider your resignation."

Kansas shook her head. She sincerely doubted that Captain Lawrence would ever want her back. He all but came out and said so, commenting that he felt she would be "happier someplace else." And he was right. She felt she'd found a home. In more ways than one.

"You have nothing to worry about there." Things had gotten very uncomfortable for her within the firehouse after Bonner was caught and arraigned. Everyone agreed that Bonner should be held accountable for what he'd done, but the bad taste the whole case had generated wasn't going to go away anytime soon. And it was primarily focused on her.

Transferring to another fire station wouldn't help. Her "reputation" would only follow her. She would always be the outsider, the investigator who turned on her own. She'd had no choice but to resign. The moment she had, like an answer to a prayer, Brian Cavanaugh had come to her with an offer from the Crime Scene Investigation unit. The division welcomed her with open arms.

"Good. I know I speak for all the divisions when I say that we look forward to working with you on a regular basis."

About to add something further, Brian fell silent as he saw his older brother walk into the center of the room. He, along with Lila and Rose, were the only other people who knew what was going on—if he didn't count the eight people waiting to walk into the room.

This, Brian thought, was going to knock everyone's proverbial socks off.

"Everybody, if I could have your attention," Andrew requested, raising his deep baritone voice so that he could be heard above the din of other conversations. Silence swiftly ensued as all eyes turned toward him.

"What's with the melodrama, Dad?" Rayne, his youngest and a card-carrying rebel until very recently, wanted to know, putting the question to him that was on everyone else's mind.

"No melodrama," Andrew assured her. "I just wanted all of you to hear this at the same time so I wouldn't wind up having to repeat myself several dozen times. And so no one could complain that they were the last to know." He was looking directly at Rayne as he said it.

"Repeat what several dozen times?" Zack called out from the far end of the room.

Andrew paused for a moment, then, taking a breath, began. "First of all, I think you should all know that your grandparents had four sons, not three."

"Four?" Teri, Andrew's middle daughter, echoed, stunned. "Where's the fourth one?"

"Let him talk," Janelle counseled.

"Good question," Andrew allowed. "The son your grandparents had after Mike and before Brian only lived for nine months. Your grandmother woke up one morning to find that he had died in his sleep. What you also don't know," he continued, raising his voice again as snatches of disbelief were voiced throughout the room, "was that, for weeks after she first came home from the hospital, your grandmother kept insisting that they had switched babies on her. That Sean—that was the baby's name—wasn't *her* Sean. Nobody really paid attention to her, thinking she was just imagining things." He paused again to let his words sink in before he came to the most incredible portion. At times, he still didn't feel as if it was real.

"Recently, people—like your uncle Brian—have been coming up to me, asking me why I was ignoring them when they encountered me on the street. Other than thinking maybe I had an early onset of dementia—"

"Never happen," Rose told him fiercely, threading her arm around her husband's waist.

Andrew grinned down at the wife he'd gone to hell and back to find, bringing her home after everyone had assumed she was dead. "Anyway," he told the others after planting a kiss on his wife's forehead, "I started my own investigation into this so-called doppelgänger people were seeing. Long story short—"

"Too late," Brian deadpanned.

Andrew ignored his brother. "It turns out that your grandmother was right, which will teach the male segment of this family never to doubt their women's instincts. I won't bore you with details—"

"Also too late," Brian commented loud enough for everyone to hear.

Andrew slanted his brother a patient, tolerant glance. "Right now, I would like to introduce you to the end result of my investigation. Everyone, I'd like for you to meet your uncle Sean—oddly enough that's what the people who raised him called him, too—and his seven kids…your cousins."

The silence within the family room was deafening as eight more people walked into the room. Each and every one of them blended in perfectly with the people who were already there.

It would have been difficult to tell them apart.

"We really *could* start our own country," Ethan murmured, remembering what Rayne had said earlier.

"I don't know about our own country," Kansas whispered in his ear, deciding that the time was right to tell him, "but we have gotten started on a family."

He looked at her sharply. "Are you—?"

She grinned broadly at him. "I am."

He couldn't begin to describe the joy he was experiencing. "*Now* will you marry me?"

Her eyes sparkled. "You bet I will."

If she was going to say anything else, it would have to wait. Because Ethan scooped her into his arms and kissed her. And he intended to go on kissing her for a very long time to come.

* * * * *

2 FREE BOOKS
AND A SURPRISE GIFT

We would like to take this opportunity to thank you for reading this Mills & Boon® book by offering you the chance to take TWO more specially selected books from the Intrigue series absolutely FREE! We're also making this offer to introduce you to the benefits of the Mills & Boon® Book Club™—

- **FREE home delivery**
- **FREE gifts and competitions**
- **FREE monthly Newsletter**
- **Exclusive Mills & Boon Book Club offers**
- **Books available before they're in the shops**

Accepting these FREE books and gift places you under no obligation to buy, you may cancel at any time, even after receiving your free books. Simply complete your details below and return the entire page to the address below. You don't even need a stamp!

YES Please send me 2 free Intrigue books and a surprise gift. I understand that unless you hear from me, I will receive 5 superb new stories every month, including two 2-in-1 books priced at £5.30 each and a single book priced at £3.30, postage and packing free. I am under no obligation to purchase any books and may cancel my subscription at any time. The free books and gift will be mine to keep in any case.

Ms/Mrs/Miss/Mr _____ Initials _____

Surname _____

Address _____

_____ Postcode _____

E-mail _____

Send this whole page to: Mills & Boon Book Club, Free Book Offer, FREEPOST NAT 10298, Richmond, TW9 1BR

Offer valid in UK only and is not available to current Mills & Boon Book Club subscribers to this series. Overseas and Eire please write for details.. We reserve the right to refuse an application and applicants must be aged 18 years or over. Only one application per household. Terms and prices subject to change without notice. Offer expires 31st March 2011. As a result of this application, you may receive offers from Harlequin Mills & Boon and other carefully selected companies. If you would prefer not to share in this opportunity please write to The Data Manager, PO Box 676, Richmond, TW9 1WU.

Mills & Boon® is a registered trademark owned by Harlequin Mills & Boon Limited.
The Mills & Boon® Book Club™ is being used as a trademark.